Billion Dollar Love Story

Copyright

Paperback ISBN: 978-1-961966-26-0

Published by: Carxander Publishing
Minnesota

Opening Quote

When your soul finds the soul it was waiting for. When someone walks into your heart through an open door. When your hand finds the hand it was meant to hold, don't let go. Someone comes into your world, suddenly, your world has changed forever. No, there's no one else's eyes that could see into me. No one else's arms can lift me up so high. Your love lifts me out of time, and you know my heart by heart.

Heart to Heart by Demi Lovato

Chapter One

✗ Jason ✗

Manhattan has always been my home. I love it. I love how busy it is. How the city never sleeps. Works perfectly for me. I never sleep. Being that I'm one of the youngest CEOs to ever grace the world and given the family I come from, sleep is a luxury I've never been able to afford.

I started my property development business just after I graduated college. Within a year, I was already successful. I can't say that I did it totally on my own. My father gave me a loan to start and used his influence and contacts to help get me up and running. It was those influences and contacts that kept me going. Their word of mouth, references, and recommendations got me to where I am today.

A billionaire. A thirty-four-year-old billionaire with a reputation of being ruthless and cutthroat. Just like my father. My brother. My family. My mafia family.

I sigh as I delve into the contract sitting in front of me. It's one of my first clients. One of my father's mafia contacts. He needs an old warehouse torn down and rebuilt into something magnificent. Something I'm known for. Taking the ugly and making it gorgeous. One-of-a-kind designs.

I'm not an architect. I contract out for that shit. But I design. I develop. I create. I have the best people in the world working for me. I'm the best in the world at what I do. It's why I'm so successful. Why I was so successful at such a young age. It's why I've stayed that way.

Which leads me back to the contract in front of me. I never wanted to be attached to the mafia. The loan my dad gave me was dirty money to me. I accepted it because I wanted to get out. I didn't want to run missions or live the life I grew up in anymore. I wanted my own life.

So, I took the loan with the intention of paying it back as quickly as possible. I accepted the clients because I knew their references and recommendations could get me where I needed to be. Out from under the thumb of the mafia.

Unfortunately, it hadn't worked out exactly as I planned. I paid off my dad quickly because the work rolled in extremely fast thanks to his contacts. I got clients who had nothing to do with the mafia, thanks to those earlier clients. But those earlier clients didn't go away. I'm too good at what I do, and they keep coming back for more.

I could turn them away. I make more than enough to get by without them. The problem is it all goes back to my family. I tell these undesirable clients I can't do their project, they go after my family.

I probably have nothing to worry about. After my brother took over for our father, he turned the Crane Mafia legit and grew it. It's far bigger than any of the mafia clients who come to me. My brother could annihilate them if they even thought about coming after our family. But doing these small projects to appease them and keep them at bay is my way of helping out since I left the mafia life.

"Mr. Crane. Your brother is here to see you," a soft, sweet voice comes over the intercom on my office phone. I smile. Speak of the fucking devil himself.

I press the intercom button. "Thanks, Nance. Send him in." I flip through the contract in front of me absentmindedly with one hand and pinch the bridge of my nose with the other. My brother breezes in like he owns the damn office.

"What's going on, Jas? Your text was a bit ominous," Ryan says. I look up at him. Ryan exudes power. He's six-five. His height itself is enough to intimidate most people. He's muscular. His broad shoulders and all around strong and defined physique could go a long way in making him pass for a linebacker of the New York Giants. I'm glad he's my brother and on my side because no fucking way I'd want to go against him.

"I try to keep my private and professional lives separate. You know that."

"Yeah?"

I sigh and hand him the contract as he sits. "I'm having a fuck of a time deciding if I want to keep some of my contracts or send them packing. That contract is a new project. Small scale for a small-time mafia."

Ryan looks the contract over. "I thought you wanted nothing to do with the mafia."

"I don't. But they gave me my start. It's been twelve years. If I start turning them away now, I don't know what the fuck they'll do."

Something I can't read flashes across Ryan's eyes as he looks at me. It's gone just as quickly. I've always been able to read him. I don't like that whatever he just thought, I can't decipher.

He swallows as he hands me back the contract. "How long have contracts like this been going on?"

"Since I started. They're all small. Flipping a warehouse, or developing abandoned lots. I don't get a lot of them anymore. Here and there." I pinch the bridge of my nose again.

"But you don't want them anymore. You don't want anything to do with them."

"I don't want to be linked to the mafia in any way at all. It's bad enough my last name is the same as yours, and everyone in the fucking world knows I'm your brother. I worked hard to make my own reputation. If anyone found out I still do these small projects on the side..." I shrug.

"I get it, Jas. We don't want Crane Enterprises getting the wrong rep."

"I also don't want my family or any of my employees getting hurt if I start denying them."

Ryan smirks. "You worried about me, little bro?"

"Fuck you."

He laughs. "I'll take care of it. Turn them down. You get any more contracts from any of them, let me know first, and then turn them down."

"Make more conflict for you. Got it." I shake my head. This is the entire reason I've kept this from him for as long as I have. I put my head down on my mahogany desk.

"Jason. There's always going to be conflict for me. But that's why I have as many people working for me as I do. Not only that, you're family. You know I'll do anything to protect my family. Give me the heads up, and there won't be conflict. I'll take care of it before it ever happens. Your employees will be safe, and so will your family."

He stands and puts a hand on my shoulder as I nod and look back up at him. He looks at his watch as I stand and grab my jacket. "Dinner meeting," I tell him.

"This late? It's ten p.m."

"What the client wants." I throw my jacket on over my white dress shirt and straighten my loosened tie. "I need to finalize the plans on this project so Jessa can get to work. This is the only time this guy can meet." I smile softly at the thought of Jessa.

Ryan catches it. Asshole. "And how is the infamous Jessa Holloway? You ask the girl out on an actual date yet? Or are you still dragging her along to these boring dinner meetings?" Ryan teases.

I laugh. "You know my rule."

"Yeah, yeah. No office dating." Ryan rolls his eyes as we head out of my top floor office into my lobby. My secretary, Nancy, is still sitting at her desk. She's close to my mother's age and is like an aunt to me, Nick, my other brother, and Ryan. She's a small woman. Not frail by any means. She could probably whoop all of us if she wanted to. I'm six feet six, an inch taller than my older brother. Nick Crane, my adopted brother and Head of Security, is six feet two. Next to us? Nancy is tiny. She yawns.

"Nancy, come on. Go home," I say with a half grin. "You work more than I do."

"I doubt that, Mr. Crane." She shuts her computer down and grabs her purse as the elevator door opens. Nick steps off.

"Ready to go, Nance?" he asks.

"Yes, sir!" Nancy smiles widely as she steps around her desk. My building is secure. She has nothing to worry about walking to her car. But I have rules. If she stays late, she gets an escort to her vehicle.

"I got her, Nick. Just get Jason to his dinner meeting," Ryan says. He offers an arm to Nancy and grins. "Let's get you out of here, huh?"

"My bed is calling my name."

"I don't doubt that." Ryan winks at me and Nick as the elevator doors close behind him.

"Is he taking care of the last few contracts you have with the mafia?" Nick asks.

"Yeah. Huge fucking relief." I grab the files for the meeting Nancy left on her desk for me and turn towards the elevator. "Did Jessa leave?"

Nick gives me a knowing smile. "Yeah. A couple hours ago."

I nod as we step onto the elevator. Ever since I hired Jessa about a year ago, she's been the only woman to occupy my thoughts. I can't get her beautiful, dark brown, silky hair or her deep blue eyes out of my mind.

I took a huge chance on her. She had very little experience designing projects and absolutely no experience leading a team. I only hire the best of the best. I'm the best. It would only make sense that the people I employ are the best. I wouldn't be where I am without one hell of a team under me.

But I needed a Project Manager. It's such an important job within this company that I took the interviews myself. Many people applied. A few had the experience I was looking for, but none had the passion.

Except Jessa.

The second I laid my eyes on her, I wanted her. I wanted everything with her. I also needed her. Her talent and passion, despite her little experience, was exactly what my company needed at the time. And I was right about her. She's done several projects over the past year, and each and every one of those clients love her work. I'm impressed with her more and more every day.

I'm also falling for her more and more every day. I've tried forcing myself to stay away from her, but I can't. Every project I've assigned her and her team, I've made sure I'm a part of. I keep giving her important VIP clients so I have an excuse to be involved. She thinks it has everything to do with the fact that the clients she deals with are high profile. Really, it's because I can't get enough of her.

I shake my head in an attempt to snap myself out of my damn thoughts. I'm her boss. The CEO of Crane Enterprises. It doesn't matter what the hell I feel for her. She's off limits. I'd never put her in a position where her talents are questioned. I don't want anyone accusing her of sleeping with the boss to get ahead in the world.

"You really have a thing for her, don't you?"

I glance at Nick. He's watching me curiously. "Doesn't matter. I can't act on it."

"She likes you, too."

I shake my head again. "You're imagining things."

"It's not hard to see." He shrugs as the doors open in the parking garage. Nick steps out first and glances around, making sure there aren't any threats. I smile.

I'm lucky. I know it. I'm lucky to have a loving and protective family despite the fact that it's the most powerful mafia in the world. I've learned how to be ruthless and cutthroat from them. But I've also learned everything else from them, too. Including how to be honest and caring. Protective.

No. No matter how much I want her, I won't act. Jessa deserves to thrive here. To show off her talents. Not to be questioned for being in a relationship with me.

Chapter Two

☓ Jessa ☓

(Two Days Later)

The sun had long ago set, and my day had ended hours ago. Yet, I'm still sitting in my office pretending to work because I know my stalker is outside. He's been texting me all night telling me so. I had a restraining order against him once. It didn't matter. He walked right through it. I almost didn't live to tell the tale.

I thought I had gotten away from him this time, though. I left my whole life behind in L.A. Packed up and moved to Manhattan. It wasn't that hard. All I had there was Cole and my job. My parents were killed in a car accident while I was still in college. Leaving Cole was hard. He was my best friend. He still is my best friend. I talk to him daily.

Maybe I should call him now. Nah. What's the use? Nothing he can do for me from L.A. He can't hug me. He can't protect me. No one can protect me.

I sigh as a tear falls from my eye. I was lucky I got a good job soon after I arrived. Cole stayed with me for a month just to make sure I was settled here. He didn't leave until after I was hired at Crane Enterprises. I wish he were here now.

I always thought the ad I saw in the paper was fate. Crane Enterprises needed a Project Manager. I had very little experience, but I fought for the position and was hired. I love it here. Jason Crane, the CEO, treats his employees very well. He's a tough boss, but no one seems unhappy to work for him. His company runs like a well-oiled machine.

It's too bad I'm going to have to run again. I really have enjoyed my time here. Even though it's only been a year.

Damn. Why did he have to find me? Why couldn't he just leave me alone? I know the answer to that, of course. It's because Alex Lang is crazy. I don't know why I stuck with him all through college like I did. I saw the signs. I just didn't want to believe that I could possibly attract someone so crazy. Someone so blinded by jealousy. Someone who would never let me go.

I broke up with him six years ago, when I was twenty-two. A year later, I took him back. I had never really stopped loving him. The way things ended with us the first time was so unfinished. I truly believed he wanted it to work the second time. And it did work for nearly four years. He was perfect. I was ready to marry him.

That was until the night we fought. He was the only man I had ever truly loved. I really thought I had anyway. And maybe I did at one point. But at the end of our relationship, it just wasn't the same. The feelings once there were gone. Fizzled.

Alex got violent when I tried to break it off. He shoved me. I got away and ran to the only other person in this world I knew I could trust. Cole. Cole helped me file a restraining order. He took me in, so I had a safe place to stay.

My phone vibrates again. It's been doing that every fifteen minutes since my day technically ended… three hours ago. I had hoped if I didn't answer, he would just give up and leave. I was wrong. I should have known.

I sigh as tears sting my eyes, and I look down at my phone. Maybe if I text him back, he'll be less angry when I do go out there. He obviously isn't going to leave.

Alex: I'm tiring of this Jessa. Get your ass out here. We need to talk. You're pissing me off.

Jessa: Please, Alex. Promise you won't hurt me like last time.

I grab my purse, jacket, and phone and take a deep breath as I leave my office and walk towards the elevators. As much as I want to, I can't stay here all night. He won't leave.

As soon as the elevator doors open, I steel myself and step inside, immediately pressing myself into a corner. I hate elevators.

It takes a second to realize I'm not alone. Standing on the other side is Jason Crane himself. He stands at six feet six. I know because I asked him one day. He's built of solid muscle and fills out his expensive, custom tailored suit perfectly.

I clear my throat and try to act normal. "Good evening, Mr. Crane."

He grunts and barely acknowledges me, continuing to read his emails on his phone. This isn't atypical. When he's deeply involved in something, getting more than a grunt out of him isn't likely.

My phone goes off again. I glance down and see another text from Alex. Tears sting my eyes once more.

Alex: Get down here, Jessa. I already told you I won't fucking hurt you. I just want to talk.

Jessa: I am coming, Alex. I'm in the elevator.

I'm fighting a panic attack. I've had them for a long time, but they really started to get bad after I lost my parents. The news of them dying landed me in the hospital. It was during the good times with Alex. The times when he never left my side. When he helped me fight through them.

Now, I fight through them alone. Sometimes, if they're really bad, I call Cole. He talks me through them. Makes me breathe with him. But I can't do that right now. Not with Jason in the elevator next to me.

I close my eyes and count backwards from ten as I try to steady my breathing.

"Are you okay?" Jason's deep voice cuts through my thoughts, and I feel him close to me. I can smell his expensive cologne. "You don't look so well, Ms. Holloway."

I nod my head and continue focusing on my breathing. The nausea is beginning, and my head is starting to pound. I feel Jason move closer to me. His cologne. Thankfully, it helps to regulate my breathing. No one's scent has been able to calm me like that. No one but Alex.

12

I force myself to breathe. No matter how well his masculine, spicy scent works to calm me, if Mr. Crane walks out to my car with me, it will piss Alex off, and I will pay the consequences.

"I'm okay, I just... don't like elevators," I say, trying to convince him as well as myself.

"Then why not take the stairs?"

"I usually do. But I don't like staircases at night much more than I don't like elevators."

I don't tell him the reason I don't like staircases at night is because Alex caught me there once. He didn't like that I was trying to avoid him.

I look up into Jason's eyes. Gorgeous. Deep blue. Deeper than Alex's. More serene. I could stare into them all day. Too bad this is the last time I'll see him. If I survive the night, I can't stay here. I'll have to go back to L.A. If Alex can find me in Manhattan, he can find me anywhere. There's no point staying here. At least if I go back, I'll have Cole. I attempt to fake a smile for Jason but fail, so I quickly look away.

"Ms. Holloway, I didn't get where I am by being stupid."

"Mr. Crane, I would never -"

"I know something is going on. You looked down at your phone. You answered a text. And then you stopped breathing. You can trust me."

"Mr. Crane. Please. I... I can't. I have to go."

I nearly sprint out of the elevator as soon as the door opens. I'm supposed to get an escort to my car if I stay late. It's one of Mr. Crane's personal rules. But I can't. I can't do that. Mr. Crane calls after me, but I ignore him. I have no choice. No one can help me now.

"Jessa! Wait!" Jason catches up to me and grabs my arm. He spins me around and forces me to look up at him. "Tell me what's happening."

"I can't," I whisper. "I can't."

"Then let me walk you to your car. I know something's wrong. Let me help."

For a few moments, I think about telling him everything. But then I think better of it. I don't want him involved. I don't want him to think less of me. I don't want him to get hurt. I want him to remember me as the good employee I am. If I survive, maybe I'll be able to get another job. Maybe he'll give me a good reference.

"I'm okay," I lie and take a deep breath. I have to keep him away. I have no choice. "I got a text from a friend. She was in an accident. She's okay, but I want to go see her. That's why I'm hurrying."

Jason studies me, like he's trying to figure out if the words I uttered are really the truth. I force myself to hold his gaze and will my eyes not to betray the fear I feel.

Jason sighs and lets my arm go. "I don't know if I believe you or not, Jessa. I'm hoping that you trust me enough to tell me if something is wrong or not."

"I promise. There's nothing wrong. I just need to get to my friend."

He watches me another moment before looking over his shoulder and sighing again. He looks back at me. "I have a second dinner meeting to finalize the plans for this big project I have you on. I can't be late, or he'll pull his account. I don't want that. He's one of our biggest clients."

"I understand."

"I want you in my office at seven a.m. I'll go over the final plans with you."

"Yes, sir. I'll be there."

Jason nods, then turns to leave. He glances back at me as he's walking away. I can see how concerned he is as he shakes his head and runs his fingers through his hair. He turns the corner towards the front of the building, and I hurry out to my car.

My heart drops as soon as I see Alex casually leaning against the hood of my car. All six feet two inches of him. His muscular arms are folded across his well-sculpted chest. His short brown hair brings out the tan of his skin. His blue eyes look like they're on fire. I can see how angry he is.

I fight the urge to throw up from the fear he instantaneously instills in me. "Alex," I whisper.

"Jessa. It's good to see you. You were tougher than hell to track down this time. Manhattan. Really, honey? You've always said you would never in a million years come here."

"I... I'm sorry, Alex. I needed a change."

"Your running is starting to upset me, Jessa. You know I'm going to find you. Why in the hell do you have to make it so damn hard?"

He hasn't moved from his position on the hood of my car. I want to run, but he knows I won't. He's too fast. He's always been able to overpower me. I'm only five foot three.

"Alex. I'm sorry. I really am. Please. I don't want to fight. I won't run anymore. Please. Don't hurt me." I'm not above begging when it comes to him.

"For Christ's sake. I told you I'm not going to hurt you. Get in the car. I'll follow you to your apartment. Try to run again, though, and I will hurt you."

I simply nod. I can do nothing else. My heart feels like it's going to beat out of my chest. I can't breathe.

I can barely see.

I'm dizzy.

I feel like I'm going to pass out.

Alex sighs. "Come here." He reaches for me, and before I have time to react, he pulls me into his arms. I try not to struggle. I don't want to upset him. "Jessa. Relax. Come on."

I take a deep breath and breathe in his fresh scent. He hugs me tightly, forcing me to breathe with him.

"I'm sorry," I whisper into his chest. My body doesn't know what to do. Being close to him… having his arms around me… scares me to death. But he's always known what to do to help me through my attacks.

It only takes a few minutes for me to calm down. Alex slowly lets me go and waits while I get in my car before he gets in his. I begin driving to my apartment. He follows closely behind. I briefly think about calling Cole, but I'm terrified Alex will see me do it.

I take a deep breath and slowly reach for my phone. Maybe I can put it on speaker and Alex won't notice. Keeping my eye on Alex's distance from me, I call Cole. The phone rings, but he doesn't pick up.

"Hey, it's Cole. Leave a message."

I nearly cry. "Cole? It's Jessa. Alex is -" My phone beeps, and I look down at it. The screen is black. "No." My phone is dead. I can't hold the tears back anymore. He was my last hope. I don't know what he could have done from L.A., but nothing can be done now.

I can't think. I feel like I'm completely on autopilot. I'm so confused. Alex scares me to death, but without him and his ability to get me to breathe, I would have passed out from fear long ago.

It's like a cycle. A never-ending roller coaster ride. I need him, but I fear him. He calms me down, but he's the reason I'm so scared; the reason for the panic.

After nearly twenty minutes, I pull into the parking garage of my secured building. So much for the extra security this building has to offer. Alex has, once again, walked right through it.

After we park and get out, I lead him to my apartment and let him in. My chest feels like it's going to collapse on itself. I feel like I'm going to black out. I need him to calm me, but I don't want him to.

"Nice building, babe. You must make a hell of a lot of money to afford a place like this. I know you have nothing left from your parent's estate."

I nod. I don't have anything left. I gave most of the money to charity because I felt like the kids of St. Jude's could use it more than I could. I kept some in a retirement account, but I didn't need the money. St. Jude's will always hold a special place in my heart because of my parents. Without them, my father never would have made it to adulthood. I loved my parents. I still do. I miss them every day since the day they died in the accident. I hope giving St. Jude's the money made them both proud.

I used what I had left to pay for this place and relocate. Cole and his department helped a lot, too. Moving to Manhattan was expensive. I never would be able to afford this place if I didn't make a lot. Mr. Crane pays me well.

My apartment is spacious and has a private balcony overlooking the city. It's also quiet. So quiet that I question if anyone will hear me scream.

I reach up to rub my chest. It hurts. "My job pays well. I was lucky to get it so quickly after moving here."

Alex rummages through my purse that I had set on the counter. After a moment, he goes to the open kitchen to get water. He returns and hands me my prescription for anxiety and the water. He waits while I take it.

"Crane Enterprises. A multi-billion-dollar real estate corporation. The CEO, Jason Crane, is worth fucking billions. Tell me, Jessa. Can you afford all of this and your fancy little fiat because you're fucking the boss?"

16

"What? Alex, no! I barely even speak with him!" I stare at him in open-mouthed shock.

He glares. "You're a whore. I knew you were. I just didn't want to admit it to myself." He's looking at me with hatred in his eyes. The same look he had the night he nearly killed me. I feel panic once more. The pill I just took seems to sit in my throat. I swallow, but it stays there.

"Alex, I swear to you. I'm not sleeping with my boss. Mr. Crane doesn't even know I exist. Please. I won't lie to you. Alex. Please believe me. Please."

"Shut up, Jessa. I don't care if you are or aren't. That isn't why I'm here anyway."

"Then why? Why are you here?"

Alex looks at me. His eyes soften. For a brief moment, I'm transported back to when we first met. Before he became the psychopath I know today.

"Because I miss what we had, Jessa. I want you back. I'm willing to start completely over and forget about everything. I want you back, babe. I want what we had back."

"Alex…"

He stands in front of me, vulnerable. The same Alex who came back a year after we broke up the first time.

But I know better this time. I won't fall for it. I'm not going anywhere with him. I'm not taking him back. It's for that reason I know instinctively I won't be making it out of this alive.

Chapter Three

☒ Jason ☒

I've been sitting in my office since seven this morning. Jessa was supposed to meet me, but she hasn't shown up. The events of last night's elevator ride play in my head. I'm fucking uneasy.

The entire encounter was odd. I don't know much about Jessa Holloway. I know I hired her because of her passion. I never regretted it. She's proven herself. She's the best Project Manager I've ever had. I've seen her ruthless side. I've seen her be just as cutthroat as me. Her confidence, abilities, and her passion is part of the reason I like her so fucking much.

The woman I saw last night was nothing more than a scared little girl. I couldn't decide if she was telling me the truth when she told me she was going to see her friend, or if she was trying to get me to leave.

I look at the clock for the hundredth time. It's already ten in the morning. The more time passes, the more I feel like something isn't right. I should have trusted my instincts because now a fucking war is waging in my gut, and I feel like something is really wrong.

I look up at the knock on my door. "Come in." Nancy enters, closing the door behind her, and makes her way to the leather chair in front of my desk. "Well? Did you find out anything?"

"She isn't here yet. She's always here by seven. She's never been late. You already knew that. She hasn't called in sick." She drops a folder in front of me and opens it. "Apparently an ex-boyfriend was stalking her. She had a restraining order. He walked through it. His dad is part of a powerful family, so he never spent any time in jail. She's run before, but he has always found her."

"This is her current address?" I ask.

"That's the address that Human Resources has for her."

"Cancel my appointments for the day. I'm going to find her."

"Mr. Larksy is in the conference room right now."

"Tell him I have an emergency, and then reschedule. I'm going after her."

"I'll take care of it."

I follow Nancy out of my office, and in a few minutes, I am striding to the security desk. Nick watches me.

"Reassign someone to the desk, Nick. I need you with me."

"What's up?" He narrows his eyes as he speaks into his radio, barking out orders to someone. I don't care who. I need him to move. I feel like Jessa's life is in serious danger. I've always had good instincts.

"Let's go. I'll explain on the way."

It only takes a minute before we're hurrying to the parking garage and to Nick's car. I didn't drive today. Whenever I have meetings with people at a location that isn't my office, like today, I take a limo. It shows power. Control.

"Alright. Where am I going? Explain." Nick pulls out of the garage and expertly drives through the thick traffic.

"I have her address programmed into the GPS on my phone. Jessa."

"What? Why? What about her? What happened?"

"She's never been late. Never missed a day. Always arrives at seven sharp. Last night, she left the office at eight at night. When I did. She got a text in the elevator, answered it, and then quit fucking breathing. As soon as the doors opened, she sprinted out and ran to the parking garage."

"Did you follow her?"

19

"Initially. She was terrified. I didn't want to terrify her more, but I felt like something was wrong. I told her she could trust me. She told me she was in a hurry to get to a friend that she was worried about. I wanted to follow her, but I had that meeting last night. I should've said fuck it because she's a no show today. I had Nancy do a little digging."

"Why Nancy?"

"Because that woman can dig shit up faster than you can sometimes."

Nick laughs. "What did you find out?"

"She has an ex-boyfriend who has been stalking her. She had a restraining order against him, but he walked through it several times. Probably why she doesn't have one now. Never did any jail time."

"Powerful family?"

"Very." I pause and force myself to choke down the anger bubbling to the surface. "He's part of the Lucinio Mafia."

Nick nearly chokes as he speeds through the streets. "Jason. Jesus. Are you fucking kidding? The Lucinio Mafia?"

I don't say anything. I don't need to. Matthew Lucinio, the boss of the Lucinio Mafia, is the man who shot my father. My father survived, but Ryan took over the Crane Mafia because of it. My dad couldn't lead anymore. Ryan didn't want to. At least not that early in his life. Fuck. Neither of us wanted to take over. But no way either of us were going to allow Lucinio to get away with it either. The dismantling of our family's legacy would have meant he won. That wasn't a fucking option.

We drive the rest of the way in silence and in record time. As soon as we pull up to the font of the building, I jump out. Nick follows me, pulling me back.

"You can't just go charging in there. We need to call Ryan."

"No time."

He looks at me before shaking his head and taking the lead. "You're answering to Ryan for this."

I shrug. "Wouldn't be the first time."

Within moments, security is buzzing us in and leading us to Jessa's apartment. Building security leaves us alone as soon as we reach the door. Nick immediately takes out his gun and puts his ear to Jessa's door before he starts pounding on it.

"Jessa! Open the door! Jessa! It's security! Open the door!" Nick yells.

It takes her a few minutes but eventually the door opens a crack, the chain lock I heard her slide into place is securely fastened. Her eyes widen when she sees me, and she tries to close the door. Nick holds it open.

"Jessa," Nick says gently. "Open the door. We're just here to make sure you're okay."

Jessa looks at both of us a moment before deciding we aren't going away. She sighs and closes the door enough to remove the chain before opening it again.

My heart breaks when she looks out in the hall, seemingly making sure we're alone. Her face and arms are covered in bruises. Both of her eyes are black and blue and swollen. She has cuts all over her hands and face. Blood mats her hair and her clothing. The outfit she wore to the office yesterday is ripped. Her skirt is torn up the side. Even her legs are covered in bruises and scratches. Bite marks.

I can't stop myself. Seeing her like that breaks me. I rush into her apartment and take her in my arms. "What the fuck happened to you, Jessa?"

She's stiff in my arms briefly before she collapses against me and starts sobbing uncontrollably. I look at Nick. He doesn't say a word as he begins a sweep of her apartment. Nick is well-trained. We all are. The three of us had a good teacher. I don't need to use any words at all. Nick knows what he needs to do. Just like I know to keep an ear open for any sign of him struggling. Or, God forbid, the sound of a silencer. They aren't really silent. They still make noise. Distinct noise.

I watch as Nick disappears down the hallway. I close the door. I don't lock it in case I need to make a quick getaway. If anyone tries to come through it, though, I'll hear it and be able to move.

Jessa clings to me, and I hug her tighter. I don't know what happened, but I will tear apart the person that dared fuck with my girl.

Chapter Four

⚔ Jessa ⚔

"Jessa. What happened to you, sweetheart?"

Jason sits on my couch and pulls me into his lap as I sob into his chest. It hurts to breathe, and my uncontrollable sobbing doesn't help. I'm nearly hyperventilating, which hurts me even more because it already hurts to breathe.

Thank God he's here. Thank God it's Jason that showed up.

"Honey, breathe. Okay? Breathe with me. Feel me breathing, and breathe with me." His arms tighten around me, and he takes a deep breath. I try, but it's shaky.

"Tighter. Hold me… tighter. Please?" I whisper.

He hugs me tighter to his chest, and I take a deep breath again. I let it out as he does, forcing myself to follow his breathing. After a few minutes, he has me breathing normally again. My panic attack subsides, but Jason doesn't let go of me.

"Please tell me what happened, Jessa," he whispers in my ear.

"Apartment is clear, Jas. We're safe for now, but I don't like this."

I jump, nearly forgetting there is someone else here.

Jason holds me close to him. "It's just Nick, Jessa. You know him. He works at the office."

All I can do is nod as I bury my face in his shoulder. I inhale his expensive spicy scent, but it's a few more minutes before I finally feel calm enough to talk. I don't look up at either Jason or Nick. I'm too scared of what I'll see in their eyes. Too ashamed of my weakness. How hard I've fallen.

"My ex-boyfriend has been stalking me. I had a restraining order against him, but he has a powerful family. My restraining order was just a piece of paper. He found me at work in L.A. He figured out where I lived. He beat me up so badly because I wouldn't go back to him that I ended up in the hospital. I was there for a month. After I recovered, I ran. I thought I could get away from him. I thought if I moved here, he would leave me alone."

I feel the tears leaking from my eyes, but I can't stop them. They hit Jason's shoulder, soaking his suit jacket. I'll have to pay for the dry cleaning. I'm sure the suit costs more than I make in a month. I shift, trying to get up.

"Don't, Jessa," he says. His voice cracks, and I look at him. I see no anger. No disbelief. Just understanding and support.

"I don't want to ruin your suit."

"Fuck the suit." He tangles his fingers in my hair and pushes my head back down on his shoulder. "What happened? How did this happen?" He tightens his grip on me once more as he cradles me against him.

Other than Cole, no one has made me feel comforted and safe since Alex. Before he switched to a crazy, possessive, jealous asshole. Jason makes me feel like I'm going to be okay. Like nothing will ever happen to me as long as he's near.

"I thought I got away. I hadn't heard from him for an entire year. I was starting to become happy. Comfortable. I love my job. I love my apartment. I fell more in love with Manhattan than I already was." I take a breath and curl further into Jason's strong and large arms. "Until a few nights ago. He got my number somehow. He was texting me."

"You started asking for escorts a few nights ago," Nick says.

I nod. "He told me he knew where I worked. Where I lived. That he was coming for me. Every time I left work or got home, he was never there. I thought he was just messing with me. Until last night. He was texting me for three hours straight. He took a picture from the parking garage at work. He was telling me he just wanted to talk. He was waiting by my car. He took a picture of that, too. I didn't respond. I just stayed in my office. But I finally had to leave. I couldn't stay all night."

"Why didn't you ask for an escort, Jessa? I was working. You know I would've walked with you to your car. You trust me," Nick says gently.

"I do. But it wouldn't have helped. He would've followed me home and been even more angry."

"Why didn't you say anything to me?" Jason asks. "I could've helped you. I could have gotten you an escort home. I would've posted security outside your door. I would've done anything you needed me to do to avoid what happened to you."

"Mr. Crane -" I begin.

"Jason. For God's sake, Jessa. Jason. It's just Jason to you."

I swallow and grip his jacket tighter. I'm one of the few allowed to call him Jason. If I slip and call him Mr. Crane, he almost always corrects me. "Jason. Don't you see? If he had seen me with anyone, it would've just been worse for me."

"How? If you had let me help you, he wouldn't have gotten fucking near you."

I shudder, feeling his anger. "I'm sorry. Please don't be upset with me," I whisper. I can already feel my heart rate spiking. I try to stay calm, but I can't handle the anger I sense from him.

"I'm not. I'm not, honey." He runs his fingers through my hair.

"What happened after you got back here, Jessa?" Nick asks.

I force myself to calm down. I have to. I know if I don't tell them what happened, they won't leave. And if they're here when Alex gets back, I don't know what he'll do to them. I have to tell them no matter how hard it is. I have to protect them from him. They don't need to be the objects of his wrath. It's better for everyone if he keeps his attention on me. I'm so thankful that Jason showed up. Being in his arms feels perfect. I feel safe, but I have to protect him. I care about him too much to let him face Alex. Even with Nick here, I don't know what Alex will do.

"When we got here, Alex accused me of sleeping with you to get this apartment and my car. I tried to tell him you didn't even know who I was, but he didn't buy it. He dropped it, but he didn't buy it. He kept saying he wanted me back. I tried to tell him we weren't good for each other, but that made him really mad. He hit me. He kicked me. I fought him, and it made him more angry. He started accusing me of sleeping with you again."

"Jesus," Nick whispers. Jason keeps running his fingers through my hair.

"I tried to tell him the truth. That I've never slept with you. He didn't believe me. He hit me more. He shoved me on the floor. Ripped my top. My skirt. My panties. And…" I can't finish the sentence. I start sobbing again.

"Did he rape you, Jessa?" Jason asks softly. I can feel him tense, but he keeps hugging me tightly and running his fingers through my hair. He doesn't know about my panic attacks. He doesn't know that what he's doing right now is keeping me from passing out again. I grip his jacket as hard as I can. Like if I squeeze tightly enough, everything will be okay again.

"No," I whisper. "I fought so hard! He was too strong. He held me down. When I screamed, he slapped me. I kept fighting him, and he kept slapping me. He choked me. I passed out. I only came to when Nick started pounding on the door. There was a note next to my head saying he would be back tonight."

There's complete silence for several minutes before anyone dares to move or say anything. I take as much comfort in Jason's embrace as I can. After last night, there's no way Alex will keep me alive. He definitely won't if he catches Nick and Jason here. I don't know what he'll do to them, but if he can do what he did to me, I have no doubt he'll hurt them. He's blinded by jealousy. He's changed so much. There's nothing but anger and hatred in his eyes now.

This… coldness.

Emptiness.

Darkness.

"What do we do, Nick?" Jason finally asks, breaking the silence.

"Well, the police won't help. She's tried that. She said it herself. The police arrest him, and he never faces consequences because of who his family is. She can't stay here. He'll come back for her. He already told her he'd be back. I doubt she'll survive the night if she stays."

"Then you're coming home with me, Jessa. Get some stuff together."

My eyes snap to his in unabashed horror. "Jason, do you not understand? He'll kill me the next time he finds me!"

"He'll kill you if you stay," he argues. He switches into full CEO mode. Commanding. Powerful. "You aren't staying here. Get some stuff together or don't. Either way, you aren't staying here."

"Then I'll stay in a hotel," I say. I have to get them out of here. Before Alex gets back. I don't know where he went. I don't even know what time it is.

"Jessa. Listen to me." Nick puts a hand on my leg as he kneels next to me. "He'll find you. Your safest option is with us. Jason's house is like a fortress. I would know because I designed it. Also, there's enough room there for me to assign a twenty-four-hour security detail for you."

I look at both Nick and Jason, unsure that either of them are real. How are they both so protective of me? Why is Jason so caring? I have to be dreaming because this is everything I've ever wanted. Him. Just him. My literal Knight in Shining Armor.

"You know you can trust me, right?" Nick asks. I nod, wiping away a tear. "Then trust me now. Trust me when I tell you that you can trust Jason. We can help you."

"Why? Why do you guys care? Why are you doing this?" I don't mean to be suspicious of their intentions, but I have to be. There's only one other person I don't question. That's Cole. But he isn't here, and there's no way he could get here before Alex gets back.

"Because you work for me, Jessa. And I take care of my people. Especially if I care about them. I don't think it's any big secret that I care about you. I know you're smart enough to figure it out." He runs his thumb under my eye and catches a tear. "We can discuss all of that later. Right now I want to get you out of here. Please go get your stuff. You aren't staying here."

After his declaration of caring about me, I don't bother arguing. I know it's futile. Maybe if I leave and accept his help, it will buy me enough time to call Cole.

I climb off Jason's lap and walk slowly to my room. I try to get a suitcase, but it hurts, and I yelp. Jason is almost immediately at my side helping me.

"I'm sorry. I should've known with your injuries you'd need help."

He takes my suitcase and puts it on the bed. I grab my necessities and enough clothing to last a few days. I stuff them as quickly as I can into the suitcase. He closes it without a word and holds out his hand to me.

Confused and unsure, I shakily take it. He leads me out of my bedroom to my living room. He doesn't let go of me as Nick leads us to his car.

We get in and take off. I glance out the back window at the life I had built for myself fading into the distance. I lean my head against the window and watch the city I've grown to love blur into nothingness as we drive.

I close my eyes. My last thought before I fall asleep is to thank all the God's for Jason Crane.

Chapter Five

⚔ Jason ⚔

She weighs nearly nothing. It's obvious the stress has taken its toll. I've seen a difference in her over the past week. She looks tired. Sick. Like she hasn't been eating or sleeping. Guess I know why.

The drive to my house isn't long, but she fell asleep anyway. Maybe that's a good thing. She needs it. I lift her out of the car and carry her to my bedroom. Nick follows with her suitcase.

As soon as I get her settled on my bed, I slip out of the room. I close the door but stand next to it so I can hear if she wakes up. Nick leans against the wall across from me and folds his arms over his chest.

"Get a security detail for her," I say as I run my fingers through my hair.

"Already on it."

"We need to contact our brother. If we're dealing with the fucking mafia, I need Ryan."

"We're really doing this?"

"You're damn right. No one touches what's mine and gets away with it. That son of a bitch is going to fucking pay."

"Yours?" Nick smirks.

I don't answer. Instead, I shoot him a grin and silently slip back into my bedroom. I don't want her to wake up in tattered clothing, so I find one of my t-shirts and gently remove her ripped top. Her bra is black lace, and I gasp.

Damn. Why did it have to be black and lace? I have to fight myself to leave it on and stop looking at how her large breasts nearly spill out of it. I've wanted to see her like this for so long, but not like this. I pull my shirt over her head and cover her.

I give myself a mental punch in the face. Why are any of these thoughts crossing my mind? After what she just went through, she deserves better from me.

After she's covered, I lay her back down. She lets out the cutest fucking whimper I've ever heard. I grin and shake my head as I, as gently as I can, remove her ripped black skirt. I suck in a breath as my eyes fall on her bare pussy.

I forgot that he ripped her panties off. I expected more black lace. I didn't expect to see her in all her glory. She waxes. Or maybe shaves. Either way she's smooth. No hair at all, and all I can think of is how good she'll taste.

"Fuck me," I whisper as I tear my eyes away. Tossing the shirt and skirt into the trash, I take off my suit jacket and lay it next to her. I could tell by the way she breathed me in in the elevator and at her apartment that something about my cologne calms her down.

She whimpers again as she curls onto her side and hugs my jacket to her body. I groan at the sight of her perfect bare ass.

"Goddamn."

Not touching her is like physically ripping my own arms off. But I'd never do that to her. I've had my fair share of women. I know my reputation. I like beautiful women. It's no secret. But I'd never take advantage of her. I already feel like a fucking prick for letting my eyes take her in when I shouldn't have been.

I head for the door. I want her to rest, and I don't want her to hear the conversation I'm about to have. I leave the door open and walk across the hall to my office. I leave that door open, too. I can hear her if she wakes up.

I sigh and take out my phone. I don't want anything to do with the mafia, but I also know I'm not letting anything happen to Jessa. I know I don't have a choice this time.

"Hey, Jas. What's up?"

"Uh… I… need your help, Ry."

"What happened?" I hear the edge in his voice. The worry.

"Jessa."

Ryan is silent for so long, I question if he heard me. Finally, I hear him telling someone in the room to leave, and then a door slamming. "What happened with Jessa?"

"She was attacked last night. Her ex. I don't know a lot about it, but Jessa said she left L.A. because of him."

Ryan swallows. "Fuck."

I narrow my eyes. "What? Something you know that I don't?"

"Yes. I was hoping you'd never need to."

"What the hell is going on? What do you know?"

"Not on the phone, Jason."

"Fuck you. Tell me what you know." I glare at the phone because I can't glare at him. I hear Jessa stir so I lower my voice. "Now."

"No. This isn't a phone conversation. I'm not debating it. I need you to trust me, and I need you to tell me what happened. Tell me what she told you."

I growl under my breath. Whatever is happening just made my brother switch into protective mafia boss mode in a matter of seconds. I don't like being kept in the dark, but I also know him. He won't tell me anything if he feels like it will endanger my life.

"Fine. She didn't show up to work today. It's unusual. I had Nancy do some digging, and I found out she had a restraining order in L.A. against an ex. Alex Lang. But that's an alias. His real name is Alex Lucinio."

Ryan sucks in a breath, then hisses. "Fuck me."

"What?"

"I said not now, Jason. What else?"

I furrow my brows. "Uh… she said he put her in the hospital. When she got out, she ran. She said she thought he was going to leave her alone. She hadn't heard from him in almost a year. Until a few days ago. He started texting her. Saying he knew where she lived and worked. She started asking for escorts to her car. He was never there, and he was never at her apartment, but she was scared. I could tell. She wasn't sleeping. She looked sick."

"What happened, Jason?" I can tell he's trying to keep his voice even and calm, but something has him on the ledge. I don't like it.

"Last night, he was there. I was late. I had another late dinner meeting. I've had them all week. Not as late as the one the other night when you were there. Anyway, I was on my way out. She got into the elevator, and she looked freaked out. Scared. She got a text. She answered it. Stopped fucking breathing. I stepped closer to her because it scared the hell out of me. She wouldn't tell me what happened. I told her she could trust me, but she fled."

"You follow?"

"No. I didn't know any of what I just told you about the ex. All I knew was she was freaked out, and I didn't want to scare her more by following her. But I should've because, like I said, she didn't show up to work this morning. She's there every day at seven. Never late. Hasn't missed a day since I hired her. By ten, when Nance got me that information, she still wasn't there. As soon as I saw the last name..."

"I know. I know, Jason. Why didn't you call me right then?"

"All I was thinking about was getting to her. I grabbed Nick, and we left. Got to her apartment, and it wasn't fucking good. She's got bruises everywhere, Ryan. He beat her up so bad, she passed out. He choked her."

"Jesus Christ, Jason. He could have still been there."

"I had Nick."

"I don't care! You knew as soon as you saw that name that you were up against a dangerous motherfucker. Don't ever go out on your own again like that. You fucking call me. I'm not playing."

"I know. You're right. I didn't think it through. I followed my instincts. I knew she needed help, and I didn't think past that."

"At least tell me you got her out."

"She's here."

"I'm sending some guys."

"Nick already has a detail coming."

Ryan lets out a breath. "That's okay for now. But you know as well as I do it's not going to be enough. I need to make some calls."

"Okay."

"Keep her there. Nick stays with you. No negotiation. No argument about how you can handle it. Nothing about his security detail. He stays."

"Got it."

"I mean it, Jas."

"I know. I got it." I rub my temple and look into my bedroom. Jess is still sound asleep.

Ryan sighs. "How is she?"

"Sleeping. But he fucked her up. I'm calling a doctor to take a look at her." We're both quiet for a moment. "You know you need to tell me what the hell is going on."

"I will. But I need to make some phone calls. I need to pull some people. I need to get security set up on our parents. I don't know what the fuck Lucinio's game plan is here. I only know part of the story, and I don't like that. In the meantime, Nick doesn't leave your house, and you stay with her."

"I will." We say our goodbyes and hang up.

I stay in my office to think. This is the smaller of the two offices I have in my house. I only use it if I don't want anyone to bother me. I have several bedrooms and rooms in this house. I own a large chunk of waterfront land. My bedroom and the back part of my house overlooks The Lake in the Upper Westside of Manhattan.

"What did Ryan say?" Nick asks, appearing in front of me. He seems to know just when I need him.

"Nothing. He said it's not a conversation for over the phone. He knows something that I don't."

"Nothing new. He always knows more than any of us. It's his job as the protector of this family."

"When it comes to Jessa, I don't like being left in the dark."

Nick is quiet for a moment as he nods. "You really like her, don't you?"

"It's no secret. You and Ryan know all about it."

"Hearing you say you like her and actually seeing it in action are two different things." He glances over his shoulder, and I look around him. Jessa is slowly sitting up on the edge of my bed. I smile as I watch her sniff my t-shirt. Nick looks back at me. "We'll figure it out."

"Ryan says you aren't to leave."

"Wasn't planning on it." He smiles as he quietly leaves the office and walks back down the stairs. I sigh and head towards my bedroom. Jessa looks up at me with wide blue eyes. I sit next to her and smile.

"How did I end up in one of your t-shirts?" she asks sleepily.

"You were passed out after the drive over. I didn't want you to wake up in your ripped clothing. So, I put a t-shirt on you." She nods as she looks straight ahead. "I love black lace, by the way," I tease.

She turns and glares at me. "I'm not wearing any underwear."

I smirk at her as I look her up and down, still teasingly. "You definitely are not." I laugh as she stands up and storms to the bathroom.

I hear the shower start, so I decide to make the two of us something to eat. By the time she's done, I have a couple sandwiches made and sitting on the nightstand next to my bed. I smile at her. She looks a lot more refreshed. More awake. She has a towel wrapped around her.

"Feeling better?" I ask.

"Yes. Um... can I ask you something?"

"Anything."

She sits on the bed next to me and bites her lip. "Why do I feel so comfortable with you? Why do I feel like I can trust you?"

"Because you can trust me, Jessa." I play with the idea of telling her how I feel, but I decide against it. I don't want to scare her.

Jessa nods and stands. She walks to her suitcase and opens it, grabbing some of her things and disappearing in the bathroom again. I sigh and turn my seventy inch, wall-mounted, flat screen on, then remove my shirt. I toss it on the chair before grabbing a pair of pajama pants and changing into them. I grab my suit jacket from the bed and put it with the shirt.

As I'm settling back on the bed, Jessa comes back out dressed in a tiny tight tank top and short as fuck shorts. My mouth goes dry as I watch her every move. She crawls into the bed next to me, and I swallow.

"I had the worst possible night and day. Yet, here I am in bed with my boss. And I'm not afraid at all. Shouldn't I be? Is something wrong with me?"

"Jessa, honey, no. I'd never hurt you. I'll never do anything without your permission." I look over at her and hand her a sandwich. "Eat something. We can watch a movie."

"Do you have Fast and Furious seven? It's my favorite of the franchise."

"I have anything you want." I quickly do a search for the movie and turn it on. She smiles so widely that for a second, I forget all the trauma she just went through. But as I put my arm around her when the movie starts, she jumps. I quickly remove it from over her shoulders and drop it to my side.

"I'm sorry," she whispers.

"Don't be. I'm the one who's sorry. That was a very natural move for me. I didn't think."

She gives me a shy smile, and I wink. We finish the sandwiches and drinks I brought up and after a few minutes, Jessa looks at me. I look down at her with a reassuring smile.

"Do you think it would be okay if you had your arm around me?"

"It's up to you." I watch her as she scoots closer to me. I give her a grin and lift my arm. She lights up as she plasters herself to my side and practically wraps herself around me. I hold her close and in what seems to me like seconds, Jessa is peacefully asleep once more.

I smile as I shift her so we're both lying down. A few minutes after I shut the movie off, I, too, drift off to sleep with her wrapped tightly in my arms.

Where she belongs.

I don't care that it seems fast. I've been slowly falling more and more for her over this past year. I've fought it for far too long under the guise that I don't want her relationship status to dictate her status among her colleagues.

But I'm fucking done pretending. This feels right. It feels like things are finally falling into place with us.

I'm just pissed off it took me this damn long to get my head out of my ass and follow my heart.

Chapter Six

☒ Alex ☒

I step off my family's private plane praying to whatever God exists that I'm not too late. As soon as I turn my phone on, it's ringing. I look down at it.

My father. He can wait. I know he's pissed I took the jet, but I don't care. I need to save Jessa from whatever psychotic plan he roped my twin brother into this time.

Jessa is more important to me than whatever he's planning. I could have taken my own jet, but I don't want him anywhere near her. Whatever I can do to thwart his plans, I'm all for. Including stranding his ass in L.A. Not only did I take his. I had mine following so he had no way but a commercial airline to follow me here. And he won't do that. He's far too good for it.

And then there's fucking Josh. My twin. I've done everything in my power to prepare him to stand up against my father. I tried to shield him from all of the things I went through. Protect him. I took many of the beatings. I made him hide. Maybe that was my mistake. Maybe I shouldn't have done that. Maybe it would have toughened him up. Made him more able to withstand our father's manipulation.

I'm the oldest. Only by a few minutes, but because of that my father thinks taking over his precious mafia is my birthright. We both went through training. We both were dragged out on missions. We both know how to kill someone and not feel a thing. But my father never wanted Josh. He only wanted one kid. A son. I came out first. I became the one heir. To him, Josh is a burden.

And fuck if he hasn't treated him like one. Josh is the one who wants control of the Lucinio Mafia. Not me. For a while, I thought Josh and I had a good plan. I'd take over Italy and the overseas operations. Force the fucker to give Josh control of the U.S. And then I'd abdicate and give Josh everything. We both thought he'd give it up. We were wrong.

Then last year, I find out that the brother I spent my whole fucking life protecting went after the only girl I've ever loved. My first love. I didn't go to Italy for the sole reason of forcing my dad to give control of the mafia up to Josh. I also left because of her.

Jessa Holloway.

I hadn't told her the truth of who I am because I didn't want the mafia life. I certainly didn't want her involved in it. I should've told her, though. I should've been honest and upfront from the beginning because as soon as she figured out who I really am, she got scared. I let her go because I loved her. I still love her.

Josh became fucking obsessed with her over the four years I was gone. I know my fucking father had something to do with it, but I still don't know what the hell he did to Josh. Josh won't talk to me about it. He's become colder. Far more unhinged. I try to bring him out of it, but he shuts down on me and becomes quiet as fuck.

Josh put Jessa in the hospital last year. Nearly killed her. He stalked her for a while before then. She got a restraining order against me, and I couldn't figure it out. I flew home immediately. Fucker had been using my name. Pretending to be me. I still can't believe it.

I put a protection detail on Jessa as soon as I figured it out. The night he got past my protection detail and beat her up was the night I decided I'd do whatever the hell I could to get her away. I went through so much work to hide her and keep her hidden, I don't know how the fuck Josh found her.

I jump in the black SUV waiting on the tarmac for me and wait until my private jet lands. I flew Cole, an L.A. police officer and member of my crew as well as Jessa's best friend, out here on my jet, just so it wasn't flying totally empty.

It only takes a few minutes for it to land, but it's a few precious minutes that I don't have time to waste. Finally, though, I watch my plane taxi to the gate. Cole pops out and runs over to me. He jumps in the driver's side and we take off. I love how he just knows we need to move.

"Hurry the hell up. I don't know what we're about to walk into."

"Want to call Gavin, Damon, and Lance out?" Cole asks.

"Not yet. I don't know what Josh has done yet."

Cole speeds through the streets. It doesn't take nearly as long for us to get to Jessa's Manhattan apartment as I expect it to.

As soon as Cole stops in front of her building, we jump out. Cole enters her security code, and we quickly make our way up to her apartment. The door is slightly ajar.

"Shit," I whisper. I have a sinking feeling we're too late.

Cole and I both take out our guns, and I cautiously open the door. What I see before my eyes as we walk in stops my heart. Upturned chairs, a flipped coffee table, dishes shattered on the floor.

Blood.

"No. Dammit, Josh. What the fuck did you do this time?"

"Now, are we calling the crew?" Cole asks.

He's barely holding it together. I can tell he's pissed off and wants to kill Josh, but I also can see that he wants to find Jessa. She hasn't answered any of his calls or texts. Not at all like her. She's said it more than once. Cole is all she has. She's never ignored him.

I take out my phone and call Lance. He's my tech guy, and he's fucking good. I need him to track Josh. I need my crew.

"I never should have left her, Cole. I was young and fucking stupid. I thought I was doing the right thing."

"You can't beat yourself up now. She needs us, and you know as well as I do that your fucking father is behind this."

I nod as Lance answers. "What's up, man?" he says.

"Lance, I need you in Manhattan. Now. Grab the boys."

"What? What's going on?"

"Josh found Jessa."

"Shit! How? We masked her fucking social. We kept her well-hidden!"

"I know. Hang on."

Cole finishes searching the apartment and shakes his head. I swallow. She's not here so we need to leave. No time to waste. We rush back to the SUV and jump in. I don't need to tell Cole to head to the hotel. I put the phone back up to my ear.

"I found out Josh left last night when I got a text this morning from the pilot for our family's jet saying the jet had returned and would be ready for me. I had no idea what he was talking about until he sent another one saying he meant that for my father. I didn't think anyone was supposed to be going anywhere so I asked him who took it and where they went. He told me my brother took it, and that his destination was JFK."

"Fuck!" Lance swears.

"I knew. I knew he was going after her. I didn't have time to find out the plan. I knew he was going after her, so I grabbed Cole."

"Fuck, man. He'll kill her this time. We all know this isn't all him, but he's become pretty unpredictable."

"I know. Track him. Find him. And get the boys. I was just at her apartment. She wasn't there, but it didn't look good. Track her, too."

"On it. I'll call you back with the track. We'll get out there as soon as we can. What hotel?"

"Ours. I don't want Josh or my father knowing I'm here."

"We'll find her, Alex."

"We fucking better. I might kill my brother this time." I hang up and take a few deep breaths. It's not going to do her any good if I'm panicking.

"What are you thinking?" Cole asks.

"I have a contact here. We need to get to the hotel. I need to call him."

"What are you going to do when we find Jessa?"

"Tell her the truth. I should've done it a long fucking time ago. She deserves to know the truth. Why all this shit happened to her. I never should've kept it from her in the first damn place."

"She's terrified of you. She thinks Josh is you."

"That's what you're here for. She trusts you. When we find her, you'll be the one to get her. You can calm her down when she sees me."

"I can't promise you I won't kill your brother on the spot when I see him."

38

"Fuck. I can't make that promise either. I know this isn't fully him, but fuck."

Cole pulls up to the valet. We both get out and grab our bags. Cole tosses the keys to the valet and we head in to the front desk.

"Hello, Mr. Lucinio," Amy, the hotel's manager, greets me. "Your room is ready for you. Will your team be joining you this trip?"

"Yes, Amy. Are their rooms ready as well?"

"Yes, sir! We never rent out your penthouse suites. They're always available for you, sir."

"That's what I like to hear. And also why I pay you and your staff so handsomely for your discretion." I give her my winning smile and a wink as she hands me my key card and gives one to Cole for his room. We head to our rooms.

"I swear if he hurt her, Alex..."

"I know. Trust me. I know." I open the door to my room, and Cole follows me inside.

"I can't just do nothing. What's the plan? We have to have one. What about Crane Enterprises? We can start there."

"We can't just go in and start asking questions, Cole. It'll raise suspicion. We don't need that. I need to make a call. We wait for the guys to get here. That's what we do."

"Alex, no fucking way! We need to find her!"

I turn to Cole. "Trust me. We will. Don't question me. I've been doing this a fuck of a lot longer than you."

"She's my fucking best friend!"

"She's my fucking first love!" I yell, losing the last shred of control I have left. "You think I want this to be happening? You think I'm okay with sitting here and doing nothing? We don't have a fucking choice! Now, let me do my damn job and find her!"

Cole looks taken aback, and I turn away, running my hand through my hair. I know my chance with Jessa has long passed. I came to terms with that long ago, but I've never stopped loving her. The girl will forever have a piece of me and has since I sat next to her on our first day of classes at UCLA, and she told me how good I smelled.

"Tell me what you need me to do, Alex. Because I don't know. I don't have a fucking clue how this is supposed to work."

I turn back to him and sigh. "I *need* to make a phone call. I need to get things in motion while we wait for the guys. I can't do anything without information. I have Lance tracking her and Josh. Patience. That's what I need from you. We'll find her, Cole."

He nods as he sinks into a chair. I head for the bedroom.

We fucking better find her. Or my father and brother are fucking dead this time.

Chapter Seven

⚔ Josh ⚔

I have her. I finally have her. Jessa Holloway is mine. Again. She isn't getting away this time. After a year of searching for her after she ran from me, she's finally mine again. I finally have what I deserve. What my perfect twin lost all those years ago.

Alex let her go. Left her unprotected against our psychotic father. It had been up to me to protect her. And I did it. For five years. I had to do it in the most unconventional way, but Alex made it be like that. He lied to her. He never told her he had a twin brother. He said it was because of the family. The mafia. He said he'd tell her everything as soon as dad gave me control. She'd be safe then.

But then he left. He left both of us unprotected against dad. He never really loved us. Dad was right about that. Alex is a selfish son-of-a-bitch. I had to pretend to be him to get to her after my dad tried getting to her. I had to protect her.

She was ready to marry me. Until my father fucked everything up. He forced me to rush things with her. He shot my only friend. All I had was Jessa. I needed her. I knew he wouldn't give me control unless I got Jessa to marry me and have an heir.

Dad threatened her. I knew I had to get that heir. To protect the woman I loved. But I scared her. All because I was upset at watching my friend get shot right in front of me. She ran and spent a year running from me. But I found her. I finally found my girl.

Manhattan of all places.

I smile to myself as I use her passcode and key to enter her building. The security she surrounded herself with is completely futile. She really should know by now. No matter how much security she surrounds herself with, no matter how far she runs, I'm smarter than her. I'll always find her.

I step into the elevator and laugh out loud. Jessa is terrified. There's a lot she doesn't know. She doesn't know who I truly am. She doesn't know about my family. It's easy to control her through her fear. She'll do anything I want her to because she thinks if she doesn't, I'll kill her.

I have much bigger plans for her than that. She can't run anymore. She'll be bound to me, and I'll finally get the one thing I've deserved all my fucking life. Control of the Lucinio Mafia. Alex won't stand a chance against me. Not with her by my side.

I want her to trust me, though. I need her to trust me. That didn't happen last night. She made me hit her. Made me choke her. She fought so fucking hard that it pissed me the hell off. She wouldn't calm down. I didn't have a choice. I had to knock her out.

I intended to take her with me right then, but not even I could stand seeing my girl bleeding all over the damn floor. So, I cleaned her up the best I could. In order to protect her, she has to marry me and have my child. If she doesn't, my father will kill both of us. I know it. She has to come with me tonight. Willing. Which means I need to tell her everything, so she'll understand the importance of it.

As soon as I step out of the elevator, I instinctively know something is wrong. The door to her apartment is ajar. I rush to it.

"Fuck! Fuck! Fuck! Fuck!" I barge inside and grab my head. This can't be happening. I should've tied her up! I should've fucking tied her to the bed!

She promised. She promised me last night she wouldn't leave. No more fucking running. She doesn't know what she's just done. She doesn't know she just sealed both of our fates!

I grab my phone as it goes off and look at it. Part of me is hoping it's her, but I'm never that fucking lucky. The text is from fucking Alex. Funny. Because I rarely ever talk to him anymore, but he still can't take a fucking hint that I don't fucking want to.

Alex: You up for drinks?

"Fuck you, Alex. I'm not up for fucking drinks. I'm not even close to L.A.!"

I ignore his text and pace the apartment, kicking chairs over as I think. Her cell. I'll call her cell and text her. Maybe Brandon can track her.

Josh: Where the hell are you, Jessa? You promised me you wouldn't run, you bitch! I will find you. And when I do, this is over. You will never run from me again, Jessa.

Alex and our dad think I'm stupid. They think I'm not capable of having my own contacts. Not near their level of intelligence. But I've watched them. I've learned a thing or two.

I look down at my phone again as it starts ringing. Alex is calling, but I send it to voicemail. I don't have time for him and his attempts at making me fucking weak and dependent on him. Instead, I call my best friend. My only friend after Keith was killed in front of me.

"Hey, Josh," Brandon chirps. "What's up?"

"I need you to track, Jessa."

"Thought you found her. What happened?"

"She got away. I made the mistake of trusting her. I shouldn't have. I won't make that mistake again. I should've fucking tied her up."

"Dude. Your dad is going to be fucking pissed. He wants her home."

"He wants the heir she'll give him. If I fail, he'll take her for himself, kill me, and then kill her after she delivers."

"I don't know man. He's fucking obsessed with her. He might keep her as his own personal sex slave."

"I wouldn't put it past him, but no fucking way will I ever allow it to happen. Just fucking track her."

"Alright. Hang on. I'm on it."

The silence of the next few minutes drives me insane. I can't believe she ran. She knew the consequences. I told her last night. I have to make her obey me. Which means I'll have to hurt her now. I can't let her think she can get away with this. Not if I have any chance of protecting her. I have to get her home. She won't be able to run from me again. I'll make sure of it this time.

"Looks like she's at her apartment, Josh."

"What? I'm at her apartment. She's not fucking here!"

"Well, her address is what's coming up."

"Fuck!" I hang up my phone and search every square inch of her apartment. I tear her clothes out of her closet and dresser. I flip the furniture that hadn't already been flipped in our fight last night. I toss her bed. Just as I flip her couch, I find it. Her phone. "Fuck!"

I throw her phone across the room. It shatters. She has no idea what she just did. If I don't bring her home, my dad will come after her. He'll kill me. Alex will get the mafia. My dad will get Jessa. Neither of them need or even care about me. Alex doesn't give a shit about Jessa.

Only I do.

Only I can protect her now.

If Alex gave a fuck, he wouldn't have left.

This is my last chance.

If I don't deliver this time, I won't see tomorrow.

Chapter Eight

✕✕ Jessa ✕✕

I struggle against Alex. I fight.
Scream.
Cry.
Claw.
He keeps coming. He pins me down and rips my shirt. I kick and bite him. "Stop! Alex! Please stop!" *I scream.*

"Keep it up, Jessa. You're fucking beautiful when you fight me,"
Alex snarls.

He rips my skirt and tears my panties. I scream and scratch him. He pins my small hands with one of his large ones to the floor.

"Help! Please! Someone help me! Alex, no! Please! No! Alex, please! No!"

Tears stream down my face as I kick. He's too strong for me. He's crushing me, and I can't get away.

No one hears my cries or screams.

"Stop! Jessa! Honey, wake up, baby."

That voice. It isn't Alex's, and it sounds so far away.

Something is holding me down. It's heavy, and I'm fighting, but I can't get it off. I'm screaming and crying, but I can't get free.

It has to be Alex. I have to get away, but he's so heavy. I can't get away from him. He's always been stronger than me. But I can't give up. I have to fight him.

"Please get off me, Alex. Please! Please!"

"Not Alex, Jess. Come on, honey. Wake up. It's Jason. It's Jason, Jessa."

My eyes fly open, and I see Jason on top of me, holding me down. His arms wrap around me, and I cry into his chest as he rolls to his side, taking me with him.

"Oh God." I grip him as tightly as I can, using him to steady me.

"I'm sorry I was holding you down, baby, but you were kicking me in your sleep. And then you started hitting, screaming, and crying. I tried to wake you up, but it got worse. I had to hold you down so you didn't give me a black eye. Or make it so I can never have kids." He holds me tightly and tangles his fingers in my hair as I attempt to get reoriented to my surroundings.

After a few moments of his steady breathing and spicy scent calming and bringing me back to reality, I loosen my grip on him. "I'm sorry. I'm so sorry."

"Don't be." He kisses the top of my head and pulls me closer to him so that his arms are engulfing me.

I curl into him. For the first time in years, I feel safe. Totally and completely safe. I don't know why, but Jason makes me feel like I'm going to make it out of this.

A long silence passes with Jason holding me close to his solid frame and his fingers in my hair. I'm so thankful that he showed up. Tears of gratitude sting my eyes thinking about it. Even after I lied to him and told him that I was fine, he still showed up. He's still the one who saved me from possibly losing my life. He stuck by me. He held me. He swept me away to the safety of his house. Given the feelings I have for him, I'm so happy to know that he cares about me.

There's so much on my mind, and I don't even know where to begin, but I've never been good at keeping my mouth shut when things are running through my head. And right now, I feel like they're going fifty miles an hour.

I take a deep breath and look up at him. "You called me honey and baby."

He smiles. His blue eyes sparkle. "Should I not?"

I feel the corner of my mouth turning up as he brushes some hair off my forehead. "I… don't know how to word everything I'm thinking."

Jason stays quiet as I bite my lip, trying to organize everything I want to say. Usually, I just blurt things out. I don't think before I speak. But with him? I can't seem to form words. Every time I try to say what I want to, I get tongue-tied. My stomach takes flight whenever he looks at me from across the room. His arms around me right now, being so close to him, has set my body alight. I feel like I'm sitting in a volcano right before it explodes.

"Everything is so different with you," I whisper.

Jason runs his thumb over my bottom lip as he watches me. He trails his hand down my arm while the other stays tangled in my long hair. "What's different?"

I shrug before I feel everything I want to say suddenly coming out of my mouth. I'm powerless to stop it, so I don't even try. "When I see you walking into the conference room, or when you stop by my office, it doesn't matter the kind of day I've had. You make it better. All I have to do is look at you. I feel like I could take flight with the amount of butterflies I get in my stomach when you look at me. When you brush by me, I feel like I could burst into flames. I feel like I could lose myself in you and never come back. Sometimes I imagine other things." I bite my lip again. "Like what it would be like to kiss you."

His smile turns into a huge grin that lights up his eyes. "Why imagine it? I'm right here."

My mouth falls open slightly as my eyes fall to his lips. I have to be crazy. Wanting to kiss my boss? Feeling like I do in his arms after everything I've been through isn't just crazy. It's certifiably insane.

Still, I watch as he leans slowly in. Inch by inch his lips come closer to mine until they're a breath away from me. I let my eyes close as I eliminate the distance between us.

As soon as his lips meet mine, my toes curl. Like the Princess Diaries kind of toe curling kiss. If I was standing, my foot would lift off the ground, and I'd let myself be swept off my feet. My lips tingle against his. When his tongue slides into my mouth and finds mine, my entire body ignites into a raging inferno of want and desire. I've felt attraction. I've felt what it feels like to want someone.

But not like this. Never like this. I feel like if he stops kissing me, I won't survive it. If he stops touching me, I'll die. I feel like I need him more than I need oxygen. Like the only thing necessary for my existence is him.

When he pulls away from me, I want to dig my nails into him and pull him back, but I force myself to stop. To act like the dignified human being that I am instead of some crazed, wild animal.

I open my eyes as I breathe in. His intoxicating, expensive cologne makes me feel like I could lose all control at any given moment, so I attempt to pull away. Putting distance between us seems like a really good idea.

Jason, however, has other ideas. He tightens his grip and doesn't let me get up. "What else do you want to say? I know there's more than just that."

I blink, completely unnerved at how intuitive he is. It reminds me of Alex, but it's different. I don't know how or why, but it's not like it was with him. Jason is intuitive and caring.

I take a deep breath. I guess I started this. "Uh… I… really like you. I feel crazy because you're my boss. I shouldn't feel like I do. Especially after everything I've been through. I feel like a stupid highschool girl who has a crush on the hottest guy on the football team. Only, it's more like you'd be the principal of the school, and the romance is strictly forbidden."

He smiles. "Interesting analogy."

I plunge forward. "I feel so comfortable with you. I feel so much more than I've ever felt for anyone. It's overwhelming. It makes me feel like a psychotic person."

"Hmm…" He cups my cheek in his palm as he leans forward. His lips meet mine in a sweet kiss. When he pulls away, he licks his lips. "Sexiest psychotic person I've ever seen."

I blush. "I shouldn't feel like this. I'm really sorry."

"For really liking me? I hope you aren't sorry for that because I happen to really like you, too." He runs his thumb over my lower lip again, and I melt into him. "A lot."

"Really?"

"What's not to like? You're beautiful. Smart. You're talented. Driven. When you aren't thinking about all of the consequences and negative outcomes, you're pretty fucking tenacious. You're an amazing woman, Jessa."

I can't help but smile as he kisses me again. As we lay in each other's arms with our lips locked together, I allow myself to forget what happened last night. For a little while, I let myself be Jason's. My head keeps making me think that he's not interested in me. That as soon as this is over, and he doesn't need to play my hero anymore, he'll leave.

My heart, though… my heart makes me believe that he's for real. That he really likes me, too. That maybe, after all of this is over, I'll finally have my happy ending.

Jason pulls away reluctantly once more. "I need to ask you something."

I'm immediately on edge. "Oh. Okay."

"How are you feeling? Physically? I need to know because your injuries look bad, honey."

I break eye contact and shrug. "I'm sore. I hurt everywhere."

"I don't want to get too personal, but I need to know. When I took off your skirt earlier, I noticed bruising between your legs. Your thighs. There's some scratches. I looked away because I don't want to invade your privacy, but it looks bad. I think you need to get checked out. Do you remember anything he did to you?"

I shake my head. "He didn't. I don't remember anything other than him beating me up and choking me, but I know he didn't do that." I sigh, deciding to be honest. "I spent a month in the hospital because of Alex. I don't like hospitals, Jason." I lay my head on his chest. "I have panic attacks. Walking into a hospital will send me directly into one."

"Then we won't go to the hospital. I'll have a doctor come here. Jessa," he begins hesitantly. "The truth is we don't know what he did to you. We need to. You don't remember a lot of it, and you told me you passed out. We need to know the extent of what he did, so we can fix it." He runs his hand up and down my back and brings his lips to my ear. His warm breath tickles it, and I smile. "I think you're fine, but we need to know."

"Will you stay with me?"

"If that's what you want. I'll do anything for you." He leans down to meet my lips as soon as I look up at him.

The kiss turns heated incredibly quickly and before I know what I'm doing, I'm pushing him on his back and straddling him. He groans as he locks his arms around my waist. I whimper when he drops his hands to my ass.

I don't want to think about last night. All I can think about right now is everything I want to do with Jason. None of them are innocent. As I kiss him, I want nothing more than to take all of his clothes off and ravish him. I want him to ravish me. Make me okay again. Make me forget.

The thoughts make me abruptly stop and sit up, out of breath. Jason looks up at me, confused. "You okay?"

"I… just..." My eyes go wide when I feel him underneath me. "You're so big."

He smirks teasingly. "I'm six feet six, Jessa. You think a guy my size is going to have a tiny dick?"

The laugh escapes before I have time to stop it. "You'll tear me apart!"

"That's what you were thinking?"

"No! I mean… yes. I mean… maybe?" It's not, but being in this position with him, it's hard to not feel his size beneath me. Especially since I can feel him hardening. Which makes me blush. Furiously.

Jason raises an eyebrow and sits up. He wraps his arms around my waist and claims my lips again. "Then… what were you thinking?"

"I'm thinking… that over the past year, I've barely learned anything about you. Yet, I feel like I've known you forever. Like our souls are connected somehow. Like over the course of all of our past lives and this one, we always find each other. And now I'm thinking, after saying everything I just did, I'm positive you have to think I'm obsessed with you or something."

He chuckles. "Have you ever wondered why I interject myself in every single project I give you? Or why the projects I give you are for important VIP clients?"

I tilt my head. "Kind of."

"It's because I can't get enough of you, Jessa. Because even though I'm your fucking boss, all I can think about is you. I fall for you a little more each day. Starting from the day I hired you. I tried to stay away, but seeing your face when I walk in the room, or listening to your breath hitch when I brush my fingers over yours… it's the best damn feeling in the world. I spend my whole day thinking about ways to get you to smile."

I look up at him, tears glistening in my eyes. I want to believe him, but I'm terrified to think that a man like him could really fall for a girl like me. I'm so flawed. "Really?"

"Really, beautiful. When you didn't show up to work this morning after everything that happened last night, I was scared. For the second time in my life, I was terrified. I thought I lost you without getting a chance to tell you how I feel. I vowed on the way over to your apartment that I wasn't going to waste anymore time with you. No more messing around. I like you. A lot. I don't care that I'm your boss. I don't give a fuck about my reputation with women. None of them matter. I've never felt anything for any of them. Nothing on the same level as you."

I can feel the smile on my face getting bigger and bigger until my cheeks physically hurt from how hard I'm smiling. "Does that mean… that… maybe you'd be okay with giving this whole thing a try?"

"Honey, it means that the second I saw you sitting in my conference room waiting for me, I knew you were meant for me. Right then, I decided I'm not giving you up. I'm not letting you go. You were mine as soon as I laid eyes on you. I'm just sorry I waited so long to say anything."

Before I can respond, a sharp knock sounds on the door. I jump and look at the clock. It feels later, but it's only six p.m.

"Hey, Jas? You two awake?" a deep voice asks.

Jason sighs. "What do you want, Nick?"

"Ryan is here. I think we need to figure this out as quickly as possible if Jessa is up to it."

Jason looks at me and softly kisses my lips. "I know it's been a hard day, but he's right. We really need to figure out a plan to keep you safe. Which means we need to get to the bottom of why your ex is after you in the first place. We need to find him."

I swallow and try to stay calm. "I don't want to find him. I want to stay away from him. I want to forget everything that happened. I want to exist in a bubble."

"I know, beautiful. But I also know that there's something going on here that neither one of us are fully aware of. We need to figure it out."

51

Jason kisses me once more, then shifts me next to him as he gets out of the bed to get dressed.

He puts my suitcase on the bed for me, so it's easier for me to rummage through. I smile to myself as I turn my back to Jason. I find a pair of jeans and smile as I bravely strip off my shorts. I'm not wearing any underwear underneath them. It's not something I'd think I'd do so quickly with him, but I really am done with all of the waiting and sexual tension between us. He's right. It's gone on far too long.

I put the jeans on, foregoing panties because I really don't like them. And I want to be different then how I used to be. I want to be more confident. For once, if I don't like something, I don't want to feel pressured, by society or anyone else, to do it.

Maybe it's because of what happened last night. Maybe Jason is helping me see that it's okay to turn over a new leaf. Maybe it's because I simply don't care anymore. I've never been rebellious. Maybe, in order to get through this entire thing with Alex, I need to be. Maybe I need to be stronger. Maybe it's time to trust Jason to do what he said he will.

Help me.

Maybe trying to do everything myself was the wrong decision. Maybe depending on Cole as much as I have wasn't the best choice. It's time to stand up for me. Do what I want. Be stronger. Braver. A fighter.

When I turn, Jason is staring at me, his mouth agape.

"What?" I smirk.

"What? You know full well what you just did. You sure know what the fuck you're doing to make a man rock hard." He crosses the room to me, and slips his arms around my waist. I love how he towers over me. How he has to bend to kiss me. I love everything about this man.

I can't believe that just last night, I was fighting to survive a psychopath. Jason Crane was nothing more than my boss. My very hot boss that I'm falling for despite myself. Now, here I am in his bedroom. Kissing him. Touching him. Confessing feelings for him.

Even more surreal to me is that he feels the same way. I'm afraid to think it's reality. I'm afraid to think that this man could be the man meant for me.

As Jason pulls me close to his body once more, I know without a doubt that even though I thought I was in love with Alex, I wasn't. I did love him, but I was never in love with him. Not like this.

These… feelings that I have for Jason. This relationship that's been growing for a year. This sense of safety and trust. This thing that writers have spent their entire lives trying to put into words.

This.

This is the love I've always dreamt of.

Chapter Nine

✗ Jason ✗

I can't believe I have this beautiful woman in my arms. This amazing woman that I've wanted just like this for so long. I'm really glad that I have the opportunity with her that I do, and that she feels the same way. I'm not blind to how close I was to losing her; to never getting this chance with her.

My only regret is that I didn't tell her long ago. Maybe if I had, she wouldn't have been in the situation she was last night. She would have been with me. Maybe she would have opened up about Alex a long time ago. I could've had all of this shit with him taken care of. I could've protected her better. My family could have protected her better.

I hug her a little tighter before letting her go. Maybe if I told her how I feel, she wouldn't have lied to me last night about what was going on. She would've trusted me.

I look down at her. "My brother. His name is Ryan. He's a couple of years older and took over the... uh... the family business."

She looks confused. "Family business? I thought you're the CEO."

"No. That's my business. I started that. From the ground up. The family business is... it's something a lot different. You'll find out."

"Maybe you should just tell me." She's looking at me apprehensively.

I don't know how to tell her that my brother is the leader of the fucking mafia. Not after what she just went through with her ex. I think she's had enough mafia for one lifetime. Fuck. I don't even know if she knows he's mafia. Her restraining order is against an alias.

"Jessa, I… maybe we should just go downstairs. I'll explain everything when we get there."

She puts her hands on her hips and plants her feet firmly. I tower over her, but I can't help but smile at the way she stands up to me. Not many people are brave enough to make the attempt. I know how intimidating I am. Yet here she is facing off with me. Goddamn, it's sexy as hell.

"If we're going to do this, I want honesty. I want to trust you and not feel like you're hiding anything from me. I've had enough of that in my life. I don't want it anymore. I have to be stronger than that. I will. I will be stronger than that."

I grin. Okay. We're doing this. "Fine, beautiful. My brother is head of one of the largest mafias in the world. My family's mafia. I left it. I wanted to be on my own. Make my own way. I'm the youngest anyway. My brother was next in line to take over. My dad always knew I wanted no part of that life anyway, so it wouldn't have mattered. Ryan would have gotten the throne no matter what. I ran missions. I did my part. When I said I wanted out, Ryan wished me well. My dad gave me a loan to help me start my company. I paid it back with interest within the first couple of years."

Jessa watches me with both interest and wonder. I expected fear, given Alex's affiliation with the mafia. But again, I don't know if she knows that. I don't even know if she knows my affiliation.

"Oh. That's… a lot to take in. I mean, I suspected, but never asked. You've done well at making a name for you. Not your family."

"I know it's a lot. I'm sorry. Ryan turned our operation legal when he took over. I'm close to him and my family, but I'm not involved." I want her to know that I have nothing to do with it. I don't want her to think I'm ever going to hurt her. Jessa doesn't say anything. Instead, she hugs me, then takes my hand, pulling me towards the door. "Does this mean you aren't pissed?"

"Why would I be? Everyone has a history, Jason. I don't care if your family is part of the mafia. If they're anything like you, I'm sure I have nothing to worry about. Besides, I'm not stupid. I know not all mafias are created equal. And I do know a little bit about the Crane Mafia."

I tug on her hand, stopping her in her tracks and spinning her around. She meets my chest, hard, and I kiss her just fiercely. "You're fucking amazing, beautiful." I tuck her hair behind her ear. She smiles up at me and kisses me again. "Before we go down there, I need to make sure you're okay."

"I'm trying to forget. I'm trying to just…" she shrugs. "I'm trying to be the woman I want to be. I don't know why last night made me want to fight. I don't know if it's because I feel like I might have some help this time. Other than my friend, Cole, I really was all alone. The truth is I feel safe with you. I feel comfortable with you. I trust you. I'm a little afraid of how I feel about you, but I can't live in fear because of what happened to me. That's not fair to you or to me or the future I want." She smiles up at me and kisses me again.

My heart beats a little faster as I'm filled with a sense of pride. Jessa may not feel it, or maybe last night made her see it, but she's strong. Fierce. With me and my family at her side, I have no doubt in my mind she'll finally see the confidence I already see in her.

I take her hand and lead her downstairs. Nick and Ryan are sitting on the black leather recliners in my living room. All of my furniture is black leather. I think the white carpet underneath is a stark contrast and works nicely in the room. Both Ryan and Nick watch as I pull Jessa into my lap on the loveseat between the recliners they're in.

Ryan gives Jessa a brilliant smile. "Hey, Jessa. I'm Ryan. Jason's older and far more attractive brother."

I shake my head. "Easy now. I finally just got my girl. I won't be losing her to you."

Ryan laughs and Jessa chuckles. The banter between Ryan and I has always been easy. We may tease each other, but when it comes to women, if one of us has a claim staked, the other one wouldn't dream of interfering.

"It's nice to meet you," Jessa says quietly.

"You okay with diving right in, Jess? We can wait a few minutes if you need it." Nick asks.

Jessa nods. "It's okay."

Nick smiles. "Okay. Your ex, Alex Lucinio. He's -"

"Wait. Stop. Alex's last name isn't Lucinio. It's Lang," Jessa interrupts.

We all look at each other until everyone's eyes fall on me. Of course they'd leave this part to me. I clear my throat. "Jessa. Baby, I had someone look into your past a little bit when you didn't show up for work this morning. I was worried. She found a few police reports from L.A. as well as the restraining order you have against him. Lang is an alias. Alex's last name is Lucinio."

Ryan shifts in his chair, looking incredibly uncomfortable. I narrow my eyes because I know he's hiding something. I know my brother.

He clears his throat. "Alex Lucinio. Also known as Alex Lang. He's the son of Matthew Lucinio, leader of the Lucinio Mafia based in L.A." He looks at Jessa. Jessa looks confused as hell. Ryan breaks eye contact. Something is definitely going on.

"Maybe you should explain, Ryan. What more do you know about the family that I don't?" I ask.

Nick leans forward. "I'd like to know. Because as far as I know, Matthew Lucinio has no kids. You told us that after he shot dad."

"What?" Jessa asks, shaking her head. I pull her closer to me. "Yes. Please explain because Alex had a family powerful enough to keep him out of jail, but he wasn't part of the mafia!"

Ryan looks back at her and then at me and Nick before he sighs. "Well. Alex Lucinio does have an alias. Several, actually. One of them is Lang."

I glare at Ryan as Nick scoffs and stands up. He starts pacing the room. Ryan watches him as he leans back in his chair.

Nick turns on him. "Just spit it out. I don't like not knowing what the fuck I'm up against just as much as you."

Ryan looks like he's picking his words carefully. "Uh... Alex was... being groomed his whole life to take over the Lucinio Mafia for his father when he stepped down. Alex didn't want it. Just like I didn't. After his senior year of college..." Ryan pauses and looks at Jessa. "Alex left. He took over part of the mafia to get his dad to back off, but it was overseas. Italy. He took off and ran his own company, one he started a few years before, while running the overseas branches of the mafia."

"What? He… he never left," Jessa says.

"Jess, he… did." Ryan hesitates and looks nervous. It's nothing like my brother.

"What the hell are you hiding?" I demand.

Ryan looks at me. "Alex has a twin. The twin is the one who wants control. Their father won't give it to him."

"So, you lied to us?" Nick asks. Ryan looks away and says nothing.

"Wait," Jessa says. "I'm so confused. Alex doesn't have a twin brother. He's an only child. I spent time at his house! His parents were always away. He said they were both very busy. But he was an only child."

"What are his parents' names?" Ryan asks quietly.

"Matthew and Rebekkah."

"Matthew's wife's name is Rebekkah," I say, glaring at Ryan. It's the same as my dad's sister's name. She's dead. We never met her. But that's how I remember Matthew's wife's name.

Ryan nods as he takes out his phone. He scrolls through it, then hands it to Jessa. She hesitantly reaches out to take it. "Is that Alex, sweetheart?" he asks.

"Y-yes…" It's a picture of Ryan and a man together in front of the Roman Colosseum.

"That's Alex Lucinio, Jessa," he says as she hands him back his phone. "Two years ago."

"That doesn't make sense!" Jessa jumps off my lap and starts pacing.

Nick collapses back in his chair. He starts rubbing his temple. "Jesus Christ, Ryan," Nick says. Ryan refuses to look at either of us.

"Ryan, you said Alex went to Italy after college. How long was he there?" Jessa asks, stopping in her tracks like she just had an epiphany.

"Four years. Something like that," Ryan answers.

"Then they can't be the same person! Alex and I broke up for a year after college, and I didn't see him at all, but then he came back. We got back together and were together for almost four years! He spent a month stalking me, and then he put me in the hospital for a month! He almost killed me! I ran as soon as I was released!" She starts pacing frantically as Ryan stays quiet.

58

I finally grab Jessa's wrist and pull her back into my lap. I can feel her out of control heartbeat, and I've noticed hugging her calms her down. "Shh, baby," I whisper, holding her tight.

"He did say he has a twin, Jessa. Maybe it was his twin," Nick says.

Jessa glares at him. "It doesn't make sense! How can I have not known the man I was with for eight years is part of the mafia and has a twin?"

"Well, I... have an idea." Ryan finally looks at her, but the guilt I can see all over his face throws me. "I don't think you're going to like it."

I level him with a glare. "You're still hiding something."

"It's not my story to tell, Jason." Ryan rubs his temple and takes a deep breath. "Alex and I are good friends. He's like a brother to me. I never told anyone of our relationship because of the rivalry between our families. I didn't think any of you would understand it."

"Son of a bitch," Nick whispers. I shake my head, but stay quiet.

"He's in Manhattan," Ryan continues.

"I know. Where the hell do you think all these bruises came from?" Jessa asks, holding out her arms and showing him her neck.

He winces. "I haven't talked to him yet, but I know he's here because he called earlier and left a message. I haven't responded because I needed to talk to you guys first and make other calls." He pauses again and sighs. "I think we need to meet with him. Together, Jessa. There's a lot you don't know."

"Not fucking happening," I growl. "I won't put her back in his hands."

"For fuck's sake. Do you think I'd put her in any fucking danger?" Ryan growls back, finally snapping. He doesn't take shit from anyone. Me included.

I let out a frustrated breath and pull Jessa closer to my chest. "What's going on with the security detail? Why aren't they here yet?"

"Because I'm here and waiting on orders from my badass big brother," Nick snarls with a glare at Ryan.

Ryan glares. "Watch your tone with me. Just because we're family doesn't mean I won't kick your ass if I need to," Ryan says. Nick says nothing as he folds his arms over his chest and keeps his steely gaze on

Ryan. Ryan stands. "Jessa, I think we need to invite Alex over here. He needs to explain. Or he needs to be here when I explain all of this."

"When what's explained?" I ask. "Ryan, fuck. This is so fucked up."

"There are a lot of things you don't know, Jessa. A lot. And I can't be the one to tell you everything. It's not my story to tell," Ryan says.

Jessa buries her head in my chest. I don't want to tell her, but I'm starting to think this is a good idea. I may be pissed off at Ryan for keeping secrets, but I trust him. I don't know what he's hiding, but I do know him. I know if he thinks Alex needs to be here, then he needs to be here.

Ryan stands and kneels in front of me and takes Jessa's hand. "Jessa, look at me for a second. Please." It takes her a few moments, but she does as he says. "I know you don't know me very well. You barely know anyone in this room. But I can assure you, sweetheart. We protect our own. I know Jason has liked you for a long time. I can see you like him just as much. If you guys are together, and that's what it looks like, then that makes you family. What has Jason told you about me?"

She glances at me, then back to him. "That you're the leader of your family's mafia."

"I am. I'm protective, Jessa. I'm protective of my family. I'm protective of good people who don't deserve bad things to happen. I'm not a bad guy. I'm not good either, but I'm never going to let anything happen to the good people in this world. If you don't trust that Alex won't hurt you, or that the three of us won't let him, I'll have some of my guys come over right now. Whatever you want me to do to make you feel safe, I'll do it. But I really think we need to talk to Alex."

Jessa stares at Ryan like she's trying to figure out what to make of him. Like she's trying to decide if he's being truthful. Finally, she sighs. "Fine. But I want a lot of your guys here. I want to be surrounded by people who won't let him near me. Because he will kill me this time."

Ryan nods as he stands. "Done. I'll make the call right now."

My house becomes a flurry of activity. As promised, Ryan has several of his guys come over, and he gives each of them an assignment. Jessa sits stoically on my lap watching it all unfold with a calculated and suspicious eye. She doesn't move, even when my arms tighten around her, and I kiss the back of her neck.

I can tell she's fighting hard to stay strong; to show no emotion. What she doesn't know is I can feel her shaking in fear. No one would be able to tell by looking at her, but I can feel it as I hold her close to me.

He won't get the chance to touch her. He'll have to go through everyone in this house, followed by my brothers, and ending with me. I don't know if it's right of me to feel as strongly as I do for her, but I don't care. She's mine.

It's my responsibility to protect her now; to show her how a real man should love a woman.

Chapter Ten

⚔ Alex ⚔

"Where do you want us, boss?" Damon Knight, a member of my crew and one of my best friends, asks. I consider him a brother.

"I need to meet someone. I'll know more after," I say. "Lance, what did you find on Jessa?"

"Jessa's phone hasn't left her apartment. I'm still getting a signal. Josh is at your family's hotel," Lance tells me.

"But she isn't with him," Gavin says. He's another of my friends. Someone I consider family. Damon, Gavin, and I all grew up together. With Josh. We were all very close. It's hard that he's not part of us anymore. "Cole had a contact with the NYPD check, just to be sure."

"Glad I chose you as the cop I bankrolled," I joke as Cole grins. "You have fucking contacts everywhere."

"Pays to be a nice guy," he says as he shrugs.

"Anyone who thinks you're a nice guy doesn't know you very well," Damon jokes. We all laugh, needing it after the day we've had.

"I need you guys to sit tight," I say as I look down at my phone. I stand and head to my room as I answer. "About fucking time you answered my fucking messages."

"I couldn't. I needed to figure out what the fuck happened. I couldn't come to you with limited information. You would have gone completely ballistic."

I sigh. He's right. Ryan Crane. My best friend. Adopted brother. Leader of the most powerful mafia in the fucking world. Right up there with mine. The Crane Mafia has outfits everywhere. Just like mine.

Ryan and I shouldn't be friends. We should be enemies. There is far too much power between the two of us, but it didn't really bother either one of us. We hit it off years ago. We became close. We've used each other for different projects and even missions. We're allies, even though he hates my dad.

I can't blame him. I hate him, too. My dad shot Ryan's dad. Nearly killed him. He's fucked with Jessa's life. Mine. He's turned my brother into something I hardly recognize. If I had to be involved in a mafia and had a choice, I'd choose his. My dad still controls the Lucinio Mafia. I have a lot of control, more than he thinks, but he still controls it.

None of it matters right now, though. I need Ryan. I need his help. No one in our families knows we know each other or how close we are, but I need my brother.

"Do you know where she is?" I ask.

He sighs. "You need to come to me, Alex. There's a lot of fucked up shit going on. Jessa is fucking terrified. I told you that you should have told her. She has no idea."

"What? You and I both thought that's why she wanted out."

"I don't think that's it, bro. Not at all. She didn't know your last name. She didn't know anything about your family except your parent's names. She told me that you guys got back together a year after breaking up."

"We know Josh was pretending to be me."

"I know, Alex. I'm saying there's a lot she doesn't know. I told her you were in Italy during that time. I thought maybe she'd realize that there was more to the story. I told her some things, but this needs to get resolved. Now. You can't hide this shit from her anymore. If you ever really loved that girl, and I know you did, she deserves the truth."

"I already intended to tell her, Ryan. I couldn't find her."

"She's at my little brother's. Get here. I'm not fucking around. I found out a lot of shit."

"Like what?"

"Just get here." He pauses. "Just know that when you do, you need to really trust me."

"You know I trust you."

"She doesn't feel safe. You're going to have a lot of guns in the room when you get here. It's the only way I could convince her to face you."

"I'm fine with that. I expected nothing less."

"You should have told her."

"Lecture me later." I head out of the room. "Text me the address. I'm bringing Cole."

"Cole?"

"Her friend. Cole. He'll go a long way in getting her to feel safe."

"I know who he is. You didn't tell me he was here. Doesn't matter. There's one more thing you should know."

"She's with your brother. I already know."

"Not just with. Alex, she's together with him."

"I know, Ryan. Cole already told me how she gushes about him. It doesn't take a fucking rocket scientist to figure it out. You said she's at his house. I can only conclude she's with him." I glance at Cole and my team. "Cole, with me. Everyone else, settle in. I'll explain later."

Cole immediately follows. Everyone else obeys my command. Cole and I head for the elevator.

"I'll text you the address," Ryan says.

"Be there in ten."

"Ten? Sure. If you can fucking fly."

"Doing one-twenty good enough for you?" I smirk into the phone.

"You're going to kill yourself one day driving like that."

"I learned from you. Besides, my skills have gotten you out of more jams than I bet you can count."

"Fuck you. Get your ass here. That's an order."

Before I can respond, Ryan hangs up the phone. I grin and look at Cole. He looks more worried than I was only a few minutes ago. He keeps his eyes straight ahead at the elevator door. His eyes are red and bloodshot.

I pat him on the shoulder. "He found her."

Cole whips his head to me, a panicked expression on his face, and I instantly realize he thinks I'm talking about Josh. I haven't told him, or anyone else, about Ryan. "What? Are you fucking kidding?" he practically shrieks.

I hold up a hand. "Hey! Hold up! She's safe. My contact. He found her."

Cole visibly lets out a breath. "Fuck. Fuck, don't ever do that again." He runs a shaky hand through his hair as the elevator doors open. We exit into the lobby. One of the staff members sees me and immediately picks up the phone. I know he's calling the valet for my SUV. We head outside and wait while they retrieve it.

"Look. What we're about to walk into, it's… not what you're used to. There's going to be a lot of people there with guns." I look over at him.

He meets my eyes. "You know I'm armed."

"I know. Cole, I've never taken you on missions. I know you know I come from a powerful mafia family, but the power my family has is nothing compared to the power my contact wields."

"Are you talking about Ryan Crane?"

We get in the SUV, and I look at him and chuckle. "Sometimes, I forget how fucking smart you are." I take off and speed through the streets, following my GPS.

"I'm a cop. She works for Jason Crane. He's well-known. His entire family is well-known."

"What do you know about Ryan?"

"He took over his family's mafia after your dad shot his dad. He turned the entire operation legit. He works with Law Enforcement. His contact in the LAPD is my Captain. He works closely with a few Lieutenants and the Chief."

I nod. "Not bad."

"I had a feeling he was your contact, but I figured you'd tell me when you were ready."

"How did you know I'd tell you at all? Gavin, Damon, and Lance don't even know, and they've been with me a lot longer than you."

Cole looks at me. "Because Jessa is head over heels for Jason Crane. You'd have to tell me eventually. I'm her best friend. Not like I wouldn't fucking find out. If she becomes serious about him, you know as well as I do I'll be meeting the family."

I drive until I reach the mansions in the Upper Westside of Manhattan. I pull into one of the most lavish mansions I've ever seen. It sits on the shores of a small lake, and the property is perfectly groomed. The mansion is classic. It shows the owner has money, but the style has a more down to earth vibe.

I smile as I walk up to the door. It's large, but it has more of a homey feel. Sort of like Jessa's parent's house had felt. The size compared to theirs is far larger, but it almost doesn't matter. It's the sense of family that's important, and this mansion says all of that to me. It's not cold. Despite the gates that we had to get through when we showed up, the mansion has a warm feel.

The door swings open, and Ryan grins at me, pulling me into a hug. "You have no fucking idea how happy I am to see you."

"I love you, too, man, but I just want to see Jessa. Where is she?"

Despite my rush, I hug him back because I really do need my brother right now. I'll never admit it, but after the tension, fear, anger, and rollercoaster of emotions I've been through today, I need the hug. It's like Ryan knows that as he tightens his grip. I sigh as I pull back after a few moments, actually feeling better.

Ryan lets me go and sticks his hand out for Cole to shake. "I'm Ryan Crane."

"Cole Westwood." Cole shakes his hand.

"You're Jessa's friend."

"Yeah. I am. I hate to be a dick, but I want to see Jessa. I need to know she's safe."

"I get that, Cole," Ryan says. "But we do this my way."

Cole glances at me, and I nod. "Fine. But if it looks to me like it's not going well, I step in. Got it?"

Ryan nods with a grin. "Got it. Just know she has six of my guys surrounding her and she's sitting on her boyfriend's lap. Getting to her isn't going to be easy, unless she specifically tells me she wants you near her. Her safety and peace of mind is what matters."

Cole watches him a moment before he sighs and shakes his head. We both step in, and Ryan closes the door. He leads us both to the spacious, surprisingly modern, living room. Cole sucks in a breath next to me when he takes in all the people in the room. He's behind the wall, so while he can see into the living room, they can't see him.

"Shit. He wasn't fucking kidding," he says to me under his breath.

66

"He's more protective than both of us combined. The more you deal with him, the more you'll understand."

Ryan clears his throat, and all eyes fall to him. He commands the room without a damn word. I've learned all I know from him. "Everyone. I'd like you to meet Alex Lucinio."

He doesn't introduce Cole, and Cole glares at him. I shake my head and keep him hidden behind the corner. He growls again and turns his glare on me. I know how much he wants to get to Jessa, but Ryan is right. We need to trust him.

I drop my voice low. "Trust me."

Cole holds my gaze a moment, but he finally relents. If he goes in there with me, it will terrify Jessa more. She won't understand why he's with her enemy. I need to explain everything first.

I follow Ryan into the room as he talks. "I asked him here because there's a lot you don't know, Jessa. I mentioned that to you. It's time you know. You shouldn't have been kept in the dark as long as you were."

"Everything better get explained because the level of fear my girl is experiencing is not something I enjoy seeing."

My eyes fall to the deep and powerful voice across the room. I don't miss the possession projected from his voice when he referred to Jessa as his. I smile because, though that was me once upon a time, I'm happy she found someone who obviously makes her feel safe.

Ryan nods towards the direction the voice came from. "Alex. This is my brother, Jason. You know Jessa. Sitting next to them is my other brother, Nick. I think everyone else in the room is probably someone you've worked with over the years."

"Why don't you take a seat, Alex? Jessa doesn't like that you're standing up," Jason growls.

I meet his eyes when the guard in front of him moves slightly and find nothing but a challenge, daring me to disobey him. He looks like he wants to murder me. I can't really blame him. I'd feel the same way. All the guards in the room are standing near him and the tiny woman sitting on his lap, wrapped in his arms. She's trembling, and it breaks me. I hate seeing her fear. It was never what I wanted.

I take a seat as far away from her as I can get. It's not far, but it's across the room. Ryan kneels in front of Jason and touches Jessa's leg. She nearly jumps out of her skin. I can hear her gasp, and her breathing starts

67

racing. My heart shatters again in my chest. I didn't think it was possible to feel that kind of pain twice in less than a minute, but here I fucking am feeling like a thousand shards of glass are sitting in my chest.

"It's okay, sweetheart. It's me. Look at me," Ryan says gently.

Jessa clings to Jason, but shakily turns her head. She's careful not to look at me. My breath catches in my throat. I hate how much fear is coursing through her right now. I fucking hate even more that it was caused by my actions. By me running away instead of fighting for her. For us.

I watch as Jason pulls her closer. Her body visibly relaxes. I'm careful to stay still. I'm so fucking happy that she's okay. Despite the bruises and scratches, she's okay. She's alive. She looks completely at ease with Jason. Like she's meant to be with him. I'm happy to see she's finally found someone who loves her in all of the ways she deserves.

But if fucking kills me all over again that she's hurt because I left. That she endured all she did because I walked away and left her alone.

"Fuck, Jessa," I say, unable to hold back anymore.

A huge sense of relief falls over me because I know that she'll be okay. She picked the right guy to fall in love with. It looks to me like Jason will do whatever he can to protect her, but what's more is she has Ryan on her side. One of the few guys in this world I don't question, and that I trust with my own life.

I swallow down a lump of anger at myself for leaving her like I did, but her very own words come back to me, easing me slightly. She's always said she's a big believer in fate. Well, fate fucked with her in unimaginable ways, but they led her to him.

I shake my head and let the relief wash over me. "Thank God you're safe."

Chapter Eleven

✕ Jessa ✕

Jason keeps me close to him. I told him as soon as Ryan said Alex was here that I didn't want him to leave my side. It meant everything to me when he promised he wouldn't. Ryan made sure to have several of his guards here. I can't believe I'm sitting in the middle of several people involved in the mafia, and that one of the two guys in the room who makes me feel safe is the mafia boss.

Jason's strong arms around me and his scent calm me, but I still can't look at Alex. The thunder in my ears makes it hard to hear, but I swear he just thanked God I'm safe. I don't understand. He must be acting. He's so good at that.

"Jessa, I can't tell you how happy I am to see you're okay," Alex's deep and powerful voice says to me from across the room.

I don't say anything. I can't. I'm frozen in fear and near hyperventilation. I'm shaking in Jason's arms. He kisses the top of my head.

"You have a lot of explaining to do, Mr. Lucinio," Jason rumbles.

I whimper, but force myself to steal a glance at Alex. He's looking at me with a strange look of peace on his face. He looks at Ryan, sitting next to him.

"We both do," Ryan says. I burrow back into Jason's chest, intent on simply listening. Ryan told me I didn't have to say a word if I didn't want to. Jason agreed.

"Jessa. Ask me anything you want. I'll tell you," Alex says quietly. When I don't answer, I hear him sigh.

"Maybe it's best we start from the beginning," Ryan says.

"Maybe that's for the best," Alex agrees. He sounds almost sad. Incredibly apprehensive.

"Alex and I have been friends for a long time," Ryan begins. "Ever since the night our father was shot."

"What? How the fuck could you not tell us?" Nick thunders.

"Nick. Enough. Hear him out," Jason rumbles. Nick growls. I sniffle, trying not to cry; forcing myself to focus on Jason's breathing. I've already taken the prescription I need to carry with me for the panic attacks, but it doesn't seem to be working this time.

"I saw something more in him. Something more than a cold-blooded killer. So, I didn't shoot him like I could have. I gave him my number instead. We've used each other on more missions than I can tell you. He's just as much a brother to me as the two of you are."

I let out a sob because I can't figure out how someone as kind as Ryan seemed to be, could talk about Alex like that. He put me in the hospital. He tried to kill me!

"Shh… I got you, Jessa. You're okay. I'm not letting anything happen to you," Jason whispers in my ear. "You're safe, beautiful."

I tighten my grip around him and nod. I can't do anything else. I don't know what else to do even if I could do something. I'm numb with fear. So much for being strong and brave.

"Ryan and I became incredibly close. By the time I met you, Jessa, I had made the decision that I didn't want the mafia life. I wanted to go to college. I wanted to get my business degree, so I could take over the legal operation that we had as well as the company I started. My father hated the idea, but he agreed to leave me out of the mafia life and train Josh more so I could focus on school. He said by the time I graduated, if I really didn't want to take over, he'd let Josh. Josh is…" I hear him take a deep breath. "He's my twin brother."

I gasp, but I still can't look at him. Ryan said he had a twin, but Alex told me that he was an only child. I never met another brother. Surely, with as much time as I spent with him at his house, I would have seen this twin!

I grip Jason's shirt and take a deep breath of my own. "I spent time at your house, Alex. What about when you got beat up, and I was there with you? Your parents didn't see you. I think your mother did once when I was in the shower. But certainly not a twin!" I'm met with silence, and when I finally get brave enough to look over at him, he's looking at Ryan.

After a few moments, he looks at me and closes his eyes, pinching the bridge of his nose. "Just… let me finish." He opens his eyes and leans back on the couch. I see nothing but pain in his eyes, and it takes me by surprise. I stay quiet, waiting for him to continue. "When I started college, I enrolled under Alex Lang. I told you that was my name, and I never told you the truth because I didn't want you to be involved with my family. I didn't want anything to do with the mafia. I certainly didn't want you to. I wanted my own identity. Something not linked to my family name. I used that alias because it's as close to real as I could get. Alexander Joshua Lucino is my real name. Alexander Joshua Lang is an alias I use when I want to be me, but not me."

I watch him as he pauses. He glances at Ryan again and leans forward as Ryan starts talking. "The longer you guys were together, the more he realized he made the right decision. His dad didn't stand by the agreement and kept pulling him back in. Fuck. I pulled him into a few of my missions because I needed him."

"I don't understand. I'm trying, but I don't," I say, shaking my head. None of this makes any sense to me.

"You will, Jessa. I promise. When I'm done, it'll make sense. But there's a lot, and you deserve the truth," Alex says.

"We needed to tell you all of that so you understand, so all of you understand, that Alex and I really are close. Jessa, remember when you went to New York for a week, and Alex said he was in Canada?" Ryan asks.

"Yes," I say, a little unsettled that he knew about it.

Ryan gives me a soft smile. "Alex was with me."

"My dad got our family involved with the fucking cartel. Ryan helped me fix it," Alex says.

I shake my head and shift in Jason's lap so that I am sitting with my back to him instead of being curled up in a ball on him. "What? I'm so confused."

"I know, Jess," Alex says. "I know. I don't expect you not to be. This is a lot to take in. Shit. I should have been upfront about this years ago. If I had, maybe things would be different."

I sigh and settle back into Jason's arms. "Just finish."

"I had intended to tell you everything after graduation. I… was… going to ask you to marry me. To come to Italy with me, but by that time, we were… drifting apart?"

I look at him incredulously. "Drifting… apart? Have you lost your mind?"

"I know, Jess. I -"

"You spent so much time berating me and telling me I was a slut and crazy!" I burst out. My entire body tenses with anger.

"Jessa, please -"

"You accused me of cheating on you with Cole!" I nearly jump out of Jason's arms, but he holds me tightly to him, sensing how angry I am. "And then you'd spent hours making it all up to me and treating me like a princess. Like nothing fucking happened!"

"Jessa! Enough! Let him finish!" Ryan commands. I immediately shut my mouth and shrink into myself. Ryan is intimidating, and his tone demands respect and obedience.

"I'm sorry, Jessa. I know you're afraid of me," Alex says. "Just please let me finish. Please?" The pleading tone of his voice is projected in his eyes. I nod. "Thank you. The day I told you to make a decision to be with me or not and you chose to leave, I left. That very day. I called Ryan, and the two of us flew to Italy. Ryan came home not long after. I stayed. I took over the overseas operation of the mafia. I ran my company. Lucinio Tech. I lived a relatively normal life. Thought about you every fucking day for a while, but I respected your wishes. I stayed away."

"That's why I told you he was in Italy," Ryan says to me. I feel a headache coming on. My head is swimming.

"Wait. Let me get this straight," Jason says. I silently thank him because I'm really trying to understand everything. "Alex, you lied about

72

your name and your family. Didn't tell her who you were because you wanted out of the mafia life and didn't want her involved. And you have a twin? Fucking convenient."

"Jason," Ryan growls in warning.

"Just finish, Alex," Nick says as he leans back on the couch and rubs his head.

Alex only nods. "About a year after I left, Josh told me he was seeing this amazing woman."

"Wait. A year? That's when you…" I trail off, all at once understanding. I look at Alex. "Oh my God."

"I didn't know, Jess. I wasn't here. He told me he was in love. He told me our parents loved her, and that dad was going to let him take over as soon as he married her. About four years later, I got a call from Lance. He's one of my friends. A guy on my crew. He told me that you filed a restraining order against me. That I shoved you and hurt you. I was confused as fuck because I wasn't here. I hadn't even talked to you in almost five years at that point."

If I wasn't already sitting, I'd collapse. I can feel my legs get numb. Everything suddenly makes sense, and I feel so stupid for not understanding it sooner.

"Josh had been pretending to be me," Alex, the real Alex, continues. "For four years, you were with him, Jess. As soon as I got back here, we figured it out. The night he attacked you, Gavin tried to save you. He had been tailing you, but he lost you and got stuck in traffic. We tracked you to Cole's house. He called me as soon as he got there and saw Josh. By the time he got into the house, Josh had already beaten you up and knocked you out."

"Holy shit," Nick mumbles.

Alex glances at him, then turns his attention back to me. I don't know what to say. "Gavin called the police and me as he was going into the house. Josh fought with him and eventually knocked him out when he was trying to help you. I got there seconds after he fled. I heard the back door close. Damon and Lance ran after him but couldn't find him. Cole showed up with other officers. We got you to the hospital, and I made the decision that you would never know any of this. I wanted you to start over."

73

"Why? Why wouldn't you just be honest and tell me everything then?" I ask. I sniffle and look down at my hands as a truly horrible thought enters my mind. "Did you ever love me?"

"Jessa, are you kidding? I loved you so much that leaving you tore me apart. I was a fucking mess. I interjected myself back into mafia life just so I had an outlet for everything I was feeling but couldn't deal with." He runs a hand through his hair.

I take a breath and loosen Jason's grip on me and stand. Everyone in the room watches me. Except Alex. He's put his head in his hands and is looking at the floor. I get down on my knees in front of him and take his hands in mine. "Alex."

He squeezes my hands and looks at me. There are tears in his eyes. "I'm sorry, peanut. I'm sorry I was too late that night. Had I just been honest with you, none of this would have happened. I just wanted to protect you. When you left L.A., I made sure your social security number was masked. Everything it came up on, Lance hid. That's how Josh found you when you were in L.A. He tracked your social security number. I took every precaution I could to make sure you were hidden. Anything your name came up on, my team removed it. Jessa, I did everything I could to make sure you were a ghost. I don't know how he found you, but I'm sorry. I should never have left. I'm sorry I wasn't there for you then. I'm even more sorry that he found you, and I wasn't there for you last night."

He hangs his head, defeated. I've never seen Alex like this. I can't help but hug him. He hesitantly puts his arms around me as I rest my head on his shoulder.

"I'm sorry, Alex."

"For what? Peanut, you have nothing to apologize for."

"Yes, I do. I should've talked to you. I should've known something wasn't right. The way I was being treated by you; the differences when it was your twin. He was a lot more cold. Mean. There was a night at the club. Actually, it was when I really started talking to Cole. Josh caught me. Of course, I thought it was you. I'd only had one glass of wine, but I was feeling tipsy. Awful. Josh dragged me outside and was super rough with me. Angry about me talking to someone else. He told me to go home. He'd see me later. Then, he walked away. It's so obvious now. I knew deep down you could never hurt me."

Alex shakes his head. "You couldn't have known. I never told you who I was. I never took you home. I kept my entire family a secret from you. Fuck, it all makes so much more sense now. The fear you showed towards me. I never put two and two together. Never in my life did I think Josh would ever do something like that to me. Or you. I should have told you everything."

"But I know now that you didn't tell me to protect me."

Alex lets go of me and slowly pulls away. "I want to show you something. Just so there's no doubt about what I'm telling you." He reaches into his pocket and pulls out his phone. He scrolls through it and hands it to me. On it is a picture of him standing next to someone who looks just like him.

"Josh," I whisper. "Seeing you next to him, the differences are so obvious."

Alex nods. "He works out more than I do, so he's got more muscle mass. He looks bigger."

"He looks colder. More calculating."

"You'd be right. That's the effect our father and the mafia has had on him."

I hand him back his phone as I stand and walk back to Jason. Alex looks far more relaxed. Ryan is less on edge. Even Jason has calmed down. I can feel it in his body as I settle back on his lap.

"That's not everything. Alex worked really closely with both me and Cole to get you here," Ryan says. "Alex told me your dream of wanting to work with a big project development firm where you could focus on designing. When you were ready to start looking for jobs, I convinced Jason to put the open position he had in the paper and online instead of hiring within or recruiting, like he usually does."

"And I made sure you saw the ad," a deep voice says. I would recognize it anywhere.

"Cole?" I ask.

He comes around the corner and smiles softly. "Hey, honey."

I waste no time jumping off Jason's lap and running to him. I've talked to him nearly every single day over the past year, but I haven't seen him since he left. I bury my face in his neck when he catches me. "I missed you. So much."

"I know. I know. I promise not to stay away so long again." Cole buries his face in my hair as he wraps his arms around me and squeezes me tightly. After a few minutes, he lets me go and leads me over to the couch Jason is sitting on, watching me intently.

When we reach him, he smiles and stands. "I'm Jason Crane."

"Nice to finally meet you. Jessa's been gushing about you ever since you hired her," he says winking at me.

I give him a playful shove. "Cole! Stop. Don't embarrass me." I feel my cheeks burning red as Jason pulls me down with him again. Cole sits in a chair near us and grins.

"So all of you were involved in this," Nick says.

"We were all involved in protecting her, yes," Ryan responds. He turns back to me. "When you got here, I had orders to keep an eye on you. Even if you hadn't gotten the job, Jessa, I would've had surveillance on you. That's what Alex wanted."

"Where the hell was your surveillance last night?" Nick grunts.

"That was one of the calls I had to make. They weren't watching her. Nothing had been going on, so they thought they could slack off. They've been dealt with."

I swallow. I don't know what that means, but the dangerous glint in his eye tells me that it's nothing good. I wouldn't want to cross him.

"That's why the past couple days when I brought up the mafia…" Jason says as he looks at Ryan.

"Yeah. I got a little strange. The mafia being involved at all in your company was an immediate danger to Jessa. When you told me what happened, I went into mafia boss mode. I arranged for guards to be stationed around your property. And then I spent the day piecing shit together before I called Alex." Ryan looks at Alex. "I wanted everyone together when I told you this."

"When you told me what?" Alex asks cautiously.

"I found out the reason Josh went after Jessa at all is because of your father."

"I knew that. I'm the one who told you."

"No. I mean, initially, Josh intended to protect her." He pauses and hands Alex a single sheet of paper. "And you."

76

I watch as Alex's face contorts from shock to bewilderment to complete rage in a matter of seconds. I look at Jason, then Cole. "What?" I ask.

Alex looks up at me as he crumples the paper in his hand. "He had a hit on me."

"What? What does... that mean?" I ask. Alex gets up and paces the room. Cole and Nick watch him, as do Ryan's guards.

"It means, his father ordered some of his guys to kill Alex if he didn't follow his demands," Ryan explains. "He was still in college when the hit was ordered."

"Demands?" I look at Alex as he meets my eyes. "What demands?"

"He wanted me to break up with you. He thought you were the reason I was so against taking over his precious mafia. He showed me pictures one day of the two of us together and told me that one of his contacts wanted me dead and intended to go through you to get to me. But this?" He holds up the now crumpled ball in his hands. "This proves that he was obsessed with you. He wanted me dead so he could have you for himself. It specifically says that you were to remain unharmed and taken to him. I played right into his hands by leaving. It left you unprotected and available to him whenever he wanted to take you. He canceled the first hit and ordered another. It says that if I ever came back, and you and I ever got back in contact, I'm to be killed immediately. The only reason I'm still alive is because he never knew I was involved in your disappearance."

"I don't know if it's true, only one person can really answer that, but it looks like Josh got involved to protect his brother. After Alex left, it was to protect you."

"But he became just as obsessed," Alex says. "My father must have done something to make him snap, because what happened to you isn't Josh. He still won't talk to me about everything, and I'm not making excuses, but there's more to this story. I fucking know it."

"Like what?" Jason asks. "Why the fuck is he so obsessed with her?"

"I wish I could answer that question for you, Jason, but I don't know," Alex answers.

"You know what this means?" Ryan asks, looking at Alex.

Alex nods. "It means we're working together."

"We need to protect Jessa and figure out what the hell is going on," Ryan says.

I look between all of the men in the room before my eyes fall on Alex. His eyes bore into mine. "It means Jason, Nick, and Ryan don't leave your side," Alex says.

"It means I'm staying here," Cole tells me.

I nod. In a matter of twenty-four hours, I've been beaten up, fallen head over heels in love with my boss, or at least finally admitted to it, and gotten involved with, not one, but two mafias. I've found out that my tormentor really wasn't who I thought, and that the person it actually was may not have been completely at fault.

I chew my lip as I think. Finally, I decide to just say what's on my mind. "The day you got beat up, or I guess it was Josh, you'd, ugh, he'd just left my apartment. I had a meeting with my boss at a job I'd just started not long before. When I got back to my apartment, there was someone waiting for me. I'd never seen him before, but he said you'd sent him. It took me a few minutes, but I followed. He said you were in trouble. In bad shape. You'd been jumped outside your house. When we got there, he led me through the back. I thought that was odd. He said he didn't want your dad to try and introduce himself. Or your parents or something. I don't quite remember. I couldn't figure out why they weren't with you. When we got to what I thought was your bedroom, I saw who I thought was you on the bed. Josh was really hurt. After I had a chance to really look him over, I saw what I swear was a needle mark on his neck. I talked myself into believing it was a bee sting or something, but it still felt very strange to me."

Alex and Ryan look at each other and both shrug. "I think that's something we should look into," Ryan says to Alex. Alex nods.

I still don't know everything that's going on. I know there's more that's being left out. I just don't know if it's because Ryan and Alex are trying to protect me, or if there's pieces they don't have to this very complicated puzzle I find myself trying to put together. For now, though, I need to trust the people in this room. I shake my head a little bit because I still don't believe that the people I need to trust, other than Jason and Nick, are the mafia.

Chapter Twelve

⚔ Jason ⚔

I sent Jessa to bed long ago. She was falling asleep in my arms, even though she was trying not to. I couldn't blame her. Besides the short nap, Jessa hadn't really slept in I don't know how long. Certainly not after being attacked. We talked to Alex long into the early morning hours. I know she wanted to stay up with the rest of us, but she really needed sleep.

I don't know what to think of Alex. I didn't get where I am by trusting blindly, but I find myself going along with Ryan and Jessa on this one. Ryan trusts Alex with his life. If it wasn't already obvious, he said it many times.

But it's really Jessa's reaction to him. She hugged him. She has no fear of him at all. I don't know what to make of this entire situation. The only thing I know for certain is that I never wanted any part of the mafia. I hated it when I was in. I got out for a reason. I'm not like my brothers. I can't compartmentalize the kills and move on with my day. It's never been who I am.

Somehow, though, I am suddenly deeply involved once more because the woman I love is inadvertently entangled with them. And fuck do I hate it. I hate that she's going through this. I hate that I'm being pulled back in.

After Alex and Ryan leave and Cole and the guards Ryan left are settled, I walk into my room. I see Jessa laying on my bed. It's almost daybreak, and I don't want to wake her, but I need her in my arms. I need to feel her next to me if for no other reason than to make sure she's safe. I strip down to my boxer briefs in the almost pitch black room and crawl in next to her.

"Fucking Christ, Jessa," I whisper growl into her hair as I'm wrapping my arms around her. She's naked, and my body instantly responds to her. I should be running the other way. Unfortunately, it's not my head that's in control anymore. It's my heart. My head tells me to let her go; that she's not ready for this, but my heart says she needs me.

She reaches behind her and brushes the back of her hand over my length. I groan, and involuntarily push myself into her.

"I like you like this," she whispers. She squeezes, and I inhale sharply. I can feel her smiling. I don't even have to see it.

"Tease," I moan as I'm kissing her neck. She begins lightly stroking me over my boxer briefs, and I groan. Everything in me is telling me that she's tired and vulnerable.

"Tease? Maybe if I stopped you could call me that."

She turns to face me, her naked and very full breasts pillowed against my chest. She stops stroking me and kisses my chin.

"Now can I call you a tease?" I grin teasingly against her lips.

She laughs and pushes me on my back. She climbs on top of me and positions herself over my cock. She leans down to kiss me while she grinds herself against me. I wrap my arms around her and move my hands down to her perky ass just as she pulls away.

"Now you can call me a tease." She attempts to climb off me, but I hold her firmly against me, pushing her against my hard cock. I question myself the entire time, but I'm following my instincts. She seems to want something, and I'm not in a position to deny my girl anything.

"Do you feel what you've done to me?" I ask her, giving her the same teasing tone she seems to enjoy using on me.

"Yes."

"And what are you going to do about that?"

"Hmm… I'm just… not sure, Jason." She's smirking, and I bite the inside of my cheek to keep from laughing. She grinds and wiggles against me as she giggles. Actually fucking giggles.

"Fuck, Jessa. What are you doing?" I cup her ass and sigh at her smooth skin against my fingers.

"Making you feel good?"

"Why are you naked?"

"Because I'm tired of waiting for you. This isn't insta-love with me. I've wanted you for so long. And now that we've admitted it…" I watch her for a moment, and she sighs. "I'm sorry. I feel so stupid. I shouldn't be acting like this after what happened. I just feel like there's a war raging inside me." She moves to stand, but I stop her. I can hear the tears in her voice. I don't like it.

I gently pull her down next to me as I roll on my side. I wrap her in my arms and tilt her chin up to look at me. "Jessa. Baby, tell me what you need. There's nothing I wouldn't give you, but I'm not going to do anything unless you ask."

"I'm just so confused about everything."

"Talk to me. Let's figure it out." She burrows into me, and I force all sexual thoughts aside as I wrap her in my arms.

She looks down at my chest before she burrows herself in my arms. I run my fingers through her hair. "Should I be afraid of you? Afraid to be touched? Shouldn't I be jumpy after what happened?"

"You trust me. It's obvious. You feel the same way about me as I do about you. We already figured that out. I'm not going to rehash it. If you're asking me if all of your feelings and your wants and needs are unrealistic after everything that happened last night with Alex's brother, I'll tell you no. I don't think they are."

"I feel so crazy and stupid."

"For wanting to feel wanted and loved by someone you care for? Especially after everything you just went through? Baby, that isn't crazy. That's human fucking nature."

"I just feel so deeply for you. It seems so against… well, everything. And it's scary because I fell for Alex so fast."

"But you didn't fall for me like that, Jess. This whole thing between us has grown since we first met. Progressed naturally, if that's how you want to interpret it. We've gotten to know each other since we've met. And yeah, we don't know all there is to know, but isn't that what relationships are all about?"

"You're my boss," she nearly whispers. "You have rules in place."

"Rules change, baby. We're both adults. We both know what we want. We have feelings for each other we've never had for anyone else. If this is what we both want, there shouldn't be anything stopping us. Including rules that I created to put barriers up between us in the name of protecting you and your reputation."

Her eyes soften in both wonder and awe. "Really?"

"Really." I shrug a little and brush my lips against hers. "I didn't want people to think I was playing favorites because of a relationship between us, baby. And I was also trying to keep you at a distance because of my feelings for you. I've never felt this way about anyone. It's pretty fucking scary for me to. I'm a one and done kind of guy. With you, I know once is never going to be enough. And I didn't know what to do with that. Honestly, I just don't care anymore. I want you. You want me. Maybe it's time to just give in and stop fighting what we both want."

"You're truly beyond my dream come true, Jason."

I smile and lean down to kiss her, pouring all of the feelings I've hidden from her ever since I met her into it. Within a few moments, she's moaning into my mouth. Seconds after that, she's wrapped around me, and I'm straining against my boxers once more.

"Tell me what you need, Jess." I give her a squeeze.

She whimpers. She rubs her legs together and pushes against me. "You. I just want you. I've wanted you for so long."

Needing no more than that to understand, I leave sweet yet searing kisses along her jawline and down to her neck. I gently nudge her onto her back and continue my trail of kisses down her collarbone. When I reach her soft and full tits, she whimpers and arches into me. I rest my hand on her hip and give her a light squeeze as I work my way from her delicious mounds to her already peaked nipples.

As soon as my tongue hits her sensitive flesh, she cries out and digs her fingers into my hair. She squirms, and I hold her down on the bed with my arm. I suck one of her nipples into my mouth and swirl my tongue around it while I tug the other one between my thumb and forefinger.

"Oh my… God." She sucks in a breath as I pull back with a grin. I blow on her nipple and lick it before moving onto the other one and giving it the same attention. "Mmm…."

"You like that?" It's a question I already know the answer to.

"Love that. I love that," she whispers. By the time I pull back, she's panting and squeezing her legs together. With patience and as much gentleness as I can manage, I lightly graze her thigh with my fingertips. I kiss between her tits.

"If we do this, Jessa, there's no going back. I don't want anyone else. You become mine. No one else gets to touch you. You don't get to touch anyone else. I'm a possessive mother fucker, and I want that commitment."

"I've waited my whole life for you, Jason," she says softly, running her fingers through my hair. I don't want anyone else either. Just you. I've known it for a long time. I was just never brave enough to say anything. I didn't want to ruin my career."

I let her pull me to her lips. As my tongue plunges into her mouth, I drop my middle finger slowly and deeply into her pussy. She gasps into my mouth, and I groan. She's tight. Wet. Waiting and ready for me.

"Jesus. You're fucking soft all over, aren't you?" I whisper against her lips. She melts into my touch and reaches down to touch me. I groan again because I'm so hard that just her touch makes me want to come instantly. "Don't, honey. I'm too close, and I have no intention of coming on your hand." I add a second finger and slowly thrust them in and out of her.

"Oh God! Jason!"

She arches into me and kisses me so hard that I nearly come all over her without her even touching me. Not fucking like me at all, but she has some strange effect on me. All she has to do is look at me, and I'm solid as a damn rock.

I slide my fingers deeply inside her and swirl them both around as my tongue entwines with hers. She tries to say something, but I catch her words with my kiss as I quicken the pace. I moan when she nearly sucks me into her tight walls.

"Jesus, you're so tight." I feel her body start singing for me as I fuck her with my fingers. Knowing how happy I'm making her is the biggest turn on I've ever experienced. Her moans, her quickened breathing, and her subtle movements all make me want her so much more.

Jessa's breathing gets heavier as her movements become more and more erratic. Her sweet pussy gets wetter and wetter the more strokes I give her. She rides my fingers and clenches uncontrollably around me as her fingers dig into my shoulders.

Once again, I find myself plunging my tongue into her mouth at the same pace I'm thrusting my fingers into her. I set my thumb against her little ball of nerves and start rubbing in smooth circles with a little pressure at the same pace I'm thrusting.

"Jason!" she screams into my mouth.

I grin because my name on her lips is everything I never knew I needed to hear. She sets my body on fire; my heart alight. I kiss down her jaw to her neck, continuing to thrust my fingers into her pussy and rub her clit. She bucks into me, holding onto my shoulders like she's trying to stay afloat in violently tumultuous waters.

I lick her neck and suck lightly right before I bite down on her sensitive skin and suck again to soothe the pain. Her walls clamp around me and she clamors for any kind of hold as I bring her closer and closer to falling off the edge of the peak I've led her to.

"Come, Jess. Fuck, I need to feel you." I crook my fingers inside her, hitting her sweet spot, and she comes completely undone.

"Ah! Jason!" She arches off the bed, gripping me tightly, and throws her head back. Her pussy spasms around my fingers as I thrust her through her release, slowing my pace with each stroke.

But I can't hold back anymore. I need to feel her; need to be inside her. I shift, pulling my fingers out of her and sucking her sweetness off them, and slide my underwear off. I position myself between her legs as she looks up at me shyly.

"You taste even better than I imagine," I say huskily as my eyes travel unabashedly up her beautiful body. When they meet her eyes, I lean down and kiss her, putting most of my weight on my elbows so I don't crush her.

I reach down and grab my throbbing cock. I slide it through her wetness and let out an inadvertent groan at how fucking good she feels. No one I've ever been with has felt like she does. I let my head drop to her neck and kiss it as she moans and writhes under me.

84

"Mmm…, Jason…," she whispers against my shoulder.

Those words are all it takes. I plunge into her in one sure thrust. "Holy fuck."

She clamps so tightly around me, I'm not entirely certain my dick is still attached to me until I feel her arch. I slide deeper. I try to stay still as she pulses around me. I know with how tight she is, she has to be getting used to my size. The last thing I want to do is hurt her. I'm sure she's still sore from the injuries she took from the beating by Josh.

"Mmm…" She closes her eyes and lets herself relax around me.

When she opens them, I smile and run the pad of my thumb over her lower lip. "Ready?"

She nods with a blush. "So ready."

She makes me feel dizzy. She's so small and fits so perfectly with me, I know she was made for me. There's no question. When I start moving, she wraps her legs around me, pulling me closer. I slide deeper with another low and possessive groan. She's so tight. So wet. So fucking perfect.

And all mine.

I lick and suck my way back to her lips, kissing her deeply as I slide my hand down to her hip. I grip it and raise her slightly. The angle causes my dick to slide even deeper inside her. I suck on her tongue with a low groan.

The way she pulses around my dick brings me closer and closer to the edge as I thrust hard and deep but slow. Each and every thrust is filled with desire, passion, and love. Fucking love because damn if I'm not already head over heels for her. Her moans and whimpers are addictive as she tightens around me.

She meets my thrusts and wraps her arms and legs tighter around me. "Oh my God, Jason. You… feel… so good."

"Fuck, baby…," I groan as my dick starts to thicken. Her pussy pulses erratically and uncontrollably around me. I can feel her thighs start to tremble as she gets wetter and wetter. "So tight and wet for me."

She's not going to last much longer, and considering how close I already was, I know I won't either. But I still thrust slow, deep, and hard. I want to feel every part of her. I want her to feel every ridge of my cock. I don't want to think about anything. I just want to feel. I want her to just feel me. All of me.

She throws her head back and arches into me again and again as I sink into her deeper and deeper. Her fingernails scratch across my shoulders. When I feel her start to come, I can't hold back. A jolt shoots down my spine. I come so hard, I see stars.

"Ah! Jason!" she screams into my shoulder. Her hips buck into me as my dick jerks inside her, filling her pussy with all of me.

My stomach tightens with each hard thrust into her as I come. "Jessa! Holy fuck!" My fingertips dig into her hip and sexy as hell ass until we're both so spent, we collapse.

After several moments of panting into each other's neck and holding onto each other as we fall through cloud after cloud on our way back down to earth, something very important sucker punches me. My eyes widen, and I scramble up, staring down at her in horror.

She furrows her brows and looks at me completely confused. "What… happened?" She tilts her head adorably as my heart starts racing at a pace to rival a Nascar driver.

"Shit. Baby, shit. I always wrap it up. I… Fuck, Jessa. I wasn't wearing a condom."

I was conditioned from a very young age to always protect myself. I've been with a lot of women over the years, and not once have I ever not sheathed my fucking dick. But that's, shockingly, not the reason, I pulled out so quickly. It's because of her. I don't know if she's on birth control. I don't know if she wants kids. I'm not ready for them in the slightest, but I sure as hell should have talked to her before losing all fucking control like that. I never lose control. Ever.

Jessa sits up slowly with a soft smile. "I'm sure, considering who you are, you're probably a little freaked out."

I take a deep breath. "Surprisingly, I'm not at all freaked out about not wearing a condom for the reasons I usually would, baby. I'm a little afraid because we didn't talk about if you're on birth control. We didn't discuss kids. Kids are something that we can talk about later, but -"

She giggles as she palms my cheek. "Jason, I'm on birth control. I have been for years. Not because I'm so overly sexually active or whatever the stigma is for women on birth control. I started it in my teens to help with cramps. And I never got off it because it regulates everything and makes things easier for me. I was one of the lucky ones who didn't have a ton of issues with it and gain a ton of weight or have hormonal imbalances.

So, I just stayed on it since it seems to be in my best interest health wise."
She kisses me softly with a smile. "So, you don't need to worry about me.
It's okay."

I relax, but only slightly. "It's not a hundred percent, though. If I'd
been thinking, it's an extra layer of protection. I'll be honest. I'm not ready
for kids. I'm not totally sure I want them at all. Maybe one day, but right
now?" I shake my head.

Jessa sighs. "I've always believed in fate." Her smile softens. "If it
happens, it happens. I'll take it as it comes, you know? I know it's not a
hundred percent. But it's been good so far. And if it fails, well, I guess it's
meant to be." She shrugs a little. I can see the hesitancy; how unsure my
words just made her.

I kiss her forehead as I get off the bed. I hold out a hand for her.
She takes it, and I pull her off the bed into me. I wrap her in my arms and
hug her tightly. "I may not be ready, and I doubt you are either, but you're
right. We'll take it as it comes. Together."

Her entire body relaxes as she lets out the breath I'm not sure she
knew she was holding. I smile as I lead her to the bathroom. We both clean
up. I feel like my face could crack with how hard and wide I'm smiling.

When we finish, she curls up under the blankets, her cute naked
ass, peeking out. I can't help but let out a laugh as I crawl in next to her.
She blushes and cuddles into me when I put my arms around her like it's
the most natural thing in the world.

I'm asleep moments later to the sound of her soft breathing; the
feel of her safe in my arms.

Chapter Thirteen

⚔ Jessa ⚔

I wake up later with the sun high in the sky. I don't know what time it is, but I'm laying naked with my back to Jason, his arms engulfing me and his face buried in my hair. His large hand is comfortably cupping my breast. I smile as I try to get up without waking him.

"Where do you think you're going?" His voice is raspy and heavy with sleep.

I laugh. "I was just going to get cleaned up."

"Hmm. Good idea." He lets me go and rolls out of the bed, but he grabs my hand and pulls me with him. I nearly have to run to keep up with his stride.

"Where are you taking me?" I laugh again.

"You said you wanted to get cleaned up." He turns the shower on and pulls me in with him. The water droplets on his body are hypnotizing, and I have to fight to keep from licking them off.

"Wow. You're gorgeous," I whisper as I watch a droplet make its way down his abs.

"Same to you, beautiful." He leans down to kiss me as he backs me against the shower wall. "Now that I've tasted you, I want you all the time." He bends to kiss my neck, leaving a trail of featherlight kisses across my collarbone to my nipples. "Only this time, I'm worshiping you with my tongue."

I gasp and throw my head back as he takes each one of my hardened peaks into his mouth in turn, giving each of them a hard suck and flick with his tongue. He nips them and continues lower with soft kisses until he's on his knees in front of me. He looks up at me and grins.

Every part of his touch is soft and sensual. It's like it's his mission to make it all about me. He moves slowly to my core as the water runs over his back. He gently licks and kisses me until I'm squirming. Just when I think I can't take anymore, he slides one finger into me and takes my small bundle of nerves between his lips. He sucks and nips at it.

"Jason!" I scream. Part of me wants to collapse. The other part of me wants to shove his face into me because whatever he's doing with his tongue is setting my blood on fire.

My head falls back against the shower wall as my eyes flutter closed. I thrust myself over his tongue. My fingers grip his short, messed up bed hair. My fingers dig into the wall behind me. His tongue swirls over my clit.

He pushes a second finger inside me and moans against me. I inhale sharply. My pussy pulses and clenches around his fingers. I tighten and get wetter for him with each thrust. When he starts crooking his fingers inside me, though, I almost lose my mind.

"Oh…," I moan and let my head fall forward once more. There's something so sexy about Jason Crane on his knees in front of me bringing me this much ecstasy.

Before I can stop it, my legs start quaking. My stomach tightens. The all too familiar tingles shoot through me until they turn into shockwaves. My pussy clamps down over his fingers. He nips my clit, and I'm done. It has to be in record time.

"That's it, beautiful. Come for me." He gives me one more lick before he takes my clit in his mouth once again. It's all it takes for me to do as he commands. As I release, my legs get weak. I slide down the wall and hang onto him for dear life. He continues pumping his finger in and out of me, allowing me to ride out the orgasm that's wracking my body.

"Oh God. Jason…"

He releases my clit but doesn't pull out of me. He lets me slide further and further down the wall until I'm on my knees in front of him. He cradles me against him with one arm while he slowly removes his finger from me and sucks me off of them. I blush and bury my face in his neck.

"Watching that is fucking hot. I'm never going to get sick of it." He leans in and kisses me. I taste myself on his tongue as he stands and helps me to my feet. He wraps his arms around me and holds me tightly for a few moments while I regain my strength. At least enough to stand on my own two feet.

"You're so amazing. That... was so amazing," I whisper.

Jason slowly releases me and chuckles. "It's only going to get better." He pushes my hair behind my ears and holds my face in his hands. He kisses me on the forehead, then steps away so we can clean up. As soon as he's done, he kisses me again and steps out of the shower. "I have a meeting I can't miss this afternoon baby. Hurry up." He swats my ass. I jump and giggle.

Holy God, this man is going to be the death of me.

XXX

I'm not entirely certain how long I stay in the shower enjoying the hot water after such an incredibly long couple of days, but when I step out, Jason is tying his tie. He looks every bit the CEO, and I fall for him even more. Crazy. I can't deny I love him in a suit.

I smile to myself as I quietly sneak up behind him, putting my arms around his waist and pressing myself against his back as I kiss the back of his shoulder. I'm not tall enough to reach any higher than that.

He holds my arms close to him, taking one of my hands and kissing it. "I could get used to this."

"Get used to what?"

"You. Waking up next to you every morning. Taking showers with you. Moments like this when you're being incredibly sweet and don't realize how sexy you are." Jason turns to me and slips his arms around my waist, lifting me off the ground as he kisses me.

I smile against his lips, wrapping arms around his shoulders. "And I could get used to this."

"Good. Because I want to be with you every day, Jessa. I want you to know what it really feels like to be loved. To trust. To not have to fear the man you're with. I want to erase everything that was done to you, baby girl. Everything."

My smile falters slightly as I remember the past years of my life. Nine? Ten? What does it matter at this point anyway? I'm torn between wanting to be upset with Alex and understanding. But what makes me the most confused is I feel like despite everything Josh did, there was some underlying cause to it. Something I don't fully understand. While I want to be so pissed off and angry at what he did to me, I almost feel like it wasn't his fault. Is this what a victim mentality is? Or am I seeing things as they really are?

I hug him tighter, unwilling to let the thoughts in my mind ruin this moment. I take a breath and kiss his chest. "I want that, too." I really, really want that, too. I want the trust. The love. The support. Kindness. I want it all, and I want it with Jason. I have to be insane because Jason is so different from everything else I've thought I wanted in the past. Yet, he's so perfect for me. He fills the broken cracks inside me that I didn't believe would ever be fixed.

He kisses me again, and sets me back on my feet. "Get dressed. You have twenty minutes before I have to go, and I want to make sure you're set without me for the rest of the day. Move your sexy ass, beautiful."

He swats my butt, and I giggle. He grins and walks out of the room. I find jeans and a black tank top and quickly throw on a bra. I get dressed before hurrying downstairs. Jason is in the kitchen talking to Nick. Jason hands me the mug of coffee he's holding. I greedily sip on it.

"Sharing coffee?" Nick asks, nearly choking as he raises his eyebrow. "You never share your coffee."

"Well, there's a beautiful woman involved," Jason says, smirking.

"Yeah. Not buying that shit. You guys are adorable," Nick says.

"Shut-up," Jason commands, using a very dominant voice that makes me shiver. We all see the smile he tries to hide, though. Where's Ryan?" Jason asks.

"Someone say my name?" Ryan walks in right on cue as I'm handing Jason back his coffee. I look up at him. He and Jason really have the tall, dark, handsome, and ruthlessly intimidating thing down. "The hell? Are you sharing your coffee? That's fucking adorable."

"That's what I said," Nick jokes, folding his arms over his chest.

"Shut-up. Both of you. What's the plan for Jess?" Jason asks, standing protectively at my side.

"Jess?" Nick laughs. "We have nicknames now?"

"Fucking adorable," Ryan says, the smirk on his lips reaching his eyes and giving him a devilish glint.

"Christ," Jason says as he rolls his eyes and chuckles. I get a sense that this entire brotherly camaraderie is normal. Jason looks down at me, almost pleading. I look back up at him, deciding to join in the teasing.

I bat my eyelashes. "What's the matter, Jas? Too shy to show everyone just how adorable we are?" I tease. Ryan and Nick burst out laughing as Jason shakes his head.

"You *are* going to pay for that," Jason says. I laugh and reach for the mug of coffee, but he holds it far above my head as a teasing grin falls on his face.

"Aww…" I pout as adorably as possible.

His grin only widens. "Challenge accepted, beautiful."

Before I have a second to understand what he means by those cryptic words, he leans down and captures my lips with his. The kiss curls my toes, and I inadvertently sigh in contentment, making both Ryan and Nick laugh even harder. Jason finally pulls away and swats my ass before handing me the mug.

"Accepted and passed," Nick laughs. I blush. Furiously.

"I have to go," Jason begins. "I rescheduled a meeting yesterday with someone who was already sitting in my conference room. If I'm late or reschedule again, he might go with another company and that would piss me off. Cole left because Alex needed him to help track Josh and get information on their father." He turns to Nick and Ryan, pointing at each of them as he talks. "You two figure it out. Let me know what the plan is. You know my preference."

And with that, my gorgeous, tall, powerful, billionaire CEO is gone. I shake my head and smile. It takes everything I am to focus my attention on Ryan and Nick instead of Jason's magical tongue in the shower this morning. Trying to hide the second blush creeping into my cheeks, I bring the mug to my lips.

"So?" I ask. "What's he talking about?"

"Well," Ryan starts, looking down at me. He leans against the counter and crosses his arms over his chest. The pose matches Nick almost exactly, and I smile. They are definitely brothers. "A few things. First, do you have anything at your apartment that you absolutely need? Valuables or heirlooms that can't be replaced?"

"Um… I have some jewelry. My parent's wedding bands that I was given after they were killed."

"Killed?" Nick asks, glancing at Ryan.

I give him a weak smile and nod. "In an accident." I look down and set the mug on the counter as I sigh. "I'm not supposed to know this, but Alex never thought it was an accident. You should ask him about that."

"I plan to," Ryan says softly.

"Looks like we go to your apartment and get what you need. I don't want to be at your apartment too long," Nick says.

"Wait," I say, looking up at them. "I knew security was going to be a thing because of the talk last night and… everything." My voice is quiet as I tilt my head. "But I thought the purpose of security was so I could go home. I mean, I really like Jason, but we've really only just started an actual relationship. Living together like I… assume… you're suggesting might ruin everything." I pause and look down. "I don't want that, you guys. I really, really like him. I'm head over heels in love with him. I have been since I first saw him, if I'm being honest."

Ryan levels me with a hard look that makes me flinch slightly. "There isn't a negotiation here, Jessa. You aren't staying at your apartment. You have two choices. You stay with Jason, or you stay with me."

I wrap my arms around myself and bite my lip. I try to keep looking at them, but it's hard. I know they're right. Josh walked right through my security. After Alex left, Josh has walked through it several times. I'd be crazy to think my apartment would be safe. Even with security. What if he's really unhinged now that I've disappeared? It would put so many people in danger.

Nick steps in. "You have the mafia after you, Jessa."

"Sweetheart," Ryan says, his voice softening. I look up at him near tears. "Your security would be sleeping on chairs. You have no kind of protection on your doors or your windows. Yes, you live high up, but you

93

never really know what someone is capable of until they actually show you. I know Alex. I don't know Josh very well. What I do know is what I've been told. "

"And I can tell you from experience, Ryan doesn't like not knowing things. Truth is, there is a lot more at stake here than just some guy stalking you. You know he's mafia, but you don't know about this mafia. You don't know the history we have with it. Things you'll learn, eventually, but not until we understand what the actual fuck is going on here."

"There are a lot of unanswered questions. I don't like that. So, you can stay here," Ryan says. "Your security can stay here. Nick put in the security system himself. It's second to none. You have your boyfriend here. Or you can stay with me. Same security system. Only difference is no Jason, and there will be a lot more guns."

"I…" I know they're right. I'm not stupid. I feel totally safe here. But I'm so afraid to ruin what I've found. I want to do things right with Jason.

Ryan sighs, and I watch as he softens. He takes a step towards me and folds me in his arms. "I hate that you have to make a decision, but it's for your own well-being. Think about it while you get your stuff. Don't worry about a phone or clothing because Jason will get all of that stuff for you." He steps back and leans against the counter again. I'm bewildered that I feel better.

"That was the second thing. After you and I go to your apartment, we'll be going shopping for clothing, a phone and whatever else you need." All I can do is nod as Nick continues. "Third is transportation. When you go back to work, you can go with Jason. I'll follow behind with a guard. But anywhere that Jason isn't with you, you have me or a guard."

Ryan lets out a breath. "Alex said you'd be pissed about that. We'll get you a car, so you don't feel like you're losing your freedom, but you don't just get to go anywhere without security. You *will* have someone with you at all times."

"You don't agree to that, you don't get a car. And that's my decision. Not Ryan's or Jason's. Be pissed at me if you want, but as your lead security, that's the deal. It's final. No negotiation."

"I thought you were getting me security. Doesn't Jason need you?" I ask Nick, overwhelmed with everything being thrown at me; terrified that Jason might need him, and he won't be there.

"Jason, Ryan, Alex, Cole, and I all talked. We decided that I'm the one they all trust to make sure you're safe if they aren't around. We keep it in the family because it's the family we trust," Nick answers. "Jason will have people with him, too. Just because I'm not with him, doesn't mean he won't be protected."

I look between the two men standing in front of me. Brothers. If not by blood then by something far stronger. I still can't believe how much my life has changed in such a short time. These two are so protective of me. I'm really just a nobody.

Just two days ago, I had no one I really thought I could count on except a man that was literally across the country. I had no one here in Manhattan I could confide in, or that I considered a friend. My day consisted of going to work and going home. I gave Crane Enterprises all of me. Every single day I showed up with a smile on my face and put my all into work. I never allowed myself the luxury of having a friend here. But I had gotten so close. So close to letting down my guard and starting to feel at home. Until Josh started texting me and flipped my whole world on its head.

Now, standing in front of me, are two people willing to not only help me, but lay down their lives for me. Not far away is Cole, my best friend and the only protector I really had for so long. I can't believe Alex has walked back into my life. I've gone from being alone to being surrounded by people who love me and want to keep me safe. It's surreal.

After a few moments, I look up at them. "I don't know what I did to deserve your loyalty, protection, and Jason, but I'm so grateful."

Neither of them say anything. They simply step forward and hug me, wrapping me in a cocoon of safety and comfort that I haven't felt with anyone other than Cole and Alex. And now Jason.

For the first time in longer than I can remember, I feel like everything might just be okay.

Chapter Fourteen

☒ Josh ☒

She's gone.

Fucking gone.

I've been near hyperventilation ever since I found out. I never understood exactly what Jessa went through when she had panic attacks, but fuck if I don't get it now. I've been trying to calm down since I walked in her apartment and she wasn't in it.

Jessa never showed up for work today. But that asshole Jason fucking Crane did. I'm sure she ran to him the first chance she got. I growl as I throw myself on my bed. My dad was so proud of me when I found her. He told me if I brought her home, he would marry us as quickly as possible and swear me in as the leader of the Lucinio Mafia. Finally. I finally had what I've wanted my whole life in my grasp. Even with Alex back, he was still going to give it to me.

Until she fucking walked away. Slipped out of my grasp.

And that's not even the real problem I find myself facing.

The real problem is I don't want it like this. I've spent nearly every day of the last year under my dad's roof. I've listened to him berate me and tell me I'm not worth anything. That I'm not as good as Alex and never will be. I can't even count the number of beatings I've gone through. They became far more frequent after Jessa disappeared from L.A. last year.

And the physical pain afterwards has been unlivable. The feeling like my blood is made of glass and veins are fire. Like some kind of poison is coursing through my body. I've nearly taken my own gun to my head countless times just to make it all stop but decided to allow myself to pass out instead. When I wake up, I hardly remember my own fucking name.

But I do remember the pain.

If I'm being honest with myself, I'm not mad at Jessa. I don't blame her for running. I don't even blame her for running to her boss. I've had the entire day and all night to think without the interference my dad is constantly running in my head. If I were in her shoes, I'd fucking run away from me, too.

It's always been like this. The longer I'm away from my father, the clearer my head becomes. The less I talk to him, the more I realize that he's the reason I have such jealousy for Alex. He's the reason I can't think for myself. I lost Keith because of him. I blame myself a lot more than I don't, but when I'm thinking clearly, I know that Keith is dead because of my father. I lost Jessa because of him. Because he was in my fucking head. I can't think when he's in my head telling me I'll never be anything without her.

As if the thought of my father conjures him up, the fucker calls. I contemplate not answering it. Part of me knows that if I do, the confusion and resentment and jealousy that I've worked through over the past couple of days is going to hit me again full force. I don't want that. I don't like not being able to think clearly.

I also know that if I don't answer, it will just be worse for me in the end. I used to be so good at fighting through the pain from the beatings. I was numb to it. All of it. Now? Now I'd do almost anything to avoid it.

Taking a deep breath, I answer the phone. "What?"

"Josh. Are you coming home?"

"Uh. No. No, dad. She… she got away."

"What? Josh, you said you had her! What happened?"

Here we go. I rub my temple. "I had to take care of some things. I had to strip her car and deal with shit, so when she disappeared, it couldn't be tracked to us. I was trying to protect the family, dad. I left her in her apartment. She was… unconscious."

97

"Fuck! Josh, do I have to do everything? Did you beat her up like I told you to? Make her fear you?"

"She already fears me from the last time!" I grip the phone in my hand tighter as tears sting the corners of my eyes. "I never wanted this for her. Fuck. Never. She's a better person than this. She deserves more."

"Stop fucking thinking of her like a person. She's a means to an heir. Nothing else. Just like your mother." The danger in his voice makes me wince. I can feel my mind going almost cloudy again. It always happens just like this with him. "You're a fucking failure, Josh. Do you hear me? You've never been able to handle anything like your brother. I trusted you to deal with this. You fucking swore to me on your own goddamn life that you could handle it. This was your last chance."

My heart stops beating. The threat isn't missed. "Dad, please," I nearly plead. "I'll find her. Get her back."

"I warned you. I told you that if you didn't get her home, I'd kill you myself. You're an embarrassment. How can I trust you to take over for me if you keep fucking up the simplest of tasks?"

I can feel myself slipping. The need for him to be proud of me. The need for him to love me and not resent me. I'd give almost anything to feel his love. Even though I know he's a horrible human being and terrible father, all I've ever wanted is for him to love and be proud of me.

"I... I'm sorry, dad." The tears I tried to hold back leak from my eyes. I swipe at them, refusing to show weakness and, God forbid, let him hear it. "I'll fix it."

"We can't allow our lineage to die out with you and Alex. You're both fucking insolent. She's the one I want to carry the heir. I gave you a chance. You failed. You better hope I don't find you because I'm done with your games." He hangs up.

I sit up. I know what he's threatening. I know that he's on his way here, and that if he finds me, he'll kill me. I know he's going to go after Jessa. I also know that if I can't find her, he won't be able to either. I'm better than him.

None of that matters, though. He's after her, and I need to find her. Maybe he'll still be proud of me if I bring her home. She's my only hope of survival.

The anger that feeds me rises to the surface once more. I don't bother stopping it anymore. There isn't a point. If Alex hadn't left me, and

Jessa had just fucking married me, I'd be leader of the Lucinio Mafia. Jessa would be safe with me. Alex would be safe from our father. Fuck. My father would probably be dead. None of us would have to fear him anymore.

We wouldn't have to deal with his threats. We wouldn't have to deal with his games, and his manipulation. We wouldn't all have to bend to his will. My mother would be safe.

I growl as the phone in the room rings. I don't know what I'm thinking anymore. I can't even follow my own fucking wild mind. Everything is such a jumbled mess that I can't make sense of it anymore. I need a distraction, and my hope is that my distraction is on her way upstairs.

"What?" I rumble into the receiver.

"Hello, Mr. Lucinio," the woman from the front desk says softly. "Your guest has arrived. Shall I send her up?"

"Give her a card. She can let herself in," I order.

"Yes, sir."

A few minutes later, Layla, the woman I always use from the Timeless Escort Service, is lightly knocking on the bedroom door in the suite I'm staying in.

"Did I tell you to knock, Layla?" I ask irritably.

"No, sir." She slowly opens the door and closes it behind her. I stand and cross the room, pulling her into a hard kiss. I need the distraction, and she's as good as it gets. I need to release the tension. I need to think without my father's fucking voice in my head. When I pull back, she looks up at me, no doubt surprised at my abruptness and neediness.

Without saying a word, I push her down on her knees, a little rougher than necessary. She makes a surprised whimpering noise as I unbutton my pants.

"Suck. Right now. Don't talk." I grab her hair and my dick and thrust into her mouth.

Immediately, I can feel some of the tension leave, and I let out a quiet sigh. Layla knows to do what I say. That's why I use her as often as I do when I'm here. Funny how I've been here many times and never fucking knew Jessa was in the same city.

I fuck Layla's mouth and close my eyes as she does something incredible with her tongue. Something only she seems to know how to do.

No one else I've ever been with does this. It's probably why she's so popular in the city. She sucks me hard. I know she senses that's what I want; need. I tug her hair so she moves off my dick, then shove it in her mouth again, making her suck me at the pace I need her to. Right before I'm about to come, I pull her back. I tug her up by her hair.

She stumbles into me. "Sir, you seem tense."

"Did I say talk, Layla?"

"No, sir."

"Then don't." I pull her to the bed and toss her on it. She bounces a little, her tits giving me a show in her tight red dress; her blonde hair bouncing across her shoulders. "You better not be wearing anything under that dress, girl."

"No, sir. I'm not wearing anything under it. I know the rules well."

"Good girl. Take it off."

She bites her lip and sits up on her knees. She pulls the dress over her head. My eyes rake over her naked body. There's nothing wrong with the girl in front of me. She's beautiful. I hold out my hand for Layla's dress. She hands it to me without a word. I take it and put it over the back of the chair. She watches my every move.

"Wow," she whispers as I pull my shirt over my head.

I smirk as I turn back to her. "Like what you see?" I stalk back over to her, and she smiles as she begins to lay back on the bed. I narrow my eyes. "What the fuck do you think you're doing?"

She stops mid-motion and looks at me with wide eyes. "L-laying down?"

"Did I tell you to lay down, Layla?" She shakes her head. "Answer me."

"No, sir."

"You know you don't do a damn thing unless I say so." I beckon her to me with a crook of my finger. She obeys and crawls to me, her perky ass in the air. I swirl my finger in a circle, signaling her to turn around. She does.

"What are you -"

"Shut-up, Layla. Stop fucking speaking unless I tell you to." I spank her. Hard.

She cries out. "Oh!" She digs her fingers into the blankets and takes a deep breath as my hand comes down hard again on her other ass cheek.

"You don't do anything I don't tell you to."

"Josh!" she sobs.

My hand comes down hard again. "Have you forgotten what you call me, Layla?" I spank her again. She screams. "Have you forgotten the rules?" I can see the red marks I leave on her ass. I can hear her cry. I've never spanked her like this before. Not this hard. But I need it. I need the control because fuck knows I don't have any. My dad has it all. It all lies in his hands.

Not Layla.

I control her. She will do whatever I want. Bend to my every fucking will, and if she doesn't, she'll get more of this. I spank her again, this time as hard as I possibly can. Her skin splits a little, and seeing the blood forces me back to myself. I shake my head slightly as I take a step away from her. Layla is crying into the comforter on the bed. Her ass is red and welted from my hand.

"Fuck." I run my hand down my face as I regain a little control. "Layla, I…"

She looks back at me, tears rolling down her cheeks. I expect her to run, and I wouldn't stop her if she tried. Instead, she slowly gets up and stands. With a shaky hand, she reaches for mine and looks up at me.

"Your dad again?" she whispers. Layla is the only one other than Alex and Brandon who knows about my father. I don't say anything. I simply nod and keep my eyes focused on her. She reaches up and runs her thumb across my lower lip. "What did he do this time?"

I pull away from her and sit on the bed, dropping my head in my hands. "Same shit as usual. He called before you got here."

She moves off the bed and kneels in front of me. "Josh, you're getting worse. You've always liked control, but you're losing it. You always get rough after something with him, but you've never done that before. You've never gotten violent with me." The words are soft, but I can hear all of the pain in her voice. Pain I put there.

"I know. I -"

Layla reaches for my dick, still out and hard. I watch her with interest and awe. How the fuck is she still here after what I just did? "Just

101

let me do this," she whispers. "Give me at least a little control. Just for this. You're wound up and you're tense." She looks up at me.

I nod, giving her the permission she seeks. I lift myself off the bed enough for her to pull my jeans and boxers down. I kick them off and lean back on my elbows so I can watch her work me. Watching is one of my favorite things.

Her mouth takes me, her hands stroke me, making me grow impossibly harder. When her tongue flicks across my tip, I groan. When she takes me in her mouth until I hit the back of her throat, I let out a sigh of pleasure. She sucks me so hard, I have no choice but to let her have her way.

I close my eyes. "Fuck, Layla. Don't fucking stop."

She looks up at me with hooded eyes, and I reach for her hair. Pushing her down, I feel my cock slide down her throat. One of my favorite things about her is that she doesn't have a gag reflex. And damn does she love my cock. I've never gotten a blowjob from anyone who can top what she does.

She slowly releases me and nibbles on my tip as her tongue finds that spot that drives me insane. I push her back down on me as I come. She swallows everything I give her then licks me clean. When she's finished, she looks up at me and stands, waiting for my next command. I stay leaning in the position she left me as I lick my lips. My eyes drop to her smooth pussy.

I slowly sit up and grip her hips. I nudge her legs apart as I let my hand wander across her stomach, dropping lower and lower until I reach what I want. She puts her hands on my shoulders to steady herself, anticipating what's to come.

"Please, sir," she whispers.

"Good girl," I praise after she does exactly what I need her to without asking.

I slip a finger between her sweetness and find her clit. I pinch it and flick it as she closes her eyes. I thrust hard and deep, watching her pussy take everything I give it. She's tight. Wet. Just like she always is for me. Perfect. "Have you been doing your kegels?"

"Mmm… Yes, sir… Just like you tell me. A hundred in the morning. A hundred at night."

I grin. "Good girl."

I bury my face between her tits as I slide a second finger inside her as a reward for doing what I say. I keep my thumb on her clit and start rubbing faster. I pick up my pace with the thrust and crook my fingers inside her. She gasps and almost immediately starts trembling for me. Her pussy clenches. I want her to come for me quickly because I want to be inside her.

No.

I need to. I need to be inside her.

I flick my tongue across her nipples and bite them. She moans and digs her fingers into my hair, pulling my head closer to her. I fuck her with my fingers with long, hard strokes twisting and crooking them until she's whimpering, and her legs are shaking.

"Tell me, Layla. Beg for it."

"Please. Please, please make me come, sir."

"Come, Layla."

I quicken my pace even more and close my eyes against her tits as I try to focus on the way she feels. But it's no use. My dad's voice hits me like a splash of cold water. Him telling me I'll never be good enough. I'm a failure. How he's never loved me and never will. How the fuck could someone do that to his own son?

Layla screams as she comes, thankfully pulling me out of my thoughts. Her tight little pussy squeezes my fingers as I pump them inside of her. She collapses against me, trembling. Needing her to anchor me and keep me from succumbing to my dad's taunts and demands, I grab her around the waist and pull her on top of me as I lay down..

"Ride me," I command her. My dick is rock hard again. I don't need her to do anything to get me back up after coming just minutes ago. My cock is just as tense as I am. It needs the sex; the distraction.

She slides down on my cock, and my eyes roll back into my head as I bottom out balls deep inside her. I give her no time to adjust to my size, which is nothing to scoff at, before I grab her hips and rock her against me.

The strokes are hard. I lift her hips and push her down on top of me with such force that I'm positive I could break the bed. I don't care. I'll pay for it. I need the pace. I need to feel her warmth wrapped around me.

"Josh! Too hard! Too ha-" Before she can finish her sentence, my hand grows its own mind. I reach up and slap her. Her head snaps to the side as I quickly sit up and grab her hips. Without pulling out, I flip her so she's underneath me. "Oh!"

"What did you call me?" I glare down at her as I pin her arms above her head. I'm still buried inside her, but I'm not moving. "Correct it. Now."

"I'm sorry, sir," she whispers.

"Good girl."

She closes her eyes and wraps her legs around me as I bend down to kiss her neck. Her tits press against my chest as I start pounding myself inside her once more. I close my eyes and push her wrists hard into the bed. I try to lose myself in her, but all I can see is my father calling in his guards to beat me down for failing once again. In my mind, I take blow after blow until I black out.

"Josh!" Layla's scream brings me back again, and I mentally kick myself for allowing myself to be sucked into the darkness again. It takes me a few moments to realize Layla is crying once more. I shake my head and pull out of her. I scramble to my feet and watch her. She's gasping for breath.

"What? What did...?" It's then I notice the red marks on her neck that look suspiciously like my hands. "No. Fuck." I reach for her, and she scrambles to the other side of the bed, curling into a ball with her knees against her chest. I don't have the strength to stand anymore, so I fall to my knees. "I'm sorry, Layla."

I should've known it was a bad time to do this. Being away from my father has started to give me a clearer head just like it always does. But I should know better than to do this until I'm out of the fog he always puts me in.

"Josh, please look at me." Layla's soft hands grab my face, and she forces me to look at her as she kneels in front of me. I hadn't realized she's even moved. "It's getting worse."

"I know." It's not the first time I've lost control like this with her. But she's never not been able to snap me out of it. When I put Jessa in the hospital last year, I vowed I'd never lose control like that again.

And I hadn't.

Until a couple days ago with Jessa.

I spent the entire day before getting to her being berated and yelled at. When I didn't answer, he texted. Everywhere I turned, I saw my father's guards just waiting for me to fuck up. He wouldn't leave me alone. By that night, I was so messed up and pissed off, that I didn't know what I was doing until it was too late. When I realized what I'd done, Jessa had passed out from fear.

I was pissed off the entire next day while I was out stripping the car and taking care of any traces of her. She was supposed to become my wife. Give me an heir, and save me from my crazy fucking father. I was supposed to have her with me to protect her from his crazy ass. At least long enough to take over the mafia. After I had taken care of my father, I could have let her go if she hadn't fallen in love with me by then.

But the longer I'm out from under my father's thumb, the more I realize how stupid all of this is. The intention for me has always been to protect her and Alex. Not hurt her or be jealous of Alex. Yeah, he left, but I know why he fucking did it.

"Josh, come back to me." Layla forces me to look into her eyes, and things become a little more clearer by the second again.

"Why are you still here?" I ask her, bewildered. "Why haven't you left? Like Alex did? Everyone I've cared about has abandoned me when I needed them."

"Not me. I've never abandoned you," she whispers.

"I just choked you, Layla. I didn't even know I was doing it. I'm so far gone right now, I don't know what the hell is going on."

"But you keep coming back. Which means your dad's hold on you is weakening again. Soon, you'll start to see everything just as clearly as you did the last time you left Manhattan."

I take her hands in mine and pull her to her feet with me. Layla isn't my type, but sometimes, I wish she were. She understands me better than anyone. She turns and bends slowly over the bed. I smile softly as she wiggles her ass.

"You're a glutton for punishment."

"I know what you need, Josh. And I'm determined to get you there before our time is up for the night. Just like I always do."

I lightly, and a little hesitantly, grab her hips and thrust myself inside her again. She moves herself back and forth along my cock until I can't hold back anymore. But I refuse to come first. I'll never come before the woman I'm with. No matter how fucked up I am.

I grunt and slam inside her as I reach around and find her clit. I feel her relax against me. She throws her head back, and I bury my fist in her hair. When her walls collapse around me, I pull her up and pull out, rubbing her clit until she finishes while I stroke my cock.

I turn her around and push her to her knees. "Suck, Layla." I thrust into her mouth and fuck her throat while she sucks me hard until I explode. As I pull out of her and help her up, she smiles and climbs into the bed. I raise an eyebrow. "What are you doing?"

"You aren't done with me yet."

"I didn't pay for you for the whole night."

She shrugs. "I have no more clients tonight."

"Layla, you know I'm not completely back yet. I'm not in control. I haven't worked out everything in my mind."

"I don't care. I'm not leaving until I know you're okay. Maybe this time, you shouldn't go back. Maybe this time you should call Alex."

"I can't call Alex. You know that."

"He's not going to turn you away."

"Lay, you don't know everything I've done. I've fucked up. A lot. Alex would never forgive me. And I haven't exactly gotten over him leaving me in the first fucking place."

"Just come to bed, sir."

I shake my head. "Blatant disobedience."

"What are you going to do about it?" She watches me through hooded eyes as I stalk to the other side of the bed next to her. I kneel next to her and spread her legs, settling my face between them.

"I have no choice." I look up at her, and give her a devilish glare. "I'm just going to have to fuck it out of you." I dive into her with my tongue, and she throws her head back.

Maybe she's right. Maybe she is the distraction I need right now. As long as I focus on her, I *am* slowly coming back to myself. I don't know if it's always been like that, or if I'm just able to think clearly enough without my father in the back of my head screaming at me. What I do know is that I can't let her leave until I'm right again.

She's all that's anchoring me right now.

Chapter Fifteen

 Alex

(One Week Later)

I'm sitting in my hotel room with my crew around me racking our brains. We're trying to figure out what the hell Josh is thinking. He has to have an angle other than an obsession with her. If it's even really a fucking obsession. I can't decide. I know my brother. I know he's not as crazy as he's portraying. I'd bet all of my money, and I have a lot of it, that my fucking father is pulling his strings. I know it.

I look down as my phone pings, alerting me of a text and interrupting my thoughts. I smile when I see it's Jessa. I've been checking in with her every single day for the past week. I hadn't gotten around to it yet today. It's been busy.

Jessa: You know, it's getting boring. Cole and Nick are great, but the other guys here are terrible conversationalists.
Alex: Well, in their defense, it's their job to protect you. Not be your entertainment.
Jessa: I need to go back to work. I'm going stir crazy.

Alex: Soon. You're still bruised. You don't want to explain that to your colleagues.

Jessa: Are you and Jason best friends now? He said the same thing.

Alex: Patience has never been your strong suit.

Jessa: Don't think I didn't notice you ignored my question.

Alex: You're too smart for your own good, peanut.

Peanut has long been my nickname for her because she is so much smaller than I am. I glance at the phone in my room as it starts ringing. The front desk only calls me if it's an emergency. I already don't like what I'm about to hear, but pick it up anyway. My crew has fallen silent.

"This is Alex," I grunt into the receiver.

"Mr. Lucinio, I'm so sorry to bother you, but there's a young lady down here begging me to let her up to your suite," Amy tells me. She sounds panicked and scared. I'm instantly guarded. "She's um… Mr. Lucinio, she looks like she's in pretty rough shape. She almost crawled in here. She can barely stand. She's exhausted. And she has a little bit of bruising. Sort of like she… was… grabbed too hard."

"Does she have a name?"

"She only said Layla before she collapsed. She's in my office."

I pinch the bridge of my nose and close my eyes. "I'll be right down, Amy." I hang up and snap my fingers at Gavin as I open my eyes. Time to get this shitshow started. "Gavin, with me."

"What's up, boss?" He's immediately at my side as we walk to the elevator and head down to the lobby.

"I don't know, exactly. Amy says there's a woman in her office asking for me, and that it looks like she's in bad shape. Name is Layla. That's the name of an escort I've used."

Gavin nods. "I don't like the sound of that." I know he means the fact that she's in bad shape and not the part about the escort.

"Me either. I didn't ask her to come here. How the fuck does she know I'm around?"

We both check our guns and have them ready as we step off the elevator. I don't even need to tell him my fear of being ambushed. He just knows. That's the best thing about my crew. They follow directions and don't ask questions. We can read each other well. We can communicate in

108

nothing but hand and eye gestures because we've been together and worked together for so long. We're brothers. Family.

It doesn't take long to see that we're in the clear, and it confuses the hell out of both of us. Uncomfortable, we keep our guns at our sides as we find Amy. She motions us behind the desk and leads us to her office.

On the white plush couch is a woman in a red dress. Her hair is tattered. She looks like she's been through hell and made it out only to be dragged right back to it again. It takes me a minute to recognize her, but it is Layla.

"Shit." I holster my gun and hurry to her side. I drop to my knees next to her and take her hand. "Layla. Hey. Wake up. It's Alex, honey."

"Alex…," she whispers. Her eyes flutter open, but she can barely get my name out. "Alex… he… Josh…"

She closes her eyes again, and I lift her in my arms. Gavin leads the way, his gun at the ready just in case this is a trap. We rush to the elevator, and he taps his key card to get us to the suite. There's no access without a key card. It's one of the things I love about this hotel. It's incredibly secure. When we get up to our floor and off the elevator, Gavin shoves the suite open. I lay Layla on the couch.

"The hell?" Damon raises an eyebrow as he leaps off the couch when we enter.

"Man, what's going on?" Lance asks me. "What the hell happened to her?"

"No idea. Get a cold cloth," I demand. I smooth Layla's hair back from her face, checking her for injuries, as Lance grabs a cloth. I roll her over on her side and check the back side of her legs as well as the front. She has bite marks and scratches everywhere. Some bruising. "Fuck. He really messed her up."

"Who?" Damon clenches his fist at his side.

"Josh," Gavin growls.

"What?" Damon looks at me. "What the hell is going on? Who is she, and what the fuck does Josh have to do with this?"

"I don't know what Josh did, Damon. All she said was his name, but I refuse to believe that he's this far gone." My voice cracks, but I don't care.

"Are you kidding?" Gavin asks in complete disbelief. "I saw what he's capable of with Jessa. You saw it. This is fucking nothing!"

I look up at him, tears shining in my eyes. "He's my brother. You know as well as I do that what happened to Jessa was just as much my fault as his. I shouldn't have left. I should've been honest with her from the beginning. And I sure as fuck shouldn't have left my father to fuck with either of them as much as he has."

Lance returns with the cloth, and I use it to both clean her face and wake her up. Her eyes flutter open. She gasps.

"Layla," I say, my voice as calm as I can possibly make it. "It's okay, honey. It's me. It's Alex."

She looks at me for a moment as she comes to, the shock from the cool cloth wearing off. She throws her arms around me as she cries. "Alex! Your dad has him under his control again! I tried so hard, but he just kept threatening Josh and beating him down!"

"What? Shh. It's okay, honey. You aren't making any sense." She cries hysterically into my shoulder and everyone looks at me for an explanation. The only problem is I don't know what the fuck to say.

"Layla. How did you know I was here? I haven't called the escort service."

"I didn't know you were here." She takes a few deep breaths and then looks around the room, seeing everyone for the first time. Her eyes widened in surprise. I take her face in my hands and force her to look at me.

"Hey. It's okay. They're with me, okay? No one here is going to hurt you."

She sizes everyone up and takes another deep breath. Her focus falls back on me. I can see she's decided to trust them, but only because she trusts me. Because I said it's okay.

"Honey, tell me what happened? What did Josh do to you?"

She shakes her head and sniffles. "When I first was sent from the escort service to Josh, I thought he was you. He explained he's your twin. He's always been as nice to me as you always are. Just more controlling, and a little more rough. The second time I was with him, he was having a bad day. He opened up to me and told me about your father. I felt awful for him."

"What did he tell you?" I gently coax.

"He said that his dad gets in his head. Makes him think crazy things. He said when he's away from him, he's able to think clearer. He thought he was being drugged by him somehow, but he couldn't prove it."

"Fuck." Gavin collapses on a chair.

"Why did he think he was being drugged?" I asked. Things are starting to make a little more sense, but I fucking hate where my mind is going.

"He said he didn't know if he was. Just that the longer he's away from him, the more he's able to think. I've always thought he was right because when I left, Josh was like a whole different person. He... was more like you." She looks down at her hands. She turns her wrists over like she's seeing the bruising for the first time. Like she was being held too tightly.

"Keep going. I need to know what happened," I whisper. I need to understand.

She looks up at me and jumps as Damon sits next to her but calms when he puts his elbows on his knees. "I've been with him a lot over the past year, Alex." She looks down at her hands again.

"Year? He's been coming here for a year?" I nearly choke. Lance is the next one to collapse in a chair. He puts his head in his hands. Gavin is near hyperventilation. How the hell did we not know he's been coming here for a year? I force myself to put that aside for now. I need to get to the bottom of what happened because so much isn't adding up for me. Layla is sobbing once more.

"Hey, it's okay, Layla. You're safe now." Damon takes Layla's hand in his. Instead of recoiling, as I expect, she gives him a grateful smile.

"Explain it to me," I say softly as she looks back at me.

"I've... been able to bring him back around. But... this time it was different. He was different. He was rougher. He lost control. He choked me. He held me down. But I was able to bring him back. He stopped. But every time I got him to come around, he would get a phone call. He didn't answer it a few times, but when he did, I watched the change in him. He grew cold and almost distant, but as soon as I started talking, it was like he hung on my every word. It was like he needed me there to keep his dad's hold from completely overtaking him. Sometimes, he'd mumble about someone named Keith. How it was the anniversary of his death. Other times, he'd rant and rave about you. How you abandoned him. Sometimes, he'd seem like he was in agonizing pain. Like it was ripping him to shreds."

She takes a few swipes at her eyes, and I glance at my crew. We've all been working tirelessly with Ryan to keep Jessa safe. I put Cole with her because she needed him. Like I would've been able to keep him away anyway. We've been looking for Josh, but he has completely disappeared. Lance can't track his phone. It's almost like it's off or something. He's not checked into my family's hotel. At least not under his name or any alias he's ever used. It's like he vanished, and it scares the fuck out of all of us.

Despite all of this shit, Josh is our brother. We love him and want to know what the hell is happening. What Layla said about being drugged is something we've all thought for a while now. Like Josh, we can't prove it.

My father hasn't left L.A. as far as we know. The family jet is still at the private hangar we use. Lance has a track on his phone, too, and, according to the track, he's still at his house. But I'm becoming more and more uneasy about that. According to Lance, he hasn't gone anywhere the entire day. That's not like him at all.

"This is getting more and more fucked up, Alex," Gavin says, pulling me out of my thoughts.

I sigh. "I know." I look back at Layla as she takes another deep breath. "Tell me the rest."

"I stayed with him. I couldn't leave him, Alex. Not like that. I tried to get him to call you, but he won't. He thinks you hate him, but he won't tell me why. He kept talking about you abandoning him, though. He kept coming back to that."

I swallow. It's something I've regretted every damn day since I came back. Probably even before that. A part of me never thought it was right that I left. But there was a much bigger part of me that believed I'd made the right decision. To this day, a war still rages inside of me.

"Where did the bruises come from, sweetheart?" Damon asks, tucking a strand of hair behind her ear.

"Every time his dad called, he got angry and lost himself. He got really rough when he held me down. But I kept getting him to come back before he hurt me too bad. I didn't want to leave him, but he made me."

"Called? He hasn't had his phone on for a week. Did he call the hotel?" Lance asks.

She shakes her head. "He had a cell phone, but he said something about a burner? I... don't know what that means."

"It means he got a phone that can't be tracked and few people have the number. Fuck, I don't know how I missed that." Lance scurries to his laptop and starts furiously typing.

I can see Damon is physically trying to hold himself back from taking Layla in his arms. If there's one thing I know about my friend, my brother, it's that seeing a woman hurt and crying is not something he can handle. His hand is shaking, and his jaw is ticking. His hand never shakes. He's always steady. But when he feels like there is danger to someone who can't defend themselves, he becomes a big pile of nerves.

I stand and pull Layla gently up with me. I lead her to my bedroom and close the door behind me. I don't want anyone to know what I'm about to ask right now. It's not that I don't trust my crew. That's my family out there. It's that I need to know for myself what the fuck is happening because I already know the answer somewhere deep in my gut, and I fucking hate it. I'll tell them after I calm myself down.

"Why did he make you leave?" I ask her as soon as I close the door.

Layla sits on the bed but winces from the pain. "He said Matthew is on his way here. He made me leave. He ran."

"Fuck." My knees nearly buckle. I focus on her instead and swallow. It's the best option for me. I need to think. "I need to see, Layla. I need to see how fucked up you are so I know if I need to call a doctor."

She looks at me for a few moments before she finally stands. She turns around so I can unzip her dress. It's not like I haven't seen her like this numerous times, but she holds her arms over her tits anyway. I look her body over. She's covered in scratches and bite marks. Some bruising. Her ass is red and has welts all over.

I close my eyes to steady myself before I make her turn around. "I shouldn't have fucking left. I could've stopped all of this." It comes out as a growl and far more forcefully than I intended.

Layla sniffles. "It doesn't matter now. He needs you, Alex. He really, really fucking needs you. He's alone out there. I don't know what his father is going to do, but he was scared enough to run and make me. I

113

prayed like hell that you were here. And if you weren't, I really hoped someone would be able to find you."

"I know. Fuck, I know." He never would have been in this situation if I hadn't left. I had always protected him when we were kids. How could I do that to my own brother? I know what my father is like. How could I let him deal with that fucker on his own? And now he's fucking running. I can't blame him. This is all my fault. "I need to call him."

"You can't. He doesn't have the same phone, and he smashed the burner phone. He didn't want his father to be able to track him."

"Smart. That's what I would've done."

"He's very smart. And he's stronger than he gives himself credit for."

I smile as I gently turn her around so I can finish my inspection. "He's smarter than anyone gives him credit for. Including me. I was so fucking pissed off at him for what he did that I barely gave any thought to why or how it could've happened. I need to talk to him."

"He needs you, Alex," she says again. "He's been alone for far too long."

"I never knew he was struggling this much, Layla. He put on one fuck of a facade."

"He didn't want to disappoint his father or big brother."

"By minutes." I gently have her sit on the bed. "You have bruising on the insides of your legs. Did he use weapons on you? Anything?"

She shakes her head. "The sex didn't hurt me. At least not much. He was hard and a little rough, but it was everything else. It was the grip on my wrists or the hold he had on my neck. He held down my legs and gripped them. He scratched me."

My expression darkens as I reach out my hand. "Let's get you cleaned up." She takes my hand, and I lead her to the bathroom. I turn the water on for her and help her in.

She turns back to me. "I'm not mad at him, Alex. I don't know everything he did to you or anyone, but I know that he needs you. I know he's not a bad person. Your dad really fucked him up. I wanted to stay with him to make sure he's okay, but he wouldn't let me. You have to help him. I really think if your dad finds him, he'll kill him."

"I don't doubt that. I'll find him, Lay."

114

She nods as she steps under the spray. I grab a towel and place it on the counter, then leave the bathroom to find some clothes for her. She wasn't wearing a bra or underwear, so I reach for the phone to call the front desk.

"Mr. Lucinio? Is that poor girl okay?"

I smile. "She's okay, Amy. I need a bra and panties for her. I know that isn't a typical request."

"Don't worry about it. I'll get it done. Is that all? I might have a few things here. She looks like she's close to my size."

"Get what you think she needs." I pause and rub my temple. "Uh… she… may need tampons or… something. I think she may have… you know. I didn't see any injuries that would have caused the blood on her leg." It's not that I'm nervous about talking about a woman's period. It's talking about it to someone other than said girl herself.

"I'll be up in a jiff."

I nod, then realize she can't see me. "Thank you."

"You're welcome." She hangs up, and I find a t-shirt before heading back into the bathroom.

"Lay?" I knock on the door and call for her.

"Yeah?"

I open the door. "I'm putting a t-shirt in here for you. I have someone coming with some women stuff. I think you might have started your period."

"Oh… yeah, I think I did. Sorry."

"Don't apologize. Look… uh… with my dick father after Josh, I don't want you out there alone. He'll do anything to get to Josh. If he thinks Josh cares about you, he'll go after you."

"I trust you. I don't have a job anymore. They fired me when I didn't show up for my next appointment. I don't know what I'm going to do, but Josh was more important. I trust you to do what's best, Alex."

"Don't worry about money. I'll take care of it. You know that. You need to stay here. You can stay with me or go with Damon. You seemed comfortable with him. He was the one holding your hand. I don't care, but you aren't leaving our sight. My father is unpredictable, and there's a lot of shit going on."

She shuts the water off. I grab the towel and wrap her in it when she steps out. She grabs another towel to dry her hair as she looks at me.

115

"He didn't rape me."

"Thank fuck for that." I give her a soft smile. "I don't feel like he's capable of that, but I don't really know right now. But everything you said corroborates what I already knew or was coming to the conclusion of." I hear a knock on the door to the penthouse. "That's your clothes."

She smiles as I turn to leave the room. I had a sick feeling all day that my father was going to come here. Now, I need to warn Ryan so he can keep Jessa safe. We need to find my brother. He's not as far gone as we all thought, and I can't help but kick myself for believing for a second that I couldn't bring him back. I never should have left them, and now it's my responsibility to save them. Both of them because losing either one of them will shatter me.

Chapter Sixteen

✗ Jason ✗

(One Week Later)

I kiss Jessa awake thinking that these past two weeks with her have been the best of my life. When we learned Josh had disappeared, Jessa stayed as strong as the diamond she is. The woman who had apparently been trying to help Josh had become pretty good friends with Jessa. They talk every day.

"You're staring again," Jessa whispers, coming out of her sweet sleep.

"I can't help it. You're beautiful." I fell hard for her as soon as I saw her. I fought it, like an idiot, but not anymore. Jessa is everything to me. I can't believe I finally have everything I've ever wanted with her.

"So are you."

I laugh and kiss the back of her neck and her shoulder. "Are you sure you're ready to go back to work, beautiful? You can take more time."

"No. I can't take more time. I need to work."

"That's the one good thing about dating the boss, beautiful. He can approve you to take all the time you need."

"And that. Right there. That's why this is such a bad idea. You and me together. You're going to start treating me differently." Jessa tries to get up.

I stop her by pulling her back to me and tightening my grip. I kiss her shoulder again. "We already agreed that you'd be moving up to my office. That will be people's first inclination we have something going on, but I don't care. I don't want you alone."

"You… are… infuriating." She tries to hold back the smile.

"Infuriating and fucking hot."

That gets her smile, but it falls quickly. "Do you… think that maybe we could do… I don't know." She shrugs. "Something just maybe by ourselves? I'm feeling pretty cooped up. I realize how necessary it is, and I love it here. I love being with you, but I'm kind of just going stir crazy. I feel like with everyone around, we haven't really gotten any… alone time."

I roll her on her back and crawl on top of her, holding my weight off of her so I don't crush her. She giggles. I lean down and kiss her as she wraps her legs around me, and I groan into her mouth. My reaction to her is unlike anything I've had towards any woman I've ever been with.

I pull back slowly. "I know this has been hard on you, baby. If I can do anything to make it better, I'll do it. You want a night alone, I'll give you a night alone. I guess not completely, but I can cook dinner. We can do a movie. It's not perfect, but I can make the guards scarce."

"You cook, too? You really are perfect, aren't you?" She smiles, her pretty blue eyes glittering.

"I mean, I'll give credit where credit is due. Ryan is the cook of the family. But I learned a few things from the pro himself."

She smiles wider and wraps her arms around me. She pulls me down so my lips meet hers again. "Thank you, Jason."

"Anything for you, beautiful girl." I kiss her again even though I really need to get up, and I know if I don't right now, I won't be able to.

I push myself gently off her, but she pulls me back down. I'm weak when it comes to her. Denying her anything she needs or wants is something I've discovered quickly I'm not capable of.

She wraps herself around me like I'm all she needs, and I plunge my tongue into her mouth. I kiss along her jawline and collarbone until I reach the delectable hardened peak I've been seeking. I take it into my mouth and she arches into me as she moans.

I kiss along her chest and take her other hardened nipple into my mouth. She gives me another soft moan as a reward. Lightly nipping her, I trail a hand down her side and shift slightly so I can slide that hand between her legs.

"Jason, please…" She arches into me as my finger slips inside her warmness. I chuckle against her nipple and slide my finger in and out. Her slight movements make me moan, and I can't help but add a second finger.

"You're so tight for me." I kiss down her stomach, never stopping my strokes. She rewards me with more soft moans and more slight movements that have me getting harder and harder by the second. I flick her clit with my tongue.

"Ah! Yes…" Jessa arches into me and my fingers slide deeper inside her. I hum against her clit as I take her in my mouth. "God, yes…"

"You taste like fucking Heaven, Jessa." I move my fingers in and out of her, eliciting more delicious moans that make me want nothing more than to feel her wrapped around my cock, not my fingers, but this is for her. Not me.

I lavish her clit with my tongue and deepen my strokes in her warm pussy. She starts moving her hips in time with my thrusts, and I give her clit a light nip. She bites back a moan as she arches her back. I feel her tighten around my fingers, and I quicken my strokes while flicking her clit back and forth and giving her long, slow licks and a little pressure.

Within seconds, she's giving me what I want. Her walls tighten around my fingers. I smile at how jealous I suddenly feel that they got to feel her come and not my dick.

Soon. Very soon.

As she releases for me, her hips jerk into my fingers. Her eyes close. She moans and lets herself do nothing but feel. A soft smile spreads across her pretty lips as she whimpers and whispers my name. I slow my thrusts more and more until she has come down.

I crawl back up her body, licking my fingers on the way. She watches me, her lips parted slightly like she's just waiting for me to claim her. I lean down and kiss her. My cock rests against her thigh as I tease her mouth with my tongue.

"Jason," she whispers against my mouth. Her nails lightly trail a path up and down my arm as I look into her crystal blue eyes.

"You're so fucking beautiful, baby." I lean down and kiss her lips softly again and again as I slip just my head inside her entrance.

"Mmm…" Her nails scrape lightly up my arms to my back.

I grin wickedly and gradually slide inside her, inch by inch, watching her intently. It's torture for me, but watching her eyes fall closed as her pussy pulses around me makes it all worth it. Eventually, I'm buried balls deep inside her sweet, tight, wet pussy.

Home. She's home.

"Fuck," I groan. I kiss her neck as I thrust slowly, allowing her to adjust to my size.

"Jason, you're…" She pants and gasps. "So, so big. I swear, I'll always be amazed at this feeling." She closes her eyes. "You feel so, so good…"

My chuckle rumbles low in my chest, and she shivers as I graze my teeth along her neck. "So tight, beautiful girl"

"Mmm… Jason."

My cock fills her as I gradually thrust faster. I'd keep teasing her if I could handle it, but I can't. I'm way too close. Jessa's hips move in time with mine until we're both a tangled mess of limbs and slick with sweat.

My cock thickens. Or maybe it's just her pussy getting tighter for me. Either way, she milks my dick with each thrust I give her until I have no hope of holding out. A jolt of pleasure shoots down my spine. My dick gets impossibly harder.

"Oh fuck, Jessa. Come, baby. Come for me." I'm sure she takes it as a command, but it's a goddamn plea. I need her to come so I can.

"Ah! Jason!" She trembles and writhes under me as she bucks into my thrusts. Her pussy clenches tight and spasms as she comes.

As soon as I feel her walls collapse, I'm gone. "Fuck…" I bury my head in her hair as she squeezes my shoulders and continues orgasming around my cock with the sexiest of sighs, screams, and grunts I've ever heard. She rips my orgasm from me, and I spill out inside her with a moan.

We both pant as I thrust slowly through our releases simultaneously helping us both come down from the incredible high. Several moments later, after we catch our breaths, I slowly pull out and gently kiss her again.

"No…" she says sadly as I leave her warmth.

I miss it instantly. "I would love to continue this, and I'm sorry I can't, but I have a couple meetings today that I can't miss."

"The price of dating the CEO," she says as sadly as possible with a teasing glint in her eye.

"Cute." I kiss her again and force myself to get up.

I quickly clean up and hurry to get dressed. Jessa heads for the shower as soon as I'm done in it. I grin as she lazily yawns and stretches. I don't miss the devilish smirk in her eyes as she licks her lips and disappears behind the door.

I can't help but laugh as I enter my closet. After choosing my suit for the day, I quickly get dressed and choose a tie from the many I own. I tie it as I rush down the stairs. I'm greeted by Nick, Ryan, and Cole.

I narrow my eyes and growl. "It's way too fucking early for this. What the fuck do you want, Ry?"

"You've always been a dick before you've had your coffee." Ryan chuckles as he smugly leans against the counter.

I don't say anything. I just reach for the coffee pot because he's absolutely right. I need my coffee in the morning or things don't go well for anyone. I pour myself a cup before taking a sip, not taking my eyes off my brother.

But the liquid caffeine sliding down my throat is too good. "At least you made coffee. Thank you."

Ryan just grins like an asshole. "Better?"

I chuckle. "Much. Now what do you want?"

"You ain't going to like it," Cole says.

I sigh. "Cole. There isn't one fucking thing I like about this entire situation. Now what the hell is going on?"

"We know Alex's dad is obsessed with Jessa, but Josh has been the wild card. It didn't make sense why he was doing what he did," Nick starts.

"Layla kept telling us that Josh had always been trying to protect Jessa and Alex, but that his dad fucked with his head," Cole continues. I raise an eyebrow. It was a theory we had when this whole shit started. Seems like we're on the right track.

"He kept taking her home in order to make his dad think that they were together to protect her from him. He was always on business trips.

121

Josh planned it that way. His mother was usually hiding, but the guards corroborated his story to his father. And he had cameras set up around the house. So, he saw Jessa around. According to Layla, things got fucked up real quick, though. Their father kept saying he would give Josh control if Josh married Jessa," Ryan finishes.

"So, Josh is obsessed with my girl because he needs her to take over the Lucinio Mafia?" I ask incredulously.

"Looks like it," Ryan shrugs.

I shake my head. "That doesn't make sense. Jessa thought he was Alex. If he took her home that much, wouldn't his parents have called him Josh? She would've known."

"Nope. Because he was never there. Josh was careful," Cole answers. "But it wouldn't have mattered. Jessa told me he told her that his middle name is Joshua. Which is Alex's actual middle name. So, his parents calling him Josh wouldn't have made a difference. He told her that's what they called him."

"It still doesn't make sense to me. At all. In all those years, she never actually met his parents." I shake my head.

"Something more is going on here," Ryan agrees.

"We need to figure it out," I say.

"I'm already on it. Right now, we need to find Josh."

I suck in an inadvertent breath. I don't trust this Josh person at all. Not after what he put Jessa through. I don't know anything about him except for what Alex and Layla have said. I don't know what the fuck to do.

"How do I play this, Ry?" I ask, meeting Ryan's eyes.

"I don't know, Jas. I'm still trying to figure out what the fuck is going on. Alex is still trying to find Josh."

"One more thing," Nick says looking at Cole.

I narrow my eyes. "Seriously? There's more?"

"Uh. Matthew is here somewhere. We think he's going after Josh, but we can't find him. Neither can Alex." Cole has the decency to look away from my cold stare as I put my mug in the sink.

"Trust me. I won't let anything happen to your girl, Jason," Ryan says to me.

I nod before turning to look at the three of them. "No one says a fucking word to Jessa. She doesn't need the extra stress. She's already freaking out about Josh being missing. I don't want her to know Lucinio is here."

"Cole and I will be with her all day." Nick pushes away from the counter and Cole nods.

I look back at Ryan. "Whatever the hell you do to make shit happen, keep it away from me and Jess. I really, really don't want anyone to know I'm involved with the mafia, but I absolutely want it kept away from her. It could ruin her." I don't need to tell him that it could destroy me, but I'm not sure I care. As long as it doesn't touch her. "I have to go."

"Jas. I got it," Ryan says. His mafia boss tone is extra prevalent, and fuck if it doesn't help me come down a little bit.

I glare at Nick and Cole. "Get Jessa to work in one piece. Neither of you fucking leave the top floor. Stay near my office and escort her everywhere. Even to the cafe if she wants to walk there to get lunch. The two of you do not leave her side. Got it?"

"Got it, boss," Nick smirks with a fucking condescending smirk. He knows me well enough to know exactly how to cut through the anger. I'd laugh, but I really hate this is even happening.

"We'll keep her safe," Cole says softly, trying to smooth my ruffled edges.

"You damn well better," I say quietly. I turn to leave as Jessa comes down the stairs. I pull her to me and kiss her a little more fiercely then I had intended. She looks up at me in surprise. "Will you do something for me today?" I ask her.

"Of course. Anything." She blinks at me, still a little shocked.

"I want you to stick as close to Cole and Nick as you can today."

"I thought that was a given, but you seem on edge." She furrows her brows in concern. "What happened?"

"I just… want you to be safe. Trust me, okay? Please?"

"Of course I trust you." Her lips meet mine as I lean down to kiss her before I reluctantly let her go.

"I love you, beautiful girl."

She blushes. I hadn't meant to blurt the words out, but I'm completely over holding anything regarding my feelings back from her anymore. It's been way too long. It's time we get over the tentativeness of the new relationship. We both know exactly how we feel about each other.

"I love you, too." Her cheeks flush a deeper shade of red as I lean down to kiss her again.

I head out the door and jump in one of Ryan's SUV's. It's bulletproof. Ryan has taken far more precautions with all of us than I've ever seen. I'm not allowed to drive any of my own vehicles just in case situations we hadn't anticipated actually happen. There was a little concern that Matthew was coming here last week, but they found him in L.A. He hadn't left but did send some guards here.

Truthfully, I don't really mind the extra protection Ryan has put in place. As our big brother, he has always protected us. Since he became the leader of the Crane Mafia, though, the protective instincts have grown tenfold. And with all of the unknowns happening right now, I'm happy as hell to have him.

Chapter Seventeen

✗ Josh ✗

I open my eyes and immediately feel sick. I can't move, and I don't know why. I force myself to take deep breaths while I try to figure out where I am and what the fuck is happening to me this time. I can never catch a fucking break.

I take a breath. There's nothing covering my head. Alright. That means I'm somewhere dark. Good thing I have a long sleeve shirt on because it's cold. I let my eyes adjust but can still barely make anything out. I can tell I'm in a room with no windows, and I'm near a wall. I'm sitting in a chair. It smells dank as fuck.

Basement?

Something feels like it's dried on my face. I attempt to brush it away, but my arms won't move. What the fuck? They feel heavy. I pause for a moment before trying to move them again and hear something like a chain. I'm handcuffed to the chair.

Panic rises as I try to break free. I yank the cuffs against the chair. It's no use, though. They're not going to break. So, I try to use the cuffs to break the chair, but after a few moments of useless movement that sap my much needed energy, I give up.

I try to yell instead. Someone has to hear me, right? "Help! Help! What the fuck is going on? Get me out of here!"

In my panic to get my hands free, I realize my legs are tied to the chair, and the chair is bolted to the ground. I'm not going any-fucking-where.

"Son of a bitch! Dammit!" No matter what I do, how hard I tug and twist and pull, I can't get free. The cuffs cut into my wrist. I can feel they've split the skin because it fucking stings. I close my eyes and take a breath. "Okay. Calm down, Josh. You have to calm down to get the fuck out of this. Think."

I force myself to take more deep breaths as I listen to my surroundings with my eyes closed. I hear crickets chirping. So, I know I'm outside. It's night. That's why it's so dark and cold. I must be in a shed. My head is pounding, but the more I calm down, the more pissed off I become.

It's all coming back now. I made Layla leave. The one person who could get me out of my fucking head and keep my father from sucking me back in. I knew as soon as she brought me out of his brainwashing, which she's gotten really fucking good at, that I'd have to run. There wasn't any other option for me. I knew then my time was up with him.

So, I ran. I left my burner phone in the hotel room. Smashed it. I bought another burner. I couldn't go to Alex because no matter what Layla said, I knew Alex wanted my head. I fucked Jessa up. Bad. It's something I'll regret for the rest of my life. Something I'll never take back and can never make up for. I know Alex will never be able to forgive me for that.

I also know I can't go to him because our father will follow. I know Alex is here. I know he's probably made contact with Jessa. That means Jessa is safe as long as he's with her. I trust that. But it also means that the hit on Alex has just become a very real threat. When he left, he was safe. If he came back and contacted Jessa, he was to be killed on the spot.

Well, he came back. He didn't contact Jessa, at least not that anyone knew. So, he was safe. He's not anymore.

Our father said he took the hit off Alex, but I seriously doubt that. I know nothing about it. I've tried to find out, but it's something he's kept hidden. I don't trust our father. Which is why I know he'd follow me to Alex. Which means he'd find Jessa and kill Alex. Then take her. I needed to do whatever I could to keep him away, and I felt like I'd been doing a damn good job of it. I had left little clues for him so he'd chase me. I'd found out where Jessa was, and I'd kept an eye on her.

I knew she'd gone back to work yesterday. Her boyfriend has her surrounded by security. Or maybe it was Alex's decision. I don't know for sure, but I know Cole is with her. I know he's part of Alex's crew.

I tug at my bindings again in frustration and sigh when they don't budge. I didn't expect them to. They're digging into my wrist and around my ankles even if I don't move. Every time I do, they dig in further.

"Fuck," I growl. My head feels like it's going to explode. It's the same feeling I have when I wake up after a beating, but I force myself to focus. I need to figure out how the fuck I got here. Things are still a little hazy, so I have to talk myself through it. I'm surprised I don't feel the other kind of pain. The pain that makes me want to jump off a hundred story building.

Jessa.

Last I remember is seeing Jessa.

Fuck, I can't believe everything I put her through. Letting my dad get in my head like he did was the worst fucking thing for everyone. I'm better than that. Alex taught me better than that. So, how the hell could I have let him get to me? Jessa didn't deserve what I did to her. It started out just fighting with her. Then it morphed into nearly fucking kidnapping her after beating the shit out of her.

Marry Jessa. Get her pregnant. Get control. Get rid of the old man. Live happily ever after. That was the plan. But it never started like that. It was never *my* plan. It never fucking should have become that. The plan had always been to protect my brother. Protect Jessa. My father was going to kill them both. No way could I let that happen.

And then Alex took off to Italy. I didn't blame him at first. Until my father got in my head and did what he usually did. He made me jealous of Alex. He made me feel like I could never compare to his perfect son. The beatings got worse. I didn't have Alex to snap me out of it anymore, but I almost didn't care. He was gone. I knew he was safe. Jessa was safe. That's all that mattered. I succeeded in my goal. I was pissed that he abandoned me, but at least he was safe.

That didn't last long. I found out my father was still after Jessa. With Alex gone, it was my responsibility to keep her safe. He left because

127

he was heartbroken. I got that. I was fucking pissed that he left me. He knew how our father was and what he'd do to me, but I got it. He'd done what I wanted him to do. How could I be pissed off at him for doing what I fucking wanted?

Over my time with Jessa, though, I lied to her. Manipulated her. I know everything I did to her was so fucking wrong, but back then I thought I was doing the right thing. I was keeping her safe. The only thing that kept me going was knowing that Alex and Jessa were okay.

Then I lost complete control. Watching my best friend get shot right in front of me broke me. I'd been with Jessa so long by that point that I'd actually fallen in love with her. It didn't start out that way. I thought I had been in love with her, but I know now that I wasn't even close. Not then. Not until the end. I really did love her then.

I was truly obsessed with her. I loved her. Pissed off at Alex and fucked up over her. That wasn't my father. That was me. And after watching my father kill Keith, I needed her. She chose that day, though, to break it off with me. I lost complete control and lost her forever. I know now I deserved it, but then? Fuck. Then I blamed her. I blamed Alex. I blamed my fucking father. But I never once blamed myself. My mind kept twisting from loving both Alex and Jessa to hating them the very next second.

And now? Hell, now, I don't even know what the fuck I was thinking.

"Fuck." I tense my arms and am rewarded by the bindings cutting into my wrists again. I let out a low growl, but it only makes more pain shoot through my skull. I let out a low sigh instead.

As if nearly beating her up after the breakup wasn't enough, I stalked her for a month and beat the fuck out of her. I hospitalized her like I'd never fucking loved her in the first place. I became what my father wanted. I became a monster. He almost gave me control that day. But his obsession with Jessa stopped him. He still wanted her. I didn't know it then, but it wasn't for me. He wanted her for her.

I was supposed to get her as she left the hospital, but she was with Cole. I didn't have the heart at that point. I was broken. Depressed as hell. I had no one. No Alex. No Keith. No Gavin or Damon. No Jessa.

I let her walk. I got the worst fucking beating of my life that night. I don't know how the hell I survived. I went through days of excruciating pain. When I came out of it, I'd wake up later in even more agony. It went on like that for weeks.

As if that wasn't enough, though, when I came out of it all, dad spent the next few months grooming me. Turning me into some jealous as fuck psychopath who was so fucking obedient to him. He'd send me to New York to deal with his operations.

I met Layla. I needed release. She was my release. She took everything I gave her and made me feel like myself. During those moments of lucidity, I started to see that the shit I was doing was all wrong. It wasn't me. Never what I wanted.

I'd go back with a clear mind, and the fucking cycle would start all over again. I couldn't let it happen anymore. I ran so I could come up with a plan. I knew if I went back, it would either start happening again, whatever *it* was, or he really would follow through on his threat to kill me. I wanted to come up with a plan to not only save my life, but also theirs. The longer I was away, the more clear things became. I may have ended up calling Alex after all. Truth is, he's all I can think of right now. He's the only one who can help me now.

I hadn't intended being caught so damn quickly. Yet, here I am. Tied to a fucking chair in the middle of nowhere. I don't know if they got to Jessa. I have no way to contact Alex, even though I know I need to. Whether he forgives me or not is one thing. I can't say that I would if I were him, but I know that if the roles were reversed I wouldn't hesitate to help him. He's my brother.

I know now that the only way my father will ever stop is if he's dead. I should have done it a long time ago. I don't know if I would have survived it, but I know that this world would be a better place without him in it. If I could have taken him down with me, so fucking be it.

It's taken me a while to come to all of these conclusions, but the more time spent not under my father's control, the clearer my head gets. I realize all of my fuck-ups. I know I have a lot to atone for. I need a fucking vacation. Anywhere. I would happily throw a dart at a map right now and go wherever the dart landed. I'd be content if it were in the middle of the fucking ocean. Anywhere to get over the stress and mindfuck of everything that's happened over the last however the hell many years. Fucking all twenty-nine of them would be fine with me.

I look up at the door being fucked with. Seconds later, it opens, and I'm blinded by light I hadn't noticed. That's why I can see slightly more. The light is peeking through a few cracks in the wall. I squint as a figure I can't quite make out comes towards me. A second one follows. I watch as the first one raises a hand. There's a shiny object in it, but I don't know exactly what. I try to bring my hands up to block the blow, but I can't.

It looks like I won't get to atone for my sins after all. Just before what I've decided is a gun connects with the side of my head, I come to the conclusion that this is the end for me. My father finally got what he wanted all these years. He never needed me.

What would it matter to him if I'm dead?

Chapter Eighteen

✗✗ Jessa ✗✗

I smile down at my phone as it goes off with a text.

Layla: Hey. I know you're busy during your first week back, but lunch?

It's my second day back, and I'm so busy I barely have time to think of anything other than the projects in front of me. A break would be a good thing. Maybe I can get my head back in the game and not feel so scattered. I glance up at Jason sitting at his desk, oblivious to the world around him. He's the perfect CEO. Nothing distracts him. Not even me. I can't say I haven't been trying. I dropped a folder in front of him a little while ago. I bent sexily to pick it up, and he didn't even flinch.

I can't seem to get enough of him. I crave him. Just looking at him makes me tingle all over. It's like I need his touch. I need him.

"Hey, Jason?"

"Yeah, baby?"

"Would you be okay if I went to lunch downstairs with Layla?"

"As long as you bring me something back. I have to finish looking over these contracts."

"And maybe not having me as a distraction will help with that." I grin as he looks up at me. "You won't have to worry about me bending over in front of you. Or making cute noises to get your attention."

Jason grins as he leans back and laughs. "You think I didn't notice all of that, don't you?"

I bite my lip with a smile. "No reaction. At all."

Jason stands and stalks towards me, a sexy grin on his face. When he reaches me, his eyes are glimmering, and he leans down to kiss me. "Text her and tell her the cafe downstairs. Half an hour."

I do as he says as he walks to his office door and locks it. I watch his every move as he walks back to me. He immediately drops to his knees in front of me and lifts my knee length black skirt. He trails a finger across the front of my satin panties, immediately causing heat. He moves the fabric aside and leans forward to kiss my already sensitive skin.

"Beautiful," he whispers. He slides a finger inside me.

I gasp and grab hold of his shoulders. "Fuck, Jason..." It comes out as a throaty whisper. Jason chuckles as he leans forward and teases my clit with his tongue. He gives me a long lick as he strokes me inside and out. I let my head fall back as I curl my fingers in his hair. "You're so good at this."

"It helps when what I'm eating tastes so fucking good." He swirls his tongue around my bud as his strokes deepen. He knows just how I like it, how I like him. He's learned me so quickly.

"Mmm... yes... Jason. Right there. It feels so good."

He adds a second finger when I tighten and clench around him. I push his head closer because I really need it, and he buries his face in me. He licks and gently bites my clit as his masterful strokes deepen and become faster.

I can both hear and feel how wet I am. I blush at the sound and ride his tongue. My pussy pulses as I clench uncontrollably around his fingers. I can't form words. I can only whimper and moan as my thighs tremble.

Knowing my tells as well as he does, Jason can sense I'm about to lose it. "Come for me, beautiful. I want to taste you."

He licks me one last time, and I give him exactly what he wants. I come for him, hard, soaking his tongue. He licks it all up. My knees go weak at the feeling of him still licking me as I reach and plunge off my peak. I nearly fall, but he catches me and takes me to the couch he has against one of the walls in his office. He kisses me, long and sweetly as he unbuckles his pants. He pushes them low on his hips, his massive cock popping out with a flick. He sits and looks up at me expectantly.

"You want me to…" I look at him slightly confused. I'm not sure if he wants me to suck him or fuck him.

He chuckles and crooks his finger at me in a 'come hither' motion. I start to take off my skirt and panties. "Don't you dare. Get your ass over here, Jessa. Hop on and enjoy the ride."

I can only laugh as I do as he says. I straddle him and he pushes my skirt up and moves my panties aside. He positions me over him. "I don't think I'm ever going to be able to get enough of you."

"You better not." He sinks slowly into me, and I grip his shoulders harder.

"God. Oh my God." My eyes roll back in my head. I see stars and he hasn't even started yet.

Jason doesn't move right away, instead giving me time to adjust to his incredible length as he grips my hips. After a moment, he starts slowly thrusting inside me and moving my body against his. It feels like he's hitting my stomach with each thrust. I could die right now and be happy about it.

"God, Jess. You're perfect." His hands slide up my body and under my silk shirt to cup my breasts, his thumb flicking my nipple over my bra.

I bite my lip as I look at him. I lift myself slightly off him. I drop, plunging him deeper inside me and nearly collapsing against him as my eyes roll back in my head again. My pussy tightens around his cock. I almost come just because I wasn't expecting how good that would feel. I've been out of the game for too long, I guess.

Or maybe it's just how he makes me feel. It's not just the sex. It's that I feel the love and passion. It's something on a wholly other level. Something I'll never be able to describe as long as I live. Words for it have yet to be thought of.

"Jessa! Holy fuck, you feel so good." His head falls back onto the couch, and his eyes close as I continue to lift myself off him and drop down. Before long, we've found a rhythm and every move we make is totally in sync. He thrusts into me hard and deep as I meet his thrusts with each bounce on his cock.

"Oh! Jason!"

He reaches between my legs and sets his thumb against my clit. "Fuck, baby. Come. Come for me."

It takes seconds before my pussy obeys his dominant command. Seconds before I'm collapsing on top of him, spasming, as waves of pleasure overtake me. Moments later, his own release hits, and he holds me close to him as he pumps inside me, filling my pussy until I'm dripping his come.

He holds me for a few minutes, running his hands up and down my back and playing with my hair as we come down.

"Oh my God, Jas," I whisper against his neck as I kiss it.

"I can honestly say I've never had sex in my office," he rumbles. "This is kind of my sanctuary."

"And here I am ruining it." I chuckle as I kiss his neck again. I love the way he smells and tastes.

"What the hell are you doing to me, beautiful girl?"

"Corrupting you."

Jason lets out a loud and hearty laugh. "Fuck, Jess. You're gonna be my undoing."

"I think I already am," I say in my sexiest and most seductive tone.

He groans as his dick flexes inside me. "Get to lunch. I have to finish these contracts by the end of the day. If you want me home before one in the morning, you need to let me work."

"Yes, sir."

He groans again and squeezes my ass as he kisses my neck. "Baby, get off me before I fuck you again."

"Tempting offer." I lean down to kiss him before I get up and straighten myself out. "How am I supposed to concentrate on lunch with Layla after that?"

"Guess you'll have to think of me the whole time." He stands and leans down to kiss me before I walk down to the cafe, Cole and Nick trailing closely behind.

XXX

After a relaxing lunch with Layla, I grab Jason a sandwich, and Layla and I head back upstairs. Cole and Nick follow a little closer than usual, and I'm suddenly on high alert as I read them. I force myself to focus on the joke Layla is telling me and laugh along with her. I can't say I'm upset about having the company of another female. I know Layla isn't either. Our worlds are now dominated almost exclusively by men.

As we step off the elevator, I freeze in my tracks. Jason is standing outside his office. His receptionist, Nancy, is behind her desk, looking terrified. Alex looks like he's about to throw up. Damon, Gavin, and Lance look just as upset.

Lance glares in our direction. "Do you not read your texts? We said keep them away!"

Nick and Cole immediately take out their phones and look at each other before Cole looks back at Lance. "We didn't get a text."

Layla and I glance at each other before making our way over to the group. Before I have a chance to say anything, Nancy has her arms around both me and Layla; hugging us close.

"Oh, girls," she chokes out over her tears. "I don't think you want to see this."

She draws us away from the guys as Alex hits his knees and dry heaves. My chest immediately starts to hurt. I've never seen Alex truly fall apart. Not like that. He's always been the strong one. Even when I knew something was wrong and he showed some type of emotion, he was always so strong. So in control.

I meet Jason's eyes. My own confusion and terror is mirrored in his. Damon breaks away from the crowd and takes Layla's hand, pulling her to him. He buries his face in her hair as she holds him close. The friendship those two have is something similar to me and Cole. I love seeing it.

Jason's strong arms are suddenly around both me and Nancy. He draws us both into him. He kisses my hair and I feel my heart rate slow. "I'm sorry, Nancy," Jason rumbles. "I'm sorry you had to see that. Take the rest of the day off. Actually, take the rest of the week off."

"Mr. Crane, you have meetings I need to make sure you're ready for. I can't take the week off."

"You can. And you're going to. When you come back next week, I'm promoting you to something more than you are. I'll figure it out. I should've done it a long time ago. I apologize for putting so much extra work on you."

135

"Mr. Crane, you don't need to do that. I'm happy to help you where I can."

"This company wouldn't run without you, Nance. You've been with me from the start. You deserve more than just an Executive Assistant position. Now, please. Go home, Nancy. Be with your family. You need them right now. I'll take care of canceling my meetings."

"Maybe I should do that before I go," she says worriedly.

"No. Go home, Nancy."

She deflates in his arm, and he hugs her tighter. A few minutes of him hugging us both, Nancy slowly pulls away. Putting up no more of a fight, she finally gathers her things and does as he says. Jason pulls me into him, both arms holding me close.

"What happened?" I ask. Instead he holds out a hand, and Gavin hands him a phone. Alex is still on his knees.

"I warn you, baby. What you're about to see… it's not good."

He hands me the phone. On it is a man tied to a chair. He has blood all over his face. It's dripping from his head. It's hard to tell what his hair color is with all the blood dried into it. I drop the phone and bury my head in Jason's chest. His arms never leave me. They tighten even more around me.

I haven't had a panic attack in a couple weeks, but I can feel one coming on. I try to fight it, but I have to know, even though I'm sure I already do. Knowing for certain will send me into a full-blown attack.

"Who is it?" I whisper.

"Alex's brother. It's Josh," Jason answers.

I let out a gut-wrenching sob. I may not know what to think of him right now. I may be completely torn on how to feel. But no one deserves that. "Why? Who did this?"

"My father," Alex says from across the room. I stop breathing and meet his eyes. He's still on his knees on the ground. Cole is next to him trying to be of some comfort.

"Breathe, baby. Hey," Jason's deep timbre cuts through my foggy thoughts, but it's far away.

I look up at him, then back at Alex, trying to focus, but I can't. The world starts spinning. I knew it was going to happen. I feel like I'm falling and floating at the same time. I watch as Alex runs towards me, seemingly in slow motion, as everything around me goes black.

Chapter Nineteen

☒ Alex ☒

I watch as Jessa's face completely pales. I'm already getting to my feet and running to her before I can even comprehend what's happening. Jason catches her before she falls just as I reach them. He looks terrified.

"She's having a panic attack," I say with a calm I don't fucking feel. I've always hated seeing her have panic attacks, but I've only ever seen her pass out from them once.

"What?" Jason looks at me in a daze.

"A panic attack. She's prone to them. Get her to your office. Go." He lifts her in his arms. Everyone starts to follow. Cole and Nick both look just as terrified as Jason and tortured as me. "No! The more people in there, the worse it will be when she comes out of it. Everyone stays out here."

I follow Jason and close the door behind us as he lays her on the couch. I waste no time checking her breathing. It's shallow, but as I reach out and touch her neck, I can feel her pulse is racing. It feels like she's having a heart attack. Fuck. Just like that night.

"Has she had one since you've been together?" I ask him. "Do you know what to do?"

"Uh… she… when I went to her apartment after she was attacked… she started hyperventilating. She told me to hold her tight."

I nod. "Do that. Where's her purse?" I look around the office. "She always keeps extra medication in there in case she needs it."

"In her desk. Bottom drawer. She grabbed just her credit card and ID for lunch." Jason pulls Jessa into his lap and holds her tightly while I find her purse.

"Talk to her. Tell her to wake up. Run your fingers through her hair. She needs to feel you, Jason. You have to calm her down, or she'll have a heart attack. Do you feel her pulse? Feel how it's racing?" I dig into her purse and find her prescription as Jason talks to her. "Thank God, Jess. Thank fucking God you still carry it," I murmur.

I hurry back to Jason as he rocks back and forth with her, running his fingers through her hair and kissing her cheek and lips. I drop to my knees in front of him.

"Come on, beautiful," he says to Jessa. "Wake up. Please?"

I reach up and touch her neck. Her pulse is still racing. "Fuck. We have to get her to take this."

"How? She's passed the fuck out!"

"You aren't going to like me much, but give her here. I was with her for four years. I promise I know what I'm doing, and there's no time to explain it all to you."

"Fuck. Just get her to come out of it. I don't care what you have to do."

I stand and take her from Jason. "Get up."

Jason stands up and watches me. I lay her on the couch and then get on top of her, putting both arms around her.

"What the hell?" he growls.

"I told you she needs to feel you. She needs to feel your strength. She needs to feel you nearly crushing her."

"How is that supposed to help her?" His frustration and anger comes out in his tone and glare.

I glare right back. "Just trust me, Jason. I'm not going to hurt her." I soften my tone as I hold Jessa tightly. "After her parents died, she had one. She realized just before that this was becoming a serious situation. She made an appointment to see someone. But then the night of the crash happened. The attack was bad. She'd had them before, but that one was the

138

worst I'd ever seen. Worse than this. We rushed her to the hospital. She was unconscious. Her heart was racing. She was barely breathing. After she came to, the doctor pulled me aside and told me panic attacks happen when the person doesn't feel safe. Her brain tricks her into believing that she's in danger. Whether it's something like she can't catch her breath, or she really is fighting for her life, doesn't matter. She thinks she's going to die in that moment, even though that probably isn't the case. She needs to feel safe. That's why she told you to hold her tightly at her apartment."

"Obviously that wasn't fucking enough this time."

"Jason, she needs to feel you breathing," I say, keeping my tone even and breathing steady. "If you're breathing erratically, like you are right now, she'll feel it, and it will scare her even more. I can tell you aren't calm, and I don't even need to feel your pulse. If you want to help her, you have to stay calm."

I can feel her heartbeat slow as I lay on top of her, holding her close. "Come here. Put your hand on her neck where her carotid artery is." He drops to his knees and does as I say. I watch him visibly relax. "See how she's calming?"

He nods and takes several deep breaths. "Thank Christ."

Jessa starts coming to, and I tighten my grip, knowing her well enough to know that she'll fight. She'll think she's in danger even though she isn't fully awake. Just as I knew she would, she wakes up in a panic, hyperventilating, as she struggles underneath me.

"No! No! Please, no!" Jessa screams and cries. I can see Jason's heart break as he watches her.

"Shh, Jess. Honey, you're safe. It's Alex, okay? No one's going to hurt you," I murmur in her ear. I hold her tightly and whisper in her ear over and over again that she's safe until she finally stops fighting me.

"Alex, what happened?" she whispers. "What are you doing?"

"You okay? Feeling like you're ready for me to get up?"

She pauses and shutters out a breath. She grips the front of my shirt tight in her hands. "Not yet. Please." She buries her face in my shoulder. "Where's Jason?"

"I'm right here, baby." He touches her arm and rubs it soothingly as she clings to me.

"What happened?" she asks again.

"Not yet. Not until you feel okay enough for me to get up."

"I'm sorry, Jason," she whispers as her nails dig into my chest. I tighten my grip around her and keep my breathing steady.

"For what?" he asks, confused.

"Everything. I know I probably scared you. I haven't told you about all of this yet. Things have just been happening so fast. And I know you're probably pissed that Alex is on top of me."

"I'm not pissed, beautiful. Alex stepped up when I didn't know what to do. Just relax, okay? Breathe. Don't talk."

Jessa takes a deep breath. Her grip on me doesn't relax, and she buries her head further into my shoulder. My scent has always been able to calm her, and I'm hoping it still can. I'm hoping that it doesn't send her into some kind of PTSD related panic attack or something stemming from what Josh did to her.

"Use your senses, Jessa," I whisper.

"I can see your shirt," she breathes after a few moments.

"What color is it?"

"Blue. Like your eyes."

"Not as blue. My eyes are really blue." I smile as she giggles. "Good. What else?"

"I can smell your cologne. I can feel you breathing."

"Good girl. What can you hear?"

"Jason. Chuckling."

"Why do you think he's chuckling?"

"Because he loves how cute I am."

Jason laughs out loud and Jessa smiles as I look down at her. Jason rubs her arm a little more. "You're not wrong!"

I feel her relax more and more until her breathing returns to normal. "What about taste? Can you taste anything?"

"My tongue. It tastes like a tongue."

I laugh. "How are you now?"

"Better. I think I'm okay now."

I slowly get off her, knowing if I do it too quickly, it could cause her to panic again. When I'm completely off her and standing, she slowly sits up. Jason is immediately sitting next to her and pulling her close. She turns and hugs him.

"I need you to take this, Jess. You're a lot calmer, but your pulse is still racing pretty bad." I hand her the pill, then grab her water bottle off her desk, and hand it to her.

As I sit next to her, she takes my hand and she leans on Jason's shoulder. As usual after one of her attacks, she looks weak and tired. "Thank you, Alex."

"No need."

"There's a need," Jason says as he hugs Jessa. "I'm glad you were here. I didn't know she kept pills. I didn't know she had panic attacks like that. I didn't know what to do. If you hadn't been here -"

"You would've called 911, and she would've been fine," I cut him off.

"Maybe, but you got to her a hell of a lot quicker than any paramedic would've. I owe you."

I shake my head at him. "It's not necessary. I may not be with her anymore, but I still care about Jessa. It might take us a while, but I do plan on still being friends. Just remember when it happens again, and you have to do that yourself, that when she tells you she's okay, you get up slowly. If you get up too fast, it can cause another attack. If she feels like she still needs you, getting up slowly also gives her the chance to pull you back down if she needs to."

"So what happened?" Jessa asks quietly.

"What do you remember?" Jason hugs her tightly.

"Seeing Josh on the phone. I don't know if he was dead or not, but it looked like it."

"He's not. My father sent me that picture as a bribe." I sigh as she squeezes my hand.

"Your father? Why would he do that?"

I look over at her as her grip on my hand tightens. "I got a text from him."

"What did it say?" she asks.

I promised myself that I'd never lie to her or keep anything from her again. So, I take out my phone and scroll to the text. I hand her the phone so she can read it for herself. I question if it's the right decision, she deserves better from me than what I gave her in the past. If I expect to move forward with her in my life in any manner, then I have to start here with the utmost honesty.

Matthew: Bring me Jessa, or I finally off him like I should've done years ago. You will bring her back here. You will marry her. You will take over like you should've done years ago, and you will give me my heir. Disappoint me, boy, and I'll make you watch while I fuck her myself. I'll make you watch as I kill your precious brother. I'll keep you alive long enough to watch every time I fuck Jessa until she gives birth. I'll make you watch as I kill her. I'll kill your bitch mother. All before I finally end your miserable life and kill you, too.

She furrows her brows, looking sick to her stomach. "I don't understand." Jessa looks at me, confusion all over her face. "What are we going to do?"

"The same thing we have been doing," Jason says as he rubs up and down her arm. "We protect you. We know you're his target. You've always been the target. Just because we have confirmation instead of suspicion doesn't change anything."

"We've always known he was involved somehow, peanut. I… just… failed to see how deeply." I pinch the bridge of my nose. "I have to send Gavin and Damon home. I need them with Marissa and Tia."

"Marissa and Tia?" Jessa asks, a little bit of hope and maybe some slight apprehension in her voice.

"Marissa. Same one from college. They got married." I smile a little. I still don't like that girl. "And Tia. She's not with Damon anymore, but she's still a close friend."

"Why, though? She isn't the target," Jessa asks, still confused.

I look at her for a moment. She really doesn't understand the mafia life. "He'll go after them next if he thinks it will get me to do what he wants. He knows I protect my own. He knows who my crew is. I've been friends with Gavin and Damon since we were all kids. They're like brothers to both me and Josh. I want us all together, so they need to bring them here."

Jason lets out a long exhale. "It's a good idea. We should all stick together from this point on. I don't want anyone else to get hurt."

I nod, gently letting go of Jessa's hand as I stand to let everyone else in the office. After they've all made sure Jessa is okay, I clear my throat just as Ryan walks in. I feel myself relax as he glances at Jessa. Jason is still holding her close and running his fingers through her hair.

142

Satisfied that she's okay, he turns to me. Ryan has always been the most dependable person in my life. I'm everyone else's rock; he's mine.

"You okay?" He watches me. I've never been able to lie to him about anything, let alone what I'm feeling.

"Now that you're here, I'm feeling a little more stable. But those texts and that pic fucked me up."

"Thanks for sending them. Glad to know you know not to hide shit from me and try to handle it on your own."

"Learned my lesson long ago."

Ryan chuckles. "You want me to tell them the plan?" I can only nod. I still haven't completely gained control over myself after seeing Josh that way. Ryan nods. "Listen up." The room silences, and all eyes fall on Ryan. "Jessa and Jason. I'm upping security."

"I think it's best if Alex and his crew stay with us. We already decided we need to stick together," Jason says.

Ryan nods. "I want that place locked the fuck down," Ryan says authoritatively. "I'm not taking any fucking chances. We've already gone up against Alex's dad once. We know what he's capable of. We know how conniving and manipulative he is."

"You think more security is necessary?" Cole asks in near disbelief. There are already a good amount of guards around Jason's house.

"You don't understand what he's capable of," Nick mumbles darkly.

"On that note, I want Layla with us at Jason's," I cut in. "Gavin and Damon need to go to L.A. to get Marissa and Tia. Cole has some cops from L.A.P.D. watching them, but they can only do so much. I don't want either of you calling Marrisa or Tia. We can't be sure the phone's aren't tapped."

"Wait. You think that sick fuck would go after my wife? Why?" Gavin asks, suddenly on far more edge than he already was.

"You know better than anyone that he'll do everything he can to get what he wants," I answer. "He knows the way to get to me is through what I love. You and Damon have people in your lives you care about. He knows I'd do anything to protect them because of their relationship with you. And you know that just as well. Our only chance is bringing everyone together and teaming up with Ryan. Mafia against mafia."

"What about Josh?" Damon keeps Layla close to him. She's plastered to his side. If she feels safe with him, I'm all fucking for it. "Fuck. We grew up with him. We know he's not the bad guy here. We should have noticed his behavior was off."

"Shouldn't we find him?" Jessa asks quietly. "Obviously he's in bad shape. He might be alive now, but he won't be for long."

One of the things I've always loved about Jessa is her heart. Despite how terrified of him she obviously is, she's still putting his well-being above her fear.

"I have some ideas, peanut. Don't worry about him. That's my job. Your job is to worry about you." I narrow my eyes at Gavin and Damon. "Why are you both still here?"

Gavin chuckles and waits for Damon. Damon whispers something in Layla's ear and nods towards Lance. She sniffles as he gets up but nods. I don't know what he said, but Lance takes his place, and Layla curls herself into his side instead. Damon follows Gavin out the door.

Jessa hugs Jason, and I lean against his desk. I don't know where my father's obsession is coming from, but fuck if I'll let it continue. It ends here. I wish I could talk to Josh about all of it. I may have thought he was unhinged, but Layla has convinced me that he isn't. My suspicions about brainwashing seem to be true. I haven't told anyone, but I also think Josh's suspicions about being poisoned are also true. Layla has given the part of me I long since stopped listening to a much louder voice. I'll have to thank her for helping me think more clearly.

I can't believe I didn't see any of it before, and it's something I'm going to have to live with forever. Allowing my brother to be preyed upon by that sick son of a bitch tears me apart just as much as Jessa being hurt and having to live through all of this shit does. I won't allow it to keep happening.

It's time for my father to meet his fucking maker.

Chapter Twenty

⚔ Jason ⚔

Jessa has been sleeping soundly since we went to bed hours ago. I hold her close. Alex warned me this would happen. Panic attacks exhaust her, and the prescription she takes exhausts her more. She was gone as soon as her head hit my arm. She hasn't moved since. I haven't moved either, only enough to pull her closer to me. I need her close to me. Seeing Alex's brother bloodied and beaten nearly to death...

That's the reason I wanted out of the mafia. Why I wanted to be on my own. I can't handle seeing either of my brother's like that. I wish Ryan would walk away. Hell, I wish Nick would quit helping him when he asks.

I rub my head. Of course, that isn't true. I do wish none of us were involved in the mafia in any way whatsoever. But if Ryan ever asked either of us for help, neither of us would ever say no. We're a family. Just like Alex and Josh.

Fuck. I wonder how different our lives would be if we all just walked away. I wonder how it would be if I really could keep both sides of me separated. But here I am. Deeply involved in something I wanted out of. Willing to walk right back into it if it means saving the woman I love.

I glance at the clock. Four in the fucking morning, and I haven't slept at all. Every sound has me tensing. Listening. I got rid of all my guns long ago. I gave them all to my brother. What I wouldn't give to have my Glock nestled snugly in the drawer next to me.

I'll have to talk to Ryan about that. I don't care if there are six armed men in my house and who knows how many more Ryan sent over to patrol the property. I learned a few things being the son and brother of a mafia boss.

Never let my guard down.

Never ever leave what's important to me, what I love, unprotected. I never thought I would fall in love. I never allowed myself to get close to any woman I've ever been with. Jessa is the first for me on so many levels. She's the exception to every rule I've ever made.

Every billionaire has the same story. A woman who took everything and broke his heart. My brother, Nick, went through it. But not me. Never me. I've always protected myself. I've always been suspicious of a woman's intentions with me after watching Nick get his heart broken by someone who drained all of his accounts. Hell. I was suspicious of them before.

But Jessa Holloway walks into my life, and suddenly all of my inhibitions are out the window. I don't know what it is about her, but I want to, no, need to protect her. I've never wanted to jump back into the mafia life, but I'd do it for her in a heartbeat if it meant saving my girl's life.

I haven't picked up a gun since I walked away. I put everything into starting my business and separating my life from the mafia. What the hell is wrong with me? Being willing to lay my life down for her is one thing. I fell and I fell hard for her. I accept that. But being willing to become the coldhearted assassin I was before I met her? That's crazy. I shouldn't be entertaining the idea, but I am. It's fucking crazy.

She stirs in my arms, and I tighten my grip. She's not getting out of this bed. Not yet.

"Are you okay?" Her soft voice is filled with sleep.

I smile and kiss the back of her head. "You're the one who just had the worst panic attack I've ever seen, and you're asking me how I'm doing?"

"Well, you're holding me really tightly. Like you're using me to anchor yourself or something. Like I do to you when I'm having a panic attack."

"I'm just not ready to let you go, baby. I'm… I have a hard decision to make."

"I hope you aren't saying what I think you are."

I glanced at her in surprise. There's no way she can know what I'm wrestling with right now. She turns in my arms and reaches up to touch my face. I turn my head slightly and kiss her palm. She runs her hand down my cheek, neck, and arm before coming to rest on my hip.

"What do you think I'm saying?" I ask hesitantly.

"That you don't want any part of this. You've spent the last several years running from the mafia. Now, because of me, you get thrown back into it again."

"You're partially right. I have been running from it since I graduated college. Probably before."

"I know. And now look at you. You've made so much of yourself." She burrows into me, wrapping her arm around me as I pull her closer.

"I don't want any part of it, Jessa, but I *am* part of it. It's part of me. I can't run from it forever."

"Because of me." She's quiet for a moment. "I understand if you want me to go, Jason."

"What?" I nearly choke as I tighten my grip on her. "Baby, that's not what I'm saying. I don't want you to go. Where the hell would you go anyway?"

"I… don't know. I'm sure I could talk to Alex and Cole about it."

"I don't want you to go, Jessa. I don't want to let you out of my arms ever again. That's not what I'm saying. I already told you I love you, and that I fell hard and fast for you. You told me the same thing, Jess."

"Then what? What's wrong? I can feel something is off with you."

I run my fingers up and down her back and through her hair before finally taking a deep breath. I have to tell her. If I don't, what the hell am I doing here with her?"

"I hope you don't look at me any differently when I tell you this." It takes me a minute to formulate my words. She waits patiently like the saint she is. "I was thinking about talking to Ryan about getting my Glock back. When I left the mafia, I gave him all of my guns. Symbolism. No guns. No mafia. I haven't touched one since. But I've been thinking maybe I should get some back. I should start carrying one again. To protect you."

She's quiet for so long I'm positive she's going to tell me go fuck myself. It's such a small thing to be wrestling this hard with myself over, but I really fucking want her to tell me it's okay. Something, anything to make this easier.

I jump a bit when she starts talking. "I'm not sure what to say. I understand why you wouldn't want to, I understand why you would. I also know how far you've come since leaving. I know you don't want to go back."

"I was going to talk to Ryan. See what he thinks."

"If you go back, it could ruin your company."

"If I don't, I can't protect you."

"I don't think you need to go back in order to protect me, Jason. There has to be another way if that's not something you want. Maybe Ryan can help you figure out the balance because I know you. I know how hard you're struggling with this."

"I'd give it all up if I had to. I would do whatever it took to keep you safe."

"I won't let you step down from your company, Jason. Not for anything. You love your company. You've worked so, so hard to get where you are. There has to be a balance. You need to call your brother and figure it out, but stepping down isn't an option. I think the real issue that you're grappling with, though, is that the mafia is your family. It's in your blood. It's hard to be away from it because you feel like a part of you is missing."

I have to smile at how caring she is towards me and my career. My needs. But I'm completely shocked that she knows me as well as she does. She's right. I do feel like a part of me is missing. I might not want the life. The late-night bullshit. The traveling all over the world to take out factions trying to take my family down.

But I do feel like I need to be a part of it in some ways. I don't feel whole otherwise. I feel like I'm on the outside looking in on my own fucking life. Like there's a disconnect somewhere. It's something I've felt for longer than I care to admit to myself or anyone. I may not want the mafia involved in my company, but I do think they're a part of my life. Me.

I groan as I reach for my phone on the nightstand. I can't put this off. I can't sit by helpless and unable to protect my girl. It's time to talk to my brother. I don't care how early it is.

He picks up on the first ring. "Jason? What's wrong?"

"I know it's early, but we need to talk."

There's some shuffling, and I'm pretty sure Ryan drops the phone before mumbling something to someone. After a few moments, he comes back on the line.

"Okay. What do you want to talk about?"

"How's Megs?" I chuckle.

"It's Jamie tonight."

I grin. "What happened to Megs?"

"She was last night."

"Man. You go through more women than I ever did and I was admittedly a manwhore before Jessa walked in my life."

"Three things make me happy in life, Jas. Beautiful women. Money. Guns. In that order."

I can't help but laugh. "You're a fucking liar. Family. Guns. Money. Beautiful women. In that order."

"Family goes on the list of things that annoy me." I can hear the smirk in his voice. "I know you didn't call to hear about my sex life. And I'm sure you don't want me asking about how that sexy woman next to you is in bed. So, what's on your mind?"

I grin, but it drops to a frown real quick. "With Jessa in so much fucking danger, I've been thinking of the best way to protect her. One of the first rules we ever learned was to never leave someone else in charge of protecting what's yours."

"You're not rejoining, Jas. I won't let you. You got out, and we're all proud of you for that."

"You went legit. It wouldn't really be the same."

"I still run a mafia. We still have a rep. People are still killed. You're staying out."

"I didn't say I wanted back in. At least not completely."

"I've known you your entire life. I know where you're going with this."

"Help me figure out a way to do what I need to without rejoining, Ry. I can't just sit idly and do nothing. There has to be a way to balance both parts of me."

Ryan is silent for a few moments as he thinks. "You can't just walk into the boardroom packing heat, Jas."

"Then, I'll take time off until this is resolved."

"You can't do that."

"Why not? I'm the fucking CEO."

"And who the fuck would take over at the drop of a hat? Nancy?"

His words slam into me. She could do it, but I can't just drop it on her. She needs preparation. Jessa kisses my chest, and I feel her smiling. I don't know how much she can hear, but it's enough to elicit a soft chuckle.

"Listen to me," Ryan continues. "As your older, more attractive, and much wiser brother, the best thing for you to do is what you already are. Run your company. Love your woman. But if you want to do something to protect her, keep a gun in your nightstand drawer. We can get you a shoulder holster so you can have one with you. When you're in your meetings, you'll have to wear a suit jacket."

"I usually do."

"Come over later, and we'll practice in my indoor range downstairs. You're rusty. And I mean later, Jas. There's a naked woman in my bed that I need to get my fill of."

"I bet you I'm still a better shot," I tease.

"Fuck you. Not a chance in hell. Come over around dinner. I'll make chicken marsala."

I laugh. "It's gonna take you until dinner to finish fucking her?"

"Not to finish. To get my fill."

He hangs up, and I laugh. Jessa is looking at me with a soft smile on her face. The sun is just beginning to rise. She looks incredible with the soft light playing around her. I reach over and grab a strand of her hair, wrapping it around my finger.

"You two have an interesting relationship," Jessa chuckles.

"Yeah, sorry about that."

"It's okay. Do you feel better about everything?"

"I actually do. Surprisingly. He won't let me back, but he knows I need something. He'll help me figure it out. As soon as he gets his fill of whoever he's with," I say teasingly. She giggles and climbs on top of me.

She runs her hands up my chest as she leans down to kiss me. I slide my hands along her legs to her sexy ass, giving her a light squeeze. "What are you doing, Jessa?"

"He's not the only one with a naked woman in his bed." She reaches down and gives my cock a couple of strokes. I moan. It's all it takes to make my dick stand at attention.

I reposition her so she's directly over me. She drops herself, and I'm suddenly nestled deeply inside her. "Fuck me, beautiful girl." I let my head fall back against the pillow, relishing in the feel of her wrapped around my cock.

"That's my intention." She sits up, straddling me and begins bouncing.

I reach up and grab her tits. "Jessa, goddamn, you feel so fucking good." I sit up and pull out of her as I get up, grabbing her hand and pulling her out of the bed after me.

She giggles. I lean down and kiss her as I grip her thighs. I lift her up, not breaking the kiss for a second. She wraps her legs around my waist, and I walk to the wall. I hold her against it, plunging deeply into her once more with a low groan.

"I love when you become all CEO and take control."

"Yeah?" I slam into her again and again. The feel of her firm body and perfectly large tits against my body as I fuck her is enough to drive me over the edge. I'll never get enough of her. "Tell me how much you like it."

"I… love… it…" Her words are staggered and come to the beat of her back hitting the wall.

Her pussy, soft and wet, clenches hard around my cock, making me impossibly harder and thicker. She tightens more and more, getting wetter and wetter with each hard, deep, and fast thrust. Her arms tighten around my shoulders as her thighs start to tremble. She bucks into me.

I groan as I slide deeper. "I love when you do that." I lift her slightly. My next thrust makes her scream my name.

"Fuck, Jason! Oh my fuck. Don't stop. Don't you dare stop!"

I growl as I kiss her neck and suck it gently. "You're mine, Jessa. All mine."

Her head falls against my shoulder as I slam into her again and again. She bites down on my shoulder with a low moan. "And you're mine."

And with that, she spills around my cock. As she pulses and quakes around me, I keep up my thrusts letting her ride through it before I finally come for her.

Chapter Twenty One

✗ Jessa ✗

I decided to stay behind while Jason went to Ryan's house. I'm not sure why, but I honestly just need the time alone. I've been surrounded by so many different people over the past weeks. I need a break. Looking wistfully outside, I decide to get some fresh air. I reach down for my shoes when I feel a presence behind me. I look up to see one of Ryan's intimidating guards.

"Going somewhere?"

I sigh. "Jason has a lot of property. I thought I'd go for a walk."

"Sure. Ready when you are."

"Actually, I thought maybe I could go myself."

"Not happening, Jessa. I have orders."

"But I'm not leaving the property," I say quietly. "And Ryan has guards all over the place. I…" I sigh. "I really just need a break from everyone. I feel like I'm going crazy."

I look down and finish putting my shoes on. I really do feel like I'm going crazy. I know all of this is necessary, but to not be able to even go outside alone makes me want to cry while simultaneously making me feel like a whiny little brat. I know he has a job. I truly appreciate all everyone is doing.

I sigh again as I look back up at the giant intimidating man looking down at me. I'm hopeful I'll at least be able to walk the property and get some fresh air. Truthfully, though, it's scary to even think about being alone, even though I know I need to for my own sanity.

"Don't go far. If you can't see a guard, you've gone too far."

I throw my arms around him. He stiffens, but I just hug him tighter. "Thank you. I promise I won't go far."

He gives me a quick hug and lets me go, pushing me back gently. "Keep in the line of sight of the guards. I'm not kidding. I don't want Nick to kill me."

"Nick? Not Ryan?"

"Sure, I fear Ryan. But Nick is one scary son of a bitch."

I look at him curiously before I turn away and make my way outside. I take a deep breath, inhaling the freshly cut grass scent as I step into the yard. The air at Jason's mansion is so much fresher than in the city.

The sun beating down on me as I walk is warm. I love it here. I love everything about this place. I love the flower garden his groundskeeper keeps meticulous. I love that there is a lake a short distance away. Everything. I love everything.

I walk slowly, enjoying the sights, sounds, smells, and all around peacefulness. Before I know it, I've reached the edge of the property. I glance back and see I've walked much farther than I intended to, but there are several guards watching me, so I feel safe. I smile and begin walking back, but I trip and fall to the ground.

"Ah! Ow!" I scream. I start to stand up, but something is holding me down. I scream again, and a hand with a cloth immediately clamps on my mouth. I smell something strong and heavy with chemicals. I cough and scream. I hear guards yelling as I lose consciousness.

My head is pounding, and I am terrified to open my eyes. I know as soon as I do, I'll throw up. I'm so cold. I'm laying down, but I'm not in bed. Whatever is underneath me is so hard. I slowly open my eyes and groan at the pain. I try to push myself up and whimper. Nausea invades my being. It's dark. I sit up, fighting the urge to throw up, and wait for my eyes to adjust.

"Hello?" I ask the darkness, quietly.

I'm trying to ignore the fact that my heart has relocated to another part of my body. I'm not sure if it's beating so fast that I can't feel it, or if it's stopped beating entirely.

Maybe I'm dead.

No one answers by quiet call. I guess I didn't expect an answer. I sigh and force myself to stand. I'm not sure it's the best idea, but I'm starting to freak out. I don't know where I am, but I know I need to figure it out. The fight or flight instinct is strong, but it's the fact that I know I'm about to start panicking that is really scaring me.

Making myself stay as calm as I possibly can, I feel my way around the wall until I think I feel a door handle. I try to open it, but it doesn't open. Of course. Tears sting my eyes. I yank on it and pull. I push and kick on it. It doesn't open.

Suddenly, the very low-pitched sound in my ears turns into a roar. My body takes over. My mind is no longer in control. The little shred of control I had is yanked so viciously from me that I almost fall to my knees.

But I don't.

I scream. "Help! Help me! Help!"

The panic.

Not here.

Please.

Not here.

I yank on the door again and again. It doesn't move a single inch. I scream again, hysterically this time. Tears are streaming down my face now. I have no control over myself. The panic. It has control. It's the leader now.

"Help me!" I pound harder on the door and kick it as I sob.

My heart.

I can feel it again. I wish I didn't. It's beating so fast. I'm getting way too much oxygen. Or not enough. Or maybe I think I'm breathing but really not.

I gasp for air and scream again.

"Help! Please! Please! Let me out! Help!"

155

"It's locked from the outside, Jessa. Don't bother. I already tried as soon as they released me from the fucking cuffs."

I recognize the voice. I'll never forget that voice. It's deeper than Alex's. I don't know how I never noticed that before. Maybe I did but ignored it. I try to breathe, but can't. I'm shaky, and my heart feels like it's in my ears.

He was hurt in the picture I saw yesterday. Really bad. He needs help. Maybe if I refocus on helping him, I can control the panic.

"J-Josh?"

"Yeah. Josh. Looks like all those guards around you couldn't help you after all. I hoped they would."

"Oh God. No. Oh my God. This can't be happening." I start coughing. "What's happening?"

Focus. Focus on helping him. He was so hurt. He has to still be.

"Jessa, relax, okay? I'm not going to hurt you." His voice holds no edge or vengeance. It's calm and deep. It's the way it was when he first came back pretending to be Alex.

I sob against the door. "You're hurt. W-we saw a p-picture of you."

"You saw a picture of me?" He sounds surprised. "How?" His voice is closer now. Like he's hesitantly inching towards me.

"I-it was s-sent to Alex. B-by your fath-er." I hiccup. "You n-need help."

"It's okay. Looks worse than it is." He's next to me. "You're panicking, honey. Let me help you."

I shake my head. "Y-you -"

"Jess." Dominance. That dominance he has that Alex doesn't. Alex has it, but not as much as Josh. "Let me help you."

I close my eyes and start sinking to the ground as I nod. I take breath after breath, but it doesn't help. "I'm s-sorry, Josh," I whisper.

Josh wraps his arms around me and sinks to the ground with me in his arms, hugging me tightly. "Just let me help you."

"I don't h-have -"

"I know, sweetheart. I know," he whispers. "I'll get you through this. I promise. What do you smell?" He rests his chin on my head and sways gently."

"Sweat. Mold. Blood." I cry into his shoulder because I know it's his.

He chuckles. "I'm sorry. I don't mean to laugh. That probably wasn't the best question to ask you. Considering the situation we find ourselves in."

"Probably n-not."

"How about this one. What do you feel?"

"Y-you. Your arms a-around me."

"Good. Do you feel me breathing?"

"Yes."

"I need you to breathe with me, Jessa."

I take a deep breath. I don't want to ask, but I'm not stupid. Josh is all I have right now, and I know I need more. I know he's hurt himself, but I need him. We need each other to get out of whatever this is alive. And it's that thought that keeps me from fearing the man with his arms around me.

"Could you… would you… possibly… h-hold me tighter."

He pulls me into his lap and leans his back against the wall, hugging me tightly to his body. Protectively. His breathing is calm, soothing, relaxing. "I'm sorry, Jess. For everything. Everything I've done to you."

"Don't." I shake my head. "Please don't. Not now. I need to calm d-down. My heart feels like it's going t-to explode. I feel like I'm going to b-black out again. Like I'm going to d-die."

"I won't let you, Jessa. I'm here. Okay? I've got you."

"I just n-need this." I put my hand against his chest and do all I can to focus on his steady breathing. "I need to f-feel you b-breathing. I need y-you to tell m-me I'm okay. Tell me I'm s-safe even if you're ly-lying."

"You are safe, Jessa. I won't let anyone hurt you. And I'm not lying about that. I won't let him near you. I swear to you."

I keep concentrating on the rise and fall of Josh's chest. He runs his fingers through my hair and keeps telling me I'm safe over and over again. I let my eyes fall closed once more. The longer I'm focused on him, the better I feel. I don't know how long it takes, but I start to relax and my breathing slows. Finally, I'm ready for answers.

"Why? Why me?" I whisper.

"Do you mean why did I do what I've done to you?"

157

"That, and why is your father so obsessed with me giving him an heir?"

I can tell he's surprised at my question. "How… did you know about that?"

"It's a long story."

He chuckles. "Not like we don't have time."

"Fine." I sigh. "Just… this is going to sound so stupid."

"Nothing you could possibly say to me would sound stupid. Fuck, Jess. Trust me on that."

"Just don't let me go, okay? If you let me go, I'm afraid I'll go right back into an attack. I'm calming, but I'm so scared right now. So, so scared."

"I won't let you go, Jessa. I don't know how much you know about this shit, but I was with you for a long time. I know how to deal with your panic attacks. I promise I'll get you through it. Just tell me what you know. I'll fill in the blanks."

"Alex. He… um… when I was released from the hospital, he and his team and Cole tried to keep me hidden. They masked my social security number and a lot of other stuff. When he found out you came here, he followed."

He's quiet for a moment. "Is that how you escaped? Alex showed up?"

"Not… exactly. My boss was worried that I didn't show up to work. I had never been late or not shown up. He had seen me in the elevator when I was texting you. He saw how scared I was. He questioned me and tried to follow me out to the garage, but I ran. He was already suspicious something was happening."

"I thought you were with him. Like together, I mean."

"Not until that day. The day after you came. I wasn't lying about that. He took me to his house. After he found me, he wouldn't let me stay in my condo."

"When did Alex show up?"

"I… am not sure I should tell you that." I'm having a really hard time sorting through the sense of safety I feel, and the overwhelming fear of him that I should feel and don't.

"I won't hurt you, Jessa," he says quietly. "I'm done with that." He shakes his head. There's a lot of shit that I don't think you or anyone else

158

knows. But I've been doing a lot of thinking. Being away from my father has given me a lot clearer of a mind and allowed me to figure shit out. My obsession with you was driven by him. I was being brainwashed and poisoned."

"P-poisoned?"

Josh sighs as he hugs me tighter. He buries his face in my hair. He doesn't have to tell me that he's seeking as much comfort from me as I am him. "I wasn't sure right away, but I've been away from him now for a couple weeks. A friend of mine sent me some information he found on my dad's computer. He hacked it. My dad keeps a very detailed journal. In it, he lists every single time he gave me this serum. I don't know what was in it yet, but it weakened the mind. He kept track of everything it did to me over the last seven or eight years. Before Alex even left for Italy is when he started it."

"Josh." My heart breaks, and I sniffle. "I'm so sorry." My entire body wants nothing more than to hug him as the realization hits me that everything he did to me wasn't his fault. I wrap my arms around him just as tightly as his arms are around me.

"The longer I was away from him before, the clearer my head got. You helped me. I started to have moments where everything he was doing made sense. I'd go back with the intention of dealing with him. And then it would all be back to like it was before. Everything would be cloudy and wouldn't make sense. The only thing that made sense to me was what he said. He'd give me goals and a purpose after tearing me down."

"That's such a horrible way to live."

"Not as bad as it was for you. I fucked you up, Jessa. I'll never forgive myself for what I did to you. I'll never expect you to forgive me."

I shake my head. "I don't want to talk about that now. You asked about Alex. Alex is friends with Jason's brother. Jason's brother was there the night Jason took me to his house. When I told him Alex was stalking me and everything that happened with him, he said it didn't add up. He called Alex. Alex came over and explained everything. Including how he had a twin."

Josh chuckles again. I feel him smile. "So, Alex is friends with Ryan fucking Crane, huh?"

I look up at him a little perplexed. "How do you know his name?"

"I'm not stupid, Jessa. I researched Jason and figured it out. Everyone knows who Ryan Crane is. It wasn't hard to put two and two together." His breathing is starting to quicken, and I start taking deep breaths.

"Josh," I plead.

He tightens his grip on me as he hugs me and regulates his breathing. "I'm sorry. That development makes things a little scarier for me."

I nod because I get it. Ryan is the leader of a huge mafia. Powerful. His mafia's biggest rival. I have to get him to not think about that. "Tell me more. About how this all started."

He sighs as he keeps running his fingers through my hair and hugging me. "I spent years being blinded by jealousy over Alex. It really didn't start until about a year before he left. It was very back and forth. Alex was always able to bring me back. After he left, I didn't have him to bring me back. My father constantly pitted us against each other. Ever since birth. Alex is a few minutes older. As soon as he came out, the mafia was his. He was the oldest. My father never cared what we wanted. He never gave a shit what Alex wanted. Alex never wanted to take over. He was forced to take as much as he did. He hated it. But I did want it. I wanted to lead."

"Alex mentioned that."

"When he met you, it only solidified his decision."

"Tighter, Josh," I whisper. My chest is starting to feel like it's collapsing. I hate feeling it. Feeling the weakness and vulnerability. Josh does as I ask, and I try to keep mimicking his breathing.

"Deep breaths, Jessa." He takes a deep breath, and I copy him. He breathes with me for a few moments. Finally, he asks, "Do you want me to continue?"

I nod. "Please. It's stupid, but you talking helps. And your grip helps, too. Please."

"It's not stupid." He shifts so he can hold me better. "Alex stopped going on missions. I stepped up. We thought if I showed my dad I was just as good as Alex, he'd finally see that I could be just as good of a leader as Alex. But our father spent more time telling me everything I did wrong, even though he set me up to fail on more occasions than I can tell you. I never did. I always completed the mission, and that pissed him the fuck off. I've always been good at thinking quickly when shit changes."

"He doesn't sound at all like the person you described him to be."

"He isn't like that guy. I lied because I needed you. I needed you to believe my family was good. Just busy. But each time I brought you home, I made sure my father wasn't there. I was careful to keep you away from my mom because I didn't want you to see the bruises he left her with. He's cold and calculating. The only reason I started fucking with you and pretending to be Alex was because he became obsessed with you. He knew about you because he'd been watching you."

"Gross." I shiver.

"It gets a lot worse, Jessa. He'd been watching you ever since you moved into the penthouse with Alex. He became more and more obsessed. By the time you graduated, Alex told him he wasn't taking over. Dad was fucking pissed at the blatant disobedience. He concocted some fucking plan to kill both of you. So, I stepped in. I needed to protect my brother. To protect you. I wasn't going to let him hurt either of you. I needed you to break up. So, I pretended to be him and acted like a jealous fucking asshole. I hated hurting you, Jessa. Fucking hated every second of it."

I can only nod as I stay silent. Josh hugs me closer to his body. He runs his hands through my hair and up and down my back. He buries his face in my neck, and I know instinctively that he's struggling with everything that happened right now. Even more than he lets on. I wrap my arms around him and hug him even tighter. It helps ground me.

Feeling him makes everything in my chaotic body calm more and more as the seconds slip by. But it's pretty obvious I'm doing the same for him. It's because of that knowledge, the knowledge that I'm helping him, that I'm able to stay relatively okay right now. Despite our surroundings.

"After Alex left, I thought that was it. My plan worked. Alex was taking over the overseas operations, and you weren't in his life anymore. Our father decided it was your fault Alex didn't want to take over. After the break-up, I thought that was it. You both were safe. But a year later, I saw some pictures of you. He was still watching you. I overheard a conversation where he was ordering his second in command to take you. I wasn't going to let that happen. I got to you first."

"That was the day Alex showed back up in my life. But not Alex. You."

He nods. "I couldn't let him hurt you, Jessa. I know how badly I fucked up. Everything should have been handled so fucking differently, but I swear that all I ever wanted was to keep you safe. The more he used whatever fucking serum he used on me to control me, the more I lost control of myself. According to the journal, he started using more on me; observing how long it lasted. He was putting it in my food. Injecting it. I never fucking expected it. After you left, it became easier for him because I didn't have anything. I didn't have you. He shot my friend. I had already stopped talking to Alex because I was so fucking jealous."

"He isolated you. Made you feel alone."

"It became easier to control me that way. Especially with the serum."

"It's so crazy. It's hard to believe."

He hugs me close as she sighs. "I understand if you can't believe that. You have no reason to trust me. I hurt you. Badly. I can never make that right. I don't expect you to believe that what I'm telling you is true."

"I didn't say I didn't believe you, or that I didn't trust you." I take another deep breath. I'm starting to feel weak. "What happened to you wasn't your fault."

"I appreciate you saying that, but I still need to take responsibility. Especially for what happened with you. I won't let him hurt you, Jessa. I'll keep you safe. I promise."

All I can do is nod. I reposition myself, so that I'm sitting between his legs with my back to him. I reach for his arms to put them back around me, and he wraps me into his embrace. "I'm so tired. But I'm so scared."

"Go to sleep, Jessa. I know the attacks take a lot out of you. I'll protect you. I promise. I won't let anyone hurt you. You're safe with me."

With his promise, I let myself drift off, his embrace keeping me warm and protectively cocooned.

Chapter Twenty Two

⚔ Jessa ⚔

I wake up, and my heart rate immediately spikes. I whimper. "Why is this happening? What did I ever do?" I whisper.

"Nothing, Jessa. You didn't do anything. This is my fault."

Josh pulls me close to him and hugs me tightly. It must be crazy, but I feel like I can trust him. It wouldn't matter anyway, though, because I know I need him. I've never been able to control the attacks no matter what Alex and the doctor's tried to teach me. Even Josh. While he's been the cause of many of them, he was also the reason I got through them.

The fear paralyzes me. My heart rate spikes so far that I black out. I'm not naive enough to believe for a second that I can do this alone. If not for Josh, I know I'd be dead. I begin to cry and shiver. I'm still sitting between Josh's legs with my back to him, but he knows me well enough to know that isn't what I need. He turns me towards him so that I'm facing him. He pulls me tightly to his chest.

"I just don't understand."

"I don't understand either, Jess. All I know is he wants an heir to take over. I don't think he even cares if Alex ever takes over. He sure as fuck won't let me. He wants someone he can mold into a version of himself. Someone who thinks like him, and does what he says."

"Why can't he just have another kid with your mom?"

"Because after me and Alex, she had a complication. She can't have any more."

"Why specifically me, then?"

"I wish I had those answers for you, Jess. I wish I could tell you everything you want me to, but I can't. I don't know. I don't know why he's so obsessed with you." He rubs his hands up and down my back. "You have to calm down, baby. I know you don't fully trust me, but I won't hurt you. I'm not under the effects of whatever the fuck he did to me anymore."

"I do," I whisper after several moments of focusing on him. He pauses in his rubbing as if he's surprised. "I do trust you. I know your dad is the reason behind this. I understand that. I understand so much more now."

He clears his throat and continues soothingly rubbing my back and arms. "I don't know if I deserve that trust, but I won't break it."

"I know."

Josh lets out a breath. "In order for you to get through this, you have to calm down. And you have to trust that I'll get you out of here. You said you trust me, so can you trust that? Can you do that for me?"

"I'm trying, Josh. You don't understand how hard I'm trying. How hard this is for me." I sniffle. "You don't understand."

I try to keep my frustration at bay because I know that getting frustrated won't help me. It will only make everything worse, but I can't. I'm angry that I can't calm myself down. I'm pissed that no matter what I do, my body doesn't listen. I feel stupid and weak for not being able to help myself. It's emotions like this that are so hard to explain to people. So difficult to make others understand. I can't just calm down. If I could, I wouldn't need a prescription to help me. A prescription I don't have right now.

"Jessa, you're right. I don't. I have no idea what it feels like to not be able to calm myself down. But I do know you're trying. And you're doing a hell of a job."

"But it's not enough, Josh. I feel like my heart is going to jump out of me. I can hear it in my ears. It's like thunder."

"I know, sweetie. We've done this before. You've always just needed to tell me what you need, right? So tell me. What do you need from me? What am I not doing that you need?"

I cry because I've never had to ask him to give me what I really need right now. He's always been able to calm me down by hugging me. Even with everything he's done to me in the past, I've never had to ask him to do the one thing I need in this moment.

It's not that I'm afraid of him. I trust him. It's that asking makes me feel even weaker. Asking makes me feel like I'm moving backwards with my anxiety. Not forward. It makes me feel like all of my improvement means nothing.

"Jess, honey, please don't cry," he whispers in my ear as he runs his fingers through my hair. "I'll do anything you need me to. You know I've never been good at letting you fight these alone. Even when I've been the cause of them. You know I can't handle seeing you like this."

"Weight. I need to feel weight."

"Weight?" He pauses as he thinks about what I mean, then leans into me a little as he holds me close. "Like that?"

"I need your weight on me."

"You mean… on top of you?"

I nod. "It's the only way. I haven't had an attack like this since before Alex left. Well, that's not totally true. I had one yesterday when I saw your picture on Alex's phone. But it's getting worse, Josh. I can barely breathe. I'm fighting, but…" I take a deep breath. It's shaky and doesn't help. I start to hyperventilate, and I feel like I'm going to black out.

Josh doesn't hesitate. "Okay. Okay, Jess. Whatever you need." He lets me go and helps me lay back on the floor. I'm so scared I'm going to die that I don't even care how dirty the floor is, or what I'm lying in. No one can possibly understand what it's like for a person who can't control their fear, as irrational as it is. They'll never understand how it feels to truly believe death is the doorstep. Not unless they've been in a situation that forces them to fully realize what it's like. Josh gently climbs on top of me, but he's holding himself up.

I reach up and pull him down. "Like you're crushing me. I need to feel like I'm suffocating. Like all I can feel is you."

"Fuck. Jessa, I don't want to hurt you."

I can't help but laugh. "Now you're worried about that?"

165

"Not fair." He chuckles at the irony and puts his arms around me. "I promise it's gonna be okay. I'll get you out of this."

"Us. Us out of it."

We're quiet for a long time. I concentrate on his breathing, his weight, and his arms around me. I focus on his skin against me. Him holding me the way I need to be. Not hesitating even for a second. My cheek against his skin. The bump I feel. Like a bug bite or something. Something I want to look at, but not right now. Right now, I just need to breathe.

Eventually, I start to feel tired again, but I feel a lot calmer. Steadier.

"How are you doing? Better?" Josh whispers in my ear.

"Tired, but okay," I whisper back. "You can get up, but will you stay close?"

"I'm not going anywhere, Jessa." He starts to move, but it's too quick.

I keep him held firmly. "Slow. Get up slow. In case I need you. So, I don't have another attack. So, my mind doesn't think what I feel is safe is leaving me."

He does as I say. I follow closely. When he's sitting, he leans against the wall and waits for me to join him. I crawl to him and sit with my back to him.

He puts his arms around me, wrapping me tightly in him. Engulfing my small frame with his large one. He rests his cheek on my head. "I don't want to send you into another attack, sweetie, but I want you to be prepared."

"For what?" I shiver as I settle against him.

"I have their pattern down. They'll be here soon with food and water. They'll cuff you and allow you outside to relieve yourself. If you fight, they'll knock you out. And when that door opens, Jess, I... I'm sorry for what you'll see. I know I'm in bad shape. They allowed me to get cleaned up after they beat the fuck out of me, but I know I'll probably look like I've been through a fucking war. I don't want to scare you."

"I don't care, Josh. After the picture your dad sent to Alex, I'm just glad you're alive."

"That's the Jessa I know. Strong and sassy as fuck."

166

"I seem to remember you hating that," I say with a small smile and soft giggle.

I feel him smile. "I never hated it. It was one of the things I've always respected and admired. But I was fucked up, Jessa. I can't apologize enough for what I put you through."

"I know. I -"

Josh puts his hand over my mouth and silences me as he whispers in my ear, "They're coming. Get back against the far corner of the wall. Don't talk. Don't look at them. Just stay over there. Let me deal with them."

He squeezes me tightly before he releases me and gently pushes me over to the corner. It takes me several moments to hear what he does. Tires on gravel. He stays right where he is near the door. Neither of us move. We listen as a vehicle gets closer. It finally stops, and the doors close. We hear their footsteps closing in before they open the door.

"Well, well, well. The infamous Jessa Holloway has awakened. You were a fuck of a run," one of the guys says. The light behind him blinds me, and I squint against it.

"Hawkins," Josh growls. "Always a pleasure. I thought you forgot about me. I'm about to piss myself."

My eyes adjust to the light, and I see Josh for the first time. I fight to keep from gasping. He wasn't lying. The blood has been cleaned up, but he's bruised and scratched to hell. One of his eyes is nearly swollen shut. His lip is cut, and his face is swollen. It's hard to recognize him.

I can't help but think back to the last time I saw him like this. This is far worse. I thought he was Alex then. I know now that it was him. I wonder how many beatings he's been through. How much strength he has to still be standing after them.

"Get your ass up then." The man named Hawkins pulls Josh to his feet and pulls out a gun. The other person pulls his as well and puts it to Josh's temple. "Run, and you die."

"I know the fucking drill. Get that away from me, Lex," Josh says to the other guy. I try to stay small, hoping they'll forget about me.

"Move, asshole," Lex says. They yank Josh away and leave me alone.

I'm tempted to run, but I doubt I would get far, and I know I would have to leave Josh. I can't do that. He doesn't deserve it. Besides, I know he wouldn't leave me. I've learned a lot about him over the past however long we've been locked in this shed together.

A few moments later, Hawkins shoves Josh back into the shed and focuses his attention on me. "Let's go, sweet thing. I'm gonna enjoy this."

I swallow hard but keep my eyes focused on the floor. Just like Josh said. Don't look at them. Don't talk to them.

"Touch her, and I'll kill you," Josh hisses.

"Relax. Boss has bigger plans for your sexy little pet. Get up, sweetheart. Hawkins won't touch you," Lex says to me.

I swallow. My heart beats faster, but I will not let it control me this time. I won't. This is our chance. I can feel it. Josh needs me. I shake my head and don't move. "I… I want Josh with me," I say shakily.

"What the hell do you think he's gonna do? Get up, or you can piss your fucking pants, darling," Hawkins yells.

I start to stand because I'm too scared of what he'll do to me if I don't obey, but I'm shaking so bad I don't even know how I make it to my feet. Josh catches my eye, giving me a subtle nod. I take a deep breath. I need to be strong right now. I have to be. For him. He's helped me so much. He didn't have to. It's my turn now.

"I assume your boss wants me untouched?" I say quietly. Hawkins and Lex look at each other, then back at me, but say nothing. I raise my head with a defiance I don't feel. "I want Josh with me. And if you don't allow that, then I guarantee your boss won't be happy with you. I'm thinking you don't want to make Mr. Lucinio angry."

"How the fuck do you know who we're working for?" Lex asked, a little taken aback.

"I'm not stupid." I look at Josh, willing a little of his strength to seep into me. "I'm taking Josh with me." I confidently stride towards Josh, portraying far more bravery than I feel.

"Fine," Hawkins growls. "If you'll feel more comfortable. What the princess wants, I guess." He waves his gun, and Josh guides me ahead of him, leaning down to whisper in my ear as we pass Hawkins and Lex. I didn't even realize that they removed the cuffs, but I thank my lucky stars they did.

"On my count, you run to the truck. Three, two, one. Run."

I don't even think. I just do as he says. I run for the truck, dodging Lex as Josh turns and grabs Hawkins' gun. He wrenches it away and

168

shoots Lex. I scream as I dive into the truck. Hawkins is wrestling to gain control of the gun. It fires a few more times, and the window next to me shatters in a hail of glass.

I feel a sting in my shoulder and upper chest. I look down and see my shirt is stained red. I touch it. It's warm and sticky. I look up as Josh opens the door to the truck. Something about his expression isn't right. He's moving so slowly. Everything happened so fast, but now it's all in slow motion.

I'm confused. "Josh?"

"Holy shit. Jessa. I'm sorry."

"What?" I shake my head as it gets fuzzy. "What happened?"

"I'm so fucking sorry."

My vision blurs again, and I shake my head once more. My throat is dry. He's talking. I see his lips moving, but I can't hear him. It's getting harder to see him.

"Josh… don't leave me." I reach for him, but he's gone. My shoulder burns. My chest feels like it's on fire. Everything is so bright. "Come back, Josh. I don't want them to hurt me. I don't want to be alone." I feel like I'm being dragged somewhere. It's getting dark again. I can't fight anymore. I can't get them off me. "I'm sorry, Jason. So sorry. I can't fight them anymore. I love you."

Everything that was once so bright suddenly goes dark.

I'm pulled into nothingness.

I don't feel anything anymore.

I can't think.

I can't hear.

I'm not even sure I'm breathing.

Chapter Twenty Three

✗ Jason ✗

Meetings are the worst part of my day. I would much prefer people just letting me do my damn job. Let my team do what we're paid to do. Most of the time, that's what happens. But sometimes, I get assholes like the one sitting in front of me, second guessing everything. Making drastic changes to the plans my team has come up with. Even though the plans include everything they requested. And more. My company is not just good. We're elite. We're an international, multibillion dollar company.

"Look," I begin as I start rubbing my temple. I have a headache coming, and I'm pretty pissed that this fucker started it. "Mr. Connor. Everything you just requested is impossible. First of all, we got permits based on the building height and specifications you requested. I can't change that now. Construction has already started. The foundation has been laid. To change it now would add millions to your budget. And you already fought with me about that to begin with."

"Mr. Crane, your job is to give me what I want."

I look at the older man in front of me and glare. I've never been one to care about age when it comes to my clients. If they're being

170

assholes, like this guy, I'm not one to sit back and take it. I have a reputation of being a ruthless businessman for a reason.

"Wrong. My job is to make certain you get everything you asked for while staying within the budget you set. If you're willing to shell out roughly four and a half million dollars for this project, then I'll see what I can do. But I highly advise against that. It puts your project on hold and adds months of unnecessary stress and work to my team. All because you want to add one more floor and five hundred and seventy five more feet."

I watch as Mr. Connor's face falls. I'm pretty sure he isn't used to being put in his place. I don't mind being the guy to do it. Wiping that smug look off his fucking face is pretty damn pleasurable and something I'd love to do all over again just because.

I lean forward over my folder that includes his contract, but don't break eye contact. One of the first rules of being a good businessman is always making sure everyone knows who the boss is. I'll never be disrespectful, but I won't tolerate anyone walking all over me either.

"Now, I'll get you your fountain, and I'll add your gym. But I am absolutely not adding another floor, and you aren't getting another five hundred and seventy five feet. You want to take your business somewhere else? I'm fine with that. But I keep all the money my team has put in already. No negotiation."

"Mr. Crane, I'm sorry to bother you." Nancy pokes her head into the conference room, and I stand. She knows better than to interrupt me if I'm in a meeting unless it's important and can't wait.

I glance towards Mr. Connor as I stride out of the conference room. "Decide what you want." I close the door behind me.

Nancy looks up at me. She bites her lip as she hands me a phone. "Ryan," she whispers nervously.

"Ryan?" I say into the phone. I can feel my heart immediately quicken.

"We have a fucking problem. Get home. Now." I don't like the tone of his voice. Nancy is already walking towards my office to get my stuff.

"What? What happened?"

"Just get here. I'm not fucking kidding." Ryan hangs up, and I stare at my phone for a second before I turn on my heel and run to the conference room.

"I'll take your deal," Mr. Connor says as soon as I walk in. "But I'm disappointed."

"Fine. I'll have the paperwork drawn up. I have to go. You can see yourself out." I don't wait for an answer.

I grab my stuff and quickly leave the room. Nancy has everything I need and hands it to me as I nearly sprint to the elevator. The ride down seems to take years. When I hit the ground floor, I run to the garage and jump in my car, speeding through the streets to the house.

What usually takes me half an hour only takes me ten minutes. I know something is going on. Ryan wouldn't have been so urgent if there wasn't. When I arrive at my house, there are more cars in my driveway than I've ever seen. I jump out of my car and sprint inside. Everyone goes deathly silent.

"Where the fuck is Ryan, and why don't I see Jessa?" I ask. All eyes are on me, and I give each of them the glare of death. I know something is wrong.

"You don't see Jessa because her fucking security team dropped the ball," Ryan says, appearing out of fucking nowhere. Nick follows, and two of Ryan's guys sit on my couch looking forlorn.

"Someone better start explaining. Right fucking now," I growl.

"She wanted to go for a walk. Lucas was in the bathroom," Nick starts. "Chris was with her, but let her go out by herself."

"I thought she'd be okay." Chris looks up. His eyes are red. "She just wanted to walk around the property. There's guards everywhere!"

"Shut up! Shut the fuck up!" Ryan's voice booms throughout the room. "Not another fucking word. I swear to God. You had one fucking job, and you failed."

"No one thought to call me or Ryan when it happened, and it's five fucking hours later! Fuck!" Nick kicks a chair and everyone in the room jumps except me and Ryan. We know what he's like. To everyone else, he's a scary mother fucker.

"Enough!" My voice is just as dangerous as Ryan's. I rarely have to use it to command anything, but when I do, people do what I say. All eyes are drawn to me. "No one has explained to me what happened. Start. Fucking. Talking."

"She's gone," Ryan says. His eyes are filled with as much venom as is in his voice. "Taken. From the outskirts of your property."

"What?" I look directly at Nick and Ryan both, attempting to figure out what the hell they're talking about, and trying to choke down the rising panic at Jessa being taken. In the end, it's the anger that wins. "How the fuck did you let this happen? Either of you! Nick, where the fuck were you? Where the hell is Alex, Cole, and the rest of them? Why is everyone here and not out looking for her? And when the fuck did this happen?"

I'm furious. I'm slowly slipping into the cold-hearted asshole I was when I was running jobs with Ryan and Nick before I left the mafia. The one who took over to keep the good person in me from drowning in guilt at what we were doing out there.

The anger slowly overtakes me, growing exponentially when I see Ryan and Nick just looking at each other. Ryan walks towards me and puts a hand on my shoulder. He's only an inch shorter than I am, but his presence is far more commanding. It has to be considering who he is and what he does.

"Sit down, Jas." He tries to keep his voice even and calm, but it only serves to piss me off more.

"Just fucking tell me!" I'm barely keeping control.

Ryan sighs as he watches me. "She went for a walk. She asked to be alone. She felt like she just needed a time out. The two guards we had assigned directly to her agreed. They stayed inside, but they still kept a close eye on her. The guards outside on the outskirts, stayed at their post. When they saw her disappear, they all started running. Except the two guards on the outskirts. They weren't there. But they were caught. It happened this morning. Just after you left for work."

"Are you fucking kidding me? Where the fuck are they! That was almost six hours ago! Why the hell am I just finding out about this now?"

"Because no one fucking told us," Nick seethes. "Ryan called you as soon as he was told. I was with him. Alex had to pull his guys to search for Josh. They're on their way back. We all thought we had enough people here to deal with the shit we had to deal with out there. Didn't think we'd be fucking betrayed by our own."

"It doesn't matter," Ryan interrupts. "I should've been informed right away by someone. There will be consequences. We have the two who betrayed us."

"Fuck!" I pace around the living room trying to think. The ocean is roaring in my damn ears. It's blocking out all else. All I can think about is killing every single person that was here and didn't protect her.

I can feel everyone's eyes on me, but I don't care. I need to get her back. I need to figure out where the fuck she is, and I've already lost so much time by not being informed right away by Ryan's guards.

I'm not paying attention and nearly plow over Tia. She gasps and puts her hand against my chest as she stumbles backwards. I grab her arm until she's steady. She looks up at me, and I can see the hesitation and fear in her eyes.

"Tia, it's okay. I'm not pissed at you," I say with a calm I don't fucking feel.

"I don't think you're going to like this," she whispers. She hands me her phone. "Damon just texted this to me. He said to show you."

Nick and Ryan each move to stand at my sides, and we look at it together. There's a picture of two dead men in front of a shed. There's glass all over the ground and tire tracks that look like they've peeled out. I sink to my knees and start dry-heaving. Ryan and Nick kneel next to me. My heart feels like it's collapsing into my chest, and all at once I know what the fuck Jessa feels when she panics.

"Fuck! Fuck! Fuck! Fuck!" I can't breathe. I see nothing but red.

"We'll find her, Jas," Nick says resolutely.

I turn my glare on him. "You fucking better. Or every single person in this room will meet their fucking maker."

I give Nick credit. He doesn't flinch. I've never been good about killing. Everyone says it's because I'm too good, and they're probably right. The truth is I'm capable of doing it. The woman I love being in danger? My family being in danger? Those are my reasons. Those are what send me over that ledge. I can feel myself edging towards it now.

Closer and closer.

Ryan stands and starts barking orders to his guards. "Call all of the hospitals. Josh was injured. Severely. We know that from the pictures. Look for him or Jessa. Go!"

People scatter, but neither of my brothers leave my side. Tia has backed away.

"We'll find her, Jason. We will," Nick growls.

"I'm fighting fucking hard not to let old Jason loose," I say.

174

Nick's eyes widen a little, and he looks at Ryan. He quickly stands and moves fast. He takes Tia's hand and leads her out of the room. He knows what I'm capable of when I'm pushed, and none of us want Tia around when it happens.

Ryan stays focused on me. "Jas. You know I got this."

"I know." I do know, but it doesn't help the fact that I'm ready to tear this entire fucking city apart looking for Jessa.

"If you know that, you know you don't need to do what you're thinking."

"I can't sit back and do nothing, Ryan."

"You have me for the dirty shit. I'll deal with the guards."

"I want her found." I swallow hard. My hands shake. It's like I'm trying to physically hold back the demons.

"Jason, look at me," Ryan says. It takes me a minute, but I do it. "We will find her. I promise."

I nod. The only thing keeping me grounded right now is that she's alive.

She got away.

I fucking hope.

Chapter Twenty Four

⚔ Josh ⚔

I speed through the streets looking for a hospital with Jessa on my lap when she stirs.

Shit.

I don't need this. If she'd only stayed passed out while I got her to a hospital, this would be so much easier. She was breathing. She was okay. She just passed out from shock and probably pain. With her awake now, I don't know what's going to happen.

"Honey, please don't have a panic attack right now. I've got my hands full," I plead with her.

Her head falls back against my shoulder just as I see a sign for a hospital. Thank God. Thank fucking God. I switch lanes and speed off the off ramp, cutting off traffic and getting a lot of honks. I don't give a single fuck. Jessa stirs again and looks up at me.

Fuck me.

I can see the panic starting. "You have to trust me. Please, Jessa. Please." I am absolutely not above begging. She watches me and takes a couple of deep breaths. "Good girl. We're almost to the hospital. Just trust me, Jess. Please."

"Okay." She puts her arms around my waist and rests her head on my chest. "Is this okay? Can you still drive with me like this?"

"You're fine, Jessa. Watch your shoulder."

"I can't feel it."

"Fuck," I rumble under my breath.

I fight to keep my breathing under control, knowing she needs me to, but it's not a good thing that she can't feel the pain. Feeling it is how you know you're alive. The fact that she can't scares me in ways I never imagined. I breathe deeply through my nose.

She mimics me. "I can hear your heartbeat," she says softly.

I smile as I focus on not killing us both. "Good girl. What else?"

"I can feel you breathing... I can hear traffic."

"Good girl. Keep focusing on your senses, Jess. Focus on me."

I fly into the hospital parking lot and head straight for Emergency. I skid, tires squealing, as I stop in front of the doors and open the truck door. I hold Jessa against me as I get out and run with her in my arms into the Emergency Room.

"Josh." Her eyes flutter closed as she whispers my name.

"Fuck, Jessa, stay with me." I slam through the doors. "Help! Help! Somebody help! She's been shot!"

Nurses and doctors all take one look at me and Jessa and immediately take action. Someone grabs a gurney, and they start to take her away after they get her on it. She's suddenly surrounded by people, and I know she's not going to handle it well while she's panicking.

"Wait! She's in the midst of a panic attack. She gets them really bad. Her heart rate was spiking hard when I brought her in., but she's in shock."

"We'll take care of her, sir," a doctor with the kindest eyes I've ever seen says.

"She takes something for it. She has a prescription, but she doesn't have her purse. I don't know what it is, but I know she's allergic to Ativan."

"I promise she'll be okay," the doctor calls over his shoulder. They lead her away, and I'm left standing with a nurse and doctor looking me over. I shake my head. "I'm fine. The blood all over me is hers. Just take me to the waiting room."

The male nurse eyes me, and looks at the other doctor, who shrugs and walks away. The nurse focuses back on me. "We have some questions and some paperwork for your girlfriend, sir."

"I'll do what I can, but I'm just a friend," I correct. I don't want him to have any high expectations of me knowing a lot of shit. I paid a lot of attention to details when it came to Jessa, but the one thing I never thought about was the name of her prescription. It seems like a big fucking thing right now, though.

The nurse nods and leads me to the waiting room. He sits across from me and asks me his questions. I answer them as best as I can, but I can't stop thinking about what I'm about to do. What I have to do. It's time for this entire thing to end. I have to come clean.

I need Alex.

As soon as the nurse finishes with me, I find a phone and dial Alex's number. I take a deep breath as it rings. I've let this whole thing get far more fucked up then it ever should have. I can't fix this on my own. I never should have tried to deal with it all by myself in the first place. If I hadn't been fucked up, I wouldn't have.

"This is Alex."

I close my eyes and lean my forehead against the wall. "Alex."

I can barely contain both my panic and my relief. I know he's going to want to kill me. Especially if he knows as much as Jessa said he does. He never let on that he knew anything that happened when he moved back to L.A. I know now that it was all so he could keep an eye on me while hiding Jessa.

Alex's silence only solidifies what I already sense. My brother is radiating anger. "Alex, just listen to me before you kill me. I'll explain everything and answer whatever questions you have, but right now, I need you. I need my brother."

"What the fuck is going on, Josh? I have intel that you and Jessa were together. I went to the location and saw two of dad's guards dead. There's so much fucking blood and glass that we didn't know if anyone survived."

I'm a little taken aback at not hearing the anger in his voice that I thought I would. I quickly shake it off. "I protected Jessa. Hawkins and Lex showed up. Hawkins threatened her. We got away. Alex. Please. I'll explain everything, but I need you."

"Where are you?"

"Bellevue. In Emergency. I didn't touch her, Alex. Please just get here."

"I know something else is going on. I know there's a lot of fucked up shit happening, and I don't have anywhere near all the information I need. I'll be there, and you know I'll listen to you. But her boyfriend just killed two people execution style in his backyard because they let dad's guys take her. I'll try to stop him from going after you, Josh, but I don't know what he'll do knowing everything you've done to her."

"I'll face whatever he gives me. Just please get here."

"Ten minutes." Alex hangs up, and I shakily walk back to sit in the waiting room.

I'm fucking exhausted. The adrenaline is wearing off, and I'm starting to feel that familiar pain I feel when I wake up from being passed out. Ever since I came to in that shed, I've been running on nothing but adrenaline. I couldn't give into it then. I sure as fuck won't give into it now. I don't think I was poisoned with anything. It's different this time. I'm not in excruciating agony I can't ignore.

I sigh and rub my head. I know Alex will listen to me, but I don't know about Jason Crane. I read him wrong. He's just as ruthless and protective as his brother. I don't know Ryan Crane. I don't need to. His reputation precedes him. No one messes with him. No one dares to.

Ryan is ruthless. Fiercely protective of his family and friends, and incredibly fearless when it comes to anything else. Those that aren't on his good side probably aren't breathing. Who knew Jason had that same mean streak? Killing two guards for not protecting his girl is something more like what Ryan would do.

I'm so lost in thought, I don't even notice that Alex has arrived. Before I have any time to react, Damon has me in his arms in a fucking bear hug that takes me so much by surprise, I forget how to breathe.

"Fucking Christ, Josh. Do you have any idea how fucked up things have been for all of us? We've been so back and forth with you trying to figure out what the hell is going on," Damon says.

"Let me go, Damon," I say quietly. "There's a lot you don't know. I doubt you'd be hugging me if you did."

"Shut-up and just let me fucking hug you. You're my goddamn brother. I'm just happy you're alive."

179

I can't help but hug him back. It's been a long fucking time since I've been hugged like this. I didn't really realize how much I needed it. Maybe if Damon is this relieved to see me and not as pissed as he should be, I'll have a chance at making things right.

I pull back after a few moments when I feel Alex at my side. I give Damon a pat on the back as I turn to my brother, ignoring the stabbing pain in my stomach, though I do flinch. Judging by the look on Alex's face, he sees it.

"Let's find somewhere private to talk." Alex leads me to a private office. I have no idea how he got the hospital to allow it, but I don't question it. Alex has always had a way. "Start talking, Josh. Fill in what I don't know. I'm buying you time by not telling her boyfriend yet."

He sits in the office chair behind the desk and motions for me to sit in the one in front of the desk. I glance at Damon. He's worried as hell. Alex motions him to leave the room giving him an order to check on Jessa and get her a private room. Damon growls, but does as Alex says. It kind of feels good that he doesn't want to leave me. It makes me feel like I'm still part of the family. Our family. The one we created with Damon and Gavin long ago.

I fucking missed it.

I sit in front of him and close my eyes a moment before opening them and looking at him directly. "I'm not going to pretend I didn't fuck everything up, or that I did some things to Jessa that I'll never forgive myself for, even though she has. I know she told you everything over these past few weeks because she told me she did. I know you know what happened with Layla."

Alex shakes his head and holds up a hand. "Don't tell me the stuff I know, Josh. I need to know everything else. Like why the fuck did this shit even start in the first place? Why pretend to be me?"

"To protect you and Jessa. Dad threatened to kill both of you because you wouldn't take over. He blamed her. And then he became obsessed with her. While you were in Italy, I saw photos of her that he fucking jacked off to."

"Why the fuck wouldn't you tell me any of that?"

"Because, Alex! Can't you understand? I wanted to show everyone that I could do shit on my own! That I could protect my family! How else was I supposed to take over if everyone knew that I always went to you for help?" I stand and pace the room. "Fuck!"

"Josh. Sit." Alex's voice is commanding, and after a few moments I finally sit. "I get it, okay? I understand. Now tell me the rest. I know there's more. I know this isn't you."

I watch him for a moment before continuing. Then, I tell him everything, starting from how I broke them up, to how I got Jessa to believe I was him. I tell him what happened with Keith being killed in front of me, and all of the beatings I took. I tell him Jessa kept me from falling apart, and how I lost control the night I put her in the hospital. When I'm done, Alex is leaning back in the chair fighting back tears.

I'm fighting them, too. I rub my eyes and grimace. My stomach clenches against a wave of nausea, and I get dizzy.

But I push on.

"After I got here, and after she escaped, dad was pissed. I knew I had to run. I thought if I ran, he'd be after me. He'd leave her alone. I stayed out of his reach for a while. I checked in with Brandon using burner phones. He'd been keeping tabs on dad, and he got word that dad found Jessa. He'd sent guards after her. I went to Crane Enterprises, hoping I could help, and I saw Jason had her surrounded by guards. I was leaving when I got knocked out from behind."

"That's when I got the picture of you."

I shrug as I look at him. "I don't know how long I was there before that picture got taken. I was handcuffed and tied up, and they beat the shit out of me a few times before then. If I had to guess, I would say I had been there almost a week."

Alex sighs. "It doesn't matter. All that matters is you're safe now." He leans forward. "Layla said something about poisoning."

I slowly nod. "I'm not looking to make excuses here, Alex."

"Josh." He looks at me sternly.

I sigh and fight through another wave of nausea. Before I really know what's happening, a stabbing pain hits my temple.

Everything immediately goes dark.

"… but I can say for certain that this has been in his system a long time," someone says. It feels like their voice is somewhere in the distance.

"Jesus Christ," Alex rumbles. His voice seems closer. "How long? Can you tell?"

"Not with certainty. Years. There's a lot of damage."

I groan and slowly open my eyes. "Fuck…" I move my hand to rub my chest, but there's something attached to it. I look down and furrow my brows at the IV sticking out of me. "The fuck?"

"Don't move, little bro," Alex says quietly as he sits next to me.

I look up at him, confused. "What the fuck?" I can see now I'm in a hospital bed. There's a doctor in the room. Damon is in a chair next to me.

Alex takes my other hand. "You passed out, man. Fucking scared the shit out of me. You were talking. Then you weren't. Doc here says you had some kind of poison in your system. He thinks it was something used in one of the wars to control the soldiers. Make them stronger. It was experimental, but fucked a lot of the guys up. They had no fucking clue what they were doing. No recollection of a lot of shit that was happening."

I just look at him before shaking my head and closing my eyes. "Fuck me," I groan. It takes me quite a while to realize I don't feel any pain. And even longer than that to remember anything about why I was in a hospital talking to Alex in the first place. "How's Jess?"

"We don't have much yet. You weren't really out that long. She's in surgery."

I nod and swallow. "The shit in my system. I got confirmation that I was being poisoned or something. It was a serum he was putting in my food, but it didn't seem to work well. He started to inject it directly into my system after a beating after I was knocked unconscious. Brandon got all of the information. There are dates and times he gave it to me. He has information on how much he gave me, and how long it lasted. All the effects it had on me including how easy it was to manipulate and brainwash me."

"When did he start it?" the Doctor asks.

I sigh and shrug as I open my eyes, tears stinging them. "He had plans about it since we were teenagers, but he didn't start it then. He had it developed and started giving it to me about three years before Alex left."

Alex squeezes my hand. "That's when you started having far more issues with him. You couldn't talk yourself out of his bullshit. You started leaning on me to bring you back more."

I nod and swallow. "The longer I was away from him, the better things got. I could think more clearly."

"I'll leave you be," the doctor says. "I have what I need. I'll do more research. Right now, let's allow the antibiotic to clear out his system. He'll be in and out of consciousness, but the serum has been slowly coming out of his system since the last time he was injected. I think the reason he passed out is more from exhaustion."

"Thank you, Doc," Alex says. After he leaves the room, Alex sighs. "Fuck, Josh. I'm glad you're okay."

"Me, too," Damon says. "You had us worried."

I just nod as I shift a little. Alex settles in a chair next to the bed. I reach up and rub my eyes. "I'm starting to feel pretty tired. But I want to get the rest of this out. They threw Jessa in the shed with me earlier today. She didn't have her medication because they took her purse. She panicked. I did everything I could to get her to calm down. She passed out from exhaustion a few times. I never let her go. I kept an eye on her. They came three times a day to give me food and let me go to the bathroom. I'd spend my time doing pushups and learning their schedule, so I could prepare myself. When they threw Jessa in the mix, I knew I was out of time. They came back a little while after they threw her in. I knew we wouldn't have another chance to get out of there. With Jess there, I knew the next visit would be from dad. I told Jessa to run to the truck. I fought."

"And killed them both."

"Yeah, but I was fighting for the gun. It was their fault they didn't think to cuff me after I took a leak. The gun went off a few times. One of the bullets hit Jessa in the shoulder."

"Fuck."

"She passed out. I grabbed her and drove, looking for the nearest hospital. As soon as I got her here, I called you."

Alex takes a deep breath and rubs his eyes. "I have to talk to Jason still. I just told him we found Jess. I didn't tell him you're here, too. I think he knows, but he doesn't give a shit. His focus is her."

I close my eyes again. I'm glad to be free of both the shed and my father's control over me, but I know it won't last. If Jason killed two people for failing to protect Jessa, I don't even want to know what his plans for me are. I open my eyes as Alex begins talking.

"Jason? Hey. Listen. I'm going to be honest. I didn't tell you or Ryan my brother is here, too, but you need to hear him out before you kill him." He pauses again and glances at me. "Uh… not the reaction I thought you'd have. He's pretty beaten up, actually, but looks okay."

"What?" I ask, looking at him incredulously.

He shakes his head and holds a hand up. "You're right. He's not the enemy, and after you hear everything, you'll feel more strongly about that." He talks a little more, then hangs up.

"What did he say?" I'm sort of afraid to know the answer.

"He isn't going to kill you." He gives me a smirk. I know he's joking to make me feel better. I love that he still knows me that well.

Relief washes over me as I let out a giant breath. "Thank fuck for that."

It's nearly twenty minutes later when the door to my private hospital room opens. I glance towards the door and see Jason walk in with Gavin and Cole. Layla slips by them both, and runs to me. She climbs into the bed gently. After what I did to her, I'm surprised as hell she's anywhere near me.

She buries her head in my chest as I gently hug her with the arm that doesn't have an IV in it. "I'm so happy you're okay, Josh. I was so worried."

"I'm okay," I whisper. "It's going to all be over soon, Layla." I look up at Jason. Layla doesn't let me go as she cries.

Jason focuses on me. "You okay?"

I nod as I hug Layla. Jason sits on the window ledge. I take a deep breath and start talking. I tell him everything, from the very beginning up until now, even though he didn't ask. When I'm done, another couple of hours have passed. We still haven't been updated about Jessa, and Jason is pacing. I don't know what he's going to do to me, or if he's going to do anything at all. Whatever he decides, though, I know I deserve it.

Finally, he breaks the silence. "Thank you."

I'm taken aback. Jason is quiet. "For… what?"

"For protecting her. I've struggled a lot on what to think of you. Between what everyone has said about you as a person and what I know happened, I really didn't know. Now, I know you're on our side."

184

I watch him incredulously for a long moment before I nod. Jason nods back. It's a silent gesture of understanding and what I hope is forgiveness. At least tentatively. He leaves the room, I'm sure to go back to the waiting room until he gets news on Jessa.

Layla stays silent at my side. Gavin, sitting on the edge of the bed, sighs. Damon leans back in the chair and closes his eyes. Alex puts his feet up on the bed and glances at the IV, slowly dripping something down and through the tubes, making its way directly into my veins.

No one says anything. We don't have to. It's time to formulate a plan. Come up with some way to take our father down once and for all. This whole thing has gone on far too long, and it's something I'll forever blame myself about.

But above all else, I'm fucking happy as hell to have my family back. My brothers. The only people in the entire world who I know I'll always be able to count on. I should have counted on them long ago. I still don't know how much of my actions were me; how much was the serum, but I do know that these guys are my circle.

Family.

I never should have doubted they'd be here for me.

Chapter Twenty Five

☒ Jason ☒

I've been pacing the room for I don't even know how long. I hit my breaking point a long time ago. This entire situation finally pushed me back to the one place I never wanted to be, but I don't care. Jessa's life is in danger, and I'll do whatever the fuck I need to do to make sure she's safe.

After I talked to Josh, I realized just how truly fucked up all of this is. Why the hell Matthew fucking Lucinio is obsessed with her is something I'm positive none of us will ever understand. I don't even think I really care. I just want him dead. We should have killed him long ago.

All of that aside, I'm not stupid. I know I'm going to have to step back from my company until this is over. Jessa is my number one priority. I've never stepped back like this before, but there's only one other person I trust who can fill my shoes. I take out my phone and make the call, impatiently waiting for her to pick up.

"Jason? Is everything alright?" Nancy asks me after the second ring.

"No. It's not. Listen. I know you aren't going to like this, and you'll fight me, but I need your help."

"Uh oh."

"Jessa is in very real danger. I know I told you she was kidnapped. We found her."

"Thank God. Is she okay?"

"She's at Bellevue. She was shot. We haven't gotten any real updates. Just that she's in surgery, and she's doing well. Until this is over, Nance, you're the only person I trust who can run Crane Enterprises as well as me. You've been with me since I started. You know the ins and outs.

Nancy is quiet. I think she's formulating an argument, but she surprises me. "I'll do it, Jason. Whatever it takes. Whatever you need."

"I expected an argument." I chuckle.

"I know the danger. She needs you, and you need to protect her. Even though your brother is very powerful. I'll do it. You kids are just as much my family as my own."

I nod. "You know you're like an aunt to us. Jess has some projects to finish. If she's up for it, I'll allow it. It helps keep her mind off shit, and it'll give me time to ease you into the position. We're hiring another receptionist to fill your position anyway since I'm promoting you. But we'll also need to hire a temp as your Executive Assistant."

"I'll start on that right away."

I look up as the doctor walks in. "I have to go, Nance. Doctor just walked in."

"Keep me informed."

"I will." I hang up with Nancy and stride towards the doctor, holding my hand to shake. He takes it. "Doc. How is she?"

The doctor looks up at me. "Very well. Your girlfriend gave us quite the scare. She was shot in the shoulder, and the bullet lodged just near her shoulder blade. It missed everything, but we don't know how. It should have hit bone and shattered, but it didn't. We were able to remove it easily enough. It took a little while because we needed to make sure there were no fragments or other damage. When she came to, she had a panic attack. We expected it after Josh's warning, so she was given Ativan by the second surgeon I had called in. It calmed her down, but sent her into anaphylaxis."

I shoot him a withering glare, and my voice becomes dangerously low. "She was allergic to Ativan? Didn't anyone check her chart? Or ask someone before you gave it to her?"

"I apologize, Mr. Crane, but she's never been here before. I knew because I was told, but I didn't know that the other surgeon directed our staff to give her Ativan. I immediately gave her a dose of epinephrine and an antihistamine. She's awake now if you'd like to see her, but only one of you at a time. She's still prone to another panic attack, and I don't want to overwhelm her."

"What are you giving her right now? For the panic attacks?" Alex asks.

"We've started her on Xanax."

"She takes Pexeva," he tells him. How the hell could I not know that?

"I'll make sure we get that switched. For now, if I switch too soon, she could get sick. I'll keep her on the Xanax for now until it's finished and see where we are. But I will make sure her chart reflects her medication accurately."

"There's no seeing where she is after it's done. She takes Pexeva. End of story. Get it done. Take her off the Xanax" Alex commands. I have to smile at Alex for being as forceful about it. I'm too fucking exhausted, and all I want is to see my girl.

The doctor nods. "I'll see it's taken care of."

He leads me down the hall and to a private room. Jessa is laying on the bed with her eyes closed. She has an IV coming out of her hand and is hooked up to a machine monitoring her heart rate and blood pressure. She looks pale and more tired than I've ever seen. I rush to her and take her hand.

"Oh God, baby. I'm so sorry. I never should've left you alone for those stupid meetings. I should've insisted on canceling them instead of giving in, but I thought you'd be okay."

"I made sure she got the private executive room your team requested. She'll have privacy here to heal. You're more than welcome to stay in the room overnight. We'll be keeping her in for observation. I'll leave you be."

All I can do is nod at him as he leaves the room. I'll have to thank Alex for thinking to get her into a private room. I was too fucked up to make that happen. I bend to kiss Jessa's hand. She softly squeezes my fingers.

"Jason," she breathes.

"I'm sorry, baby. I'm so, so sorry." I lay my head on her stomach as I caress her hand.

"Jason…, it's not your fault."

"The guards that betrayed us are no longer with us, Jessa. I'm sorry they didn't protect you."

"Jason…, you… didn't." She looks at me with so much love and concern that it nearly breaks me.

"I wish I could say I didn't. But I did, and I wouldn't take it back for a second. You never should've been alone."

"It was my fault. I begged Chris to let me go. I walked too far. I was too far away from the guards."

"Stop. Jess. It's not your fault. They were supposed to protect you. That's what they were there for. They failed. There were two guards at the edge of the property who helped Matthew's people get to you. There was a lot of confusion. They caught the two guards that helped him, but no one called Ryan when you went missing." I watch as her heart rate spikes. "Shit. I'm sorry, baby."

"No, Jason. It's… okay. It's not that."

I start tracing small circles on the top of her hand. "What? What is it?" The doctor and a nurse come racing into the room.

"Sir, you'll have to leave," the nurse says as he starts checking her monitors.

"Like hell. I'm not going anywhere."

"You're agitating her! You have to go!" the nurse barks.

Jessa starts to hyperventilate and fight the doctor as he puts an oxygen mask on her. The nurse grabs my arm and tries to drag me out. I turn and rip my arm away, shoving him back.

"No! No! Stay! Please!" Jessa screams. She starts crying, and I grab her hand once more.

"I'm right here, beautiful. I'm not going anywhere. Okay?" I reach up and stroke her hair as I glare at the nurse, daring him to touch me. "See? I'm right here. I'm staying by your side."

The doctor watches her monitor as her heart rate drops to a more normal level. He turns to the nurse. "Never, ever do what you just did again. Find out what's going on above and beyond anything else. You caused her far more stress than necessary. Out. Right now." The nurse glares at him but leaves. The doctor turns back to Jessa. "How are you feeling? What happened?"

"I started thinking about the person who brought me here. I wondered if he was okay. He had a lot of blood on him, too."

"Josh is okay, beautiful. He's with Alex, Gavin, Damon, and Layla."

She looks up at me with tears in her eyes. "He saved me, Jason."

"I know, beautiful. He told us everything."

After a few moments of observation, the doctor leaves the room again, and I'm alone with Jessa. I lean down to kiss her hand, and then her lips before I sit on the bed next to her.

"I'm sorry. I shouldn't have wandered off by myself. I thought it would be okay just being on your property. With all of the guards. I just wanted a minute alone."

"You should've been safe at home. It wasn't your fault, baby. Don't apologize for wanting to go for a walk on our own property. This never should've happened."

She smiles softly and reaches up to touch my face. I didn't shave this morning, and I'm pretty sure my stubble is rough. "Our property?"

"Well, it's your home, too, right? You've been living there for a couple weeks, and I know how much you love the place. Honestly, I like it better with you in it. More of a home."

"I do like it a lot. It feels more like home than any place I've been before."

"I hope that it still does when you're released from here. If it's not then I'll take you wherever you want to go."

"Even Paris?" she jokes.

I smile. "Even Paris." I lean down to kiss her. Paris doesn't sound like a bad fucking idea to me at all. At least it would be away from here and away from Alex's and Josh's crazy as hell father. It might be easier to keep her safe in another country than here.

Maybe I should book the flight now…

Chapter Twenty Six

⚔ Jessa ⚔

(One Month Later)

It's been nearly a month since I got shot, and my shoulder is almost fully healed. Jason is more perfect every day. He's attentive to my every need. He's even been taking me out on dates. Nick and Ryan are always with us, and Alex, Josh, and Cole are always around somewhere. Between the six of them, Jason included, they trust my security and safety to no one.

Layla and I have become incredibly close. We live together with Tia. We even have lunch together nearly every day. Sometimes, even Tia joins us for that. It's nice to have girl time. I'm not as close with Marissa as I used to be, but we're trying. She was my best friend in college, but after everything that happened, we fell apart and stopped talking.

Everyone staying under Jason's roof, even Ryan, though he has his own impressive home, has made even Marissa and I start working on our relationship again, though. Jason has also become close to Alex, and even Josh. We've all become like family, and I love it.

191

We're all on edge, though. We haven't heard anything from Matthew. Ryan, Alex, and Josh all have their ears to the ground, but we all feel like it's too quiet. I want to come up with a plan, but everyone is telling me to leave it alone until we figure out his plan.

To get my mind off of everything, I've gone back to work. Jason told me he's planning on taking a step back from the company, but I told him to wait until we have a plan or know Matthew's. He's been spending a lot of time preparing Nancy to take over.

I sigh and focus on the plans in front of me for a new account we just picked up. A huge plaza. The client wants it to have a hometown feeling with a touch of upscale elegance. I don't even know what that means, but I'll try. If they can dream it up, I can make it happen. After all, that's what Jason hired me for. To turn ideas into reality.

I allow myself to get lost in the plans. Soon, I'm standing over my desk, drawing. I don't hear Jason come in, and he startles me when he slips his arms around my waist from behind. He pulls my backside to him. I can feel how hard he is, and I blush.

"You're so beautiful. Do you know that?" he murmurs into my hair.

"Well, my boyfriend tells me every day," I tease with a soft smile. "I'm starting to believe it's true."

Jason laughs and leans down to kiss my neck. His hands trail to my stomach, and he whispers in my ear, "Your boyfriend is a lucky, lucky guy."

"Oh, believe me. He knows he is."

Jason laughs again and hugs me tightly to him as he looks at what I've done so far on the plans. "Is this the Lexington project?"

"Yeah. I'm having a bit of trouble with it, though."

"Doesn't look like it. Where's the trouble?"

"Well, I have the small town feel down. That really wasn't an issue. I'm trying to figure out how to tie in the upscale elegance. I was thinking about bringing it down to my team to brainstorm ideas."

"Not a bad idea. But not right now."

"Why not right now?" I ask as he starts moving side to side with me and kissing my neck. I close my eyes and lean into him as I tilt my head to the side to give him more access.

"Because I want to make your boyfriend jealous."

I giggle. "Oh…, I'm not sure that's a good idea."

"And why's that?" He continues kissing my neck. He starts nibbling on my ear and kisses down to my shoulder.

"Because he's kind of scary when he's angry."

"Oh yeah?" He moves to the other side and continues the same motions. "So am I."

"Not as scary as him. He once killed two guys because they didn't protect me like they were supposed to."

"Yeah? Well, I'd do a lot more than that for you." He spins me around in his arms and leans down, his lips stopping a breath from mine.

I smile at him and slide my hands up his chest as I wrap my arms around his shoulders before leaning in the rest of the way to take my kiss. Jason's hands slip down my backside to my thighs. He lifts me in his arms as he kisses me. My legs automatically wrap around his waist as my arms grip onto his massive shoulders. The injury from the bullet wasn't nearly as bad as everyone thought. I already have an almost full range of motion. It still hurts a little to lift a lot, though.

He carries me around his desk before setting me on top of it. "My desk has never looked so good," Jason says huskily.

I giggle. "You've had me on your desk before."

"Correction. I've had you bent over my desk before." He sits in his chair and takes my shoes off before trailing his hands up my bare legs and kissing each of my thighs. He reaches under my skirt and takes my panties off. "I love you in black lace."

"I know. That's why I bought them." My tone is teasing, and I'm rewarded with his easy, deep laugh. It sends shivers all over my body.

He pushes my skirt up, leaving my bare ass on his desk and the rest of me completely exposed for him. "Lean back, beautiful." I lean back, but prop myself up on one elbow so I can watch him. I don't trust my arm that much yet. He pulls me to the edge of his desk. I love watching him work me, just as much as he loves watching me when I'm sucking him. "Do you have any idea how hard you make me?"

He doesn't look up at me. Instead, he focuses between my legs. He runs a finger from my clit down to my center and pushes it inside me.

"Ah… yes… Jason."

He leans down and licks me from my center to my clit and swirls his tongue around it while his finger thrusts slowly inside me. "You're so wet, baby girl."

"For you. Only for you. Please don't stop."

"No intention of doing something as foolish as that." His breath is hot against me. He kisses each side of my waxed pussy before delving his tongue against my clit once more.

"Jason... Oh, yes. More. Please, more."

"I know what you like, beautiful. You'll get more." He thrusts his finger inside me a little harder.

I gasp and arch into him. "Holy shit, Jason! Jason, oh my God! More. Just like that."

I start rocking against him as he puts more pressure on my clit. He adds a second finger, moving them both inside me hard and fast, twisting them both and crooking them against me. I arch off the desk.

"You feel fucking amazing. You taste so sweet."

"Jason! I..." I buck into him, riding his fingers and arching for his tongue to keep licking me. "I'm gonna come. Don't stop. Just like that. Please don't stop!" I'm so, so close.

"Fuck, baby. You look so good when you're about to come for me."

"Oh... Jas..." My pussy pulses around his fingers. My clit throbs for him.

"Come for me, sexy girl. Give me what I want."

My stomach muscles tighten, and I feel myself clench around his fingers. Seconds later, my pussy starts spasming as I come for him. "Fuck! Jason... oh God, Jason." My hips jerk into his fingers and tongue.

"I'm not done," he growls into my pussy, making me moan louder as I come hard for him. He licks everything I give him, but it's not enough. It's never ever enough.

"Thank God. I can't get enough of you. I can never get enough of you. I've wanted you so badly today."

"Oh yeah? And what have you been thinking about me doing to you?"

"This. You and me. Just like this. Please, Jas. Don't make me wait." I watch him as he reaches down and frees his beautiful, massive cock for me. He stands and wastes no time slamming inside me. I sigh in pleasure. "Oh…, Jason. So good. It feels so good!" I start moving with his frantic pace, matching each of his delicious thrusts.

"Good fucking Christ, baby. You're so soft and fucking tight."

"I just feel that way because you're so thick and big." I moan as he growls and angles my hips up slightly as he drills into me harder and deeper. I fall back against the desk and let him own me. I love when he controls everything. "Fuck! Oh fuck! You're so big. So hard! Oh!"

"I know what you like. What drives you crazy."

"You. You drive me crazy."

"Fucking right. Say you want me, Jess."

"I want you!"

He reaches down and rubs my clit with his thumb as he plows into me again and again. The sensation, coupled with his deep thrusts, makes my stomach start to clench as the familiar tingling between my legs starts. I feel myself start to tighten around him. Clench. Pulse uncontrollably.

"Tell me how much you love my dick pounding inside you, beautiful."

"Oh!" My eyes roll back in my head. I can't think of anything other than how he rocks my body. "I love your dick. Fuck, Jas! Harder! Please, please, harder. I'm so close." I'm losing all control, lost in him.

"Me too, honey." He pounds himself into me deeply as his thumb strokes me faster. "Come, baby. Now. Right fucking now."

I throw my head back and arch as my release takes over me. I clench around his cock, feeling him come deep inside me. He slams his hands down on the desk as we both moan. Our hips buck into each other. I barely withhold the scream bubbling up my throat.

Jason slows his thrusts after he fills my pussy with his hot come. He pants against my shoulder as I whimper and catch my breath while we both come down. Every orgasm he gives me is better than the last. I'm pretty sure the next one will make me black out or something. It always feels so, so good.

It takes him a few seconds before he can physically pull out. When he finally does, it's slow as he stands. He packs himself away and plops in his chair, gently pulling me onto his lap.

"How am I so in love with you in such a short period of time?" I ask as I cuddle into him.

"Good question. Why do I feel the same way?" He blesses me with a sexy, pussy-soaking grin.

I wrap my arms around his neck and kiss him, deeply and passionately before getting off his lap before I beg him to fuck me again. "Back to work, boss," I joke. "I need to figure out this uptown elegance thing."

Jason laughs. "You'll figure it out." He smiles as I lean down to kiss him once more before turning to his desk to grab my panties that he left there. He takes them before I have the chance.

I give him a quizzical look when he puts them in his pocket. "What… are you doing?"

He reaches between my legs and flicks my clit. I moan and almost come again.

"That sound. I love when you moan for me. And I love having easy access. Now, get to work, Ms. Holloway. You said you have a brainstorm session to lead."

I laugh. "Yes, Mr. Crane. Right away, sir."

"Fuck me, Jessa. The way you talk."

I laugh again as I kiss him before standing and turning to gather my drawings. Just as I'm leaving, the new receptionist buzzes him.

"Mr. Crane and Ms. Holloway? There's a Mr. Lucinio on line one for you."

"Thank you, Claire," Jason says. He meets my eyes, and I need no words. I immediately open the door and pull Nick inside Jason's office before closing the door again. He gives me a confused look as Jason puts the call on speaker. "Mr. Lucinio. How may I help you today?"

"I believe you have something that belongs to me, Mr. Crane." The voice on the other end of the line sends chills down my spine. I hug myself. Nick is standing so close to me that I can feel his body heat.

"Matthew," I whisper. I can feel myself starting to shake. Nick drops a hand to my waist and pulls me back against him.

"Oh? And what exactly is that?" Jason's cocky CEO demeanor slides into place, but his eyes tell a completely different story as he looks at Nick. There's a fire and a danger in them that I knew existed but had never seen before now.

"That beautiful girl standing in front of you right now. Tell me, Mr. Crane. Was the sex good? I'm excited to know what I'm in for. Is she as wet and tight as I imagine? Does she taste as sweet?"

Jason spins around and looks out the large floor to ceiling window behind his desk. "Where the fuck are you, you son of a bitch?"

"Close enough to know that Jessa's black lace panties are in the left pocket of your pants."

"Fuck," Nick growls. He moves himself in front of me and pulls me close to his back. I plaster myself to him.

"Why don't you come hang out in my office for a bit? Let's see if you make it out alive. Spoiler. You won't." Jason's voice is low and dangerous. I start to feel dizzy. I take deep breaths to steady my racing heart. I use Nick's scent to calm me.

Nick reaches his hand back and takes my hand. "Stay against my back, Jess. Feel me breathing. Focus on that."

I do as he says, burying my face in his back. "Okay."

"Don't worry, sweetheart," Matthew says sickeningly. "We'll be together soon."

"Touch her, and you better hope you're a praying man. Because I'll tear you apart," Jason seethes between clenched teeth.

"Better calm her down. I'd hate to lose her before I get the chance to fuck her." The line clicks, and my knees buckle. Before I can hit the floor, Nick turns and catches me, pulling me close to him.

"Not happening, Jessa. Understand? He's not touching you," Nick whispers.

Jason gently takes me into his arms. "I won't let him. We won't let him." I bury my face in Jason's chest when he turns me into him. He runs his fingers through my hair.

Nick puts his hand on the small of my back. "He's just trying to scare you. He won't get anywhere near you." Nick gives my back a gentle squeeze.

At that moment, the window behind Jason's desk cracks as something strikes it.

I scream and bury myself in Jason's strong arms, covering my ears.

"Is he fucking shooting?" Nick asks.

"Bet he didn't count on triple-paned bulletproof glass," Jason chuckles.

More bullets hit the glass, and I scream with each shatter. The window cracks in each place the bullets hit, but it doesn't break.

"Let's go. We need to get out of here," Nick commands. They both shield me with their body as they usher me out of the office. The receptionist is wide-eyed, and Nancy runs out of her new office.

"I heard screaming. What's going on?" she asks frantically.

"Matthew," Jason says darkly.

"What? How?" Nancy is very obviously confused and scared. Her voice is an octave higher than normal.

"Not sure." The danger in Jason's voice should scare me. Instead, I'm comforted. "We need to get home. Nance. Let's go. You're coming with. We need to talk. Claire, we're leaving for the day. All of us. Get your stuff. I'll have security escort you and stay with you at home."

Claire whimpers, but quickly does as she's told. Nick is on the phone with Ryan as we all head for the elevators. I swallow a few times trying to control the impending panic attack. I need to focus on something else. Anything else.

A plan. We need a plan.

It's time. We can't let this asshole control our lives anymore.

No. This ends.

Now.

Chapter Twenty Seven

⚔ Josh ⚔

Alex and I look up from the couch as Jason and Nick slam through the door, ushering Jessa and Nancy inside. Ryan is right behind them. I shoot Alex a freaked the fuck out look as he jumps up.

"The fuck?" Alex chokes out as he rushes to Jessa's side. I follow. Jessa is hyperventilating. Her panic attacks have always broken me. He takes her purse and starts digging for her prescription. He thrusts the purse into my chest as he takes out the bottle. Jason is holding her close to him, whispering in her ear. "Jess? Honey, take this."

Jason hands her the pills, and I hand her my water bottle, suddenly thankful I'd been nervously playing with it before they walked in. She takes it shakily, and I look up at Jason. "What the hell happened?"

"Matthew," he growls. Jessa immediately collapses and starts crying. Ryan grabs her and leads her to the couch away from all of us. Jason gives him a thankful look as he rubs his forehead. "She was good. She held it together until we were about halfway home. Then she lost it. She started crying and shaking, and I can't calm her down."

I glance over at Ryan. He's pulled Jessa into his lap and is rocking her. I give a silent sigh of relief. She's calming down, and that's all that matters to me right now.

"He called Jason's office," Nick starts. "Just after they had sex on his desk. He was close enough that he could watch them. He knew Jason had put her panties in his pocket. He knew which fucking one."

"Hey! Go in the fucking dining room." Ryan shoots us a glare. He's holding Jessa tightly to him and keeping her head on his shoulders with his hand firmly in her hair.

"You're right," I say as I lead everyone into the dining room.

We all turn back to Nick when we get there. He lowers his voice, even though he doesn't need to. "He knew Jason ate her out. He asked him if she's as tight as he thought. He asked if she tasted as good as he thought."

"What the fuck?" Alex shakes his head in complete astonishment.

I feel the bile rise in my throat and have to choke it down before I puke. "Fuck, he's gotten worse," I say as I collapse in a chair.

"That's not all," Jason continues as he sits across from me and leans back. He looks up at the ceiling. "He was watching when he called. Nick stepped in front of her. She started having a panic attack. He could see her. He told me to take care of her because he didn't want her to die before he got the chance to fuck her."

"Jesus Christ," I say with disgust. "I should've fucking stepped in a long time ago. Fuck, I'm so sorry." I put my head on the table. This never should have gone on this long. I fucked up so fucking badly. All of this is completely my fault. I feel a hand drop on my shoulder.

"I know what you're doing right now, and you know no one in this room blames you," Alex says.

"He's right. We're over that. Past it," Jason tells me. I know the words are true, but I guess I needed to hear them. Alex sits next to me as I lift my head again. Nick sits next to Jason.

"We need a plan," Alex says. "We should've listened to Jessa a long time ago. Between me and Ryan not being able to find that son of a bitch, and not hearing from him at all for a month, we should've fucking had a plan by now."

"Hard to come up with a plan when we have no idea what *his* plan is," Jason says.

"Like or not, we need to come up with one now," Nick says. He stands. "We need Ryan."

I sigh as we all walk out to the living room. Jessa appears to be asleep on Ryan's lap. He has one arm around her and is texting with the other one. The look on his face makes my eyebrows raise as I glance at Alex. Alex cocks his head to the side as he sits on the couch across from him. Jason sits next to him and gently pulls Jessa into his lap. Nick and I take chairs. We all watch him, waiting until he's done. It's like he doesn't even know we're in the room, and he has a stupidly sweet smile on his face.

Finally, Alex clears his throat. Ryan looks at him and glares. Alex chuckles. "You good, man? Looked like you were texting the love of your life."

"Fuck you," he growls as he puts his phone down. "Jessa told me what happened. We need to come up with a plan."

"We know. We already decided that," Nick says, still staring at him curiously. "What was that all about? I don't think I've ever seen you look like that texting anyone."

"First of all, it's none of your fucking business." Ryan glares as his phone goes off. He glances at it. "Second, don't fucking start. She's a girl. And when I say girl I mean a sixteen year old girl. Let it go."

I raise my eyebrow and bite my lip. I know the look he had on his face well. I saw it whenever Jessa texted Alex. Ryan is in love with that girl, whether he wants to admit it or not.

"Sixteen?" Jason asks a little incredulously. "Why are you talking to a sixteen year old?"

Ryan sighs. "Not that it's any of your business, but she's the daughter of a girl I dated -"

"Dated?" Alex interrupts. "You've never dated anyone."

Ryan glares again, and Alex immediately backs down. I can't help but smile at the effect the guy has on everyone he's around. My brother doesn't get intimidated by anyone or let anyone order him around. He's different with Ryan.

"Do you want me to answer the question, or are you going to bust my fucking balls all day?" No one in the room says anything as Ryan shoots each of us a deadly glare. "Her father killed her mother a couple years ago. I've been looking out for her ever since."

201

I smile and nod, deciding to bail him out. "Everyone done fucking around? We have shit to do."

Jason sighs. "I don't want Jessa down here for this."

"Take her upstairs. You don't need to be here for it either." Ryan glances at his phone again as Jason gets up, carrying Jessa with him. He walks up the stairs, and we all stay silent until he's out of sight. Damon and Gavin come in from outside.

"We got a text," Gavin says. "What's up?" They both sit. Alex fills him in as we all settle in for a long night.

✗✗✗

I've sat listening to Ryan and Nick hashing out a plan to take my father down for the past three hours. Damon, Gavin, and Lance have all chipped in ideas. Layla, bored out of her mind, is curled up in a corner of the couch listening to everyone. Marissa is in the bedroom she and Gavin are staying in. Nancy shut herself in Jason's office to make phone calls to fix the window and whatever else she does. Tia couldn't keep her eyes open anymore and is curled into a chair. She wanted to stay and help. Damon tried to bring her to her bedroom, but she told him no. We've all just let her sleep. She seems comfortable.

Alex has been up the entire night, so we all forced him to go to bed. He was no help in his state anyway. Jessa and Jason are hopefully sleeping. None of us want Jessa to be a part of the planning. She doesn't need the stress after all she's been through. We can tell her later.

I'm frustrated as hell. I shake my head and stand. I have to get out of here. My head is spinning. I want to say something, but I don't want to step on anyone's toes. I can't figure out if Ryan trusts me or not, even though Alex and Jessa have both told me he does. It's hard knowing how badly I fucked up and feeling like everyone is suspicious of me. I've been doing everything I can to make it right, but I feel like it's not enough. It could never be enough.

I lean on the counter in the kitchen and drop my head in my hands. I don't know how long I stay like that, but I jump when I hear Layla's soft voice behind me.

"Are you okay? You've been in here for a while."

I take a deep breath before raising my head again. "I'm fine, Layla. I'm just not entirely certain what to say out there. I can't tell if anyone actually trusts me, or if they're just saying it. Not like I deserve it anyway." I don't move from my position, but I can feel Layla watching me.

"Josh, I think you're feeling really guilty about everything that happened. I think everyone out there understands that. I don't know how anyone else feels because I'm not them, but I can say that you haven't offered your opinion. Maybe you should."

I chuckle. "And you think they'd listen?"

"I think you know your father better than anyone else does. I think they'd be stupid to not listen to you."

I nod and look down at my hands as I fall silent. They're a little stiff. My left one shakes. Doc said it's the effects of serum. The longer I'm off it, the better I'll get. The blinding headaches and immense level of pain in my stomach will go away. The shaking will stop. I'm not holding out a lot of fucking hope right now. Too much on my damn mind. Too much fucking guilt.

After a moment, I take another deep breath and shake my head, but I don't look at her. "I'm sorry, Layla. I was fucked up. It's taken me a long time to come down from the serum. I won't make excuses for my actions. I knew what I was doing in a way. But I am sorry. You didn't deserve what I did to you."

She touches my arm, and I make myself look at her. "How many times are you going to apologize?"

I smile softly. "I have done it a lot, haven't I?"

"I know you're sorry. But you forget that I know what you were going through. I was there. I saw it, Josh."

"It's not an excuse. I'm better than that."

"I know you are. I've seen that, too." We look at each other for a few moments before she drops her hand from my arm. She leans into me and stares straight ahead at the wall. "Josh, I don't know everything. Just what I've seen. I know what your father did to you was so fucked up. It was mental and physical abuse as well as emotional. Telling you how worthless you are, and how you'll never live up to his expectations. He was controlling you with Jessa. He was using her to make you think that he would love you if you did what he said. The serum on top of it all. That's a horrible thing to do to your child."

203

I stare straight ahead trying to reign in my emotions. She's right. Everything she said is exactly right. I came to that conclusion in the shed he had me put in. It was a fuck of a way to realize that my father never loved me. That my whole life spent trying to gain approval, acceptance, and any kind of pride out of him was futile.

"That's only part of what he did. It wasn't just poisoning. He beat the fuck out of me regularly. Not just a few times, Lay. There's so much stuff it would take me all night to tell you."

She gives me a sad smile. "Do you remember when we first met? When you were kissing my back and asked about the scar I have near my spine and shoulder blade?"

"You told me you got injured skiing."

"I lied. That was the story my uncle made me tell."

I look down at her. "What?"

She turns after a moment and jumps up on the counter. She takes a deep breath before fixing her gaze on the wall. "My parents were killed in a drive-by shooting outside a theater in Brooklyn. According to their will or whatever, my aunt and uncle got custody of me if anything ever happened to them. Not long after, my aunt died of breast cancer. Very quickly. She was diagnosed and died within two weeks. My uncle blamed me. He said if I hadn't distracted them both, they would've known something was wrong and been able to catch it before. He stabbed me. Left me to die. I was only fifteen."

"Holy shit, Layla. I'm so sorry. Why didn't you tell me that?" I pull her close because I refuse to allow her to go through telling me that and not have some kind of comfort.

She smiles sadly as she buries her face in my neck. "After she died, my uncle spent the next three months berating me before the stabbing incident. He told me I was nothing. I was a disappointment. A curse. That my parent's death was just as much my fault as his wife's death was. Every day. Every second of the day. Eventually, I believed it. Before he stabbed me, he spent the day beating me."

"Layla." I pull her into me and hold her even more tightly.

"After I recovered, the state placed me in a foster home. I was forced into a life of slavery, basically. I was like Cinderella. When I was seventeen, they made me become an escort. And that's what I've done for the past eight years. I wanted to go to school. Be a doctor."

"Fuck, Layla. I... I don't know what to say. I feel even worse for treating you the way I did."

She buries her head in my shoulder. "I didn't tell you that to make you feel bad, or more guilty. I told you that to make you see that I understand. I always have. I spent years thinking I wasn't good enough. That I deserved everything that happened to me."

"You didn't. You didn't deserve any of that. You didn't deserve what I did or what your uncle did, Layla."

"I know that now, Josh. Honestly, it took you and this family to make me see that I *am* better than how I was treated, or the life I was forced into. I just want you to know that you are, too. Don't let your father control your life. And don't let what everyone may or may not think of you stop you from speaking up. If you do, it's just your father controlling you. You can't let that happen." She smiles at me as she pulls back.

I push her hair out of her eyes. "Thank you for telling me all of that. And for letting me apologize again."

She pushes my hair back. "You're welcome. Can you help me down?" I step back and lift her off the counter, setting her gently on her feet. She gives me another smile as she turns and walks towards the living room, but back before she leaves the room. "You're better than your father, Josh. Show them."

I take a couple of minutes to compose myself before I follow her. As I enter the living room, everyone is still hashing out ideas. I loudly clear my throat, and all eyes fall on me as the room goes quiet. "You can't just go in there guns blazing. You won't win, and a lot of blood will be shed. My father has very powerful and ruthless people behind him. He'll see you coming a mile away. It's what he expects. We need an actual plan."

"What the fuck do you think we're trying to do?" Ryan glares at me.

I sigh but refuse to back down. It's not who I am. Not who I'll allow myself to be. I'm fucking Josh Lucinio.

"If you have something better, please. Regale us." Nick swipes his hand across the room as he slightly bows like he's giving me the floor to use as my speaking platform. Layla gives me an encouraging smile.

I smile back as I cross to the center of the room. "Actually, I do. We give him exactly what he wants."

Everyone in the room stares at me like I've lost my mind. It's Ryan who breaks the silence. "Are you fucking insane?"

I chuckle. "No. I'll give you a second to think about it. You'll see I'm right."

He clenches his jaw, and then sits back and folds his arms across his chest. "Well? What's this brilliant plan, wonder kid?"

I give him a cocky, defiant smile. "He wants Alex to take over for him. It's been his dream since Alex was born. He wants Jessa at Alex's side. He wants the two of them to give him an heir to take over after Alex."

"Wait," Ryan holds up a hand. "It seems to me he just wants Jessa."

I shake my head. "He wants an heir. He's obsessed with fucking Jessa, but he wants that heir. He wants assurance that after Alex is ready to step down, he'll have someone else to take over. He wants to know the Lucinio Mafia is set for years. So we give him what he wants. Jessa trusts Alex. Alex won't let our father touch her. We need to have Alex bring Jessa home under the pretense that he's giving in. To protect me. Our father knows that I'm Alex's weakness. He'd do anything to protect me. That's why he went after me and threatened me." I pause and wait for everyone to catch on to what I'm saying.

Nick eyes me before he takes a deep breath and leans forward. "After he gets Alex and Jessa, his guard will be down. We could go in then."

Ryan rubs his temple. "We'd have to be stealthy. Infiltrate the house."

I nod and continue. "Once Alex and Jessa are in, they're our way in. They'll give us a signal that it's time. When the house is quiet, we infiltrate. We take him out. Leave my mother alone. She isn't part of this. Never has been. He's hit her just as much as he did me."

Everyone looks to Ryan. It's obvious he's the final say. He leans forward. "This could work, but we have a lot of work to do. We can't do this without Jason, Jessa, and Alex, so they need to be onboard. In the meantime, we need to explore other options."

"There is no other option," I say simply with a shrug. "You don't know my father like I do, Ryan. You think your father was ruthless when he was in your position? Or your grandfather? My father is both of them combined. Multiplied by a thousand. You've been against him before.

You've seen what he's capable of. I know you have a mean streak. I know Jason does. Hell, even Nick has a reputation. I know you all get it from your father and grandfather. But I'm telling you. You go in there and try to shoot the place up, you won't make it home."

They all stare after me as I turn and leave the room without another word. I head to the guest bedroom I'm staying in and close the door. I lean against it and take a deep breath. I wasn't intending on being that commanding, especially with Ryan in the room.

But if he doesn't do what I said, my father will win, and Jessa, Alex, and I will die.

Chapter Twenty Eight

✗ Jason ✗

It took me nearly four hours to get Jessa to sleep. The medication helped with her panic attack, but she was upset. She felt violated that we had been watched. I can't blame her. Fuck, I felt the same way. She's terrified he's going to get to her somehow. I drew her a relaxing bubble bath in my jacuzzi tub, but she didn't want to be alone. So, I sat on the edge with her, and we talked until she was ready to get out. I gave her a massage, and we talked more until she finally fell asleep.

She has been sleeping for a few minutes, but I haven't gotten up. I'm still rubbing from her naked ass all the way up to her neck. I need to talk to Nancy and the guys, but I don't want to leave her alone. I sigh at the quiet knock on my door. Jessa, thankfully, doesn't stir as I get up, and I'm grateful for that.

I open the door and glare at Ryan. "What?"

"Did I wake her?" He keeps his voice low, and I glance over my shoulder. She's still sleeping.

I shake my head and slip out of the room, closing the door quietly behind me. "No. But it took me a long time to get her relaxed enough to sleep. What's going on?"

"We came up with a plan. But we need to talk about it."

"Then talk." I lean against the wall.

"I mean all of us." Ryan points towards the door to my bedroom. "Jessa included." I just look at him. I say nothing, but he knows as well as I do that he isn't going to go near her right now. She needs the rest. Finally, Ryan shakes his head. "All of us, Jason."

He turns and walks back down the stairs. I take a deep breath and check on Jessa again before walking down to my office. Nancy is sitting at my desk with her laptop in front of her. She barely looks up at me, and I have to smile as I sit down in a chair in front of her.

"Making yourself at home, I see," I say as I chuckle.

"I have a contractor coming to deal with your window tomorrow. All of your meetings for the next month are on my calendar. I've emailed and called everyone regarding the change. No one has an issue. I've reassigned all of Jessa's projects to her team and put her assistant in charge of them. Tomorrow, I'll grab the drawings she's working on and give them to her team. I have a budget meeting set up with the CFO. He had requested to meet with you just before today's events."

"Sounds like you've been busy." I fold my arms over my chest and lean back in the chair.

She finally looks up at me. "It's time, Jason. We knew it was coming. You've prepared me well. The company will be in good hands, but it's time this issue is resolved once and for all."

I smile. "When this is over, remind me to thank you for stepping up."

She gives me a soft smile back. "My salary for that time is already in place. It just needs your signature."

"Whatever contracts you sign, whatever business you bring, I'll give you a bonus. I don't know if you read completely over your contract, but I had legal add in that stipulation after we talked. Part of your salary."

She blushes. "The salary is enough, Jason. I don't need a bonus."

"Your husband just had a major surgery. You've been paying a nurse to take care of his needs while you've been working. And you've been paying out of your pocket because his insurance doesn't cover that. You gave your son most of your savings so that he could take care of his newborn after the death of his wife in childbirth. The kid has a lot of health issues, and you've also been covering the bills piling in because his insurance ended with the loss of his job. You need the bonus."

She shakes her head. "I don't want you to feel like you're obligated to help my family. The salary bump is really enough."

"Nancy, you've been with this company since day one. I've told you this before, but I'll say it again. You're just as much family to my family as we are to you. I'm giving you the salary. And you are getting the bonus. And if you need anything else, just tell me. Medical bills. Mortgage. Food. Clothes. Car payment or insurance. I don't care. I can afford it. Believe me. I have more money than I know what to do with, and if I can use it to help you, I won't hesitate."

Nancy falls silent and looks at the ground. When she looks back at me, there are tears in her eyes. "Do you really mean that?"

I smile. "You're like my aunt, Nancy. I would do anything for you. We all would. If I can help, I'll do it. Are you behind on anything?" I tilt my head a little. I know the answer. I know she is. I just don't know what. She looks at me a moment before sighing and looking away. "I'm gonna find out eventually. I'd rather it be now. Before things get too bad."

"They already are," she whispers.

I narrow my eyes. "Nancy… what? Tell me."

"With everything going on with Jessa and this mafia thing, I didn't want to bring it up, but I was going to ask you for an advance on my pay. I've been paying my mortgage, and my son's, as well as the medical bills for my husband and grandchild. I was doing okay for a while, but with my husband's nurse and his added medical bills, I can't keep up anymore."

"How far behind are you?"

"A lot." Her cheeks flush, and I know she's embarrassed.

"Nancy." It's rare I ever have to use a commanding tone with her, but I do it now.

She takes a shaky breath. "My house is going to be foreclosed on… at the end of the week."

My mouth nearly falls open. "Christ. Why didn't you tell me?"

"You've had your hands full. And this is my issue. You shouldn't be responsible for my issues."

I shake my head and choose to completely ignore her statement. "I'll get your house caught back up. I'll pay your husband's outstanding

210

medical bills and your grandchild's. Going forward, I'll pay for your husband's home care and your grandchild's medical care."

"That's too much, Jason."

"Nancy. Come on. Do you know my net worth? Do you know my family's net worth? I'm not trying to brag here, but none of us are hurting for money. You know as well as I do that if Nick or Ryan knew any of this, neither of them would hesitate to do exactly what I'm doing. Your loyalty, your time, and friendship over the years have meant everything to me and my family. Let me do this."

In response, Nancy breaks down in tears. I don't hesitate. I stand and walk around the desk. I sink to my knees, taking her in my arms, and hug her as hard as I dare.

"Jason," she whispers.

"I'll catch you up, I'll get all your outstanding bills paid up. Utilities, credit cards. Just tell me what you need, okay?"

She nods into my shoulder as she cries tears of relief. After a few minutes of letting loose, she pulls back and grabs a tissue from the box on my desk as I stand and go back to my chair.

"I don't know what to say." Nancy dabs at her eyes.

I smile. "You don't need to say anything." I give her a few moments to compose herself before continuing. I clear my throat. "In the top drawer, there's a stack of paperwork. Right side. Grab it, would you?" I say with a mostly hidden smile. She does as I ask. Her eyes widen when she realizes what it is, and she looks up at me. "If anything happens to me, I want to make sure that my company, you, and the rest of my employees are taken care of. Other than Ryan or Nick, there's no one I trust in this world to take over for me more than you."

"Jason... I... I don't..."

I stand and walk around the desk once more. I lean down and kiss her on the cheek. "The order is Ryan, followed by Nick, and then you. If anything happens to us, the company belongs to you. I need you to think it through. My signature is already there. It just needs yours. Get me a list of all of your outstanding bills as well as your son's by tomorrow. Mortgages included. I'll take care of everything. As soon as you make a decision and read things over, let me know. If you agree, sign the papers and turn them into legal."

"But what if nothing happens? I don't want to take over if nothing happens."

"You won't. This is just a precaution. In case it does. I need my bases covered. I need to make sure my company is protected. That you are. That my employees still have jobs. I don't want to pressure you into it, but with what's going on, I can't give you a lot of time."

She only nods. I bend to kiss her cheek once more before leaving her in my office. When I reach the living room, Jessa is sitting on the couch between Alex and Josh. Damon is sitting next to Tia in one of the oversized chairs. Layla and Marissa are sitting on the floor. Gavin is sprawled across the smaller couch. Nick and Ryan are sitting on another couch, and Lance is sitting in front of my fireplace. I raise my eyebrow as Damon motions to the other oversized chair.

"Probably want to sit down for this," Damon says.

"Are we about to discuss this infamous plan?" I ask.

Alex looks at me while I sit and hands me his phone. "That and more. I already showed this to Jess. That came through after you brought Jessa upstairs. Read the text before, too."

Fuck. For fuck's sake. Not only was he watching, but he took pictures. He threatened Josh and Jessa yet again. I hand Alex back his phone, and Jessa comes to me. I slip my arms around her waist as she settles in my lap. I kiss her shoulder. "When did you wake up?"

"A few minutes ago," she says softly. "Ryan said you were talking to Nancy."

"Just squaring the company away." I kiss her neck as she smiles and leans her head on my shoulder.

"Josh came up with a plan. We've all thought it through. Looks like it could work," Gavin says. Everyone sounds exhausted. I can't blame them. So am I.

"It's the only chance we have. It will work," Josh says confidently.

"Well? What is it? By the way you guys are acting, I'm pretty sure you know my feelings about it already."

Alex sighs. "No one likes this plan, Jason. No one. We're all trying to come up with other options. The truth is, Josh is right. It will work, and it's the only chance we have."

Ryan cocks his head to the side. "How do you know the plan already?"

"He's my brother, Ry. You think he didn't tell me?" Alex scoffs.

"Right. Of course. Because he can't follow simple instructions and let us all talk together about it," Nick snaps.

"Stop it!" Jessa barks just as Ryan opens his mouth. Jessa sits up and levels both Nick and Ryan with a glare that could probably melt steel. "Both of you! He's fucking paid for everything he did in spades. I'm so sick of you, Ryan, cutting him down. It's been a month! I realize you're having a hard time deciding if he's for real or not, but he is! If it wasn't for him, I wouldn't be here!"

"You're damn right you wouldn't be here! He got you into this whole fucking mess! And the rest of us, too!" Ryan yells back at her, giving her his own dangerous glare.

Jessa jumps to her feet before I have a chance to stop her. Before any of us know what's happening, Ryan has also jumped to his feet. I just stare in fascination as my five foot three inch girlfriend faces down my six foot five inch brother.

Over the past month, we've all come to trust Josh. Nick still holds reservations about him. Ryan, on the other hand, is still very suspicious. I'll hand it to him, though. He's attempted being civil, but it's been a task for him. I've tried talking to him. So has Jessa, but Ryan has always needed to form his own opinion of people. With Josh, he's still on the fence.

"I would be dead if he didn't do what he did in that shed!"

"He's the fucking reason you were in that shed! It's his fault his father is obsessed with fucking you in the first fucking place!"

I can see the exact moment Jessa has reached her boiling point.

She slaps him.

Hard.

My mouth drops open.

No one says a word.

Ryan's head is turned to the side. He slowly turns back to her. I can see he's pissed, but she doesn't back down. Instead, she steps closer to him and pokes her finger into his chest as she talks. He glares down at her hand. I'm ready to step in if I need to, but seeing my girl face down my mafia boss, older brother with no fear is sexy as hell.

"It's *not* Josh's fault that his father is a fucking psycho. I don't hear you blaming Alex, and by your logic, he's just as much to blame, if

213

not more. He brought me to his attention first just by being with me, didn't he? You do remember it's his father, too, right? So, if Alex and I were never together, I never would've been involved with Josh or his father, right?"

"Jessa -" Ryan starts.

"No. You don't get to talk. You're done talking until you apologize to him for treating him like a third-class fucking citizen. He's here trying to help us and make amends for his actions. He's admitted to his mistakes, and he's apologized for them. More times than he should have to. He's set himself against his asshole father. He's had his life threatened. He's been poisoned; brainwashed, and he's still fucking here, helping us come up with a plan. I don't care if you don't trust him or not. At least treat him with fucking respect!"

"Jessa -" Ryan begins again.

"It's what you, Jason, and your entire family stand on, Ryan Crane. Jason's come around, but even if he hadn't, he'd still treat him with dignity and respect. Not once has Jason ever been disrespectful or talked down to him or even about him. Maybe you need to get over yourself and take a page from your little brother's book. Apologize, Ryan. Or I will personally figure out a way to do this on my own!"

Ryan's eyes widen in shock as Jessa turns to Nick and glares. He hasn't moved, and it's obvious he's just as surprised as everyone else. No one dares talk to Ryan like that. I smirk and choke back a laugh as I cross my arms over my chest. This is amusing to me.

"Jessa -" Nick holds up a hand in an attempt to stop her tirade, but it doesn't work.

"You too, Nick. Your comment was rude, disrespectful, and out of line. I'm so fucking disappointed in you because you and Josh actually seemed to be getting along fairly well. I will not have disrespect and all out rudeness happening here. In my presence or not. He's laying everything on the line for us. The least you can do is give him the fucking respect he deserves and stop being an asshole to him." She continues to stare both of them down until they both relent.

Nick looks over at Josh as Jessa glares at him. "Josh. I apologize. She's right. I shouldn't have said what I did. I'm fucking tired, and I took it out on you."

"Apology accepted. I appreciate it," Josh says quietly, just as in awe of Jessa as I am.

Jessa turns to Ryan and crosses her arms. I can see right away he knows how right she is. He sighs. "Fuck. I'm sorry, Josh. I know I've been an asshole, and you really have done a lot to help us out. In order for us to do this, we need to be on the same team." He glances at Jessa before looking back at Josh. "I'll be honest, trusting you is a bit difficult, but I'll be respectful of you. You deserve that much after getting Jessa out of that shed and protecting her."

"Apology accepted." Josh clears his throat. "I understand. Trust has to be earned, and I have a long way to go. I promise you, all of you, that I really am on your side. I'll do whatever it takes to take him the fuck down."

Jessa nods, satisfied, and returns to my lap. She glares once more at Ryan. I slip my arms around her waist and lean in to whisper in her ear. "You're fucking sexy as hell, beautiful. Do you know that?"

She giggles and wiggles against me. I'm instantly hard and groan. She kisses me, and we both turn to Alex as he starts talking about the plan.

"Alright, listen up. My father wants me to take over for him. We all know that he wants Jessa at my side. He wants her to have my child, and he wants that child to be my heir. To take over for me. His legacy is sealed. His mafia is in good hands. He knows I don't want it. So, he has spent years tearing Josh down in my absence. Making him promises that he never intended to keep all because he wants to make sure his legacy is locked down. So, the plan is to give him what he wants. He wants me and Jess. Let's give him me and Jess."

My mouth drops open, and I cough. "What? That's *not* fucking happening."

"Alex won't let anything happen to her," Josh cuts in. "If my dad thinks he's getting what he wants, it gives us the opportunity to take him down for good. His guard will be down. At least after a couple of days. Alex and Jessa are really going to have to sell it. Alex will have to show him that he's serious about doing this because he truly wants to protect me and Jessa. He has to show that he knows this is the only way."

"But he knows she's with me!" I protest. He has fucking pictures. "This is never going to work."

"Actually," Ryan says as he sits back down. "We're going to make it look like Alex threatened to kill you. Jessa is only going along with this to protect you, but she quickly falls back in love with him because she never got over him. Alex was her first love. Matthew will drop his suspicions after a couple of days. When he does, we go in."

"Alex can shoot us a text when the time is right, and we can plan our attack," Josh continues. "He'll let us into the house in the middle of the night, and we'll take our father out."

"It's going to be a war no matter how we play this. We'll need a lot more guns," Alex says.

"You'll have them," Ryan promises.

"Fuck. Just wait. Wait a second." I hold up a hand as if it will somehow make everything make sense. "How long will you both be in there?" I ask. I can feel a headache forming. I hate everything about this plan. Jessa being close to that fucker no matter who's with her is not something I want at all.

Josh sighs. "A week at most. Probably less."

Alex looks at me. "Jessa will be with me at all times. I won't leave her alone. She'll be with me in my room at night. She'll be at my side at all times. I'll keep her safe, Jason."

I chew the inside of my cheek and look at Jessa, silently asking how she feels about this.

She gives me a soft smile and kisses me softly. "I hate that Alex and I are using ourselves as bait, but I trust him. I know he'll keep me safe. And I think Josh is right. I think this is our only option at this point."

I sigh again and close my eyes as I start rubbing my forehead. "I still don't like this."

"None of us do," Ryan agrees.

"Josh stays here," Alex says. "No negotiation. I have to make it seem like I'm keeping him away. For his protection. I'll tell him that until Jessa and I are married, I'm not bringing Josh home. He'll believe it because he knows I'm fiercely protective."

Josh glares. "I'm going to be there to take him down."

Alex looks at him. "You can't come back with me, Josh. If he's watching, and we know fuck well he is, and he sees you go back with me, it'll raise immediate suspicion. You can leave with Jason a couple days after Jessa and I leave. Not until I know you aren't being watched. It would ruin everything if you came back with me. He knows how protective I am. There's no way he'd believe I'd throw you in the mix unless I had assurance of your safety. And I wouldn't until I'm sworn in as the new leader. That won't happen with me, but it will with you. You'll be sworn in the very day after he's taken down."

Josh continues to glare at Alex, but nods. Jessa looks at me. After a few minutes of silence, I sigh and pull Jessa close to me. She wraps her arms around my neck, and I bury my face in her hair, kissing her neck.

"Let's do it," I damn near whisper. "I'm never going to like it, but fuck. This has to end."

Chapter Twenty Nine

✗ Jessa ✗

(Two Days Later)

A couple of nights later, I step out of the shower and wrap a towel around myself, taking another towel and drying my hair. Jason has spent a lot of time at the office and has barely spoken to me. He's not here when I go to sleep, and he leaves before I wake up. I've tried calling him during the day to say I miss him, but he either doesn't answer or the call is hurried. I send him cute texts to let him know I'm thinking about him, but he never responds. I don't know what I did to upset him.

Tears sting my eyes as I finish drying my hair. I spend some time brushing it out before making my way to the bedroom. Jason not only hasn't talked much to me, but he also hasn't touched me since the night we talked about the plan to take Matthew down. The very next morning he kissed me before he left and started acting strangely after that. I didn't understand it then. I still don't now.

I sigh as I start rummaging for something to wear to bed when my phone goes off with a text message. I ignore it as I get dressed, and then crawl under the covers. I grab my phone, expecting something from Jason.

I let out a strangled sob when I see a picture of Jason in his office locked in a passionate embrace with a woman I have never seen before. More strangled sobs follow with each picture that comes in. Of Jason touching her. Jason kissing her. I throw my phone against the wall and scream.

A moment later, there's a knock on the door, and I glare at it. "Go away!"

"Not happening. Are you okay?"

"No! I'm through with Jason. I'm through with all of this!" I jump off the bed and start throwing clothes into a suitcase. Ukraine sounds far enough away.

"Jess? I'm coming in, okay?"

"Just go away!" I scream as I sob uncontrollably.

"Still not happening."

I hear the door open, then close. I glare at the intruder as I continue throwing clothes around. Alex takes in the sight of me and my phone on the floor near the wall where it hit.

"What happened?"

I don't answer, and he picks up my phone. The screen is cracked.

"Jessa, what happened?"

I still don't answer, call me childish, and he walks to me, taking my hands and stopping me from throwing my clothes in the suitcase.

I yank them away. "Just look at the messages if you want to know so badly! I never should've fallen for him. I was better off alone!" I yell. He looks at the phone and sighs before opening the messages. His eyes widen, then darken with anger as he growls. "See? It was too good to be true. I never should've fallen for him. It was too fast. She's gorgeous. There's no way I could even come close to comparing to her."

I sink to my knees and cry ugly tears, but I don't care. Alex has seen me at my worst. If I can't cry in front of him, I wouldn't be able to cry in front of anyone.

Alex sits next to me on the floor and pulls me into his lap. "Jess, listen to me. You're beautiful. You know that. Don't ever think you aren't. Ever. Do you even know who that message was from?"

"Does it matter? He's all over her." I sob harder as I grip his shirt.

"Yes. It does matter. You're missing a huge piece of the fucking puzzle, peanut."

I continue to sob as he hugs me. "I don't care. There's no mistaking that he was kissing another woman."

"Peanut. I don't know the whole story. But do you know the number?"

"No."

"My father."

I stop breathing. "W-what?"

He hugs me tighter as I start taking a few deep breaths. "It's my father, Jess. There's more going on here than you think. I don't know what, but you need to talk to Jason."

"H-how? How did he get my number?"

"I don't know, peanut. I don't. But we'll get you a new one. After this is over. New number and everything. He's probably tapping your phone. He wants you to call Jason. He wants you to break up with him and run." Alex sits with me on the floor for a few minutes as I calm down. "I think you should give him what he wants. I don't know what the fuck Jason's problem has been these last couple of days, but call him. Tell him he needs to come home. You have to talk."

"He won't."

"Then, I'll step in. Put it on speaker."

I sniffle and grab my phone from him to call Jason. I'm amazed it still works. It rings a few times before he picks up.

"I'm sorry, Jess. I have a lot of work to do. I can't leave Nancy with all of this. I'll see you in the morning."

"You've told me that the last two days. Yet, you make sure you're gone before I wake up. And that you don't come home until late. And I finally figured out why." I look up at Alex. He gives me an encouraging smile and nods to me.

"I just have a lot of work, Jessa. Things are tough. Especially with my project manager not here. I'm going to have to hire someone."

"Why? So, I'm not around to interrupt you fucking that gorgeous blonde you had in your office tonight?"

"What? Jessa, what the fuck are you talking about?"

I choke my anger and confusion down. "You need to come home, Jason. Now."

He growls low under his throat. "First of all, I don't take well to demands. Second, there is no one else here."

220

"The pictures on my phone say differently." I allow the anger to seep out a little because if I don't, I'm going to start sobbing like a child again. "So, if you aren't here within the next hour, Jason, finding another project manager will be the least of your worries. I'll leave. You won't see me again."

"Jessa, I don't know what pictures you're talking about." I can hear the fear creeping into his voice.

"Just… we need to talk." I hang up the phone and sag against Alex. "I don't have the strength."

"You aren't alone. You have me. This is the perfect opportunity for us to start our plan, peanut. I really do think something else is going on. We'll find out. But my father just gave us our opening."

✕✕✕

I'm waiting in the living room for Jason when he gets home. It takes him less than an hour. More like twenty minutes. I'm curled up on the couch with my phone clutched in my hand. I've made everyone else leave the room. I need time and privacy with him.

When he enters the room, I say nothing. I just hold out my phone. The picture of the woman is on my screen. Jason furrows his brow at the crack on my screen but says nothing as he looks at the picture.

"Scroll through." My voice is quiet, barely above a whisper. I can hardly even hear myself.

Jason scrolls through the pictures before taking a deep breath and sitting next to me on the couch. "A couple of years ago. I met this woman. Jill. She was fun to be around, and I broke my own rule. I took her out on a third date. I typically take a woman out once. Maybe twice if I like her. Never three. I've never wanted a relationship. Not until I met you, Jess. After the third date, I guess I got bored. She didn't want to give it up. She called a few times after I broke it off. Showed up at my office a few other times. I always told her the same thing. Not interested. Leave."

I can feel him looking down at me, but I say nothing and don't return his gaze. I keep my eyes on the floor and flick my nails against each other as tears prick my eyes.

He takes another deep breath and runs his fingers through his hair. "She showed up at my office tonight. I told her the same thing I did before.

Except this time I told her that I have a girlfriend who I love. She kissed me. Surprised the hell out of me. I pushed her off after I regained my composure. She came at me again, and I put my hands on her waist to hold her back. I tried to let her down easy and guided her to my door. She tried the kiss again, and I basically shoved her out. That was it. That's all that happened."

I still say nothing, but I do lift my eyes to the wall and stop playing with my nails.

He puts a hand on my leg, and my heart skips a beat. It always skips a beat when he's near; when he touches me. "Jess. Baby, you have to believe me. I don't know where those pictures came from, but I would never do anything to hurt you. I love you. Seeing how upset you are is breaking my heart, beautiful."

"It doesn't explain your absence. How you've been avoiding me." I can't meet his eyes.

"You're right. It doesn't," he says quietly. I wait for him to continue, stubbornly refusing to look at him. "It's because I'm scared, Jessa. I'm scared that I'm going to lose you. So I pushed you away, and that was wrong of me. You didn't deserve that. You deserve someone who can be strong for you. I just showed you how weak I am, and I'm sorry for that."

"You're not weak, Jason. I would never think that of you. You're the strongest person I know." I glance at him, taking a deep breath. I climb on top of him, straddling his lap. I take his face in my hands and kiss him. "Promise me something."

"Anything if it means you're not leaving me."

"Promise me that you'll never push me away again. That you'll talk to me if something is upsetting you."

"I promise."

I smile and kiss him again as his arms wrap around me. Our kisses are slow, passionate, and filled with the love we hold for each other. I don't know how long we're in each other's arms, but we're interrupted by someone clearing their throat.

"Go the fuck away. We're busy," Jason growls. He goes back to kissing me, ignoring our intruder who laughs.

"I hate to interrupt. Really. But this entire thing with the pictures gives us a golden opportunity," Ryan says.

222

It's my turn to growl. I turn and glare at Ryan. "How do you know about all of this?"

"I know everything, sweetheart." He gives me a cocky grin.

"What he means is I told him." Alex materializes behind Ryan, and I shoot him a withering glare. He gives me a dazzling, and just as cocky as Ryan's, smile.

"It really is the perfect time. Lucinio's expecting a fight. So, let's make a show of her leaving. With Alex," Ryan says.

"I hate you right now." Jason shoots daggers at his brother.

Alex laughs. "Give them an hour. Is that enough time?" Alex winks.

I scoff. Jason stands with me in his arms. I instinctively wrap my legs around his waist, and my arms around his neck as he carries me upstairs, not saying a word to anyone.

When we get to our bedroom, he tosses me on the bed, and we waste no time stripping our clothes off.

Jason grins as he stalks towards me, pushing me back on the bed. "You're beautiful, Jessa. I'm sorry for hurting you by avoiding you like that."

"I forgive you. Please don't do it again."

He dips his head between my thighs and licks me. "I love you."

I arch into his tongue. "I love you, too." He ducks his head again and licks slowly, sending shivers throughout my whole body. I can feel him smiling against me "Stop grinning like that, you cocky bastard."

He knows I'm teasing him, and he hums against me, sending new sensations through me and making me sigh. "I think you like it too much." He swirls his tongue around my bud at the same time he enters one of his long fingers inside me. I arch off the bed, and he gently sucks and gives me the strokes I love so much.

"Mmm... Jason." My pussy pulses softly around him.

"Yes, baby?" He enters another finger.

"Oh, God." I moan, and he chuckles as he licks up and down from my pussy to my clit, and then gently bites my bud as he pushes deeper inside me. He crooks his fingers against my spot as he nips me. "Jason!" I don't expect, and can't stop, the waves of pleasure that crash over me. Jason laughs as he continues to lap up my release. "I'm... I'm so sorry."

"For what, beautiful?"

"You… just hit the right spot, and I couldn't help it."

He kisses up my stomach, pausing to ravish each nipple, and continues up my neck and jaw. He smiles before he kisses my lips. I feel his hard length against my leg, and I shift, wrapping my legs around his waist.

"Jessa. You're so perfect."

I smile at him as he glides into me. "So are you."

I'm rewarded with a killer smile as he wraps his arms around me and buries his head in my hair. We move together until our bodies are slicked with sweat, and we're panting. Our grip on one another has become stronger and harder. Jason's thrusts have become more frantic. My pussy tightens and clenches around him erratically.

We need no words. There are none to say. Our bodies say all they need to. How much we love each other. Need each other. I can feel he's ready, just as he can feel me. Our bodies tense as we buck into each other again and again. We break at the same time with screams and moans as our hips jerk against each other.

After several minutes, as we lay in each other's arms, Jason reluctantly rolls off me, gently pulling out of me, and pulls me to his side. "I don't want to let you go. I don't want you to do this. Maybe we could just leave. I'll fly you around the world, beautiful. We can stay hidden. Use my brother's unlimited resources and protection."

I shake my head as I trace random patterns on his arm. "You know that's not the answer."

Jason sighs and buries his head in my chest. "I know. I don't like the idea of you being away from home. So close to that son of a bitch."

"I'll have Alex," I say quietly.

"Doesn't make me feel better. You're gonna be three thousand miles away from me. I'll have no way to protect you."

"Ryan will be there. And a lot of his guys will be there."

"I know, Jess. But I won't be."

"Jason." I run my fingers through his hair. "I'm just as scared as you. Probably more. But you're being watched. We know that's true now more than ever. If you fly out there at the same time, he'll know something is off."

"While all of that is true, it still means nothing. I don't like that I'm not there if things go down."

224

"I don't either, Jas. But this is the only way we're ever going to be free." I hug Jason and kiss his head as he kisses between my breasts.

This.

I'm going to miss this.

Being in his arms is like nothing I've ever felt. I feel safe and secure, but also treasured and cherished.

I just hope that it's not the last time we're lying like this together.

Chapter Thirty

⚔ Alex ⚔

My family's private jet is just about to land, and I hate to wake Jessa up after the day she's had. The fake breakup with Jason in his driveway went just as I had hoped. I had gotten a text from my dad before we even arrived at the airport about it. He especially loved the picture sent to him by whoever he had watching Jason's house of Jessa running into my arms. I read the text he sent again and growl dangerously.

> **Matthew: It's about time you see things my way. I knew it was only a matter of time. Can't say I'm not upset about not being able to fuck her tight pussy. Maybe I still will.**

I never responded. I'd much rather make my position clear as soon as I see the smug fucker.

I clench my fist. I moved Josh to Ryan's. I had to make a show of moving him some place to make my story of protecting him more plausible. We stopped at the family hotel and checked him in. What my father doesn't know is that Ryan was waiting there to take him back to his place.

Gavin, Damon, Lance, and Cole all came home on Gavin's plane. I needed to make it look like I was pulling totally out of Manhattan. What my father doesn't know is that I'm allied with the most powerful mafia boss in the world, and that he has guards all over Josh. My father isn't getting anywhere near my brother again.

I also had my mother pulled right from under his nose. I used some guys who are close to him and work my mother's personal security detail. He has no clue they've been on my side for years. I've always known my mother's whereabouts, even if my father, and later Josh, lied to me about them. Ever since I was seventeen-years-old and following my mentors advice on making my own allies within my father's mafia. Ryan Crane is fucking smart.

My dad had no idea that her personal security brought her to a safehouse. One that belongs to Ryan. Not me. Not my old man. It's completely separate from anything to do with the Lucinio Mafia or anyone involved in it. They were under orders to make sure they weren't tracked or bugged. When they left, they made sure they weren't followed. Then they took one hell of a roundabout way to the safehouse just as an extra precaution.

My mom is out of harm's way. Just as Jessa and Josh are. And he knows damn well he won't see either of them until he meets my demands. He knows he's not the one in control anymore. What he doesn't know is that in a few days, he'll have met the end of the road. He won't be seeing mom, Josh, me, Jessa, or anyone else ever again.

Ryan also made sure Jason had security, even though he didn't want it. He finally relented after Jessa started begging him. Jason needs to go about business as usual. We used the pictures my father sent as the cause for the breakup. Jason needed to portray that cunning, ruthless as fuck business man who didn't give two shits about anything but his company.

Jason's complete indifference to Jessa and the breakup played into her running to me when she found out about him. I told my father that neither of us had ever stopped loving each other or truly moved on. I told him we wanted to be married as soon as possible and until that happened, and he gave me the reins, Josh would stay hidden. My father knows how protective I am, so my threat to kill him if he touched Jessa or even attempted to find Josh played right into that.

The text still pisses me off, though. The fact that he has the balls to send it after my threat shows how smug and completely insane he is.

227

I look down at Jessa as she sleeps soundly next to me and sigh. I reach out and run my fingers along her cheek. She stirs and opens her eyes wide. I can't help but smile. She's always been the most beautiful woman I've ever seen. Just because my feelings for her have changed doesn't mean that has. Jessa is truly gorgeous.

"We're landing, peanut. My father will be picking us up."

"So it's showtime," she says quietly.

I nod sadly. I still hate that she's in this mess at all. "He has it in his head that we're together, Jess. We have to sell that."

"I know. I understand." She smiles softly at her hands. "It's the only way."

"We have to try to make it seem as natural as we can. He only sees what he wants, but I want to make sure he doesn't pick up on any awkwardness between us."

"We were together for four years, Alex." She chuckles. "It'll be fine."

"I know, Jess." I take her hand in mine, and she looks up at me. "We have to act like that in front of him. Just as in love. He's crazy, Jessa. I wouldn't be surprised if he completely forgot we were ever apart. When we go to bed, we'll be in the same room, but I don't doubt he'll sneak in just to see if we're sleeping together in the same bed."

She reaches up to palm my check. "I know, Alex. Really. I know. I trust you. Honestly, I'd be terrified to sleep alone anyway. It gives him too much of an opening to take me and do whatever sick thing he wants to." She drops her hand and sighs heavily as she leans back in her seat again.

"Which is another reason you'll be sleeping with me. I want you in my arms. If he gets any ideas, he not only has to get past me, but also through me. If my arms are wrapped around you, he won't be able to take you anywhere to do anything with you. I'll feel it if you move." I smile as reassuringly as I can. She squeezes my hand as she shuts her eyes tightly. The plane touches down on the runway. I chuckle as I put one arm around her, letting her keep a hold of my hand. "You've always hated flying."

"Do you know how many planes have crashed on takeoff and landing?" She squeezes my hand tighter as the plane bounces, ever so slightly, and slows down.

"Not near as many as the media would have you believe. It's okay, peanut. Trust me. You're safe."

"You say that now." We hit a bump, and she squeaks, digging her nails into my hand. I let her because I know it makes her feel safer. A few moments later, we stop. I help her up as she grabs her purse.

"Ready for this?" I ask, giving her hand a squeeze.

"No. But we have to do this." She gives a resolute nod. "We can."

"Damn right." We walk out of the plane hand in hand. As I warned, Matthew Lucinio is standing next to a long black limo looking more smug than I've ever seen.

"Son! Jessa! It's nice to finally meet you! After so many years! Let me have a look at you!" He takes her hand and spins her in a circle as soon as we reach them. It takes everything I am to not pull her away from him, but as soon as he finishes her spin, I do just that. I guide her into the limo as I glare at my idiot father. "Oh, come now," he rumbles with a dangerously lustrous look.

"Don't touch her. You've done enough. I fucking mean that. She's mine, dad. Not yours. Not Josh's. Mine. She's always been mine. Always will be."

My dad has the audacity to smirk. "There's the Alex we all know."

I give a murderous look. "Fuck you, dad. Don't touch her again."

I climb into the limo behind Jessa and wink at her. She smiles. I make a show of pulling her into my lap as my dad gets into the limo. I continue my show, and run my hand up her leg, resting it on her hip and giving her a light squeeze as I look in her eyes. My dad doesn't notice I'm actually watching him and his reaction. He's practically panting, and I want to punch him. Jessa leans close to my lips and kisses me.

It's just as soft and sweet as I remember, and I involuntarily groan when she pulls away. She smiles at me, and I lean in to kiss her again. I pull away, and she leans her head against my shoulder. She does exactly what I told her to and completely ignores my dad. I shoot daggers at him until we arrive at his house.

"Fuck... I haven't been here in six years," I rumble.

I refused to come anywhere near the house after I came back. I met my mom for coffee a few times. Josh a couple of others. But I only ever had contact with my father over the phone. I wouldn't allow him to get any reason to think that he had control over me at any time. It was all on my terms.

"I love this house. I always have." She says the words so honestly I can't help but kiss her neck. But forcing myself to stay in character is another story. I hate this place.

"Well, if you still want me like you said you did when we were fucking on the plane, this place is about to be all yours, gorgeous," I say with a smirk.

My dad's eyes nearly bulge out of his head at the thought of Jessa and I on the plane. I have no doubt that he is replacing me with himself in his head, and it makes me sick. Too bad I can't shoot the fucker right now.

Jessa smiles at me, bringing me back from my thoughts of violent vengeance. "It's always been you, Alex. No one has ever compared."

I give her my most arrogant grin. "Well, in all fairness, you've only ever had Josh and Jason. Compared to me, there's definitely no comparison. I'm a thousand times the man they are. Combined."

She drops her voice to a sexy, sultry tone. "You've always known exactly how to make me happy. How to satisfy me."

I kiss her again as I give her hip a squeeze to let her know she's doing so well. "You're mine. You belong to me."

I brush her lips with mine again. My dad is beaming, and I choke down my temper as we all get out of the limo. I put an arm around Jessa and immediately started scanning the property for guards. It'll take a couple days to get everything down. I just hope everyone can get through this.

✗✗✗

I set Jessa's suitcase on the bed as she closes the door to the bedroom. She falls against it and takes a long, deep breath, letting it out slowly.

I glance at her and chuckle. "Want to take a shower? You look like you could use it."

"I'm exhausted. I feel like I haven't slept in a week. But I don't want to sleep because it's like four in the morning here. We'll probably be expected to be awake soon."

"Well, if you want to sleep, I wouldn't mind. I think I slept maybe an hour on the plane."

"Are you saying the unbreakable Alex is... tired? Have I found a weakness in that indestructible armor?" She smirks at me.

I shake my head. "So funny. Ha. Ha." I grin as she laughs, and I open her suitcase. "How about we put our stuff away, and then take a nap?"

"Sounds like the best plan you've ever come up with."

I laugh, and we work together to put our clothes away. She leaves out something to sleep in and starts walking to the bathroom when I hear a subtle noise outside the door. I grab Jessa around the waist and pull her close to me. She hits my chest hard.

"What are you -"

I cut her off with a kiss just as my door flies open. Her eyes go wide, and I can tell how surprised she is until she hears my father's voice.

"Are you guys settled? We have wedding planning and a coronation to deal with!" He sounds far too excited. I pull slowly away from Jessa, not taking my eyes off my father. I keep my hands tightly at her waist and don't let her turn around, even though she tries.

I glare at him. "First of all, fucking knock. Second, we're busy. Third, I love mom, but she should be asleep. It's fucking barely four in the morning. We're about to take a nap. Leave. Don't barge in here like that again."

He glares. "We can't just throw this shit together at the drop of a hat."

"We can wait until I'm ready to do it. After we get some sleep. Don't like it? You can do it yourself. Jessa and I don't give a fuck about a wedding or the coronation."

"When did you become such an asshole?"

I grip Jessa tighter. "The day I found out you were fucking with my brother and my girl. That's when I became such an asshole."

He glares and looks at his watch before raising his eyes back on me. "Ten a.m."

I say nothing. I wait for him to leave the room. I keep my arms locked around Jessa and listen for his footsteps to fade as he walks away. When I don't hear him anymore, I release her and stride to the door, quickly flipping the lock. Jessa watches me, nibbling her lip.

I turn back to her. "My dad has a key, so locking the door gives me a heads up if someone is trying to get in."

231

"At least we'll have a heads up," Jessa says quietly.

I smile. "I know this is hard, peanut." I walk to the bed and start picking through the things Lance gave me to check for cameras and bugs in the bedroom.

"What are you doing?" she asks, curiously.

"I don't trust my father. Not even a little bit. Lance gave me some shit to help me check if he's watching or listening."

Her eyes widen. She presses her lips together when she catches my subtle hint to not say too much more than what we have. Normal conversation. It's what I've kept this at because I know my father. I don't have a single doubt in my mind that he put up small, hidden cameras and audio equipment all over my room.

What I'm doing right now gives me one more piece of power over him. I'm sure he doubts I'd be smart enough to do this, but he won't be able to deny that me doing it makes me even more ready to take the reign from him.

Jessa stays quiet as I start walking the room with the equipment. Sure enough, one of the devices flashes at me, signaling a bug. Jessa gasps as I chuckle. I'm pretty sure she thought I was kidding about the lengths I feel he'll go to keep an eye on all of us.

I find the tiny bug on the inside of the lampshade. "Clever dad. But I'm fucking smarter than that, asshole." I drop it and stomp on it as I twist my heel, destroying the bug. Whoever he has listening just got some major feedback in their ear.

We all agreed we need to make a big show of this. Lance made sure that whatever this little scanning thing is works, whether the bug is giving a signal or not. It picks up the transmission frequency, but it also picks up a tiny amount of some other material that apparently comes in all listening devices.

I don't pretend for a second to know anything about that stuff. I've always been into protection. Firewalls. Virus and malware. Protection against hacking. Funny that I have a hacker on my team who could more than likely get through anything Lucinio Tech develops.

Listening devices and how to find them when they are off or on has never been my thing. I took a crash course in this from Lance before we left. I would've been able to figure it out if I hadn't, but it's nice to know some of the inner workings and what to look for.

After I walk through the room and find several bugs and cameras, I take another lap. Jessa is staring at me with wide eyes. I've crushed twelve cameras within the bedroom and the bathroom, one of them being in the shower, and several small listening devices. It's beyond sickening.

"Is that it?" Jessa whispers when I start putting things away.

I chuckle. "You can speak freely, peanut. Not screaming or loud enough for him to hear you if he's standing by the door, but normally." I grab my desk chair and wedge it underneath the doorknob.

"In the shower." Jessa hugs herself. "Gross."

"Very much." I turn on my stereo and find my favorite radio station. I turn it up loud enough that anyone listening from the hall won't be able to hear more than the music if she and I are speaking in a normal tone.

She watches me and shudders. "Ick. I feel like he just violated me again."

I nod and wrap my arms around her. "You're safe, Jess." I sway gently with her and rest my cheek on her head as I hug her back. "There aren't any more cameras. I assure you. And I'll check every single time we re-enter the room. He won't see or hear anything we do or say. I promise."

She just nods as she yawns. "I don't think I can function any longer. I'm just foregoing a shower."

"Fair plan."

I lead her to the bed. We both crawl in fully clothed. Neither of us have the energy to change. I yawn as I pull the covers over us and pull her close to me. She settles into me and sighs. "He really is so crazy. It's scary."

"I know, but I'll protect you, peanut. I won't let him near you." I hug her a little tighter and closer and feel her relax more.

"So…, what's the plan? What do we do now?"

"I have to spend some time observing. I need to see if he has guards around the property. He expects me to have my crew around, so I'll get them over here later. I need to know if he's still got eyes on Jason's place now that we've all left."

"What do I do?"

"Stay at my side. Your job is to be a dutiful mafia wife. You do what I say when I say it. You portraying being a submissive girl to the big, powerful mafia boss will show him that this is serious. I'm really serious about taking over, and you're really serious about me."

"That doesn't sound like me."

I chuckle. "What you'll actually be doing is observing. If you see something, tell me. Even if you don't think it's significant, or feel like it's stupid. Tell me anyway. I'd rather you tell me something I already know than not tell me something I may have missed that's important."

She nods and cuddles into my arms. "Okay. I can do that."

"Other than that, sleep. We both need it."

She nods, and I close my eyes. It isn't long before she's passed out. Knowing she's safe in my arms as she sleeps gives me comfort, and I drift off quickly after her.

Chapter Thirty One

☒ Jessa ☒

(Three Days Later)

A few days after our arrival, I lay still as a statue in Alex's arms in his bed as my eyes adjust to the dark. I just woke up, and I swear I heard something. I hold my breath and listen.

Something makes a thudding noise outside the bedroom door, and I turn to wake Alex. I tap his shoulder and whisper, "Alex! Alex, wake up."

"Shh, Jess. I'm listening," he hisses against my ear as his grip around me tightens.

I should've known. He's always been a light sleeper. I curl closer to him. He squeezes me comfortingly. I try to keep breathing as shallow and steady as he is as we hear another thunk. It's louder than before and closer. Alex reaches under his pillow and grabs the gun he keeps there as he brings his lips close to my ear again.

"Go into the bathroom. Close and lock the door. Don't open it for anyone but me. Code word is peanut. If you hear me, but I don't use that word, don't open the door. Got it?"

I nod. "Got it."

"Quietly. Don't make a sound. Go." He gives me a gentle nudge, and I silently tiptoe to the bathroom. I close the door behind me and lock it with a whisper of a click. I don't turn on the light. I don't dare. Instead, I close my eyes and listen.

It feels like I've been in the bathroom for hours. I start to feel cold, and I'm forced to find a towel in the dark. Something, anything to wrap around me to keep away the chill. I'm scared to feel around and knock something over, but I'm shivering. I don't want my teeth chattering and giving me away.

I briefly consider running hot water and sitting in the tub to stay warm, but I know that running water would be an instant giveaway to my position. I'm mad at myself for my choice in sleepwear. The short bootie shorts and tank top I have on are thin. It's what I always wear. I didn't think. Not only does the thin material leave nothing to the imagination, it also provides no warmth.

After I quietly find a towel, I wrap it around my shoulders, hoping to stop the shivers. The tile on the floor is cold, too. I shift back and forth before deciding to move my way towards the shower where I know there's a bathmat. When I feel it under my feet, I breathe a soft sigh of relief.

I shiver for I don't know how much longer when I suddenly hear shuffling outside the bathroom door. Someone tries to open it. I hold my breath as I think of anything I can use to fend off whoever is trying to get through it. I want to sink to my knees and cower in fear, but I refuse.

"What the fuck do you think you're doing, old man?" Alex growls viciously. I almost sink to my knees in relief.

"Alex! I was just using the bathroom, but it seems the door is locked." Matthew's voice is sickeningly sweet, and I immediately want to throw up.

"You can't use your own bathroom?" Alex questions.

"Alex, put the gun down, son. Your room was closer. That's all. I didn't think you'd be this upset with your father using the bathroom."

"Helping you with that chest. It was a ruse so you could sneak in here with Jessa, wasn't it?"

"Alex, put the gun down. Jessa isn't even in here."

I can practically feel Alex's anger slamming into me in waves through the bathroom door. I can't see him, but I know him. I know how protective he is, and I know he's seething. What I don't understand is why I'm not terrified of him. I never have been terrified of Alex. At least not when he was Alex. It was after. It's obvious Alex can be just as scary as Matthew and the Lucinio family. Yet, here I am feeling safer than I ever have.

"I suggest you leave before I do what I should have done years ago." Alex's voice is dangerous. I tighten the towel around my shoulders.

"You think you can shoot me? I'm your father!"

"And she's my wife. Or damn near. I'll do anything to protect her. Even if it's from you. Get out."

"Are you aware how many guns you'd have on you if you pull that trigger?"

"Doesn't matter. You'd be dead. And she'd be safe."

"You'd kill your own father for some whore?" Matthew scoffs.

Something slams against the door with such force that I feel it throughout my body. I jump, covering my mouth with both of my hands to stop the scream. There are a few more thuds and grunts. I'm sure the two are grappling and fighting, but I have no idea who's winning. My heart says Alex, but tears sting my eyes anyway.

"Gavin!" Alex yells. "Get in here!"

There's more scuffling, and then I finally hear footsteps pounding into the room. Silent tears are streaming down my face. I keep my hands covering my mouth so no one can hear my gasps and whimpers.

"What the hell?" I hear Gavin's voice and give a silent thank you. At least now I know Alex has backup. There's another loud thud against the door like someone is being slammed into it. "What the fuck happened?"

"He came in here after Jess." Alex is gasping for air, and I whimper again. The thought of him being hurt shatters me.

"Where is she?" Gavin is panicked.

"Bathroom. I had her hide in there when I went to investigate that noise."

"What the fuck is he thinking? Is he insane?"

"I think insanity has long sailed. Get him the fuck out of here." Alex coughs. A few moments later, there's a soft knock on the door. "Peanut? You can come out now, honey."

I lunge for the door and unlock it, launching myself into his arms. He catches me and hugs me tightly. "Are you okay? I thought he was beating you up!"

"Me?" He laughs. "Jessa, have you seen me? I'm twice his size. He got a good hit in and had me in a headlock at one point, but he doesn't stand a chance next to me. Don't worry."

"What was he doing? Why was he even in here? What happened?"

He releases me and looks down at me. "He just wanted to get to you. He knew I'd investigate what the noise was, and you'd be here by yourself. He didn't count on me being smart enough to stick close or having you hide." He sighs and looks longingly at the bed. I shake my head and start walking towards it. He follows, and we crawl in. "Four in the morning is too early for this shit."

"Do you really think we'll be able to fall back to sleep after that? My heart is racing."

Alex tugs me closer to him and wraps his arms around me. His body wrapped around me is instantly soothing. "I have the guard's schedules down. My father isn't watching Jason anymore. He can't find Josh or my mom."

"How do you know?"

"I have a few sources who are close with him."

"How do you know they aren't telling you what you want to hear?"

He chuckles. It rumbles through my back, comforting me more. "That doesn't typically happen, Jess. Not only do I have leverage over them, but people don't tend to fuck with me."

I snuggle into his arms and sigh. "Sometimes, I forget the power you possess. I don't know how I got involved in mafia families, or why I'm not afraid. Well, of anyone except your dad."

He kisses the back of my head as I close my eyes. "My father has his guard down. I think we need to get everyone out here now and end this. Tomorrow would be perfect."

"Why tomorrow?"

"Because Sunday is my coronation."

I crease my eyebrows together in confusion. "Wouldn't he have more guards because of that?"

"He's cocky. He's getting what he wants, Jessa. He'll have more guards the day of. Not the night before."

I chuckle softly as I feel myself start to drift. "You've thought of everything."

"That's my job. Time to round everyone up and end this thing once and for all."

"Mmhmm…"

I lay in Alex's arms feeling safe and secure for the time being, but as I begin to fall asleep, I can't help but fear what's to come.

I know what happened between the Lucinio and Crane family many years ago. With Ryan in control of Crane Mafia now and having grown it to epic proportions over the years, I have no doubt who will come out on top.

The real question that weighs on my mind is will all of us survive it?

Chapter Thirty Two

⚔ Josh ⚔

I pace around Jason's living room waiting for Ryan. He called me over four hours ago and told me to meet him here. It didn't take me and the numerous guards he has on me long to get here, but he still hasn't graced us with his cocky presence.

I look at my watch. "Fuck," I mutter. It's already after two in the morning. I look over as Jason strides into the room carrying a couple sandwiches and coffee. I narrow my eyes. "Really? Food at two in the fucking morning?" My stomach picks that moment to betray me and growl. Loudly.

Jason laughs as he hands me one. "Yes. I'm fucking starving. And so are you, if that loud noise is any indication."

I can't help but laugh as I sit on the couch and take a bite out of the sandwich. I let out an involuntary moan and sigh as I chew. "Fuck. Prime rib is my favorite."

"Mine, too."

Jason and I eat in silence for a few moments before his phone starts ringing. He wipes his hands and answers it as he swallows the last bite of his sandwich.

"Where the fuck are you? I've been calling and texting for the past three hours." Jason glances at me as his expression darkens. "Fuck, you're not kidding, are you?" He sighs and rubs his temple. "There's no other option, Ry. We need to finish this, and she needs you." He leans back in the chair and takes a swig of his coffee while I watch him. I'm completely baffled. "See you soon." He hangs up.

I finish my sandwich. "What was that all about?"

"Long story, but to make it short, my brother has a thing for this girl, even though he won't admit it. She was just in a fucking fire, and he doesn't want her to be alone."

My eyebrows shoot up. "Oh, shit. She okay?"

"I guess we'll find out. He's on his way."

I nod and grab my coffee. I take a sip. Hot just the way I need it to be. "So, what's with this girl? Why doesn't he want to admit how he feels? Is it the same one he's always texting with a dreamy expression on his face?"

Jason smiles as his front door opens. "You see that, too, huh? You'll see."

I look up as Ryan walks in. A girl that can't be legal yet clings to him, and my eyes widen in shock. It has to be the sixteen-year-old he mentioned was just a friend. Obviously, I'm not the only one who saw through that shit.

The girl is exotically beautiful, even though she's crying hysterically and wearing nothing but thin pajama bottoms and a tank top. She has long, dark locks and wide dark eyes. She can't be more than five feet. Ryan engulfs her.

I completely understand why Ryan is head over heels for her, but I definitely understand the implications. "Fuck," I whisper.

"Jas, can you grab some of Jessa's clothes for her?" Ryan chokes out.

I've never seen him in a state where he doesn't exude control. Right now, I can see he's losing it and needs someone to step in. I don't want to say he might be about to cry, but I swear to fuck he is. Jason jumps up and jogs up the stairs.

I clear my throat. "Ry, why don't you take her to the guest bedroom I was in? It has a shower. She can get cleaned up while Jason gets clothes."

Ryan nods thankfully as he starts leading her down the hall. "Thanks, Josh."

I nod. A few minutes later Jason comes down with clothes. I direct him to the guest bedroom. He comes out moments later and sits. I finish my coffee and then set it on the table. "She really is young."

Jason nods. "Long, long fucking story. You only know a few pieces of it. I grilled him later on."

It takes Ryan a little while to come out. The girl is with him, refusing to let him go. He sits on the couch and tugs her down next to him. She curls into his side, and he puts an arm around her. She's calmed down considerably, but she's still gripping his shirt tightly in her palm.

"I just got the call," he says softly. He looks down at the girl before hesitantly looking back up at us. "I got everything taken care of. We need to leave now and get set up. I had some of my guys doing surveillance while Alex and Jessa have been staying there. All we need to do now is some observation. We go in tonight. After the sun sets."

The girl next to him whimpers a little, and we all fall silent. "I don't want to be alone," she whispers.

Ryan runs his fingers through her hair. "I know, sweetheart, but I don't have a choice. My family is in trouble."

She nods as she wipes her eyes. "I know. I understand."

"I'll bring you to my house on the way to the airport. You'll have Renza and her parents until I'm home."

I clear my throat, touched at seeing whatever the fuck is happening. I hate to interrupt, but Ryan needs this. "My dad's guards are loyal as fuck."

"We expected that," Jason says.

"We expected viciousness and loyalty for sure," Ryan says.

"You should also expect a shit ton of guards." I lean forward.

"Why?" Jason furrows his brow.

"Alex's coronation." Ryan sighs. "I have a lot of my guys there, but you're right. I think I need more guns. If it were me, I'd add more guards before the coronation. Peace of mind."

"I'll update the number of people traveling," Jason says as he takes out his phone.

Ryan stands near the door whispering in the girl's ear as he holds her close and sways with her. Every now and then, she nods and sniffles,

242

but her grip on him never lessens. Several moments pass as Jason updates numbers. Ryan finally leads the girl outside.

Within a few minutes, we're all piling into vehicles and driving to the airport. The girl is on her way to Ryan's house. Ryan is quiet as hell, lost in his own thoughts. I'd hate to leave, too, if the woman I was obviously in love with just went through a traumatic experience.

But the one thing at the forefront of my mind is finally ending my father once and for all.

As soon as we get to LAX and get off the plane, we all gather around Ryan. I take my place next to him because fuck if anyone here thinks I'm going to let him take total control of this mission. I don't care who he is.

"Everyone get checked into your rooms. I want you all to rest up. Be ready tonight," Ryan commands. "I'll take Josh, Jason, and Nick with me now. We need to stake some shit out."

I'm impressed he included me. I smirk to myself and bite my lip to keep from laughing. I'm not big into movies but there was one line of one that I don't know the name of that sticks out in my head. It's perfect for this situation.

Damn. What was that movie? *The Godfather*? No. Fuck, that ain't right.

Casablanca. That's it.

Maybe this will be the start of a beautiful relationship.

Hours later, the sun long set, I lie prone between Ryan and Jason on the ground. I'm getting more and more angry as the minutes go by, but I tamp the anger down and use it to center me. I've always been able to use it to my advantage. It makes me better on missions. I learned from Alex. He's always been able to shut everything else off and use that anger to make him lethal.

"Are you ready to do this?" Ryan asks. I don't take my eyes off my father's house.

"Six guards outside patrolling. Six on the outer perimeter. Thirteen inside. Two teams. You'll be leading one. I'm leading the other. Alex shuts his light out, we go." I keep my voice low and even, but even I can hear the furious edge.

Ryan chuckles. "You keep saying you'll kill your father if you come across him, but that's not going to be as easy as you think."

I chance taking a glance at him. "I know you don't know me as well as my brother, Ryan, but I won't hesitate to take the shot. This has to end. He's hurt so many fucking people, and he's gotten away with it for too long. I should've been brave enough to take him out years ago."

"You would've been killed instantaneously," Jason says.

"It would've stopped Jessa from getting hurt." I shrug.

"Still not the answer," Ryan says as Alex's light in his bedroom goes out.

"Time to do this." I silently get to my feet. My team follows.

Ryan's follows him. Together, we creep towards the house, silently shooting guards on the way. My dad has twenty-five guards here. I'm positive it's more than Alex anticipated, but he got us numbers to verify, which was very helpful to us. We outnumber my father's guards by three times.

After all of the guards on the outside have been taken out, Ryan and I split off. "Team Two, on my six," I growl into my earpiece.

Like a flock of geese, my team obeys. Ryan's team breaks off and follows him. He takes the front. I take the back. When I get to the backdoor, I look at my watch and wait impatiently. We decided on 1:27 in the morning to attack. It needs to be coordinated and stay on schedule in order to work, but the seconds ticking down so slowly piss me the fuck off.

Finally, the time comes, and the door opens. Damon stands on the other side and ushers us in. I follow stealthily behind him as he glances back at me. "We'll run into guards on the way to the meeting point. There's a total of thirteen," he whispers.

"We took out all twelve outside," I whisper back.

"That just leaves what's in here. Twelve down here, one upstairs. The one upstairs was paid off by Alex to watch your father."

As we round the corner, we meet a guard. I shoot. We all have silencers, so despite the soft pop, everything is relatively quiet, and no one is tipped off to our presence. After taking out a few more guards, we reach the meeting point at the bottom of the stairs.

A guard comes up behind Alex, who opened the door for Ryan, catching him off guard. Alex grapples with the guard for his gun. I shoot. The guard slumps to the ground, and Alex bends and puts his hands on his knees, panting.

"Fuck. Holy fuck," he gasps.

"You good?" I ask as I pat him on the back.

"I'm good."

I glance up the stairs before looking back at Alex. "Where's Jessa?"

"Locked in my bathroom upstairs. Anyone other than me, you, Jason, or Ryan go through that door, she screams. Her codeword is peanut. Say it before you enter, and she'll open the door. She's hiding in the cubby hole I always made you go to."

I nod before turning to the rest of the team. Time to split into smaller ones. "Lance and Gavin. Take your teams. Do a sweep. Make sure we're clear. Damon, take who's left, and do a sweep upstairs." I point to two random people. "You two. You're with me, Ryan, Alex, and Jason. Cover us while we go after our fucking father."

Everyone follows my orders. I'm sort of surprised at how natural they come. I usually take a back seat to someone like Ryan, or even Alex. Not because I'm afraid of them, but because I trust them to lead. In this case, it isn't that I don't trust them. It's that I want to become more comfortable in this position. I need to if I expect to take over and be anywhere near the type of leader Ryan or Alex are.

They do their sweep as we head upstairs. Alex takes out a straggler guard. After what seems like an eternity from when we left our hiding places to now, we finally get to my father's bedroom.

I signal for Ryan's guards that are with us to stay outside and guard the door. We enter the room and all flank the bed. That's the plan. Surround the son of bitch with guns drawn. But there's a huge fucking problem.

No one is in the bed.

I look over at Alex. "What the fuck?"

245

He looks just as confused as me. "Where the hell is he?"

"Check the bathroom," Ryan commands. "Any other rooms connect to here?"

"His office," I growl dangerously.

"He also has a hideaway room," Alex says.

"I got the bathroom." Jason walks towards the bathroom.

"I'll take the office," Alex says.

"That leaves us the hideaway." Ryan looks at me. "Where is it?"

I walk over to my mother's bookshelf that lines an entire wall and grab an elephant statue. I pull it forward. A door to the left of the bookshelf slides open. Ryan and I each enter with our weapons at the ready, but my father isn't in the room.

"Did he get tipped off somehow?" Ryan shakes his head in confusion as we leave the room.

"No one knows about this except my team," Alex says, joining us in the bedroom. "We made sure our phones weren't tapped. The only phone he tapped was Jessa's, and I removed that tap myself. The room was bugged and had a lot of cameras, but I checked every time we went back in there for anything else he may have tried to sneak by me. He tried a few times, but I found them all and crushed them."

"Where the fuck is he?" Jason asks as he walks back into the room.

"He had to have known somehow. He had to have gotten out." I grip my gun tightly. I want to rip apart the entire house to find him.

"No way, Josh. You know we have people out there. There are a lot of fucking eyes on this house. There's no way he got by us," Ryan says.

"Is there anywhere else he could hide?" Jason asks.

"Damon, Gavin, or Lance would've seen him," Alex answers. "They've been on him all day. The only time we didn't have eyes on him is when we let you guys in and broke into teams. Even then, I had a guard that I paid off watching him."

"Where's the guard?" Ryan asks. It dawns on all of us at once.

"Fuck! He wasn't out there!" Alex glares at the door.

"Then where is he?" Jason looks panicked.

"My guess is your father knew he was watching him. I bet we find him in a room nearby," Ryan says, trying to remain calm. I walk to the room across the hall and cautiously open the door. Ryan covers me. Sure enough, the guard is lying in a bloody heap on the ground.

246

A thought strikes me, and my heart starts slamming into my ribcage. "Where's Jessa?" I start moving towards the door, and Alex looks at me like I've lost my mind.

"I told you. She's locked in my bathroom. In the cubby hole I always hid you in."

At that moment, we hear a blood-curdling scream. My erratic heartbeat comes to a complete stop, and I quit breathing as I sprint out of the room.

"Fuck! Alex! Fucking get in here!" Damon yells from Alex's bedroom. Jessa screams again as we all start pounding down the hall.

I get to the bedroom first. Jason follows and Alex is close behind him. Ryan tries to get in before me, but I shove him back. I hear footsteps pounding up the stairs behind us, but all I can think about is getting through the door.

"What the fuck? I heard a scream that could've shattered glass!" I glance at Nick as he runs up behind us.

"He's fucking got Jessa!" Ryan yells. I can't breathe as I back up. Ryan immediately understands what I'm about to do. "Now!" he barks. We both kick the door at the same time. The frame splinters, but the door doesn't open. "Again! Now!" Ryan commands. We do it again.

A third time.

Fourth.

Finally, we're able to get the door open enough to shove our way through the door. I don't know what he had in front of it, and I don't care.

"Jessa!" I shout as we all rush into the room.

She's tied to the bed. Damon is knocked completely unconscious, and my father has his hands all over Jessa. He's cupping her pussy over her jeans, and I see red. I run to the bed. I yank my father off her and throw him against a wall with such intense force the wall ends up with a hole in the shape of his body. Jason runs to Jessa, and Alex joins me. He delivers a hard blow to my father's stomach. My dad's eyes nearly bulge out of his head in both shock and pain.

I smile with a sick glee. "I'm really going to enjoy this," I growl satanically.

"I told you if you fucking touched her, I'd kill you," Alex growls just as dangerously.

I throw our father on the floor and kick him so hard in the face, I can hear bones crack. Alex kneels next to him and pulls him to his knees. I smile sinisterly and kick him in the chest. He gasps. I punch him in the face several times in rapid succession. Alex watches me as I unleash everything I've had pent up for so many years.

All the hate.

Anger.

The fear.

Rage.

It all comes out as I beat my father down like he's done to me so many times.

"Finally. Finally after all these years, I get my revenge," I snarl.

I blackout as I hit and kick him. I know I'm screaming, but I don't care. I feel the hot tears rolling down my face, but I do nothing to stop them. I'm going to beat him to death, and I don't give a shit what kind of person that makes me. There's no one in this room who would blame me for what I'm doing. I know that.

I keep hitting and kicking, screaming all of my rage out, and not coming out of it until I feel myself being pulled off. I distantly hear Ryan's voice, but it takes me a long ass fucking time to stop fighting against him. My eyes are solely on my father. I watch the asshole slump to the floor as Alex gets up and stands in front of me.

"Josh. Look at me, bro. Hey… come on… look at me."

Breathing heavily, I blink a few times at Alex's voice. My arms are immobilized behind my back, and I glance back at Ryan. I pant.

"Josh. Me. Focus on me." Alex snaps his fingers.

I focus back on him as I shake my head. "I'm here."

"Thought I lost you for a minute there." Alex puts his hands on my face as Ryan lets me go.

I look down at my bloodied mess of a father. Jason is holding Jessa's face close to his chest. Damon is coming to, and the rest of Alex's team, my brothers, have made their way into the room. I don't know when.

I take a deep breath and look at my brother. "Jessa needs to leave. Now."

He nods, not taking his eyes off mine. He knows me. He knows me well enough to know I'm not going to hold back. She doesn't need to see what's about to happen. She doesn't need to see my father getting everything he deserves and so, so much more.

"Jason, get Jessa out of here. Bring her to one of the SUV's out front," Alex says.

Glancing at Jessa, I move towards my father. Alex and Ryan follow. We all hide the bloodied heap that is my father as Jason picks Jessa up in his arms and carries her out of the room. When she's gone, Ryan and Alex each take a step back. They know I need this. They understand I need to be the one to take the kill the shot.

I turn to my father and take out my gun. I aim at his head. Through his swollen, bloody eyes, I can see them widen in shock and realization.

"Josh," he sputters. He tries to hold up his hands but can't. He's too weak. Just like he made me feel over the years. "Please."

"You'll never get to hurt me again, you fucker." Words I've wanted to say for longer than even I realized. "You'll never get to touch Jessa or my mother again." Words I didn't know I needed to say. "You'll never get to threaten my brother or take another goddamn thing from me." Words that spilled from my heart. I narrow my eyes into a vicious and dangerous glare. "You'll never get to see the light of another day. I hope you burn in the hottest part of fucking Hell for everything you've done." My voice portrays all the rage and darkness I feel. All the pain and torment he's caused me over the years. "And I hope to hell that when I finally get down there myself, you'll be ready for me. Because that's when I'm going to tear you apart."

"Josh. No -"

I start shooting. I don't stop until my gun clicks, but I keep pulling the trigger, unblinking. Eventually Alex grabs my wrist. He says nothing as my eyes meet his. Ryan nods. They both lead me out of the room.

"Want a cleanup crew?" Gavin asks me. Me. Not Alex. Me.

I shake my head. "Fuck a cleanup crew. Burn this place to the ground."

"What about your mom?" he asks. "We'll need to get her a place."

"She needs to start over just as much as Josh," Alex says quietly.

Gavin only nods as we all leave the house.

A few minutes later, I look up as Alex hands me a pack of matches. "Thought you'd like to do the honors," he says. "Everyone is out. All of the dead guards are inside. The house is covered in gasoline. We cut

249

the gas lines so gas fumes are leaking into the house. We can watch it for a few seconds before we'll have to get the fuck out. It'll be an epic explosion."

I nod and light a match. I watch the flame for a moment before dropping it on the ground. It ignites a path of gasoline beginning at my feet. Moments later the entire house is engulfed in hot flames. It doesn't take long for the flames to grow into an inferno.

Alex tugs me into an SUV. As we pull away, I look behind me as the house does just what he says it will.

It blows up in fiery colors. The explosion is so fierce, the ground beneath us rumbles and shakes like we're driving along in a mini earthquake. It's a good thing we're far enough away because pieces of the house fly into the air like flaming torpedoes.

I hear sirens in the distance and can't help but laugh. By the time they get there, nothing will be left.

Not the house. Not the guards.

Not my father.

Nothing.

Chapter Thirty Three

☒ Jason ☒

It's hours later when we pull up to the hotel. We left the house, but neither of us would leave anyone behind. We pulled over outside the gate to wait. The house was fully engulfed when we all left and burned to the ground as we started driving away, everyone following. All of our vehicles with all of our guards drove away in some kind of fucking funeral procession. The explosion was the perfect ending to a long battle.

I carefully get out of the SUV. I refuse to let Jessa go. Which is just fine with us both because she refuses to let me go, too. Ryan and Nick are both standing together by the door when I get out, cradling her in my arms.

"She okay?" Nick asks. He brushes a strand of her hair out of her face as she clings to me.

I'm thankful they became so close. Even before Jessa and I were ever together, they had some kind of connection. Nick has been just as good for her as Cole. I look up as Alex and Cole run up to us. Josh is following close behind. He looks at me.

I smile. "She's good. Thanks to you."

Josh nods as Cole hugs Jessa despite her being in my arms. I have to shift a little, so I don't drop her at the extra weight. Ryan pats me on the back. Alex gives Jessa's leg a squeeze. Jessa hugs me tighter. I've gotten pretty good at reading her. I know she's overwhelmed, but I need to talk to Josh.

I look at Nick. "She needs to get out of here."

"Give her here. I'll get her settled in the room."

Jessa looks up at me as I start giving her to Nick. I lean down to kiss her for the hundredth time since I got her back. Letting her go is physical torture, but I want her out of here. She needs to be. "Cole, go with them." I command. Cole nods, seemingly grateful I gave the order for him to be with his friend. I watch as Nick and Cole take Jessa safely inside before I turn to Josh.

"Look, Jason, before you say anything -" Josh starts.

I hold up a hand to stop him. "Josh, I'm not going to say what you think I am." I hold out my hand to shake his.

He looks down at it a moment before he slowly takes it and clears his throat. "Whatever it is, I'm sorry."

I shake my head and can't help but smile. "Josh." I feel the tears sting my eyes as I shake his hand. "Thank you. Thank you for saving her. Thank you for being with her in that shed. Thank you for hearing her scream and getting that fucking asshole off my girl. I know I've been a hard ass. I know I was cold towards you while I was trying to figure you out, but you redeemed everything in my eyes." My voice cracks. "Everything."

"I... uh... I don't know about that. I have a long way to go." He nearly chokes on the words.

I pull him in for a hug and stand there for several moments with him, both of us taking whatever mysterious thing we need from each other. I know he did a fucked up thing, but he did it all with good intentions. Even if it spiraled out of his control.

It's not surprising really. He was being poisoned for years. I don't know how he had the strength to fight back the way he did. To find a way out. If I'm honest, I'm in awe of his courage and the amount of willpower it took to shake free of the control. I will forever be grateful to him for saving not only himself, but the love of my life, too.

Alex clears his throat. "I'll take care of Josh," he says. "Ryan, get Jason upstairs. Jessa needs him."

"Couldn't agree more," Ryan says. He pats me on the back again as Josh and I release each other. We head into the hotel.

I say nothing until I get to the elevator. "Fuck, what a night. I didn't think I'd ever get pulled back into mafia life." I lean against the elevator wall.

"I never wanted you to. It's my job to deal with this. The only reason I let you is because Jessa was involved. It's family. You're just like me. You'd do anything for family."

"You wouldn't have been able to keep me away," I say softly. I'm starting to feel the exhaustion.

"Don't I fucking know it."

"I'm going to marry her, Ry."

Ryan's head whips towards me. "What?"

I nod as I smile and take out a little black box from the pocket of my tactical pants. I open it, revealing a one karat diamond ring on a platinum band. "Yes. I'm going to marry her."

Ryan chuckles. "Never fucking in a million years did I ever think that was going to happen."

"Neither did I." I glance at my brother and see him looking down at the floor with a faraway smile on his lips. "Looks like you aren't far behind me."

He shakes his head. "Arianna is off limits. She's too young for me and far better than all of this. That girl has dreams to get away, and I'll do what it takes to make it happen."

"Love is mysterious, Ryan." The elevator doors open, and Ryan steps out before me, glancing around before he allows me off. It's a habit. Him and Nick have always gone into rooms before me and checked our surroundings before they let me in. I've learned to accept it.

"Love isn't for me. I live a far too dangerous life to bring anyone into it."

"Ryan, I don't think you'd be able to stop it if you tried." I open the door to my room and look back at him as I gesture into it. "I couldn't."

Ryan says nothing as I walk into the room behind him. I close the door behind me and secure it before I head to the suite's bedroom. Nick and Cole are sitting on the couch. I completely forgot about them. All I want right now is Jessa.

They both get up and leave without me saying a word. Ryan leads them out after he does his own sweep of the suite. I go back to lock the door behind them, then make a beeline for the bedroom. Jessa is curled up reading a book.

She looks up as I close the door behind me. "Everything okay?"

I smile as I kneel down next to her. She gives me a quizzical look. I take her hand. "When I first saw you, I knew there was something special about you, Jess. I paused in the doorway the day of your interview. I don't know if you knew that. You took my breath away. All I saw was the back of you. If I'm being honest with myself, I was in love with you right then. You hadn't even turned around.." I take out the ring and slide it slowly on her finger as I watch her face. Her eyes light up and widen as she looks at it. "Marry me. Let's spend the rest of our lives making each other the happiest we can possibly be. And then some."

Her other hand goes up to her mouth, and she nods as tears well up in her eyes. "Yes. Jason, yes!" She throws her arms around me, and I climb into the bed next to her, hugging her as tightly as I can. I bury my face in her hair and breathe her in, thankful to have this beautiful woman in my life.

✗✗✗

(Three Weeks Later)

Less than a month later, I look up as Jessa's music starts. *When I Saw You* by Mariah Carey. The song is perfect for us, but I pay absolutely no mind to it. Not when the most beautiful woman I've ever seen has locked her eyes on mine and is walking down the aisle to me.

Her white, low-cut dress clings to her hips. The satin material moves with her every motion. Her hair flows down her back in cascading waves. The diamond encrusted tiara she wears on her head catches the light and somehow makes her look more radiant, if that's even possible.

"She's fucking beautiful," Ryan whispers next to me. I can't speak. I can barely even breathe as I watch my soon to be wife stop in front of me. We didn't want to wait to get married. We know we're it for each other.

"Who gives this woman to this man?" the officiant asks.

"We do," Alex says as he motions to Cole.

Cole puts Jessa's hand into mine and looks in my eyes. "Take care of her. I don't care that your brother is some big bad mafia boss. I'll kick your ass if you hurt her."

I laugh as I nod. "Understood." Cole and Alex both smile as they take their seat. I keep Jessa's hand in mine as we stand in front of the officiant. He goes through the beginning of the ceremony, but I doubt Jessa has heard a word he's said. I know I haven't.

I glance at him as he clears his throat. "The rings?" Ryan materializes next to me with the rings, and we each do as we're told, slipping them onto each other's finger. We repeat our vows to each other in a daze.

I can't see anything but her. I can't take my eyes away from hers. I can only hear her breathing; my own heartbeat. All I can feel is her hand in mine; her breath against my skin. All I can think about is her soft voice telling me how much she loves me; how she'll love me for the rest of her life. When the officiant tells me to kiss my bride, Ryan has to push me forward slightly because I'm so lost in her, I don't even know where I am.

When my lips meet hers, she lets out a soft moan as she closes her deep blue eyes. Cake batter lip gloss. I fucking love it. Her tongue slips between my lips and teases mine. I deepen the kiss, lifting her petite body off the ground as I wrap her tightly in my arms. I'm vaguely aware of the applause and hoots and hollers. I barely feel Ryan patting my back.

I reluctantly pull away and set her gently on her feet. "I'll love you all my life, Mrs. Crane."

She reaches up to touch my cheek. I lean into her satiny smooth hand. "And I'll love you for all of mine, Mr. Crane."

We walk hand in hand up the aisle as everyone starts throwing pink carnation petals in the air. Jessa laughs as they land in her hair and on my shoulders. We run out and jump into the waiting limo.

Jessa curls into my lap and tilts her head up to kiss me. I can't believe how far we've come in such a short period of time. It's only been a couple months since that fateful day forced me to admit just how much I love this woman.

How much I need her.

I can't live without her, and I don't want to try.

Thank fuck I won't ever have to.

Jessa is the perfect love story.

My perfect love story.

The End

Bonus Chapter!

✗ Josh ✗

(One Week After Jason's and Jessa's Wedding)

I scrub my hands over my face as I plop myself down in Gavin's office chair. I lean my head back against the cold leather and close my eyes as I shake my head. "Fuck," I whisper to the room.

Moments later, I hear the door open, a low chuckle, and another soft click as the door closes once more. I don't bother opening my eyes. I know it's Gavin. "You look comfortable," he rumbles.

"Restless. Fucking restless," I answer.

Gavin sits as I open my eyes again., rubbing them. "Did you think about what I said?" He folds his arms over his chest.

"About taking a vacation? Unwinding?"

"It's a good idea. Considering what you've been through, I think time to yourself might be wise. Clear your mind. Doc says you're clear of the serum. You should be feeling more like yourself. When you come back from relaxing, we can do what Alex suggested. Train. Get you back in mafia shape."

I chuckle as I lean forward. I rest my arms on the desk and fold my hands. "I was never *out* of mafia shape."

Gavin smiles, but it's pained as he looks at my hand. "How's the hand?"

I sigh as I flex it. I'm coming back to myself little by little. The pain I was feeling over the past several weeks has lessened immensely. The only thing I feel now is frustration, emptiness, and a blinding rage.

And numbness in my hand. "It's getting there." It's a fucking lie. It's not getting there. I can barely grip my gun with it.

"Doc said it would take time. Train. Get back the muscle memory."

"Yeah." I remember him more talking about nerve damage that could be permanent and the possibility of me needing to train myself to shoot left-handed instead of right. I stand and walk to the window that overlooks his property.

I've been staying with Gavin and finding a place for mom and I to live. She's struggling as much as I am, but on a whole different level. I have Alex, Gavin, and Damon. I have Cole and Lance. I have her. I have Ryan and his family, who have come to accept me just as much as Alex.

She only has us. Her four boys, as she calls us. Me, Alex, Damon, and Gavin. Sometimes, she includes Lance and Cole in there. She's never really had the chance to grieve for the loss of her family. They all abandoned her before marriage and never bothered to try and help her afterwards. I'm going through a lot of emotions right now, but she's going through many of the same.

She also wants nothing at all to do with the mafia. Whenever we try to tell her anything about what happened that night, all she says is she trusts us and doesn't want to know. It works out well for all of us. We don't want her to know anyway.

But I refuse to allow her to be on her own. She's insistent that she needs her own space, but she'll have all she needs. Just in my home. Not like I'll be there much anyway. She'll have people there to protect her when I'm not with her. She won't be completely by herself. If she feels anything at all on the inside as what she portrays on the outside, I honestly fear for her safety. From herself.

I turn with a raised eyebrow when I hear something rustling behind me. Gavin is sticking a world map on the accent wall behind his desk. When he's finished, he bends and takes something from the bottom drawer of his desk.

"What are you doing?" I ask.

He shrugs as he opens a box. He takes out a single dart. "Getting you the fuck out of here. You need it, Josh. You know it. We all know it. Time to quit talking about it and do it."

I bark out a non-humored laugh. "I can't just up and leave, Gav. What the fuck? Do you know how much shit I have to do now that I'm officially sworn in?"

"Yep. I do. But it can wait. Me, Ryan, Damon, Lance, and Alex can start weeding out the good guys among the bad within our mafia while you're gone."

"And how would that look? Alex doing my job? A guy from another mafia helping him out? While I'm off fucking running away from it all?" I shake my head. "No. No. Fuck no. Not happening."

Gavin sighs. "Dude. You know how I feel about you. You know you're like my brother. You know how fucking guilty I feel for not seeing the shit that was happening. We all do. I'm not telling you this as a friend or as some dude who works for you. I'm telling you this as your brother." He pauses as he plays with the dart in his hand. He takes a breath. "You've been through more shit than any of us can imagine, bro. Nobody, and I mean no-fucking-body, is going to fault you for needing to take a fucking breather to get your mind right. A week. Hell, a month. Just… anything, Josh. Anything to just be on your own working through this. Write shit down that you want to come back and talk to us about. Fuck, I'll even let you yell and scream at us. But you need to… just…" He trails off and shrugs.

I lean against the window and fold my arms across my chest as I nod. "I get it, Gav. I do. But I can't just leave. There's a lot of work that needs to be done."

He nods. "I agree. But you're not in the right frame of mind for it."

One thing I've always liked about Gavin is that he always tells it like it is. It's one of the reasons I've been toying with an idea that I've been struggling to ask him. I don't know if the two of us are, or ever will be, back to the point we once were. I'm holding out a small glimmer of hope, but I have far too much guilt to believe the four of us will ever be that close again. Like we were growing up.

I chuckle and shake my head as I walk towards him. "Fucking

260

asshole. You did that on purpose."

He feigns shock but smirks. "What did I do?"

He knows, but I fill him in anyway as I take the dart and point it at him with narrowed eyes. His smirk turns to a full grin. "You just made me realize how much I'm wrestling with an immense level of guilt and very low confidence in myself."

He mock gasps and puts his hand over his heart. "I did all that?"

I laugh, genuinely this time. "You know you did." I look down at the dart in my hand. "Which is why…" I pause and take a shaky breath. Gavin says nothing. He just watches me. I smile a little and meet his eyes again after a few moments. "What do you think about being my second in command?"

He grins and gives me another mock gasp. "You mean you're choosing me over Alex fucking Lucinio? I'm so honored."

I laugh again. "You know he doesn't want this."

Gavin smiles. "So, you want to subject me to a life of servitude to your ugly, vindictive ass?"

I laugh. "I'd believe all that sarcasm, but you live for this shit. You're just as fucked up as me. You followed Alex because he's family, but you love this as much as I do."

He grins. "What can I say? I'm a glutton for punishment. Of course I'll be your second. You can swear me in and all that shit before you get out of here." He turns towards the map. "Now. Take your shot, Lucinio. You're going wherever the dart lands. I'll make the arrangements myself if it means you do what you need to and take a damn break."

I laugh, feeling a little better and a lot grateful that Gavin pulled me out of my funk. I turn towards the map and eye where I want it to land so I can aim. "Where's Alex?"

"With your mom. They're looking at a penthouse for Alex. He doesn't want a house."

I chuckle. "He never has. He likes penthouses. I don't get why he doesn't just use the one above his office at Lucinio Tech."

Gavin laughs. "That's what Damon and I told him before he left. Honestly, I think he's just entertaining your mom at this point. She's having fun helping him find a place. He hasn't shown her the one above his office yet."

"She's just happy to have him home. She had me this whole time, despite everything. She's missed Alex a lot. Fuck, she's missed all of you a lot. So, have I." I give him a grin and aim for Rome.

He grabs my arm. "We missed you, too. Now, you know me well enough to know I ain't fucking allowing you to just pick a place and aim for it. I've played darts with you enough to know you won't miss. Shut your eyes."

I groan and do as he says. But I memorize the map first. It's like my mind takes a snapshot of the room and map, calculates where I am in relation to the map, then figures out exactly how I need to line up my shot.

"Fine." I shift slightly and go to aim again, but Gavin is way too much of an asshole to just let me go to Rome.

"Yeah. Right. I also know you can hit a bullseye with your eyes closed. Fuck all of that." He grips my shoulders and spins me in several circles.

"You asshole. Fuck you." I smile. "What if this lands in the ocean?"

"Then… I guess you'll be buying a yacht."

I laugh. "I hate boats."

"Oh, I know. But I don't make the rules."

"I changed my mind. I'm using Lance as my second."

Gavin laughs. "You are not. You love me too much. You know I'm made for a job like this. Besides, I can guarantee Lance would make himself as annoying as possible because you took him away from his precious toys." He stops me. "Now. Keep your eyes closed."

I growl low, but I keep my eyes closed. I'm a little dizzy, but I focus on the snapshot in my mind and stumble just a little as I widen my stance. I let my body relax and focus on Rome. Rome is peaceful this time of year. I need that. Peace.

I let out a breath and let the dart fly. I open my eyes with a grin, confident I hit Rome. "See? Fucking…" I trail off with wide eyes when I see where the dart landed.

Gavin lets out a roar of laughter. "Gainesville, Florida!"

"Where… the… fuck… even is Gainesville, Florida?"

"Well, according to the map? Northish. Cheer up. It's home of the Florida Gators. You love that team. Go to a game. I'll get you tickets. I know of a club there, too. Quiet, but the show is nice."

"I'm not going to a fucking strip club."

He laughs. "Not a strip club. You'll like it. It's upscale. Which means good beer."

"Do you even know me? I hate upscale shit."

"But you'll love this place." Gavin has the audacity to wink as he turns to leave. "I'll get it set up! You get packed, boss!"

"Don't fucking call me boss!" I yell after him. His laughter fades down the hall. I grunt and glare at the dart that betrayed me. "Gainesville." I shake my head. "Maybe I'll just change the flight plan."

✗✗✗

I sigh as I get off the plane after it lands at Gainesville International Airport. Apparently, there's some kind of law against changing a flight plan in midair. According to the Captain, anyway. I know better than that, but Gavin must have ordered him to not do it no matter how damn much I protested or threatened. I guess he still knows me pretty well and knows I wouldn't shoot the Captain for not doing what I say, even though I did tell him I would. He just laughed. I need a new staff.

I grumble as I climb into the backseat of the idling SUV. The driver says nothing as he waits for my luggage to be loaded. I didn't bring a lot because I really don't want to be away for that long. I'll concede I need the break, but I won't disappear for a long period of time. Definitely not when we're in a transition stage.

Gavin is right, though. Hell, they all are. Even my mom has told me I need to get away. It was probably her pleading more than anything that finally got me to relent to Gavin in the first place, but I won't tell her that. She'll think she can make me do anything. The thought makes me smile a little because she knows she can. Out of the four of us, I'm definitely the mama's boy. The toughest by far, but I'd kiss the ground my mom walks on if she asked me to.

The driver hands me an envelope as he starts driving. "There are tickets to the Gator's home game this Saturday in there. There's also a membership certificate to Sapphire's."

"What's Sapphire's?"

"It's a really good restaurant to start. The burgers and steaks are to die for. But getting a reservation is impossible unless you're a member.

You'll like it. I don't like to make promises, but hell. I'll promise you on that. I'd be jealous as hell of the membership, but I got one myself."

"Must be the club Gavin was talking about," I mumble.

"Uh. Yeah. Club. Sort of. It's a club where submissive women can find dominant men. If you're into that. Or where submissive men can find dominant men or women. Or -"

"I get it. I get it," I say, cutting him off with a hand up. I chuckle and shake my head. Fucking Gavin really does have my number. I guess he knows I lean more towards submissives. Not just women I can dominate and control in bed. Though, that's fun, too. At least for a night.

A few minutes later, the driver pulls up in front of a building. I'm impressed by how discreet it is. Most of the clubs I'm used to like this in L.A. are a lot more flashy. Definitely not as covert. And there are usually long lines to get in.

"When you go in, give your last name to the hostess and tell her you're on the red list."

"Got it." I shake my head. Red list. Red room. So fucking cliche. I start to get out of the SUV.

"I'll be parked across the street."

I nod and close the door behind me. I shove the envelope in my back pocket as I stride towards the door. Just as I'm about to open it, though, a guy with a scowl on his face strides out. He's pulling the most beautiful woman I've ever seen, Jessa included, behind him. Her hair is tied loosely to the side of her head. She's wearing a purple t-shirt that clings to her curves with a pair of black skinny jeans that look as if they're painted on. She's not wearing an ounce of makeup. Her beauty is breathtaking and completely natural.

But there are two problems. The first one is that she's obviously trying not to cry. The second is that she's tense as fuck and biting her lip so hard, I can see the blood. Which means this entire situation is all wrong.

Instincts kick in. I follow them like second nature. I take her hand and tug her gently but hard enough towards me that the fucker pulling her with him releases his grip. She slams into my chest with a squeak and wide eyes.

The idiot she's with turns towards me with fury in his stare. "What the fuck?" he growls.

"Lyric!" someone yells as they come out of Sapphire's.

I don't look at him, though. My eyes are focused solely on the douche glaring at me. "Walk away," I say through gritted teeth with a dangerous tone. "Now." My hand falls to her hip. I pull her closer as she turns her face into my chest.

She needs to feel protected. It's obvious I portray that to her. What I'm shocked as hell to feel, though, is the instant connection I have with her. My hand on her hip. Her pulled into my body. The way she just... fits. The way every part of me reacts to her. Like she's already mine, even though I don't have a goddamn right to feel any kind of claim on her. I don't even know her.

But I'm not the only one who seems to be having a reaction. While the shiver down my spine and the quickening of my pulse was all internal, Lyric shivers and burrows even closer. I can feel her heartbeat. My mind is trying to convince me she's just panicking, but the dominantly possessive motherfucker is screaming she's feeling the exact same thing.

I found my girl and wasn't even looking.

It all forces me to take a deep breath. I have to do something to control myself and get my body in check before it betrays me.

The guy takes one look at me and runs the other direction. The person who ran out after the girl, whose name must be Lyric, stands next to me glaring after him. Lyric cries quietly as she grips my shirt. I don't think anyone would realize it's happening, but I can feel the subtle rise and fall of her chest against mine.

"Jesus, Lyric. I'm sorry. That happened so quickly. I spilled a drink and broke a couple glasses in my rush to get out here," the guy says.

"Kieran! Get your ass back in here!" someone else says as he pokes his head out the door. "Fuck! We're getting slammed in here!"

"Hang the fu-"

"Go. Go, Kieran. I'm okay," Lyric whispers. She doesn't move. "I'll text you later."

Kieran, obviously torn, looks between Lyric, me, and the dude yelling at him from the door. "Fuck." He runs his fingers through his hair.

"I got her," I say. "It might not mean much, but I got her. She's safe. And judging from the fact that she hasn't moved, I'd say she feels it. Go by her body language. Not my words."

After a few moments, he leans in and kisses Lyric on the head. "I'll call Luca. Are you going home?"

She shakes her head, keeping her grip on me tight. "He's not there. He's out of town. I... don't... I can't... be..."

"Alone," Kieran finishes. "Fuck."

"Kieran! Come on!" the guy yells again.

I shoot him a glare. "Get back to the bar!" I command dangerously.

He glares right back but goes inside, leaving us alone. Kieran rubs up and down Lyric's back as he looks at me. "Can you just stay with her until I get off work? Her brother is out of town. She's..." He sighs.

I look down at Lyric before back at Kieran. "I get it. I understand. A woman I'm close to has similar things happen. I got her."

He nods and hugs Lyric. "Call me," he whispers in her ear. She nods. He hurries inside.

Lyric lets out a breath and sniffles. "This always happens, you know. You should run away."

I raise an eyebrow and glance across the street. The driver is watching intently, ready to step in if he needs to. Good. I like efficiency. "Why would you say something like that, butterfly?"

She sniffles and looks up at me. "Butterfly?" she asks quietly. Her eyes are as beautiful as she is. Hazel with flecks of gold. Mesmerizing.

The girl is astonishingly pretty. I could stand here and look into her eyes with one arm around her waist for the rest of my life. It gives my other hand freedom to do whatever it wants. Like brush across her face, or push stray strands of her soft hair out of her eyes. Much like it is right now. It's when she leans into my hand that I jerk back, though.

I realize far too late, and only when she flinches, my mistake. "I didn't mean to do that," I say, voice raspy. The fuck is the matter with me? Why am I stumbling all over myself? I've never in my life been like this with a woman.

"It's okay," she whispers as she looks down. She has no idea I can feel the shaky breath she inhales and exhales slowly. She looks back at the building. "I can probably hang out in the breakroom until Kieran is done."

I clear my throat. "I don't want that. Not at all, butterfly." I wait until she looks back up at me. "But if that's what you want..."

Holy shit, please say that's not what you want, I think to myself.

She looks down at her feet. When she realizes she's still gripping my shirt, she yanks her hand back with wide eyes. "I... don't... want that."

I glance back at my driver then down at her. It gives me a chance to gain my damn confidence back. "I just got into town. I don't even know where I'm staying. Want to take me on a tour? I have a driver who probably could, but you're a lot prettier and more fun to talk to." The words come out confident, cocky, a little dominant, and a lot flirty. No one would ever be able to tell I'm shaking inside, terrified she'll tell me to go fuck myself.

She nods. "I'd like that," she says so softly and submissively that my dick is instantaneously standing at attention. Christ, I had no idea how much I needed a woman like her.

Without another word, I lead her to the SUV and help her inside. I climb in next to her and direct the driver to go wherever Lyric wants him to so she can show me her favorite places around the city. I could listen to her talk every second of the day. As she's telling me about the places we stop, I barely take my eyes off her long enough to look at what she's showing me.

A little voice in the back of my head asks me what the fuck I'm doing. I'm not ready for this. I'm not ready for a relationship. I'm not even ready for a quick fuck. I know as sure as my own damn name that one time with this girl would never be enough anyway. She'd never be a one-night stand. Which is why I have no right at all to be in this SUV with her.

But there's no way I'll be able to walk away.

XXX

Much, much later that night, or really early in the morning by what the alarm clock in my suite says, Lyric and I are tangled together in my bed. Our lips crash together. Our tongues dance a sexy Rumba. I suck lightly on hers as I tangle my fingers in her hair. I lock my other arm around her beautiful, petite body and hold her against me tightly.

Lyric moans and spears her fingers in my hair. She tugs lightly as her other hand grips my shoulder. She grinds herself against my dick, and I groan, kissing her harder and deeper. I arch into her and let her dry-hump me until I know neither of us will last much longer.

"Way too many clothes," she whispers against my lip.

I kiss down her jaw to her neck. "Couldn't agree more. Lose

267

them."

She sits up, straddling me and pulls her shirt off shakily. My eyes zero in on her perky tits clad in a purple, satin bra. There's no underwire, like most I've seen, but it still hugs her like a glove and supports her supple tits enough to make my mouth water.

I sit up, pulling off my shirt and tossing it. She wraps her arms around my shoulders and grinds down on me again as she starts kissing me. Holy hell, I can't get enough of this girl. She was shy when we were driving. Even shyer when we got out and started walking around a park. When we got up to my suite, everything I said made her blush.

But when I kissed her, it's like I opened Pandora's Box. She let everything loose. I can tell she's completely inexperienced. She's probably never had sex with anyone in her life. But she kisses like she's letting her heart guide her. For everything else, she's given complete control to me.

I fucking crave it.

I flick the clasps on her bra and pull it off. She releases her grip only long enough for me to remove it and throw it with the rest of our clothes. Her tongue plunges back into my mouth. I've learned really quickly it's her way of wanting me to dominate the kiss. Me to lead her.

So, I do.

I grip her hips and flip her. She falls on the bed with a squeak I'm coming to find is one of her sexiest sounds. I immediately straddle her, pinning her wrists above her head, and lean down to kiss her. This time, it's my tongue that plunges into her mouth. Her eyes fall closed. She totally submits to the kiss, tangling her tongue with mine again, and softly whimpering.

"I can't get enough of you," I rumble as I kiss down her jaw to her neck. I smile when I reach her carotid artery. Her pulse is thrumming for me. "How submissive you are. How responsive you are to me. How fucking good you taste."

She writhes, arching into me, but I reach down and splay my hand just under her stomach right at the waistband of those sexy as fuck jeans I'm about to peel off of her. I push her gently down, pinning her to the bed while I kiss down her collarbone to her perfect, already hard peaks.

She tries to arch into me, but I hold her down. "Josh…"

"I'm taking my time with you, butterfly. Be my good girl, and I'll make it all worth the wait."

Her breath hitches, and she jerks when my mouth finally reaches her sensitive nipples. I let my other hand trail up her body until it reaches her other tit while I lick her nipple. She shivers then jerks again when I suck one into my mouth at the same time I tug the other and roll it between my thumb and forefinger.

"Ah! Oh!" She moans. Her head falls from side to side. I kiss across her chest to her other breast, switching the hand I'm holding her wrists with, and lavish that one with the same amount of attention. With my free hand, I tug her nipple and play with it while I'm sucking the other one.

"You're fucking soft everywhere."

I nip her nipple. She gasps. I let go of her wrists, and she immediately has her fingers in my hair. The other grips the sheets as she whimpers. I kiss down her stomach, pausing at her bellybutton as I flick the button on her jeans open. I tug down her zipper as I kiss and lick her skin, giving her soft nips here and there.

She really is soft everywhere. Her skin is silky smooth. She's small. She could stand to gain weight, but she's still perfect to me. I lick my way down lower, expecting to find a pair of silky panties to match that satiny bra, but I'm very surprised when my tongue meets even more soft skin.

Fuck. She waxes.

I look up at her in shock. "No panties?"

She blushes a furious shade of red as she looks down at me. "They make me feel uncomfortable," she whispers in utter embarrassment.

I groan and grip her hips as I kiss her thigh. "I really want to taste you, Lyric. I want to be your first."

She gasps. "How did you…? I mean, I'm… Just… how?"

I can't help but laugh at her adorableness. "Am I wrong?"

She shakes her head, blushing even darker. "No, but I…" She closes her mouth.

I raise an eyebrow. "But you…" I don't like the tears that immediately fill her eyes.

She sits up so quickly that she almost falls backwards. "This was a mistake," she whispers. She shakes her head and tries to pull away.

Knowing exactly where her mind just went, I do the one thing I know she needs. I struggle slightly with myself, but it's not exactly with her consent. But if she freaks out or says no, I'll stop in a heartbeat.

I dive into her pussy with my tongue. I know the reason she thinks this is a mistake is because she thinks she's inexperienced. That I won't want her because of it. She's thinking that because I picked up on her being a virgin means she's doing, or has done, something wrong.

What she doesn't know is that I picked up on it because of the attentiveness to what she's doing. She hesitated in kissing me, but quickly gained confidence in that. When we got to the bedroom, she immediately went for the button on my pants, but shied away from it. Most would think it's her natural submissive nature, and it might be a little because of that, but it's more. Lyric has an extreme innocence about her. Exasperated by the submissiveness.

She's fucking perfect.

"Oh fuck! Josh!" Lyric falls back on the bed as I lick her. Her fingers spear my hair and tug. I groan into her pussy, sending vibrations through her. She bucks into me with a sexy little whimper.

My tongue darts in and out of her pussy as I suck and nibble. My dick strains against my jeans until I have absolutely no choice. I reach down and push my jeans down. Lyric fumbled with my zipper and button earlier, but she finally got the zipper down and the jeans undone. And then I ravished her mouth again until we both forgot what she was doing.

Thankfully, she did that part for me, though. It's easier to pull my cock and start stroking. I growl and groan into her pussy. She moans and whimpers as my voice sends vibrations through her. I start stroking my dick with one hand. With my other arm, I position it over her stomach and hold her down gently. I set my thumb against her clit and rub in smooth circles. I give her a little pressure and rub at the same furious pace I'm tongue fucking her.

"Ah! Oh, Josh…"

"Holy fuck…," I groan. I stroke my dick faster, twisting my wrist and squeezing it. Her sweet moans and sexy whimpers are enough. But her pussy clenching and gripping my tongue as it erratically pulses makes my dick thicken almost instantly. Fuck, I wish it was my dick inside her instead of my tongue. It might kill me, but I'll wait. I know she'll be worth the torture.

"Josh… Sir… I'm… I need…"

I groan into her pussy at hearing her call me sir. "Not yet, baby.

I'm almost there."

"Yes, sir... Oh!"

I groan again. Sir. It's the sexiest fucking thing I've ever heard. If I didn't already think this beautiful woman was perfect for me, I would now. My cock thickens even more as I stroke myself faster and harder, nipping and sucking her pussy.

She gets wetter and wetter as she writhes and bucks into my tongue. When she clamps down on me is when I know she's done. Which is all good with me because I'm there. My spine stiffens. My dick hardens impossibly more. My stomach clenches. A jolt shoots down my spine straight to my dick.

"Oh, Josh... Sir! Please! I need to come, sir! Please, please," she begs.

Her begging is what sends me violently careening off the ledge, but I won't come before she does. "Come, butterfly. Let me see this pretty little pussy come for me." I lick her furiously as I rub and flick her clit.

"Ah! Josh! Sir!" Lyric screams and pants. Her stomach clenches as hard as her pussy. "Josh!" She grips my hair tighter. She pulls me into her pussy, and I grin as I lick her, suck, and nip. I keep stroking my cock as her release washes over her.

Needing to feel her come completely undone, I release my grip on her. Just like the good girl she is, she gives me what I want. She bucks her hips into me with every spasm of her pussy. She soaks my tongue and arches into me when I start lapping everything she gives me up with low moans and groans.

Finally reaching my own limit, I kiss her pussy and pull back slowly as she comes down. I settle myself between her legs. She watches me shyly and curiously. Her pretty eyes travel down my body and to my cock. I stroke it a little faster, but I don't take my eyes off hers.

"Holy fuck, Lyric," I moan as I start spurting all of me onto her stomach. Jets of my come hit her skin. She whimpers. For a second, I think I fucked up, but then I see her lick her lips. It's not possible for her to be any more perfect. "Fuck, baby."

I slow my strokes as she trails her fingers through my come. She slowly brings her fingers to her mouth as her eyes gradually meet mine once more. She sucks me off of her with a soft smile, and I about lose another load.

"Yummy," she whispers.

I grin and shake my head. "It's not possible for you to be any more fucking perfect, butterfly." I don't bother packing myself away as I crawl off the bed. Instead, I drop my underwear and jeans. I walk to the bathroom naked as she gasps.

I quickly clean myself up as I let the water in the sink run for her. When it's warm enough, I wet down a cloth. On my way back out, I grab a bottle of water from the minifridge in the bedroom. I put it on the nightstand and crawl back into the bed, settling on my knees at her side. I start cleaning my come off her stomach.

"Why do you call me butterfly?" she asks shyly.

I smile. She asked earlier, but I never told her why. Distractions and all. "Because you're beautiful. And I can sense a transformation on the horizon for you. Hell, for me, too. Because butterflies are a symbol of transformation and hope. You, baby, are my hope."

I lean down and kiss her forehead before getting up. I hand her the water bottle after opening it for her and head for the bathroom once more. I rinse out the cloth and hang it to dry. By the time I reach the bed again, Lyric is shyly snuggled under the covers. I crawl in next to her and pull her into my arms.

"You saw all of that so quickly?" she asks with a yawn into my chest.

I hug her tighter. I haven't told her a lot about myself yet. I'm not even sure where I want to start. All I know is I felt something right away with her. If there's one thing I've learned over the years from Jessa, it's that fate always plays a hand in everything. I may not understand it. I don't even trust it. Leaving my future in the hands of fate is some kind of fucked up bullshit I'll never be a part of.

But not even I can deny that fate has a hand in a lot of life. I wasn't going to come to Gainesville. I planned on Rome. Italian girls who have no fucking clue who I am. Someone I can leave after I'm done. Peace. Relaxation. As far away from all things Lucinio Mafia as I can get.

That dart landing here was complete fate. I did everything in my power to make it land where I wanted it to. But if it had, Gainesville would have never been on my radar. I wouldn't have shown up when I did at Sapphire's and seen the girl of my dreams being dragged outside.

Fuck. I wouldn't have felt the connection I did with her. I don't doubt for a second this connection is once in a lifetime. I thought I felt it with Jessa at one point, but it was nothing like this. It didn't feel like a zap of electricity so powerful that I was thrown backwards from it.

I won't say Lyric is the love of my life. This isn't like it was with Jessa and Jason. Not an instant love kind of thing. But I can say that this is worth exploring. Because connections this strong don't just happen with everyone.

It feels different with her.

I chuckle a little bit as Lyric drifts off. It feels good with her.

It's right.

Next In The Crane Family Series

The dark and sexy Crane Family Series continues with *Be Mine*.

I'm perfectly content being a billionaire CEO. A bachelor playboy. The tabloids call me a Bedroom God. I relish it.

Until Breetana flips my entire world upside down.

Hiring her as my Executive Assistant is both the best and worst decision I've ever made. Breetana is everything I've ever wanted in a woman. She's beautiful. She stands up to me. Doesn't take my crap.

But one phone call changes my entire life. Something in Breetana shifts. She suddenly transforms into a scared, jumpy girl instead of the fearless woman I'm falling in love with.

No way I'm leaving her alone to deal with whatever demons she's hiding from me.

I didn't expect to be thrown into a world of crime, mafias, and the cartel, but I don't care. Breetana is worth the risk.

She's become my everything, and I won't let anything or anyone hurt my girl.

~ This book is a steamy CEO/Mafia Romance that has dark and violent themes, emotional abuse, mental abuse, mentions of physical and SA from the FMC's past, and strong language that may not be suitable for all readers. ~

Order *Be Mine* Today!

The Crane Family Series

Available Now

The Reluctant Mafia King
Sweet Lies
Billion Dollar Love Story
Be Mine
Protecting Her
Dangerously Forbidden Love
His Heart
Love In The Dark

Box Sets Available

The Crane Family Series

Other Books By Melony Ann
The Beautiful Dream Series

Available Now

Loving You
My Love, My Heart
Softening Lyric
Undercover Temptations
Captain Charming
Breaking Boundaries
Crashing Into You
Tactical Inferno
Ravishing Our Queen
Cherished By The Texan
Unveiling Our Passions

Box Sets Available

The Beautiful Dream Series: Box Set: Part 1
The Beautiful Dream Series: Box Set: Part 2

The Deimos Trilogy

Available Now

Connor's Legacy
Aryan's Alpha
Kade's Redemption

Box Sets Available

The Deimos Trilogy

The Forbidden Temptation Series

Available Now

The Detective's Forbidden Temptation
The Running Back's Forbidden Temptation

The Lucinio Family Series

Available Now

Rising From The Ashes
The Player's Rebel
Encrypting My Heart

Multi Author Series
Piper Falls: Firehouse 49

Available Now

Ignite My Fire by Melony Ann
Regain My Fire by Kindra White
Playing With My Fire by D.L. Howe
Fight My Fire by Darley Collins
Against My Fire by Anneke Boshoff
Relight My Fire by Louise Murchie
Harness My Fire by Ayana Lisbet
Quench My Fire by Havana Wilder

Let's Be Friends

Follow me on

Bookbub

Facebook

Goodreads

Instagram

Tik Tok

Visit my website
www.melonyannauthor.com

Subscribe to my newsletter and get a FREE never-seen-before NOVELLA
just for subscribers!
https://www.melonyannauthor.com/exclusive-content

Join my Facebook Reader Group!
Jason's and Melony's Sizzling Book Nook

The official Crane Family Series Playlist on YouTube
https://youtube.com/playlist?list=PLGEiD5wbQmDc78K7gNeODh-
janqmIFiie

Dedication

You're the only match to our heart; our soulmate.

Acknowledgements

Brad - You're my life. My love. My heart and soul. I love you.

Laura - You're such a beautiful being. A beautiful soul. Thank you for everything you've done and continue to do for me. I'm so glad to have you in my life. I love you so much.

Jay - You've always been something hovering on best friend and so much more. I will forever be grateful that we took the leap. I love you.

Ayana - You'll never know how much I appreciate you for keeping me on the right track and being my sounding board. You're such a kind soul, and I love you!

Anneke - How do you manage to keep me from spiraling into the deep abyss of my failure thoughts? I don't know. But thank you for doing it! I love you!

Jason - I don't have a clue how we got to where we are now, but I'll forever be grateful to you. You've become such a huge part of my life, and I wouldn't have it any other way.

To the Bookstagram Community.

To my family.

To all of those who believe in me and support me.

To all of those who don't.

Cover by: Carter Cover Designs

Edited by: Alyssa Skaggs

About Melony Ann

Melony Ann began writing short stories and poetry as a child. She continued honing her craft over the years until she took the plunge and began publishing her work, despite having severe anxiety.

Melony writes contemporary romance stories that are full of suspense and a lot of steam.

When she isn't writing, she is loving her family and working to make her life something she deserves.

Melony believes that if her writing can inspire just one person, then all of her hard work is worth it.

Her hope is that her writing allows each and every one of her readers to escape for a little while. To dive into a different world one book at a time.

www.ingramcontent.com/pod-product-compliance
Lightning Source LLC
Chambersburg PA
CBHW051533260626
47170CB00003B/917